Also by Gary W. Evans

Moonshine Melody

Death by Payback

Death by Poison

Death by Drowning

Cold Case Chase

The Terror Returns

and more on the way!

COLD CASE CHASE

GARY W. EVANS

Library of Congress Control Number: 2020912666

ISBN 978-1-7331826-7-6 Paperback

1

I t was the day after the day after the Great Moonshine Blast, as the news media had taken to calling it. At seven in the morning Al was at his desk and already looking for a new assignment—anything but busting stills. Once again, he had stopped for pastries, and, once again, Chief Brent Whigg's shadow fell across the desk as Rouse poured his first cup of coffee.

"Just what the hell are you doing here, Al?" The chief's face wore a grim look, eyebrows deeply furrowed toward his nose—potentially conjuring a storm in the vicinity of his desk.

Al went into full-on sun lamp mode.

"Hi, Chief. No real reason to stay home," he said brightly. "Jo Anne already had plans and Charlie was going to work, too, so I just thought, well, there must be something I could start looking into here." Then, alertly, "Please, help yourself to coffee and a doughnut and tell me what's on the docket."

Whigg shook his head, marched out of the office, head down, returning seconds later with the cup he had used for what seemed his entire career—and never washed. In fact, when things were slow, like as not, someone would suggest a pool to guess the depth of the sludge in the mug. Whigg helped himself to coffee, reached into the box, extracted a jelly-filled Danish, then slipped into a chair in front of the desk.

"So what's your appetite?" The chief was staring at him intently while blowing on the liquid in the cup.

"Appetite? For a case you mean?"

"What else would I mean? Hell, I can't even get you to take a paid day off. You beat me to work and you're lookin' like a greyhound on a rabbit. Hell, yes, a case."

"Whaddaya got that's hot?"

"Jeezus, do ya think I'da asked if there was somethin' hot? You just took care of the only thing that's been on the front burner for the last month and a half. I'm not about to beg for a crime wave just to give you something to do, you know."

"'Course, I know, Chief." Al wanted to laugh, but the look on Whigg's face didn't appear as if he was in the market for a joke. "I just thought something might've happened in the last week that needed some attention."

"Not a single thing. And if you ask me, that's a great thing. At least I think it is, because budget time is still four months away and no one's breathin' down my neck at the moment."

Al leaned back in his chair and let the air settle, and a thought surfaced from somewhere in the back of his mind. It was worth a try.

"You know, Chief, I've always wanted to work a cold case—I mean a real cold case … like something that happened years ago that people still wonder about."

It hit them both at the same time.

"The Sovereign case." Al's whisper was just audible.

The chief stared back. "Yeah. The Sovereign case."

It was as if a ghost had just walked into the room. Whigg said slowly, "I'm almost afraid to suggest it. But you and Charlie have a long history of working well together. You've closed some dillies. Nothing in the category of Sovereign, mind you." He let out a low whistle. "It'd be a good one to look at, though, that's for sure. But we'd have to do it very, very quietly. Don't wanna rattle the whole damn town all over again."

Al rolled his eyes. "For dead sure we wouldn't want the town newshounds to get a sniff of it." Then, savoring the thought, "But I'd love to take a crack at it."

"You know, Al, that kidnapping occurred in 1979, September 1979 … La Crosse's month of infamy."

"I know the date, Chief. Every cop in La Crosse knows that date.

Hell, every cop in the whole state knows that date." As if on cue a siren wailed somewhere in the distance. But the detective was in another zone altogether. "Wouldn't it be great to put that one to bed? Wow, how amazing would that be?"

Whigg thought hard for a moment. It was obvious the wheels were turning. "That's just a few months shy of 41 years ago. We were little kids. Hell, my mom and dad were just starting their business. I'm guessing yours were newlyweds."

"Pretty much, and I know exactly what mine were doing 41 years ago—they were changing my diapers. But there's not a cop in the whole state who hasn't heard the story … hasn't thought about the case … hasn't wondered what happened to her."

"Both of her parents are gone now. Coupla siblings, I think. They'd be in their late forties or fifties, maybe?" Whigg was still mulling it. "It would be a tall order to solve that one."

"Chief, if nothing's cooking right now, maybe Charlie and I could take a look—just kinda quiet like. It would still leave us open for anything new that comes up, right?"

"Yeah. That wouldn't be a problem." The chief fiddled with his tie, rubbed his hands on his coffee cup, and lapsed into what appeared to be deep thought. "That case has been looked at several times … with zero results … nothing." He paused. "But there are new tools now. And we still have all the evidence under lock and key." Then he seemed to make up his mind. "So, I guess you could have a look into the case boxes anytime you ask."

"Then I'm askin', Chief."

It was a done deal.

"I'll make the call, then. You want it delivered here? Or do you want to go over to the warehouse and look at it all there?"

"Might as well start that way, over there. If I find anything, or if Charlie is interested, we can always have it moved over here."

"Sounds good. Well, the day is moving on. Guess I'd better get ready for the bloodhounds. They're still looking for some more moonshine burger."

The chief rose, thanked Al for the coffee, and then began to move toward the door and his meeting with the news media.

"Have a good day, Chief. I'm gonna go sniff around the Sovereign case."

The chief closed his door. Al sank back in his chair, closed his eyes and began to think.

Nearly 41 years ago. Wow, my folks had just had me, their first baby, when it happened—the babysitter kidnapping that shook the city … the whole state. Everyone knew about it. Every parent was paralyzed at the thought of it. People still talk about it from time to time. And every now and then someone writes about it, too.

Well, better ring up Charlie.

His fingers punched in the familiar numbers and Charlie answered, his voice booming through the earpiece. Al moved the receiver away from his ear.

"'Was damn sure I'd hear from you today," said his good friend and sometimes partner, La Crosse County Chief Deputy Charlie Berzinski.

"And here I am. Just like a bad penny, Charlie."

"Speaking of bad penny, did you see what that hemorrhoid at the *La Crosse Tribune* wrote about us this morning? Now wasn't *that* a damn hatchet job? 'Badgered,' my ass. We gave those guys every damn chance to surrender and they made the choice to blow themselves away. I tell you, Al, these media types these days are novices—nothing like the guys we used to work with. Like Rusty Cunningham. What a peach he was. Prince of a guy."

"Charlie," interrupted Al, "this isn't about the *Tribune*—or moonshine, even. It's about something new … or old, actually … 'something I think is exciting."

For just a moment, Charlie was silent. Then he said, "New and exciting, huh? Those words are music to my ears. Sure as heck, if we don't come up with something, Dwight'll have me working at a minor robbery, like some kid who stole a neighbor's underwear. Whatcha got?"

"The Chief thinks it might be a good change of pace if we take on a cold case—and the one he's giving us has been cold for a long, long time. It's so cold, it would probably be classified ice age."

"That old, huh? Only one case in La Crosse that qualifies. The kidnapping, right?

"You got it. Man, you're on top of it this morning."

"Al, I'm always on top of it, you just don't give me the credit I deserve."

"You know, Charlie, that's probably true—I don't give you enough credit. You're a great guy, loyal as can be, diligent in everything you do, and a terrific partner. None of the things we've done could've been done without you."

Al could almost picture the big guy swooning as he dished it out. Charlie was a big man: 6-foot-5, at least, 300 pounds, almost all of it muscle, and a great guy to be around. And when they were on a case, he was a heat-seeking missile.

"Well … um … Al, you don't wanna go too far with that, ya know. It might go to my head."

"It may well go to your head, Charlie, but knowing that head—and how hard it is—it's not likely to sink in."

"S'pose you're right. Well, enough of that. This case?"

"Chief thinks that maybe the new technology that came in a few years ago may provide a starting point for something that may lead somewhere."

"Jeez, do you think so, Al? That case is, what, thirty-some years old?"

"More than forty years ago, Charlie. Can you believe it?"

"Wow, that's ancient history range … I wasn't even a gleam in my father's eye.

"C'mon, Charlie."

"Well, damn near, Al. It was … uh … that was …"

"Forty-one years, Charlie."

"Well, yeah, forty-one. I would've been … ummm … two years old."

"Okay, I'll buy that. Are you in? I think if you're interested, Brent is going to call Dwight to tell him what he'd like us to do."

"Jeez, have him do it quick. The Sheriff's gonna send me outta here soon … likely to a place I don't wanna go. I'm sick a' doin' rustlers and moonshiners."

"But we did it well, didn't we?"

"We did. But was it really that important? Well, s'pose it was, but I wanna bite into something really important."

"How does kidnapping sound … and murder?"

"Magical," said Charlie. "Just point me at it."

"Will do. More later. I'll let Brent know to call the Sheriff."

2

Al strolled down the hall and caught Whigg just before he was going into his morning news huddle.

"Charlie's in, Chief. Can you give his boss a ring to clear it?"

"I'll do it right after the news conference."

The chief pulled a tiny notebook out of his breast pocket and began to search for a pen.

"Damn, where do they always go?" he wanted to know as Al handed him a writing tool.

"Keep it, Chief. Just don't put it with the other 200 pens I've given you in the last year."

"Two hundred, my ass …" he began, then stopped, looking at Al and noted carefully, "I don't think it's 200, but it's more than a few."

Al clapped his boss on the shoulder and turned to go back to his desk.

As he did that, Chief Whigg called out, "I decided to have the files brought to you. No place to work in the warehouse. The last dated evidence files should be over before noon, Al. I told 'em to take them to your office, okay?"

"Yup. Good thinking."

As Al was nearing his office, he noticed two guys straining to keep their loads on the dollies they were pushing, each one piled high with boxes. They saw him, continued to his office, then stopped.

"Where 'you want 'em?" Hank Schultz, the evidence archivist, wanted to know.

"Not sure where I'm gonna put 'em. What do you have altogether … ten cartons?"

"Oh, hell, this is just the beginning—we've got twice as many left over there," said Hank, tipping his load to a stop on the floor in front of the office. "Chief said to bring you the latest first. It's all pretty old, though. I think this is enough for now, don't you?"

"Well now, I'm gonna hafta think a minute. Tell you what, put 'em on the table in here," said Al, pointing to the conference room across the hall. "I'll get the space approved, okay?"

"Whatever you want," agreed Hank. "We'll just stack these in order on the table."

By the time Al had put a two-month hold on the conference room and returned to his office, the table was covered almost two-deep with cartons. Hank and his partner were just dropping off a few more.

"I think there are two more," Hank told him, "that qualify for this set. I'll have those over here in a minute."

"Are they in some sort of order?"

"Yup, just the way we pulled 'em off the shelves. We placed them front to back in here, starting at the far end of the table, so I'm guessin' the stuff on that end of the table is the latest."

"Thanks," said Al, pushing past the two men into his office, where he sat down and stared back across the hall at the mountain of evidence resting there.

All that, and we still didn't find her. Damn ... wonder if it'll be different this time?

He picked up his phone. "Charlie, you're not going to believe it. The evidence files fill the entire conference room across from my office. Might as well be climbing Mt. Everest. As soon as you hear from Dwight, let me know."

"I'll do it. I'd really like to start takin' a look, so I hope I hear from him soon."

Al had settled down at his desk when the phone rang. "I'll be right over. The sheriff just came in to tell me he was making me available to you folks—until something new breaks over here. It's been damn quiet, so I hope it stays that way. Okay if I come now?"

"Sure. In fact, I'm just getting ready to go across the hall myself. I think it's going to be a long few days, based on what I see, but hopefully the evidence boxes will have something in them that will give us an idea where to start. See you soon."

Al rang off, then turned to the credenza behind his desk to brew a cup of coffee in the well-worn-but-faithful Keurig machine that he had purchased at the old Dayton's store in Valley View Mall the first year they came out. She was ancient, but she worked.

He selected a hazelnut K-cup from the holder, then also grabbed a breakfast blend for Charlie. He brewed himself a cup, left a clean cup next to the dispenser for Charlie, and headed across the hall.

He entered the room that served for small-group meetings and stared for a few seconds at the stacks of cartons on the table, and more on the floor. It was stunning. The room began to feel kind of dark and foreboding. Then he looked up, smiled to himself, shook his head, and went back to the door to turn on the lights.

He walked around the table, reading the labels on several boxes to orient himself, and selected the one on the end with the label "September 1979." Looking around, he finally plunked it in a chair near the end of the table—there being no available surface space—and settled into an adjacent chair.

He opened the box and found a folio of reports and notes and began to read. Soon he was back to that late summer Saturday, September 15. The city was "agog" with excitement—he read in a yellowed and frayed edition of the *La Crosse Tribune*—about the La Crosse Indians football team. The big headline was the game that would be played that night between the La Crosse State Indians and River Falls, the first game in the new stadium.

La Crosse State Professor Himo Swiggum had to search hard for a babysitter (everyone was going to the game, he found) before encountering biology Professor Richard Sovereign. And, when discussing his plight with his quiet but friendly colleague, Himo found out that Richard's daughter, Shirley—a sophomore honor student at Central High School—would be available to babysit.

Prof. Swiggum immediately finalized a commitment, arranging to pick up Shirley in time to show her around and introduce her to baby Janis Swiggum before the Swiggums left for the big game.

He had just gotten into the more substantive reports and notes when a giant shadow fell across the table. "Hey, can I come in?"

"Hi, Charlie," he said, looking up. "You caught me in the excitement of a home football game played at UWL 41 years ago."

"So ya started without me." But there wasn't any sincere regret in his voice—Charlie was taking in the peaks and cliffs of cardboard. "Find anything interesting yet?"

"'Haven't gotten to the event." Al held up the sheaf of papers he was reading. "Just got to the point where the girl's dad and a colleague had agreed to a babysitting deal. So, no, I'm not ahead of you."

"Where do you want me to start?" Charlie was examining the brief inventories that were pasted onto every carton. After looking over a few boxes, the big man paused and looked over at Al.

"Where did you start?" he asked.

"At the beginning, Charlie, September 15, 1979."

"How about I take the next one?"

"That'll be good. I think there are four cartons from the night of the kidnapping. I took the one on top. Why don't you take the next one down."

Charlie grabbed the carton and carried it to the other side of the table, where he put it down in another chair and sat down, catty-corner from Al.

For nearly an hour the two lawmen sifted, sorted, read, and made notes—then, on his third carton, Charlie looked up at Al and said, "I think I may have something—at least something worth looking into."

Al paused, papers still in hand, and looked over at Charlie. "Apparently there was a group of girls who ran around with Sovereign," Charlie said, looking at the report in front of him. "And it sounds as if they sowed some wild oats together. I wonder if any of them is still around?"

"Names?" asked Al.

"One's a Mary Nordstrom. Then there's a Kenjit Gustafson, a Jane Seward and a Tandy Sorenstam. When the detectives talked to the Seward girl, she said that during sleepovers they would pull all sorts of pranks. One night they slipped out of the house before dawn, rode bikes to the pool in their pajamas, and went swimming. According to Seward, they came back dripping wet and snuck back into bed.'

"Sleepovers," remarked Al.

"Are you where I am?" asked Charlie.

"I don't know. Where are you?"

"Whaddaya bet the swim was a skinny dip?"

"Yeah, you're prob'ly right. I doubt teenage girls would have jumped in in their P.J.'s, but they might have had to use them to dry off. Note the names—we'll check on 'em."

Charlie briefly left to pick up sandwiches at Buzzard Billy's, but the two went back at it with papers in one hand and a sandwich in the other. When quitting time rolled around, Al leaned back in his chair, put his glasses on the table, and rubbed his eyes. Charlie stretched.

"Not bad for a first day," remarked Al. "I think you may have uncovered something we need to check on. I'm pretty satisfied that the evidence was preserved, too. The blood that was collected from the yard at the Swiggum house and the side of the garage of a neighbor, Eugene Downer, was properly stored and may still be good for DNA testing. We need to find out if any DNA tests were done."

"Hell, Al, DNA didn't come along until … shoot, sometime in the 1990s or early 2000s, right?"

"It might have been earlier than that," said Al, "I'm gonna have to check. But it was a long time between the kidnapping and DNA testing availability, that's for sure. I'll be looking into it tonight."

"And I wanna track down those friends," reported Charlie. "They may have more to tell now that 41 years have passed, they're prob'ly still alive and around."

"But right now," announced Al, "I vote for a beer at Schmidty's. It's quittin' time."

"Sounds like a wiener," said Charlie, rising from the table and grabbing his jacket.

3

Al was thoroughly engrossed in his work the next morning when Charlie walked in and sat down. "How're things?" asked the deputy.

"Well, there's sure as heck a lot of stuff here. Every time I look at a new piece of evidence I wonder what the hell were they thinking. Why didn't they …? And then I stop and remember this was 41 years ago and the tools we take for granted weren't available then. Like this shoe for instance …"

Al held up a large, somewhat tattered, black tennis shoe. "I came upon this in an evidence container marked a week after the kidnapping. When they found this, it was on the shoulder of Highway 14 about 11 miles from La Crosse and near Coon Valley. My first thought was, 'You idiots, why didn't you do DNA testing.' Then I remembered—there was none."

"But has any testing been done since it's been available?" Charlie wanted to know.

"None that I can tell," said Al. "By the way, Charlie, I did look into your question on DNA testing. As it happens, the first time DNA was used in a court case was in 1986 in England. A molecular biologist was asked to verify the confession of a 17-year-old boy in two rape-murders, according to Google. But it was some years later before DNA became a real police tool."

"I knew you'd research it, Al. You're great at things like that. You know, I also spent a lot of time thinking about DNA testing and the other tools that have come along. And, although people before us have looked at this case from time to time, I think we should just start over. We should take every piece of physical evidence we have and put it through DNA testing and see if we can get it run through the CODIS and NDIS systems. It might not help, but then again, it just might provide a key or two. You know, DNA in that shoe is still alive, Al. Whaddaya think?"

"I think that's brilliant," said Al, rising to his feet and pacing around the conference table. He had paused now, his hands on the back of a chair, his brows knitted, his eyes closed. After a minute, he straightened up, looked at Charlie and said, "Do you think we can find either her brother or sister? I think they are still alive. We'd need a swab from either one of them to pin down her DNA to compare with all the blood samples that were preserved."

"I think looking for next of kin—or even their kids, for that matter—would be a great next step. We'd get her nailed down and then go from there."

"Okay, then we need to go back through what we have already done and pick out the things that were preserved. We have blood samples. We have the tennis shoes which, by the way, match a plaster cast made of footprints left in the dirt outside the Swiggum home. We should label each exhibit, put the items in a separate carton and continue our trek through the evidence files."

"Good idea," agreed Charlie. "But how about I see if I can locate either Steven or Ellen Sovereign. Based on what we know, Steven would be about sixty-one now, so he should still be alive. Ellen is probably in her late forties—she looks like she was much younger— maybe seven or eight in the picture we have."

"I think that's a solid step. You get going on that, and I'll keep digging through the boxes, okay?"

Charlie quickly got busy. He limited his immediate search to trying to find out more about the youngest of the four Sovereign children. Ellen was six when Shirley was taken. She would be forty-seven or forty-eight now. Where might she be?

Charlie made quick work of the puzzle. Using the police databases, the information from the La Crosse Public Library, and from the *La Crosse Tribune*—and the notes made by earlier investigators— Charlie quickly ran down the remaining family members.

The parents, Richard and Edith, were dead and buried in Colorado. Steven, the surviving son, had gone to Australia and made his home there. Charlie omitted him from consideration, mostly because of distance. He found Ellen in Connecticut. Married now for many years and the mother of several children. Her married name was Pettit.

Charlie looked up from his laptop and waited for Al to finish what he was doing. "I found the sister. She lives in New London, Connecticut. She and her husband have four children, three of them boys. How do you think I should go about the next step?"

"Well, we definitely need her DNA." Al was thinking now. "She wasn't old enough to be cooperative in the initial investigation, was she?"

"The notes don't say that, but I'd guess that would be a 'no.'"

"Where's the brother?"

"The notes I found in here say Australia."

"Guess that means we have to try the sister first, since she's closer. Do you have email addresses?"

"For the sister, yes; brother, no."

"Then let's compose a friendly note to the sister and see if she will cooperate."

"Al, I'm not much good at writing. This is probably going to take your touch."

"Okay, no problem. I'm at a good spot for a break, anyway."

Al moved his chair away from the table where he was sifting and sorting evidence and walked to Charlie's side of the table. Standing behind the deputy, he said, "Write down the name and e-mail address and I'll go across the hall to my office and write a note."

He took the information Charlie gave him, walked across the hall to his office, typed up the note, and sent it off on the ether-waves. Then he returned to the conference room.

"Anything else?" he asked.

"Nothing helpful," replied Charlie.

"I guess right now it all hinges on the sister. We have plenty of evidence here that could provide information, but without a DNA result from her sister, we are dead in the water. I have plenty of items that hold testable blood samples, but nothing that would hold up in court. The problem is, every item that we have is suspect. We have clothing that we think is Shirley's that could be tested for skin cells to run a Trace DNA, but none of that will hold up unless we have a DNA sample that is indisputable proof that it is from her or her family."

"How much more evidence do you have to go through?" Charlie had stood at his place and was stretching.

"I think I have all of it cataloged and bagged. Let's see, what time is it?" Al looked at his watch. "It's 3:20."

"It might be enough time to listen to the last great piece of evidence." Al walked to his side of the table, dug in one of the boxes, and emerged with a CD. "We need to listen to this. This is the digitized version of a reel-to-reel tape that surfaced in 2004 after some publicity about the case appeared."

"Wow. How long is it?" Charlie wanted to know. "I think I'd rather start the day with it tomorrow than end the day with it today. I didn't really get a good night's sleep last night, and if this thing has useful information on it, I won't sleep tonight, either. Whaddaya think?"

"Okay, we'll save it for tomorrow."

"Good," agreed Charlie. "Then I am gonna head back and see what my desk looks like. It's nice to get a break from the usual kind of investigative work, but I hate to have my desk get 'way ahead of me."

"Great idea, Charlie. I'm sure mine could benefit from a look, too. 'Wanna catch a beer later?"

"I guess I'll pass. Kelly is making pot roast for dinner and I promised I would be home early. The kids are coming over, too. They really like Kelly. And now that they are sort of on their own and away from Charlene, I like them, too. They're no longer whining babies about everything."

"Good for you, Charlie, good for you," said Al, pleased for his friend that this second marriage seemed to be working well for him. "Then you just get going, clean up that desk, and head home. We'll see you in the morning."

With Charlie gone, Al tidied up the conference room, leaving the CD atop the pile for the morning, then tended to his office, returning three calls. As he was thinking about leaving for the day, a shadow fell across his desk. He looked up.

"Hey, Chief, how are you?" he said as Whigg entered.

"Doing well," said his boss. "How's the Sovereign case coming?"

Al paused, trying to put a feeling into words. "You know, Chief, something about this case seems to be talking to me. It's like there's something there … like we're going to get somewhere this time. Seems like it just might be around the next bend, so to speak."

"Good feeling, then?"

"Absolutely," agreed Al. "And tomorrow could be a key. We're gonna listen to the CD of the tape first thing in the morning."

"Ah. You know, I think I heard it once, but it's been a long time. Mind if I sit in?"

"Heck no. It would be good to have you. Plan on around 7:30."

4

When Charlie walked in the next morning, Al already had the CD player on the table and plugged in. "Where ya been?" he asked, slightly irritated that it was already almost 8 o'clock and the Chief had already looked in once.

"God, Al, this case has sat here for 41 years now, do you think another day or two is gonna to make a huge difference? And if you have to know, I stopped at Ma's to grab a bite to eat 'cause I know you're gonna work my ass off today and that means no lunch stop—or at least I'd bet on that. How long's the tape?"

"Looks to me like we might have at least a coupla' hours of material. And just so you know, I was thinkin' about you, pal. That bag is filled with Fayze's pastries, so help yourself and we'll get started."

"Aw, that was thoughtful, Al. But right now I'm stuffed. Ma's. Besides, you know Kelly has me on a diet."

Al looked at his larger friend, a smile wreathing his face.

"Before you say anything, you must notice that I have lost some weight."

Al gave him a once over. "You know Charlie, you're right, you *have* lost some weight. And it is noticeable. But most of you is muscle anyway, something that has always made me envious. So if you have a little flab around the edges, it isn't noticeable. But I'm not going to get in the way of Kelly's efforts, either."

Just then Chief Whigg walked in. "Ready to go?"

"Just about to start, boss. I was gonna grab a Danish and hit the button. Have one, yourself."

"I will, but you'll have to start without me. I have a regular date with the Fourth Estate about this time every morning, as you know."

Whigg fished out two jelly-filled Danish and then quickly made his exit, with a wave and a wink at Charlie, before Al was any the wiser.

Al regained his chair, reached across the table from the boombox, activated the play button, then pulled the pastry bag over to claim his prize—and came up empty, except for chocolate donuts. He snorted, "Damnit, Chief!" Charlie laughed as the room filled with the sounds of a bar.

After a few minutes of the usual bar room sounds—people laughing and talking, someone calling for another round of drinks, the clink of empty bottles being removed—the band started up. The country western group was loud and enthusiastic, but nothing could make up for what they lacked in talent—the lead singer whined a familiar tune, but in an unknown key, and the lead guitar strayed into riffs far beyond the limits of his ability—all of which irritated even Charlie's untrained ear.

"Is this the best we've got?" he asked Al. "If I have to put up with much more of this, without fortification, it's gonna be a really, really long day."

"Sorry, pal. It is pretty awful, but this is what we signed up for when we took these fancy jobs—lots and lots of pain interrupted by a few moments of pure pleasure in catching the bad guys. We just gotta handle it."

Charlie sat back and closed his eyes. When Chief Brent Whigg looked in about an hour later, he was sure the big guy was sleeping.

"Better wake your partner up," he suggested to Al. "Looks like he's out for the count."

"Who the heck's disparagin' me now?" Charlie tipped his hat back on his head, sat up straight, and looked the interloper in the eye. "Chief, I just want you to know that some folks listen better with their eyes closed. I'm one of those."

"Well, pardon me, Deputy Berzinski, I didn't even know it was you," said Whigg in mock surprise, "but I would have sworn I heard a snore coming from under that hat. I don't know whether I'm sorrier for insulting you or for waking you up from such peaceful slumber."

"Aww, Chief, you always give me a passle of crap," asserted

Charlie, "and here I am such a devoted and humble servant of the people."

Whigg's eyebrows shot up in surprise—then he sputtered with a rumble of laughter that started deep in his diaphragm and surfaced in a belly-laughing, knee-slapping fit. Al and Charlie both watched with open awe—a truly great performance.

Abruptly the chief stopped and pulled a perfectly straight face into a look of concern. "A bit tender this morning, aren't we deputy?"

Charlie quickly recovered and then huffed, "Now, no offense, Chief, but every time I come over here, you guys pick on me unmercifully."

Al couldn't help joining in with mock empathy. "Awww, poor baby. We're so sorry little fella."

"Dammit, Chief, now see what you started." Charlie was on his feet now, face red and hands clenched into fists.

"Easy, big guy," quipped Whigg, placing a hand on Charlie's shoulder and guiding him back into the chair.

Still sputtering, Charlie declared, slamming his fist on the table, "I was not sleeping! Get it? Not sleeping! I was concentrating … like I do when I'm deep in thought."

"Okay, okay." The chief backed off and softened his tone. "Charlie, I was just having fun with you. Sorry to have poked you in the wrong place this morning."

"Aww, chief, it's okay. Maybe I'm a little sensitive … but I wasn't sleeping … honest."

"And I believe you. So tell me, how far did you guys get on the tape?"

Al was again all business. "We're about 45 minutes in. Nothing yet."

Charlie frowned in concentration, "You know, Chief, I'm sure the detectives back then knew it might be a great lead, but, in the notes, they played it down—saying that since everyone was dead and buried there wasn't any reason to take it any further."

Al was learning forward, hands on his coffee cup and staring Whigg straight in the eye. "Chief, we're not going to accept that claim. We're going to see what we can come up with. Want to hear it with us?"

"You know, I want to and I wish I could. I'd love to be doing some real police work." The chief slumped a little as he responded, as if there was something he wanted to get off his chest. "But I opted for this damn administrative stuff when my wife and kids got on me to find a better, safer job. That was back in Detroit, nearly 20 years ago now, and we had just gotten into a shootout with the mob. One of the bullets took a piece out of my arm and Janet and the kids didn't want to see me in that position again. But the fact is, I love police work and being a paper pusher is only tolerable because I get to work with great people."

"Chief, I'm gonna take that as a compliment." Charlie now was all smiles, and he gave Whigg a fist pump. "I'm sure your job does get boring. But, remember, so does ours. It's fun to close cases, but it's a grind getting to that point, don't you think?"

"I suppose it is, Charlie, but okaying overtime requests and vacation slips just isn't my way of effectively fighting crime."

The chief had risen now and was moving toward the door. "And, as if the paperwork isn't bad enough, I gotta go back and see what all the Woodwards or Bernsteins came up with on this moonshine story before they print it."

"Good luck, boss." Al was smiling as he said it, but it was a wry smile, because he knew what his boss was going through. Al just hoped this wasn't a serious funk because he thought Brent Whigg had done a monumental job of creating a smooth-running, highly effective department. As the Chief lumbered off, Al wondered, *have I told him what a great job he does? If I have, I can't remember the last time. Better put it on the to-do list.*

"Okay, Charlie, ready for some more music?"

"God, do we have to? Why aren't the good parts marked so we could just go there?"

"Sorry, big guy, they didn't make any notes on where the conversation was on the CD. We just have to listen to it in its entirety."

"Okay, hit play." Charlie slumped back in his chair as the sound of music—still country western, and still not particularly good country western—filled the room. But this time he left his hat on the table.

As the band droned on, Charlie wondered aloud, "So, Al, this thing surfaced in 2004?"

"Yup. A guy named Duke LaDoux brought it in on one of his trips home to Hazard."

Charlie thought a minute. "And the back story is that he was taping bands in his bar down there back in the early 80s … when he let the tape run one night?"

"That's it. Actually, La Doux fancied himself as a country singer," Al recounted, "and from time to time disappeared to make another run at stardom. He and his brother owned the bar, and the brother would run the place while La Doux was gone. This tape was made in the old movie theater that he had remodeled into a bar. Apparently when he wasn't playing music, he worked as a carpenter—although I guess he did better in the music industry than anyone else from Hazard. He says he played with all the stars in Nashville."

"*Really.* Is he still around?"

"He's old now, probably nearing eighty, but the last time anyone from here—the department, that is—talked to him, he had all his faculties."

The music went on and on—heavy on the beat and light on musicianship, flaws the quality of the tape exacerbated. After three bands had played, there was a lull—with only the bar sounds and the steady scratching of the old reel-to-reel tape. Then several male voices were heard.

Al hit the pause button, looked at Charlie, then rose from his chair. "Time for more coffee. Looks like we're getting to the part we need to hear, and a fresh cup will make that even better."

Charlie got up and the two officers walked across the hall to Al's faithful Keurig machine.

"Wouldn't it be great to break this thing?" Charlie was excited now as he waited his turn at the dispenser.

"It would, that's for sure. Let's pay careful attention."

Charlie added two lumps of sugar to his coffee, along with a generous pour of cream, stirred it with a pencil, and the two headed back across the hall.

5

"You know, Al, I was thinkin' about Hazard as we were listening to the first part of the tape. It's a nice little town. Coupla highways run through there, and they have the Kickapoo River. I like the place. Kelly and I go down that way every once in a while. It's a pretty drive, and we like the little cafes there. But if there was something bad goin' on there, and we find it, the town'll prob'ly go crazy, and not in a good way."

"I agree, and I mean no disrespect, but little towns like Hazard, away from a major population center, are sort of just aging in place."

Charlie sipped his coffee and wondered aloud, "Hazard is what, 800 people?"

"A little smaller, I think, and shrinking."

"Yup, aging in place is a good term for it. It could use a shot in the arm, but I'm not sure a murder is a good one."

"Well, we'd better get on with the show," said Al, reaching for the tape machine and hitting the "play" button.

After a minute or two of bar noise and static, a conversation between bar patrons was suddenly and startlingly clear.

"Fluery," said one deep bass voice, "you've been around these parts a long time?"

"Sure have." The second male voice was high pitched, and slightly slurred—as if the speaker was trying hard to get his words out. "Ever since birth. Not much I don't know about."

"You was once a rum runner, weren't you?" asked a third person, another man.

"Now, Weepin' Willie … you know better'n to bring that up,"

said the man named Fleury, still dragging his words. "Was a long time ago."

"Tell you what, beer's on me if you tell us the story," said the man with the deep voice.

"Gene, yer a damn … good man," Fleury gushed. "And a cold Leinies might just loosen me up enough to talk about it."

"Bring this man a Leinies," said deep voice, Gene. "And set some up for the rest of us, too."

The tape rasped on without words for the next few minutes, then Fleury was heard again, "That's … damn good. Haven't had a cold one a' those for a long time, Gene. Yer a good man."

"So we was talkin' about rum runnin'," said Gene. "You did that, too?"

"Sure did … used to haul booze made around here … took it to the boys down at the drunk ward … Mendota State Hospital."

"In Madison?" asked Willie.

"Yup … Madison," said Fleury. "Them boys was always thirsty … bought the booze for a dollar a gallon and rebottled it in quarts or pints … sold it to them guys for $15 a quart … pints for $5. Made enough to keep me in booze."

"You were involved in a lot of other things, too, weren't ya?" asked Willie.

"You name it … I done it," Fleury boasted. Al could almost see his chest puff out. "Handled lots of big deals."

"You was a cab driver, too, wasn't ya?" asked Weepin' Willie.

"Oh, that was a fun job … yeah, 'carried lots of young kids from La Crosse down here to wet their whistles. Didn't much like haulin' 'em home, though. They was almost always sloshed." Fluery paused, taking his time. "We'd get halfway back to La Crosse, and they'd holler to pull over so they could puke. Had to wash the car almost every trip …" Then he added, "The girls was the worst."

"You hauled young girls?" asked Gene.

"Well, not babies … but young teens, yah …"

"Ask him about the Sovereign girl." encouraged Willie.

"Sovereign girl … what Sovereign girl?" Gene wanted to know.

"You know, the one they say was kidnapped? She ain't been found to this day," said Willie, "But Fleury says he knows all about that deal. Don'tcha Fleur?"

"Well, um…I don't much like talkin' about that … but maybe for another cold one, I could remember a little about it."

"Oh. *That* girl!" said Gene. "The babysitter who was kidnapped? That the one?"

"The very one," replied Willie. "Fleury brought her down here that night, didn'cha Fleur? Didn't take her home, though, did ya?"

Fleury lowered his voice to a slow whisper. "Shit … I don't really like talkin' about this. 'Never know who's listenin'.'"

"I thought you said a cold one would wet your whistle and maybe loosen your tongue." The response came from Willie.

"Well … 'beats emptyin' glasses in the morning when cleanin' up to get a little nip."

Al shuddered and then muttered, "Yuck!" Charlie laughed.

"Sshh." Al motioned for quiet as Fleury spoke again.

"Ahh, that's good," Fleury let out a long burp that would have won high fives at an 8th grade lunch table. But the bar group wasn't interested. They wanted the story.

"The Sovereign girl?" Willie prodded.

Fleury's response was just above a whisper. "That was a bad one." His voice faded in and out as if he was searching his memory. "Took those two wild-ass Overland kids up to La Crosse that night. They was high before I even picked 'em up … I didn't want to go, but needed the money … and they seemed flush."

"You had that two-tone late-model Buick, didn'cha?" Willie again.

"Best damn car I ever had … 1961 Super 8 … hotter'n a pistol, that car. Had 'er up to 130 several times. Went like a banshee." Fleury had clearly revived and relished the new topic.

"The Sovereign girl?" Gene was a bird dog on the hunt.

"Oh, yeah, her." Fleury paused. "Well, apparently Billy Overland had met her a few nights before when her and some other girls come down here to have a few."

A long silence ensued.

Gene finally ended it. "And?"

"Well … Billy, he was pissed and all drunked up. Said he had a date with this chick he had met on Wednesday. Wanted to go up there and find her 'cause she said she'd got tied up babysittin', and he wasn't havin' any of it … There was some sorta big football game that night, if I 'member correct. Said he'd give me $10 to take 'em up there. That was big money then." Fleury apparently faded into thought. "Still is."

More silence. Sound of water running and glasses being put in a sink.

Gene spoke up again. "Then what?"

"Well … 'drove aroun' a while … Then we finally found the house she was at. Billy went up to the door and talked to her … she sounded madder'n hell that he was there. When he come back to the car, he was wild mad. Told me to go around the block, then had me stop in the driveway of a house behind where she was."

Fluery seemed to speak more freely, as if reliving the scene.

"Then he and his brother Tommy got out and told me to wait. I was damn scared that I'd get caught and arrested. But I waited. They was gone about a half hour." Fleury lowered his voice. "Then I heard something like a scream, and here they came back, dragging this girl. She was bleedin' bad from a cut on her head. Billy and Tommy shoved her in the back seat. Billy got in back with her and Tommy got in next to me. They told me to drive. I backed up in a hurry and got the hell outta there."

More silence until Gene prodded him for more.

"Nope … don' wanna talk about it anymore. It was a bad night— blood all over the car and them two wild-ass boys acting like big-time hoods. Shit, I was so damn scared. Talkin' about it makes me sick … and thirsty."

"Nina, bring us another round!" Gene yelled, apparently to the bar maid. Soon there was the sound of glasses sliding on wood. Gene told her to add the round to his tab.

Now there was silence, just background bar noise.

"Okay, Fleury. Keep talkin'."

"Geez, youse guys ..." Fleury was whining now, and Al and Charlie could almost see him twisting in his chair.

"C'mon, we're waitin'. Time's a wastin'." Gene again.

At this point, Fleury seemed to sincerely regret this part of the story, letting out a long breath, then continuing in a quiet, shaky voice. "Well ... those Overland boys, they dragged her off into a house down by the river—a fish shack, I think. They was in there quite a while. But they had paid me another $10 to wait, so I did. I finally dozed off ... they was in there a long time—coupla hours at least."

"Then what?" Gene's voice was more eager now.

"They come back out, draggin' her again. She was all messed up. They threw 'er in the backseat, Billy got in with her. She had blood ... all over her face and ... she didn't even try to pull her dress down ... underwear was gone ... more blood down there." Fleury sucked in his breath.

"Jeezus. Then what?" Willie this time.

Fleury went quiet.

"C'mon ... talk. You got this far, finish it." Gene speaking.

After a long shuddering sigh, Fleury continued. "Took 'em into the hills south a' here. To one of them tabacca sheds ... you know ... the kind they used to, ah ..."

"Dry tobacco?" asked Gene.

"Yeah." Fleury's voice was flat with resignation, as if ready to be done with it. "They was gone 20 minutes. Two boys come back—no girl. Took 'em back to Hazard. Dropped 'em off."

At that point the tape went dead.

6

Al sat forward staring at the recorder, his face a mixture of horror and disbelief. Charlie leaned back, put his hands behind his head, was silent for a minute. "Now, whaddaya make of that?"

"Well, if that drunk, Fleury, can be believed, I'd say that was the end of the Sovereign girl." Al was red-faced, obviously angry as he got to his feet and strode to the window, hands behind his back. He stared outside for a few seconds, then turned back to Charlie.

"Do you think any of those people are still alive?"

Charlie looked up and shook his head. "Those guys'd be damn old, wouldn't they? That tape was made in … what … mid-80s?" Charlie paused. "Hell, that's fortyyears ago, and they sounded old *then*."

Al thought for a moment. "Yeah, you're right. That'd … maybe … make those guys in their 90s … maybe more. Pretty damn old, if they're alive. Except for those Overland boys. They might still be around."

"You know, Al, the bar maid … what was her name … Tina or Nina or something like that … she sounded younger. She likely is alive. We prob'ly need to take a drive down there and see what people might know about those guys, and maybe see if they also remember *her*."

"I agree." Al recounted the list, ticking the names off one by one as he held up four fingers. "We know there was Gene … Fleury … Weepin' Willie … and Nina. Whoever they are now, or wherever they are, regardless, Hazard is a small enough place that everybody knew everybody. We have to try and find 'em, or at least someone who knew 'em."

"I'm pretty sure the bar is still there," Charlie offered. "'Used to be known as the Worn Saddle. It's changed hands a few times and has gone by a few different names, too. I think it's now the Rusty Nail, or somethin' like that. 'Don't know who owns it, though."

"Well, why don't we schedule a ride down there tomorrow? We can make a day of it—hopefully a short day. Tomorrow's Friday and I'm sure as hell ready for the weekend."

For the balance of the afternoon the two friends search through the written records and examined evidence contained in sealed bags in the boxes. By the end of the day, they had a series of evidence they wanted to send out for updating what could be known with trace testing and biometric analysis. With DNA testing improving every day on stains from tissue and body fluid, there were items in the boxes that the officers wanted to be analyzed.

Of particular interest were the oldest samples that had been found shortly after the kidnapping—panties and a bra, and the two tennis shoes that had been found along Highway 14 south of La Crosse. They already knew that the blood found on the bra and panties was the Sovereign woman's blood type, but they wanted to test for a DNA match. There were other items that should provide what was needed to determine if the clothing items were hers. They also wanted to test the dirt on the tennis shoes to see if it matched dirt at the kidnap scene.

"If we get it in today, it should be back in three, four days," said Charlie. "In the meantime, we have some things to do before the weekend. Hope the weather is nice for our little outing to Hazard. And I gotta get in touch with Ellen—the sister, too. Have you heard back from her?"

"Crap, I haven't checked my e-mail all day. Maybe I have a response to my note." Al leapt from his chair and walked across the hall and activated his computer. He rapidly clicked through what Charlie presumed were messages, then suddenly stopped. "It's here," he exclaimed. "Got something back. Let's see what it says.

> *"Dear Detective Rouse, I am amazed that anyone still cares what might have happened to Shirley all those years ago. She was nine years older than I am so she was my big sister heroine. At the same time, being reminded of her disappearance and likely death is not something I like to talk about. In fact, yours is the first inquiry I have returned. I am torn about providing the sample you seek. On one hand, it's simple and insignificant in the grand scheme of things, but on the other hand, it puts something of me into the middle of this, and that gives me pause. I have been debating with myself all day whether I should do this and why. I have decided to provide what you want IF you agree to two conditions: that you will never contact me for anything else, AND that you will never share with any other agency the fact that I gave you this sample—legal or not. Ellen Pettit*

When he had finished reading the message out loud, he swiveled back to face Charlie. "Now how in the hell am I gonna answer that?"

"Whadda mean," protested Charlie. "She's gonna help us. Man, in my book that's great. Whadda ya mean how are you gonna answer that? You're gonna thank her and tell her about what we are going to send her and how to use it. That's what you are gonna do."

Al's face had turned red as Charlie berated him over the question he asked. Now he responded. "Charlie, did you listen to her message?"

"Of course I listened. It was wonderful. I loved it—every last word of it."

"Then you didn't listen very closely. Did you hear the conditions? We will never contact her about anything else. And we will never share the fact that she gave us the sample with any other agency. Were you listening? How can we accept those conditions?"

Charlie hung his head. Then looked up, a sheepish grin on his face. "I guess I didn't listen very good, huh? I'm really sorry Al. I guess I stopped listening when she said we could have the sample. But here's what I think—I think we should lay it out for her … just like you said. I bet you win her over. Al, you're really good at stuff like that."

"Gee thanks, Charlie, but every time you praise me there seems to be work involved. Why is that?"

Charlie looked contrite, then brightened. "But Al, you're really good with words. Bet you can bring her around."

Al turned back to the computer, put his hands on the keys, thought for a moment, and then began to write.

> *Dear Mrs. Pettit, I am very pleased that you will allow us to have a swab taken that will help us with DNA testing, but we cannot accept your offer as it stands. You see, we can't meet your conditions. What if your sister is found alive and wants to see you? If we contact you that will violate your first condition, because it will likely be the result of the swab you provide us. The second condition is equally as prohibitive. We are going to employ as many agencies as we believe can be helpful. Certainly the FBI, other Wisconsin police agencies, and the Department of Homeland Security will also be contacted. So it appears we are at an impasse. We definitely need the sample, but unless you relax the conditions, we will have to decline. That will be a shame, because new evidence and new tools have been found since your sister disappeared. These new tools may help us solve the case. If you change your mind about the conditions, please let us know. Respectfully, Detective Al Rouse and Chief La Crosse County Deputy Sheriff Charlie Berzinski*

He read the message to Charlie, then said, "Well?"
"Perfect. That'll do the job," prophesied Charlie. "Send it."

Al read it one more time, silently, corrected a typo and hit the "send" button. "Done," he said, turning back to Charlie.

"Time to quit for the day," said Charlie, looking at his watch. "Ma's at 6:30?"

"Sounds good," replied Charlie. "See you then."

The two friends and officers met the next morning at Ma's, as they had agreed.

"'Need some food to put muscle on these bones." Charlie was smiling as he looked up at Ma, who was standing at their table, hands on her hips, a red-and-white checked apron tied around her ample waist.

"Charlie Berzinski," she said, giving him a good looking over in front and behind, "I'm not sure there's room for muscle on those bones a' yers, given all the fat that's hangin' off 'em."

"Aw, Ma, c'mon, you know better'n that. There's no fat on this old boy—this here is solid muscle. An' that's the long and short of it."

Ma smiled, wet the tip of her pencil, and got ready to write. "Charlie, the customer is always right … sometimes. What'll ya have this mornin'?"

"I'm real hungry, Ma. Real hungry. I think I'll start with a tall stack a' pancakes – buckwheat, if you have 'em. And some sausages with the cakes. Say about six of 'em. Then how about three eggs— over medium—with five strips of bacon. And, probably four slices of toast. Better make it wheat. Kelly's been on me about my weight again. Do you still have some a' that butterscotch pie left from yesterday? Cause if you do, I'd like a real big piece. I think that'll do it. I'd like some grits, too, but I better call a halt with what ya got there, okay?"

Ma studied the deputy and said, "Ya know, Charlie, it's impressive how you can hold back like that when you really put your mind to it." Charlie lit up, then thought about it. Ma turned to Al and smiled. "And what about you, detective? Something a little less Tyrannosaurus Rex, perhaps?" Al choked back a laugh and ordered two eggs, scrambled, two strips of bacon, and two pieces of wheat toast.

Ma turned to say something else to the deputy sheriff, but Charlie pretended to study the newspaper and dismissed her with a small wave of his hand, then winked at Al as Ma left.

"You guys never get beyond hassling each other, do you?" Al was grinning at his buddy, who now was rearranging things on the tabletop. He moved the ketchup bottle within reach, along with the hot sauce bottle. He pulled the salt and pepper closer and checked to make sure the syrup bottle was filled to his satisfaction.

Half an hour later the two were in Charlie's SUV heading out of town on Highway 61, bound for Westby. Merle Haggard's iconic, rich baritone was on the radio and Charlie was singing along. Al was enjoying the summer sunshine and fresh air, his arm resting on the rolled down window.

"Ya know, we can turn on the air. I like listenin' to the Hag, and I could hear better if you rolled the window up."

"Aww, Charlie, it's a great day. Cool mornin' and the air is sweet. You should try it."

Reaching Westby, Charlie turned onto County Road D, a scenic road that wound through the narrow ridges and steep-sided valleys of Coulee Country toward Hazard. Some 20 minutes later, he slowed as they came into the small community as County Road D became Main Street. Charlie drove through town, pointing out various buildings to Al.

"There it is." Charlie was pointing now. "That's the bar where the recording was made—at least I think it is"

"Looks kinda quiet. In fact, the whole damn town looks quiet, if you ask me."

"It's a nice town. And nobody asked you, okay?"

"If you say so, Charlie. Where we gonna stop?"

"Well, it's just after nine. Bar's not open yet, I'd say. How about a cuppa coffee at the café?"

"Sounds good."

After they had gone through town, Charlie turned around and headed back in from the other way. He guided the SUV into the last parking spot outside Brosi's, which appeared to be a popular restaurant on Main Street.

The two entered to find the café full with seating at a premium. They took the last two spaces at the lunch counter and hadn't waited two seconds when the plump, smiling waitress—her blonde hair frozen stiff in a hairnet—plunked down two cups of coffee and asked what else she could get them.

"What kinds of pie do you have today, darlin'?"

"Aww, Charlie, you sure know how to make a girl feel good. Good ta see ya, too. Today we' got apple, blueberry, cherry, lemon meringue, sour cream raisin, and …"

"Stop right there. Make it an extra-big piece of sour cream raisin, Judy."

"And for you?" She was waiting for Al.

"Just coffee, thank you."

While Al sipped his coffee, Charlie inhaled his pie and engaged the people nearby in conversation.

"Who's been here a long time?" was his opening gambit. Several people raised their hands. Charlie looked them over and said, "We're following up some leads in a case and we think some folks from around here might have played a part many years ago. Does anyone here recognize the names Gene, Fleury, Weepin' Willie, Billy Overland, or Nina?"

As Al looked around, one red-haired young boy—probably eight or nine, with a face full of freckles—was as studiously attentive as anyone Al had ever seen. And he had his hand up. Al smiled and gently said, "Young man, most of the people we're looking for likely were very old when you were born. Probably not something you can help with."

"No, no sir, I can. I know the name Nina … heard my dad say it a number of times. Last name was Ganz or Ginz, or something like that. My dad said she was a real looker, too. Worked as a bar maid at the Nail when it use'ta be the Saddle. I'm pretty sure that's the only time I've heard the name Nina."

Al was taken by surprise. "Well, listen to you—I think you're absolutely right about being helpful." Al was all smiles now as he stood and moved to stand by the boy. "You say your dad talked about her?"

"Yup, sure did."

"Is he around?"

"Well not right now, he's workin'. Won't be home 'til almost suppertime … 'bout five o'clock is when he usually pulls in."

"Do you suppose he'd talk to us … uh…"

"Jeremy. My name is Jeremy Simmons. My dad's name is Bart. Sure, he'd talk to you. He likes to talk."

Charlie stepped in then, shaking his head at Al and scowling. "Jeremy, I'm Charlie. Y'know, we didn't plan on staying around all afternoon. Do you s'pose your dad would talk to us on the phone?"

"Dad don't like the phone. Bitches about it all the time. Too damn many telemarketers, he says. Sure you can't be around?"

"If we have to, we will be, Jeremy." Al was back in the conversation now and making sure that Charlie didn't get in the way of a useful interview. "Tell me, Jeremy, is there a good place you like to hang out here?"

"You guys like pizza?"

Now Charlie was all ears. "Pizza? Why sure, we like pizza, doesn't everyone?"

"How about ice cream?"

"Heck yeah, ice cream is great … especially after pizza." Not surprisingly, Charlie was suddenly in complete alignment with a nine-year old foodie.

"Well, if ya like pizza and ice cream, best place around is the Goose Barn. It's just a few miles outa town. Ya gotta car, right?"

"We do," said Al. "It's a big police vehicle."

Jeremy's eyes were the size of dinner plates. "With a siren and red lights?"

"Yep," Charlie answered. "Tell you what, Jeremy, we're gonna finish our coffee and pie, but, if you walked over here, and you want a ride home, Al and I will give you a lift. That way we'll know where to find you and your dad later. Sound good?"

Now Jeremy was bouncing on his toes. "You'll give me a ride? In your police car?"

"That's what I said, m'boy. Just give us a few minutes."

Back at the counter, Al got a refill and Charlie again looked over the pie menu. "That sour cream raisin was a good sample. Now how about a slice of the lemon meringue … and a piece of the midnight chocolate." He looked down at his new pal Jeremy, who was standing close by—not letting them out of his sight. "Would you like some?"

"Don't much like pie, but maybe when we go for a ride in your car, I could get an ice cream. Chocolate's my favorite."

A smile streaked Charlie's face and caused wrinkles around his eyes. The thought crossed Al's mind, not for the first time, that Charlie loved kids and he loved to make them happy. Kelly had remarked once that he was never very far from his own "inner kid."

Charlie said, "I bet we could arrange that."

When the deputy turned from Jeremy he saw a wizened man with a long white beard a couple of stools down studying him closely. Charlie looked him in the eye and said, "Hi, how are ya?

"Jus' thinking about wha'cha asked when yez come in? Ya mentioned Billy Overland, right?"

"Sure did," said Charlie. "Do you know him."

"Did … did know him," replied the old man. He was a wild-ass kid like you wouldn't believe. He and his brother Tommy—was a year older'n Billy—got killed in a car accident out at Beeches Corners about 20 years ago or so. Nothin' lost, if you ask me."

"Those were the only Overland brothers around here?" broke in Al.

"Only ones I knowed of," said the old man.

As Al walked over to talk more to the old fellow, Jeremy was pulling on Charlie's belt.

"Hey there," admonished Charlie. "Don't be fiddling with that belt. Maybe the gun will go off."

Jeremy backed away in horror. "I was just wonderin' about that ride, mister," said Jeremy looking up.

"Oh, the ride. Sure, we can go now if you're ready," said Charlie, bringing a grin to the boy's face.

Al was more skeptical. "You think riding with us would be okay with your folks, Jeremy?"

The boy looked at him, incredulity marking his young face. "Are you kiddin'? Course they wouldn't mind."

"Well, how about you call 'em and find out." Al took his phone off his belt, handed it to Jeremy and waited. Nothing happened.

Jeremy stared at the phone.

"Need a little help?"

"Yeah, this is 'way fancier than mom or dad's phone. How do I work it?"

"What's the number?" As Jeremy related it, Al punched it in, hit call, and handed the phone back to the boy.

A few seconds later the boy became animated. "Hey, mom, guess what? I'm down at Brosi's. I met these two cops and they've offered me a ride home … No, I'm not in trouble." Al and Charlie looked at each other over Jeremy's head with suppressed grins. "Honest. They want to talk to dad when he gets home. Is it okay if I ride with them and … maybe … go with them to get an ice cream out at Goose Barn?"

Jeremy listened for a minute, then handed the phone to Al. "She wants to talk to you."

"Hi, ma'am. This is Detective Al Rouse with the La Crosse Police Department and I'm with Deputy Charlie Berzinski of … oh, so you know Charlie?" Al looked at Charlie, who shrugged with feigned modesty. "Is it okay if we buy your son a cone and then bring him home? … Yes, he's been very good … No, this wasn't his idea … Yes, ma'am."

Al smiled as he put the phone away. "Your mom says okay, but just a single scoop so you don't ruin your lunch, okay?"

The boy nodded happily. In another half hour or so, Jeremy had successfully navigated Charlie to the Goose Barn and to the ice cream counter inside. He badly wanted two scoops, but Al reminded him of his mother's admonition. In the SUV on their way back to town, Jeremy, who had waited as long as he could, pleaded with Charlie: "Can we turn on the siren? Please …"

"Oh, sure! But just for a second." Charlie hit the button and the truck cabin was suddenly throbbing with the screaming screech of the siren. "Okay, turn it off here." Charlie pointed to the button. Jeremy pushed it, and, in the sudden quiet that enveloped them, Jeremy let out a long sigh of satisfaction. "That was *wonderful.*"

Neither lawman could suppress a smile at that—nor did they try.

Al finally said, "Well, Jeremy, we better get you home. Tell Charlie how to go from here."

As they pulled up to the nicely appointed brick home, Al opened the car door and Jeremy jumped out, clutching the crotch of his jeans as he ran for the front door. "Gotta go … bad."

Just then Jeremy's mother came out, smiled and waved at Charlie as Jeremy dashed past her into the house. Al and Charlie got out of the car and made their way to the porch.

"Hi, Mrs. Simmons, I'm Al Rouse. Jeremy tells us that your husband might know a Nina who used to tend bar at the Saddle?"

"And I'm Martha." The woman shook Al's hand, then greeted Charlie before turning back to Al. "Yes, Nina Ganz apparently was a rather well-known bar maid at the Saddle. But that was a long time ago—before my time, that's for sure. Bart is quite a bit older than me, and he's talked about her many times—Jeremy's right about that. Bart won't be home until five or so. He works for the county."

Charlie, who had been listening intently now joined the discussion. "Do you suppose we could stop back later to talk with him? We don't want to disturb supper, though."

"Well, if you get here about 5:15, it should be perfect. We won't be eating until six or so."

"Thanks, Mrs. Simmons," said Al. "We have some things to do, but we'll see you a little after five, if that's okay."

"Perfect."

The lawmen returned to the SUV and made their way back to the downtown area.

Charlie broke the silence. "Now what? We got five hours to kill."

7

I t was just after five when Charlie pulled the SUV to a stop in front of the Simmons' house. A black Ford pickup was parked in the drive and a man was seated on the steps at the side of the house. Clad in blue jeans and a dirty T-shirt, he looked as if he had just arrived home from work.

"Mr. Simmons … Bart?" Charlie was walking up the driveway with Al.

Simmons unfolded his lanky frame and stood up as the lawmen approached. "You must be the cops that befriended Jeremy. Wife said you'd be stoppin' by. I'm Bart Simmons." Charlie shook his hand and introduced himself, Al followed suit, and Bart picked up where he left off. "How can I help you?"

"Well," began Charlie, "We're sorta here by accident after bumping into Jeremy at Brosi's this morning. We were asking about a Nina Ganz, and Jeremy said you knew her."

Bart Simmons allowed a slow grin. "Jeremy might have stretched that a little, but, yes, I know her … at least of her. She's a relative. Grew up here then left for brighter lights, I guess. Not sure where she is now, but the last I heard she was bartending in Vegas. Hasn't been around here for years."

"Know who might have some idea how to reach her?" Al reached in his pocket for a notepad and pen as he talked.

"I'm probably your best bet. I think we got a Christmas card from her this last year. Martha almost never throws anything, so she might be able to find it for us. There could be a return address I suppose."

Simmons opened the door and shouted, "Martha, we got company." He turned, motioned to the two lawmen to come in, and continued, "Jeremy's cop friends are here trying to get in touch with Nina." He turned to look at the lawmen, shrugging his shoulders. Charlie nodded affirmatively as they came through the door and closed it.

"I told 'em we got a Christmas card from Nina. Any idea where that might be?"

As Al and Charlie followed him into the kitchen, his wife greeted them waving an envelope she had pulled from the built-in shelf organizer over a tidy kitchen desk. "This what you're looking for?"

"Told 'em you never throw anything. Let's see. Yup, there's an address ... 4867 Tropicana Way, Henderson, Nevada." Al took the envelope, writing down the address before handing it back. Bart continued, "Don't know if she's still there, but it might be a place to start."

"Tell us about Nina," Charlie suggested, looking for a little more to fill in the picture, as he and Al lounged against the cabinets in the spacious kitchen of the well-maintained rambler.

"Well, she was a wild one, or so I was told." As Bart talked, his eyes closed, as if he was somehow transporting himself back to the 1980s—an era that passed just after he was born. "Ma said she was beautiful ... long blonde hair, great body, dazzling blue eyes. Said she was always jealous of her little sister. Apparently all the boys followed her around. She was hired at the Saddle for exactly that reason, Ma said. But, gosh, Nina must be about in her 60s now. Not sure she ever married." Bart checked the envelope again. "The return address here says it came from Nina Ganz, so maybe she never did."

Al had taken careful notes as Simmons talked. Now he said, "Bart, have you ever heard the names Gene, Fleury, or Weepin' Willie?"

Simmons thought carefully. "Not familiar with Gene or Fleury, but I heard a Weepin' Willie. He was the town drunk. Never had a job, other than cleaning up the bars in the morning. The way I heard it, he did those jobs so he could drain whatever beer or booze was left in the glasses on the bar. God, can you imagine ..."

Simmons shuddered at the thought, and Al and Charlie just shook their heads.

During the next several minutes of questions and conversation—Charlie doing most of the talking, Al doing the writing—Simmons told them he had last seen Nina some 30 or 35 years ago when he was still in high school. "She was still a looker, I'll tell you that." He was smiling now. "Ma was right, she did have a killer body." He rolled his eyes as he thought about the aunt he hadn't seen for a couple of decades. "If you talk to her, tell 'er hi, will you?"

"We will," promised Al, putting his notepad back in his pocket and following Charlie out of the kitchen toward the front door. "And we are definitely going to try and talk to her … if we can find her, that is."

"Oh, we'll find her." Charlie was in full-on Golden Retriever mode.

They bid their good-byes to the Simmons, then drove slowly through Hazard as they headed back toward La Crosse.

"I guess Nina will be our first item of business Monday morning?"

"Yup, Charlie, if that address was only a year old we have a good chance to get a hold of her. Why don't we have breakfast at Ma's Monday morning and then you can come in with me and we'll try and find her, okay?"

"Sounds good. I'm sure I'll be hungry. Speakin' of hungry, we better hurry. Kelly's makin' roast chicken for dinner. I don't wanna be late for that." It was as good a reason as any to push the speed limit.

In record time, Charlie dropped Al at his house, waving to Jo Anne who had come out to greet them as they arrived. Al barely had time to get the door closed before Charlie was backing out of the driveway. "Say hi to Kelly," Jo Anne shouted to Charlie as he sped off.

"He's in a hurry. Kelly's making roast chicken and he doesn't want to miss it. You know Charlie."

"I sure do." She was smiling as she pulled Al into the house behind her.

"Mmm, smells good."

"Roast chicken here, too." She was giggling now. "Must be a

conspiracy—maybe you should investigate." Al laughed and pretended to go for his notepad. Things were looking up.

8

When Al reached Ma's Monday morning, Charlie wasn't yet there. That allowed Al to find a table and settle down for a few minutes with the *Tribune*, the La Crosse morning newspaper. He had just finished the news section when Charlie came in and sat down.

"Just out of curiosity, how was the chicken Friday night?"

"Best ever." Charlie was huffing from the exertion of hurrying into the restaurant. "When it comes to cookin', Kelly's the best."

"Well, guess what? Jo Anne *also* fixed a chicken—was pretty damn good, too. I think those girls were in collusion. I don't suppose you *also* watched that mushy Hallmark movie afterwards?"

"As a matter of fact, we did." The light dawned on Charlie's face as Al grinned. "Well ain't that a funny coincidence?"

"Like I said, collusion. We're being managed. But I can't say it's such a bad thing, since the rest of the evening turned out better than I would have expected," Al allowed with a smile.

Charlie let out a laugh, "You old dog—'looks like we both got what we had comin', so to speak."

When Ma came to take their order, she wondered at all of the laughter going on between the two, but this time she kept her questions to herself.

For the next half hour the two friends talked over breakfast—the usual two eggs, bacon and toast for Al. Charlie had a four-plate special—capping steak and eggs, hash browns, and ham, with a waffle.

As they were finishing up, Charlie burped, begged pardon, and asked, "So do you think we'll find 'er?"

"I imagine you're talking about Nina Ganz. If she's alive, we'll find her. I think we start by looking her up on that Whitepages web-site and see what we find."

"Good idea. I'll be over at your place after I run by the office."

"Sure. See you there."

Half an hour later, Al was in front of his computer. Charlie was looking over his shoulder. "There she is ... that must be her ... born in 1961. Still lives at 4867 Tropicana Way in Henderson, Nevada. Should we give her a ring?"

"You guys going steady?" Chief Whigg poked his head in the door.

"Oh, hi, Chief. C'mon in. We've been tracking down people from the tape made in Hazard and we think we've found the former bar maid. We talked yesterday with her nephew. He gave us a tip, and we think we've found her in Nevada. We were just going to call her."

"Interesting." Chief Brent Whigg mopped his head with a hanky, put it back in his pocket and lounged on Al's desk. "Give 'er a ring. I'm gonna listen for a while. See what she has to say."

Al dialed the number on the screen, then waited for a message "the-number-you-have-dialed-has-been-disconnected." But the phone rang once, then twice, then, "Hello?"

"Hi, there. Is this Nina Ganz?"

"That *was* my name but it's Nina Severin now. I got married four months ago. Who is this?"

"This is Detective Al Rouse with the La Crosse Police Department in Wisconsin. And before you ask, nothing is wrong, we just wanted to ask you a couple of questions."

"Me? I haven't been in Wisconsin for more than 20 years."

"So we've been told. We talked to your nephew Bart Simmons Friday. That's how we found you were in Nevada."

"Oh, yes, Bart. He's my older sister's boy. How is he?"

"He's great, Nina—and he said to say hello. His whole family is fine," Al volunteered all of the family news to save time and get down to business. "But we're hoping you might tell us a few things about a conversation taped in the Saddle Bar back in the 80s."

The chief and Charlie could hear the woman laugh as Al turned on the speaker, then told Severin the chief and Charlie were with him. "Nina, Charlie and I are looking into a cold case—the Shirley Sovereign kidnapping in 1979. Do you remember it?"

"Sure do. Happened when I was in middle school. Shook everyone up in my hometown. But what would I know about that?"

Al explained that he and Charlie had found the tape in an evidence box, which had led them to Hazard and Jeremy Simmons, who took them to his father. "Bart told us you were a bar maid at the time."

"Okay ..." The woman's response was hesitant.

"I think the quickest way to clarify the issues is for us to play the tape for you," Al told the woman. "Have you got a few minutes?"

"Absolutely, now that you have me intrigued."

Al cued up the tape, then played the conversation for Nina.

When the pertinent pieces had ended, he asked, "Remember that?"

"Gosh, no ... what a horrific story. If I'd actually heard what they were saying I'm sure I would have remembered it. That was more than 30 years ago, wasn't it?"

"About that," Al told her. "We didn't really think you'd remember, but is it possible you remember the people recorded on the tape?"

"Oh. That's easy, and I'm surprised I remember them all, except they were mostly regulars. The Gene is Gene Baner. He wasn't a regular, but he came in often enough, and was fairly well known. Fleury is Fleury Michaels. He was a railroader. He'd be in on weekends when he was home. I don't know Weepin' Willie's last name, but he was a dear old man. He'd clean the Saddle every morning ... and the other two taverns in town, too. He'd be drunk by nine from the leftover beer and booze. People always teased him 'cause they knew if they called him a drunk, he'd start to cry. That's why he was called Weepin' Willie."

"I don't suppose you'd know if any of these people are still alive?" asked Al.

"No, they were pretty old back then, so I'd be surprised if they are."

"Did any of them have children?"

"Boy … I don't know. I know Weepin' Willie lived with his sister. I don't think he had a wife. Fleury was married. His wife Ella was twice as big as he was. 'Used to beat him up if he got drunk, which was often."

"And Gene?"

"Gene … he was a real nice guy. Had done time in prison. The story was he had killed the sheriff and the sheriff's son. All I know about that was that everyone was grateful. The sheriff was crooked, and so was his son, or so I heard." Then she thought a minute. "You know, come to think of it, I'm pretty sure Gene had a daughter, but I never met her. She must've left with her mother, I think. Gosh, I'm surprised any of that came back to me. But maybe the daughter might know something, if you can find her."

The conversation continued a few more minutes, then Al gave her his number and asked her to call if she thought of anything else.

When he hung up, he looked at his colleagues. "End of the line? Whaddaya think?"

Whigg looked at Al and Charlie. "Well, I think looking for the Baner daughter is the only course of action there is. Unless you can dig up something else. I've got to be elsewhere—good luck guys," he said as he left.

Charlie was thinking hard as he fiddled with his coffee cup while seated on the other side of Al's desk. "Well, how about we check birth records? Seems to me we'd find her either in Vernon County or La Crosse County." As he twirled the cup, a large blob of coffee hit the desk and splattered all over the area.

Al was up in a flash, getting napkins from the credenza behind him. "Dammit, Charlie. This is a good mahogany desk."

"Cripes, Al, lighten up." Charlie carefully mopped up the mess, took aim at the waste basket behind Al, and let fly—right into Al's lap. "Oops. Sorry pal."

Although Charlie's apology was contrite, when Al looked up, he saw the grin his deputy friend was trying to hide behind his fist.

"Ya know, Charlie …" he began, as he carefully removed the

offending soggy missile and put it in the trash, and then took a long look at the unfortunate spot on the crotch of his pants. "… I just picked these trousers up from the cleaners Saturday."

"I'm really sorry, Al. I'll pay for the next cleaning job. But it isn't like I did it on purpose."

"Well, you're a notoriously poor basketball player, and I can't think why you even tried to make the shot—except you always do, and miss!"

Al sulked for as long as it took to mop off his trousers. Then, stoically, he straightened up and grabbed a pen. "Vernon or La Crosse birth records … that what you said? Makes sense. You take Vernon and I'll look at La Crosse. A female named Baner or a child born to a Gene Baner and his wife."

For the next hour, Al pecked away at his computer, exploring the La Crosse County data base, while Charlie did the same for Vernon County on his I-pad.

Al sighed and finally gave it up, brushed again at the front of his trousers that had dried. "I've been through every birth record there is for La Crosse County and there's nothing here. You having any better luck?" Al looked across at Charlie.

"Not … yet. No, nothing yet. I'm near the end of 1957." And then—perhaps a redeeming gift from the basketball angels—Charlie said excitedly, "Wait a minute! By golly, I think I found it, Al. Vernon County, December 4, 1957, Gene and Janet Baner, Hazard, Wisconsin, a girl, at Vernon Memorial Hospital. Let's see what else I can find."

"Good work! How did you go about that?"

"Well, I was pretty sure that Hazard once had a weekly newspaper. I checked that first—after the general Vernon County stuff. Bingo. There it was under announcements. That's gotta be her. But how the hell do we go about finding where she is now?"

Al perked up. "Those old weekly papers had a local news column. Why don't you search those from the birth day forward? I'm guessing they had her baptized. That will tell us her first name and get us going on the trail to finding her."

Charlie looked up and scratched his head. "Guess that's why you're a chief detective and make the big bucks, right?"

"Right." Al was shaking his head as he replied. "I thought chief deputies made the big bucks."

The two lawmen razzed each other back and forth until Al drew them back to seriousness. "Okay, baby girl Baner, born December 4, 1957. Now we need a first name."

Charlie began to peck away at his I-pad, looking through the weekly paper columns for anything about a baptism, starting in December '57. Silence settled over the office. Al busied himself looking at the *Hazard Enterprise* records starting in 1974. He was searching for graduation records, marriage license, anything that would tie back to the Baner girl.

After half an hour, Charlie straightened up, stretched, then asked Al what time it was.

"Approaching 11:30."

"Almost lunchtime. Are we gonna order in or eat out?"

"I'd prefer to eat here and keep going. This is pretty tedious work, and if I move away from it, I might never get back in the groove."

Al stretched, straightened his tie, rested his chin on his hands for a moment, then looked up. "Wanna split a pizza?"

"Sure, that'd be great! I eat anything—don't say it—so just order what you want and I'll split the bill. I'd like a 1919, though. Better'n that crap you have in your coke machine."

"1919 … what's that?"

"Root beer, fer godsakes, where 'you been livin' for the past 20 years? It's the best root beer there is … on tap."

"Okay, I'll ask. How about Big Al's? It's nearby."

"Fine. Oh, just a minute here …"

Al stopped dialing and looked at Charlie, who was staring intently at his computer. After waiting for a while, he asked, "What?"

"Shh, don't bother me, just order the pizza. I think I got something here."

After Al confirmed that Big Al's did, indeed, have 1919, and ordered a large "the works" pizza and a half gallon of the root beer, he looked back at his buddy, who now was scribbling feverishly on a note tablet. "And?"

Charlie didn't look up.

"Charlie, are you here?"

"Oh, sorry. Did you get it ordered?"

"Yup—and a bucket of 1919, too—but what is so interesting?"

"I think I found it in the Vernon County paper, March 23, 1958. 'The daughter of Gene and Janet Baner was baptized Sunday at United Methodist Church. Sponsors were Albion and Adele Spencer. The Baners, in honor of baby girl Barbara Ann, entertained friends and relatives at their home following the service.' That's the report."

"Great! That's it. That's what we were looking for. Good sleuthing, pal. Hmm, Barbara Ann Baner ... a name. Now maybe we can run her down."

9

l walked into Ma's the next morning feeling right with the world. He and Charlie'd had a good day the day before, he and Jo Anne enjoyed a La Crosse Community Theater production of "Cats" last night, and he thought that in Barbara Ann Baner they had developed a solid lead in the Shirley Sovereign case.

Charlie was waiting for him at a table by the window. "Ma, the prodigal son has showed up." He beamed at Al, who now was looking around. Spotting Charlie, he walked over. "Hey, you're early. What's up? Special day?"

"Nope, just ready to get going on the Baner girl. Wanna see if we can find her."

"I'm sure we can. Twenty years ago, it might have been different."

"Twenty years ago … like when we were young?"

"Whaddaya mean, 'when' … I don't feel old. We're still young, aren't we?"

"No, we're not … at least I'm not. Kelly has me on a diet. I tried a workout last week and damn near died. I'm old, fat, and outa shape. And that's a fact."

"Just for the sake of argument, Charlie, if you're like me, you're definitely out of shape. And you're big, too, yes, but you're not fat. And you're certainly not old. What are you … 42 or 43?"

"Forty-three and I feel a 104."

"That's probably the workout hangover. If you keep it up, you'll get over it."

The waitress gently elbowed Al toward a chair so she could set a plate in front of Charlie. The single poached egg, one strip of bacon, and one piece of rye toast looked somewhat lonesome on the large plate.

"Eating healthy, too, I see?" Al pulled out a chair, sat down, and the waitress filled his coffee cup, then waited for his order. "The usual, Sandy. Thanks for the coffee."

"So, Charlie, you up for another day in front of the computer? I jotted down some databases that I think might have something on Barbara Ann. Funny, isn't it? She's all of a sudden become someone alive."

"How old would she be?" The look on Charlie's face indicated he was computing, but Al beat him. "If she was born December 4, 1957, she'd be 63."

"Is that right?" Charlie was squinting. "Or would she be 62 … hasn't yet reached 63, has she?"

"You're probably right. Okay, born at the end of the year, she's 62. She should still be alive. And if she is, we can find her."

Back at the office, Al suggested Charlie start with the 1975 Vernon County newspaper again. "Look at May and June, see if you can find a list of Hazard High School graduates. If you find a list and she's not on it, try 1974. Maybe she was a whiz kid."

Al began to look at the Vernon County Clerk database of marriage licenses issued in the late 1970s. He began in 1977 and worked his way forward.

"Bingo!" Charlie was smiling and pointing at his screen. "Barbara Ann Baner was a member of the Class of 1975 at Hazard High School. Actually, there's a whole article about her in the 1977 newspaper archive that came up first. You won't believe it. Wanna see her?"

Al walked around the desk to where Charlie was seated and craned his head over Charlie's shoulder to see where he was pointing. As he found the subject of Charlie's search, he looked at a smiling girl with blonde hair. Her even white teeth went with the rest of the image. She was quite beautiful, even with a hairstyle that no longer was in vogue.

Al gave a low whistle. "Wow, a real beauty."

"She is, isn't she? And she's got the credentials to prove it, see?"

Charlie moved the screen so Al could read the caption under the picture. "'Miss Vernon County, 1976, runner-up to Miss Wisconsin, 1977.' Damn right, she has the credentials." They were both stunned as they stared at the screen.

Al wondered aloud, "We started out looking for a 'baby girl Baner' and wind up with an almost-Miss Wisconsin? What are the chances of that?"

Charlie mused, "A real beauty queen. With that kind of distinction, she shouldn't be hard to find."

Al moved back to his position, energized now by what he learned about Barbara Baner. He continued his Vernon County search, looking for marriage records up through 1980, but finding nothing.

He turned to the law enforcement databases he had identified as possibilities, and still found nothing. Meanwhile, Charlie had exhausted his links, too.

"Almost lunchtime." Al stretched while he looked at Charlie. The usual smile was absent. "What's the matter?"

"I'm on a diet, remember? I brought a tuna sandwich. The only thing good about the sandwich is the green pepper Kelly put on it to mask the tuna taste. She insists I have to have it. And so, I will."

Al settled for McDonald's, and when the two got back from the short trip up the street, both got back to work.

The search plodded along until suddenly Al straightened up, then bent to look closer at the screen. "Wow, Charlie, you gotta hear this … the Baner girl changed her name in 1983 to Forsythe. So, she's Barbara Forsythe now. Wonder if I can turn her up on Google."

Charlie by now had left his chair, moved to behind Al, and was bent over to see the screen.

Al hit the keys and waited. In 0.34 seconds, Google popped up a photo of the stunningly attractive woman. The headline beneath the picture read, "Forsythe named general manager of Miss America."

"Wow—she just gets better and better-looking." Charlie continued to stare at the image until Al elbowed him in the ribs.

"Stop drooling, we've got work to do. Now that we know who she is, let's see what we can find. Why don't you go back to the newspaper archives and see if there's a search function. Plug in Barbara Forsythe and see what you find. I'll stay with Google to see what else I can turn up."

For half an hour the only sounds in the room were the click of computer keys, an occasional exclamation as a new fact turned up, and Charlie loudly sipping his coffee. Finally, Al called a halt.

"I think we now know where to get some of what we need. Miss America is headquartered in Atlantic City, New Jersey. I'm gonna call their HQ and see if I can find out where she is. Once I know that, maybe we can arrange a time we can talk. Why don't you pick up where I left off on Google? I was just getting into some pretty interesting reports, I think. Here, let me help you find where I am and you can take over there."

Al leaned over to Charlie's computer, erased what he'd been looking at, and began the Google search that would take Charlie to the reports he'd just found.

"There," he said a minute or so later. "This one looks really interesting. It's a long interview at the time she was named general manager in 1987. She then became president and is CEO now, so they must've been pretty happy with her. See if there's anything of interest in the interview while I try the headquarters to see if she is still around."

Charlie looked at Al with one of those why-do-you-get-all-the-great-assignments looks, then turned back to his screen and began to read.

Not two minutes later, he said, "Holy cow!" Charlie was on his feet. "Al, you gotta see this. It is a bombshell."

"Whaddaya got?"

"Look here, it talks about why she changed her name. Man, this investigation is taking on a whole new complexion, if you ask me."

Al rolled his chair over as Charlie sat back down and they began to read together. Charlie had focused on a small section of the long interview that Al had found in one of the trade journals. The reporter, a Mark Plenke, did the interview in Q & A format. The article was published in 1987.

Q—What is the biggest decision you have made in life?

A—I grew up in a small town in Wisconsin. It was a horrible, mean-spirited place and I hated it; couldn't wait to leave. When I finished second in the Miss Wisconsin Pageant in 1977, I felt it was my big break. I did a lot for Miss America back then and it paid off in a job. My parents were wonderful people and I loved them dearly, but my father had gotten into trouble as a younger man and it haunted him. No jobs, then no good jobs. We always struggled. After I came to New Jersey I wanted a fresh start, so I changed my name. It almost killed my parents. They thought I was ashamed of them. In reality it wasn't them, it was where we lived and how people acted.

Q—How people acted?

A—I was always that poor little girl ..."Isn't she pretty, but, my, what a past." I guess it was my parents, but it wasn't their fault. It was where we lived. Some people in that town were just beyond redemption.

Q—Would you tell me what was bad about it?"

A—I shouldn't, I suppose, but someone should've done something about the things that happened there. I wonder if it's still the same. I left in 1977 and I've never been back. My folks are dead now, so there's no reason to return and every reason to stay away.

Q—You sound like you have some-thing to say, but you won't say it. Isn't that contrary to the new Miss America culture you are putting into place?

A—You're right. It is. Women need to speak up. Well, the town where I grew up seemed like it was filled with bad men. It wasn't just one or two, it was the culture of the whole town. When I began to develop a figure, the boys played their usual games, but it was the men in town who were the worst. I couldn't go into a store without being harassed by the owner or manager. A poke here, a pinch there, suggestive remarks. But the worst part was, even in our high school, there were several young women who disappeared without a trace, never to be found. I don't know what happened to them, but some people said they thought they were probably murdered. And no one was able to do anything about it.

Q—Why didn't someone go to the police?

A—The police? (A laugh.) They were the biggest part of the problem. I had two classmates who were raped in squad cars. And with me, they tried ... boy how they tried. One night one of the police officers held me down and started stripping off my clothes. But I had learned to fight like a man and kick like a girl. Let's just say he couldn't stand up straight for a week. I left at the earliest chance and never looked back.

The report went on to other topics at that point. But the revelation in the story seemed to be taking them from a simple line of inquiry to complicated allegations of corruption in Hazard. The lawmen both felt the same punch in the gut. Suddenly it was something more than a kidnapping and possible murder of one La Crosse resident.

Al and Charlie stared at each other. Al took a deep breath and let it out slowly.

"Charlie, this feels a whole lot bigger than the Sovereign case, not that I'm minimizing that one, but do you really think she's right when she talks about the police raping girls and then young women disappearing?"

"Yeah. And this is gonna sound strange coming from me, but maybe we're thinking about running before we walk here."

Al twirled his pen in the customary fashion, rolling it between his fingers on one hand and popping it up ready to write. After enduring a maddening minute of pen-flipping, Charlie snapped and reached over and grabbed the pen out of Al's hand. "Hey, Rouse. Did you hear what I said?"

"I did hear, actually. And you're right. We'd better fill in the blanks before we go racing off on another serial killing mystery trail."

Al thought for a few minutes, then said, "I think we should try and get in touch with Barbara Forsythe and see if we can arrange a phone call for the three of us. We'll get to know her a little better—at least get a feel for her character—and maybe be able to question her more thoroughly about the accusation of rapes and disappearances. Make sense to you?"

"Sure does. Let's call her."

Al was already at the keyboard, Googling the Miss America Pageant number. Only seconds had elapsed when he started writing it down.

"Got it, let's call her." He moved his desk phone nearer the two of them, then dialed the number, and put the phone on speaker.

"Miss America Pageant, this is Jacquelyn. How may I help you?"

"Jacquelyn, this is Al Rouse and Charles Berzinski calling. We are law officers in Wisconsin and we'd like to speak to Barbara Forsythe, please."

"Oh, my, law officers. I will put you into Ms. Forsythe's office. Her assistant is Kathy."

Three rings later and a voice said, "Barbara Forsythe's office, Kathy speaking. How may I help you?"

Al introduced himself and Charlie. "Kathy, this is Detective Al Rouse with the La Crosse police, and I'm with Deputy Sheriff Charlie Berzinski of La Crosse County, Wisconsin. We've been researching a possible crime committed several years ago. And, as we looked through files, we found an interview that Ms. Forsythe did with a Mark Plenke in the late 1980s. The interview has piqued our interest and we wonder if we could set up a time for a phone call with Ms. Forsythe."

"Goodness, what an odd request. I've never had one like this. May I put you on hold for a moment, please?"

"Certainly."

The room was filled with upbeat music—a rendition of, "*It Takes A Woman*" from "*Hello Dolly.*" Soon Al was tapping his pencil in time with the music and Charlie was whistling. The song had almost played through when Kathy came back on the line.

"Gentlemen, Ms. Forsythe expressed great relief that someone from law enforcement had finally called her to follow-up on the interview—even if it was some 30 years in coming. But, hopefully you can understand that she is concerned that you are, in fact, law officers."

"Understandable," said Al. "I anticipated we might get that question. Tell you what, give me a couple of minutes and we will photograph our credentials and email them to you. Will that work?"

"Perfectly, and since she was confident you would do that, Ms. Forsythe said she would await your call tomorrow morning at 10. That would be nine your time."

The call ended, Al and Charlie put their shields and pocket-fold credentials on the desk, Al snapped a photo with his phone. Then he called in the office receptionist to snap a picture of him and Charlie. He attached both photos to an email and sent them to the address Kathy had provided.

He and Charlie waited five minutes, then he called the direct line Kathy had also provided and confirmed that she had received the photos.

"Barbara will be looking forward to talking to you tomorrow," she told them sweetly.

10

"Are we ready?"

For the past hour, Al and Charlie had been planning for their interview with Barbara Forsythe. They were seated in the conference room across the hall from Al's office, having shifted several boxes to make space at the end of the table. The receptionist had just come in and connected the conference phone. Al was fidgety as he talked with Charlie.

"I think so. I can't think of anything we have overlooked, can you? By the way, do you know how to work that thing?" Charlie nodded at the telephone as he talked.

"I think so. Looks complicated, doesn't it?"

"Sure as heck does. Glad it's not me operating the damn thing."

With 9 a.m. showing on his watch and on his computer, Al turned the phone around, then punched in the number.

Before the first ring was completed, a voice said: "Barbara Forsythe." It was a pleasant voice—very feminine, but assertive. Overall, it created a favorable impression.

"Ms. Forsythe, Allan Rouse and Charles Berzinski here. I am with the La Crosse Police Department. Mr. Berzinski is the La Crosse County sheriff's chief deputy."

"Gentlemen, good morning. How about we dispense with the formalities. You can call me Barbara or Barb. The latter is preferred. May I call you Al and Charles, or ..."

"Charlie, ma'am," said Charlie jumping in.

"And, Charlie, that will be the last 'ma'am' I hear from you, all right?"

"Yes, ma'am ... oops, sorry."

The lilting laugh made both men smile.

"Now how can I help you … no, first let me tell you how grateful I am for your call. I thought the chances of anyone contacting me were long gone."

"Barb, we are investigating a very old cold case—the disappearance of Shirley Sovereign in 1979."

"I remember it well. I was gone from the area by then but my mother was very shaken by it and made sure I got all of the news clippings. I remember even seeing some TV reports on the case. I came to wonder if it was somehow linked to the disappearance of young women I knew in high school."

"That's why we're calling." As he talked, Al was studying the notes he and Charlie had made. "As you know, we read the interview you did for a trade journal in 1987."

"I remember it well. Mark Plenke was a nice young man. I had just been elevated to a management position with M.A. and he had arranged to interview me. I debated whether to say anything about Hazard and the problems I experienced and observed."

"It may prove fortunate for us that you decided to tell what you experienced. But let me explain." Al was again studying his notes. "Charlie and I took on the cold case as kind of a break from routine police work. As it happens, the trail of evidence led us to Hazard and, ultimately, to you when we realized the story we were following might have died with your father and his friends."

"My father? Surely you don't think he had anything to do with the kidnapping?"

"We don't, Barb, but he participated in a conversation at the Saddle Bar that was recorded some years ago. The people he was talking with made it seem as if they knew about the kidnapping and what happened. We reached out to you because you are the only person who might be able to help us learn something about events at the time, and possibly information on the others in that conversation."

"Gosh, I don't know if I can help, but let's talk anyway. There are some things I do know."

Charlie moved a bit closer to the phone, and slid forward on his chair. "Barb, Charlie here. On the tape Al refers to, it seemed apparent that the other two men on the tape might know something. Their names were Weepin' Willie—Battaglia, maybe—and Fleury Michaels."

"My goodness, I haven't heard those names for years and years. I loved Willie. He was a very kindly man with a bad, bad habit. I didn't know Fleury personally, but I knew who he was."

"Fleury was involved with the kidnapping event, we think," said Al. "And Willie apparently saw some of it, because we think the girl was brought back to Hazard in a car that Fleury was driving."

"That's … shocking." A long silence ensued as Al and Charlie waited for the woman to continue. "But in thinking about it, maybe it's not so surprising. It wasn't uncommon for young women to disappear back in those days. I personally knew three of them."

"So there were three disappearances that you knew of?" Al was again participating and both lawmen huddled closer to the phone, as if they could draw the words out of the instrument.

"Yes … yes, there were. They were the kinds of girls that drew less attention than they deserved, as if they were invisible. They were— how should I put it—girls from less prominent families … girls with reputations that were rumored as questionable. I'm not sure that was deserved, though."

"Would you tell us everything you can remember?" Al and Charlie both had notepads and pens out now and were feverishly making notes as Barbara Forsythe talked.

"Hmmm, let's see. From the time I was a freshman in high school until I graduated in 1976, there were three girls that I went to school with who vanished. I remember being upset that nothing seemed to be done about it.

"I remember talking to my parents about it. My dad was vehement and said that I should forget it and keep my mouth shut. I was just starting in high school, and I pushed him on it, I remember, and he took me aside and told me there was a bad group of people in Hazard who probably had something to do with it. He said my talking about it might result in my vanishing, too. He literally scared me into silence."

"Did he say who the men were?" asked Charlie.

"He didn't use names but he did imply that that they were among the bigshots in the community. Later I came to assume they were some of the business owners. I can tell you that, when I lived there, it was a dangerous time for young women, especially those who had developed—well, let me be honest here, and use an entirely inappropriate Miss America term—'boobs.'

"I was an early developer, and I paid for it, too. Whenever I went into a store by myself, which I tried not to do, I was pinched, prodded and, frankly, felt up. It was awful."

"Barb, that's assault." As Al spoke up, both he and Charlie were shaking their heads. "The article said that going to the police would have been useless, because you felt they were involved."

"They *were* involved—definitely!" The statement was delivered with force, the venom dripping off her words.

"Tell us more," said Al.

"Well, in addition to the three girls who vanished—one freshman, one sophomore, and one junior—there were two girls in my class who were raped by one of the county patrolmen. He'd give them a ride, allegedly providing them a way home, then he'd drive them out of town someplace where he threatened them until they did what he wanted … which, of course, was sex."

"Were these things reported?"

"No, Al, they weren't. There was such an element of fear across the community that no one spoke up. The things I'd hear grown men say to me when they'd pass by on the street were horrific. Even the leers were terrifying."

Barb had been speaking so fast that she paused to slow down. "I brought it up to my mother once and she sat me down and told me exactly what I had to do. She told me to avoid the stores where I had been molested. She promised to try and be with me whenever I needed to go downtown." Barb laughed. "It's pretty hard to avoid going downtown in a town the size of Hazard. But she told me never—under any circumstances—*never* to accept a ride from any policeman."

"Barb, you must have had some idea of who the bad guys were. I know the sheriff down there—Rudy Svendson—and he's a good guy. And he's been the sheriff for a long time."

"I don't know that name, Charlie, and I'm glad to hear that things in that area are better. But the attitude there was so pervasive that I doubt it could be totally gone. And I don't plan to find out. Dad died in 1983. He'd had a hard life. When he was only 21, dad shot the sheriff and the sheriff's son."

The tone in her voice took on a tinge of sadness. "Dad spent 12 years in prison and then was released when it was finally proven the shootings were self-defense and warranted. His sentence was commuted and his record washed clean. Didn't help much when it came to finding jobs though. He was always the guy who shot the sheriff. I think his inability to provide for his family—in the way he knew he could have—contributed to his death.

"He and mom moved to Wyoming in 1981. They had a nice place in a small town and they were popular. But dad was old by then, and he was unable to handle jobs that would have paid well. Then a heart attack finally took him at 83. Mom died seven years later of a broken heart. She stayed in Wyoming—I couldn't get her to move in with me."

"Thanks, Barb, that fills in some of the puzzle. But think hard now—do you recall anything about the kidnapping that might have linked it to Hazard?

"Hmmm, no, not that I can think of. Hmmm, just a minute—there might have been something, but let me see if I can recall how she said it. Seems to me mom once said something odd about the search being in the wrong place. They had searched every square inch of La Crosse. But she said something that went like … 'They need to get down to this area and look at the tobacco barns south of here.' I'm sure it was something like that. The implication may have been that she was brought to Hazard, and killed, and her body hidden."

"You don't remember if your mom said anything about *who*, do you?"

"Charlie, I don't … I just don't remember."

The three talked for the next half hour about Hazard, Barb's leaving, her involvement with the pageant, and how she missed the beauty of Wisconsin—but not the atmosphere.

"Lots of buildings and concrete around here. Nothing much to look at, to be honest."

"Well, if you ever want to visit, let us know, and we will make sure you have an escort at all times."

"Doubt that's going to happen, Charlie," she said with a low laugh, "Unless maybe a woman from Wisconsin wins the pageant. Thought that might happen a few years ago when the contestant from Arcadia was ranked very highly. She would have made a great Miss America, but for the reasons we've talked about, I was relieved when she didn't win."

"Tell you what, Barb, I'm going to send you an email, through your assistant, Kathy, and provide you with our contact information. If anything pops into your mind, please let me or Charlie know. And thank you so much for your time and your help."

"The pleasure was mine, gentlemen. I hope someday I get a chance to meet you—just not in Hazard."

The conversation ended, Al pushed the phone aside, and rocked back in his chair. "Sort of makes you feel ashamed to be a cop. Do you really think there's still something going on down there?"

"And if there is, who the hell we gonna ask about it?" Charlie's face was red and he looked as if he wanted to punch someone.

But Al knew he was right—where would they go for information? "What about Martha Simmons?" he wondered aloud. "They were nice, helpful folks."

"Wouldn't hurt to ask," said Charlie. "You thinkin' of another ride?"

"I am."

As Al leaned back, preparing to expand on the idea, both men were startled by the shrill of the conference phone.

<hr>

"Now who in hell has *that* number?" Al's eyebrows were knitted together in puzzlement as he reached for the phone."

"Al Rouse."

"Al, Barb Forsythe. I just thought of something that might be interesting."

Al quickly hit the speaker button. "I just hit the speaker, Barb, so Charlie can hear, too."

"I was thinking back to my high school days and it seems there was a guy named Gettenburg, or Gantenbine, or something like that. First name was Jake, I think. One time I heard dad tell mom, when they didn't know that I could hear, that Jake what's-his-name was probably involved and the law guys had made a miserable situation worse. That's all I've got. Don't know if it's important or not, but it was a name that popped up and thought I would give you a call."

Both men thanked her.

The call ended, Al looked at Charlie. "A lead, Charlie, an honest to goodness hard lead." He looked at his watch and shook his head in amazement. "That took two hours. How about an early lunch?"

"Let's make it quick," said Charlie. "I have mine."

He held up a small paper bag.

"So do I," said Al, holding up a bag roughly the same size.

"We gotta hunt this guy down, Al. Something might still be going on—or at least was going on—that's bad news."

"I agree. We'll get at it right after lunch."

11

"I wonder if we should talk to Brent and Dwight about where we are?"

"That's pro'bly a pretty good idea," said Charlie, settling into the chair across from Al's desk. "We're wadin' in deep water here, given what we've found. Check and see if Brent's available, and when I know that, I'll call Dwight."

"Back in a minute." Al went out the door and turned toward the police chief's office. Charlie grabbed his cell phone to be ready to call Dwight, then began checking new messages. Thankfully there weren't many. He had just read the first one when Al hustled back into the room.

"You won't believe it but Brent and Dwight are meeting in the chief's office. They want us to come in."

"Great." Charlie left his chair and moved down the hall with Al.

Police Chief Brent Whigg had moved two chairs nearer his desk for them, and when they entered, he closed the door.

"You guys look pretty serious." Whigg made the observation as he settled into his chair behind the large desk.

"It is serious," said Al, "and we need some advice. You both know we have been looking into the Sovereign kidnapping case. We started with the tape you gave us, Chief, then began to see if anyone who was on that recording was still alive. We found the bar maid by accident as we visited Hazard. A youngster—a relative of hers—overheard us and said he knew the woman we were looking for. When we contacted her, she tried to be helpful but didn't remember the tape. She remembered the people who were involved, though, and said she thought that one of them, a Gene Baner, had a daughter."

"And what a bombshell that turned out to be." Charlie was sitting on the edge of his chair as he entered the conversation. "As we looked for her, we found out she left Hazard and now is the general manager of the Miss America organization. She's real good lookin', too, finished as runner-up for Miss Wisconsin. And she told us why she changed her name. We had found that she is now named Barbara Forsythe—but that's the least of the news."

"Folks, she told us Hazard had—and maybe still has—a network of really bad guys … the reason she left town," said Al, breaking in. "She also alleged that, while she was in high school, three students disappeared and have never been heard from since. But the stinger is, she also said that two students were raped … by officers, in the back of squad cars."

Relaxed until now, Brent Whigg vaulted nearly out of his chair. "Did I hear that right? Three girls gone and two others raped by the police? Did she really say that?"

"Chief, she was adamant … the town was, she said, a den of vipers. She said she left as fast as she could after high school and—though it was traumatic—changing her name was the first thing she did. And, yes, she said three disappearances and two rapes."

The four lawmen sat there thinking about the situation. Charlie was the first to speak. "The question is, what the hell do we do now? First of all, those alleged disappearances and rapes occurred more than forty years ago. Are the people still around? And what about the police? Can't really talk to the locals. Not sure about the sheriff and his deputies, either, although the sheriff is a good guy. He's been in our office a few times. He mighta been around back then, but he sure as heck wasn't sheriff."

Chief Whigg was the next to speak. "Well, we've got an honest-to-God conundrum here. We have no jurisdiction in the place. We were okay talking to people because of the Sovereign case, but now we're on the edge. Gotta think about this a moment."

Sheriff Dwight Hooper got up and began to pace. A long, lanky man, he covered the big office in about two steps before encountering a wall and turning around. After a couple of laps, he stopped.

"Charlie is right about the sheriff being a good guy," he said. "His name is Rudy Svendson, and as far as I'm concerned he's a straight-shooter. If he's mixed up in any of this, I'd be shocked."

Al was also on his feet. He stood there a few moments, hands in his pockets, then said, "So, unless I'm mistaken, the only official we know down there is the sheriff. We think he's a good guy and but we're not ready to bet the farm on that. Outside that, we have Bart and Martha Simmons. They seem like good people, but how do we know? And then, there's Barbara Baner Forsythe—who certainly sounds sincere and seems like she's got her shit together, but we've never seen her face to face, nor had a chance to study her as we questioned her."

"So here's what I'm thinkin'." The chief was hunched over his desk, making notes as he talked. "I think you have to get Barb Forsythe back on the phone. You need her to name names. I'm surprised you didn't push her for those when you talked to her, but I can understand with the situation that you didn't. Might be better, in fact, to schedule another session with her. Think she'd consent to a video interview?"

"Chief, I don't think that's a good idea," said Al, chiming in. "If we want her to name names, I think we can finesse the situation better in a simple phone call. A video interview could feel stilted … could cause her to clam. We have a rapport with her, I think. Do you agree, Charlie?"

Charlie nodded and Al continued. "I say we call her assistant, tell her we'd like a little more time with her boss, and see if she'll set something up for us."

"I think that's good, Al," said the sheriff. "A phone chat would be the least off-putting. Brent, I think we should let these two go with that strategy. If we get some names, maybe we can get back together and talk some more."

Al and Charlie stood, thanked their bosses for their time, and headed back to Al's office to make another call to Atlantic City.

"You call her, Al," said Charlie as they reached Al's office. "You've talked to her the most."

"I'll give her a ring." Al checked his watch and was surprised to see it was after three. "Not sure we'll get her, 'though. It's after four in Atlantic City."

"Well, give her a ring. We should get Kathy if we don't get Barb."

They sat and Al dialed the number.

"Barbara Forsythe's office, Kathy speaking."

"Hi, Kathy, Al Rouse and Charlie Berzinski calling again. I'm surprised to get you, given the time. We are interested in a short visit with Ms. Forsythe."

A lilting laugh came over the speaker phone. "Detective Rouse, this is the middle of our work day. We're always here until seven or later."

"My goodness, what kind of work hours do you keep?"

"Twelve-hour days are the norm around here. But Barb makes them fun, so time passes quickly. Speaking of time, Barb is in a meeting that should be breaking up. Give me a second to check."

In less than a minute Kathy returned to the phone. "Al, I am going to transfer you to Barb now. I think she was ready to end the meeting and you gave her a good excuse. One moment."

"Hi, detective, what's up? Didn't expect to hear from you again today."

"Hello, Barb. Charlie and I just finished up a meeting with our bosses and, at their urging, we decided to call you back. Charlie is here, too."

"Hi, Charlie, how are you?" The voice was so sweet, smooth, and sexy that Charlie just melted on the spot.

"I'm great. Just great."

"So how can I help you gentlemen this fine afternoon?"

"Barb, as you might imagine—for two cops from La Crosse—the notion of invading Vernon County is sort of a sensitive one. We can't just go into the county and start talking to people. So, our meeting just now focused on how best to go about it."

"And?"

"And we're hoping you'd be kind enough to give us some names or a name that we can start with. We'd, of course, like to know the names of the young women who vanished—but even more important are the names of the rape victims. We're assuming they are still alive and we'd like to talk to them. And, your sense of the bad cops and the good cops would also be a place for us to start. If we get some names, it would be helpful."

"I thought you might be calling to ask for this information. I've been wrestling with myself all afternoon about how to respond. Here's what I decided: I can't open my mouth and make accusations if I am unwilling to back them up. You called at a great time. I just ended a boring meeting that gave me plenty time to think. So here you go, get your pencils and paper ready."

"Where do you want to start?"

"How about at the beginning," she said, then took a deep breath.

"The beginning it is," said Al. "You're on."

"Well, when I was in school in Hazard, all the girls knew the town cop and the two sheriff's deputies who most frequently were in town were bad news. They leered at all the women, tried to get them into their cars. I knew two girls who got into those cars and paid the price."

"What happened?" Charlie was practically in the desk phone.

"Well, Pam Wiseman told me she lost her panties out by the dump and just escaped being raped by the town cop. His name was Paul Amundson. The other girl, Judy or Julie Overhaug, escaped when the sheriff's deputy had removed his gun and was busy taking off his pants. She was naked in the backseat, also at the dump. She told me she started screaming, ran from the car, and kept screaming. The deputy, she said, drove past her at a high rate of speed. His name was Abraham Svendson. I believe his son is the sheriff now. Okay, that covers a couple of things. The two women who were raped were Helga Meyers and Jodie Olson."

"What about the women who vanished." Al was totally engaged as he talked, feverishly writing notes and making sure the recorder was operating.

"Two sophomores and a freshman, actually. It's been a long time, but I think I remember their names. Sandy Meulemans, Victoria

Weinandy, and Missy Flanagan. And, much later, I'm sorry to say, another girl vanished in 2004—Molly Grisham. She was only 15 years old. Molly was the daughter of my mom's youngest sister, and it broke my heart."

Al finished writing, sat back in his chair and unconsciously began to twirl his pen. "Barbara, these names are very helpful. Do you know if any of their relatives still live in Hazard?"

"The only ones I'm sure of are my aunt and uncle. Beth and Bill Grisham. They were very broken up about Molly's disappearance. She kind of got involved with a rough crowd. As for the other girls, the assumption when the three went missing at the same time was that they left together."

After a break in the conversation, Barb again spoke up. "I think that's about what I know, Al. When I left Hazard, I guess I never looked back. I feel badly now that I didn't spend more time with my folks, but when I left I wanted as far away from Hazard as I could get. As I look at it now it was the right decision, but I made some mistakes."

"Barb, don't beat yourself up too much. We can understand why you'd want to be gone. Charlie and I are going to start looking into this. I promise to keep you posted if we turn up anything."

As Al hung up the phone, he turned to Charlie. "What say we call the Simmons and see if Martha might know Beth and Bill Grisham and, if she does, would introduce us to Beth? I would have asked Barb, but I sensed she hadn't stayed in touch."

"Great minds think alike." Charlie turned back from the window where he stood. "I was just thinking what a small world it is—Martha Simmons was key in helping us find Nina, and now she will hopefully help us meet Beth and Bill Grisham."

Al was already at work on his computer. "I have Simmons's number," he said looking up. "Why don't you call her?"

Charlie punched in the number Al provided, listened, then said, "Mrs. Simmons ... Martha ... it's Charlie Berzinski. We talked a day or so ago. Yes, yes, we did—we got ahold of her. She was very helpful. Now we hope we can prevail upon you for more help. We're wondering if you know Beth and Bill Grisham. You do? Great. Any chance you might introduce us?" There was a pause as he listened. "Yes, we understand Molly went missing. We'd like to talk to her about that." Another pause. "Yes, ma'am, we do understand the sensitivity of the matter, and we will be very circumspect."

When Charlie used the word 'circumspect,' Al raised his eyebrows. Every now and then his buddy surprised him with his intellect.

The conversation soon concluded and Charlie looked a bit smug when he turned to Al. "Martha will either arrange a meeting or else be there to make the introduction. She thought she might invite Beth over to her house—the Grishams live in Richland Center now. She was thinking we can meet with her there. Okay with you?"

"Absolutely."

"She will give me a call when she has it set." For the next few minutes they straightened up the conference room, and, as they were ready to leave, Charlie's phone rang.

"Oh, hi, Martha. Didn't expect to hear from you this soon. Sure glad, though." He paused. "Good news? Oh, great … tomorrow afternoon? Yes, I'm sure we can be there. 1 p.m.?"

He looked at Al, who nodded. "That will work, Martha. We sure appreciate your help. See you tomorrow." Charlie was about to ring off but stopped. "A question, sure … Beth Grisham wants you to sit in on the talk? I don't think that will be a problem, Martha." And after looking at Al, "No, Martha, no problem at all. Okay, see you tomorrow … and we thank you again for your help."

"So, a session tomorrow with Beth Grisham, right? I imagine it's still a difficult thing to talk about, but I hope we can get some kind of insight on what might've happened—after all of this time."

"Martha told me she's glad someone is finally looking into Molly's disappearance. Said she'd help to try and make sure Beth tells us the whole story."

"Great job, Charlie. Until tomorrow, then."

"Yup, see you late morning. Need to make a stop at the office before coming over."

12

Just before noon the next day, with Al behind the wheel of an unmarked police car, Al and Charlie headed down Highway 14. It was a beautiful day. A few cumulus clouds hovered overhead in a deep blue sky, the result of an evening thunderstorm the night before. The countryside was a study in green—from the fields of corn waving gently in the breeze to the shorter soybeans that looked vibrant and healthy.

"You know, Al, I think it was right about here that the bra and panties we believe belonged to Shirley Sovereign were found."

"You're right. And that bridge we just passed was where the tennis shoes were discovered. Speaking of which, we need to check on that. The DNA testing on those items should be complete. We need to see if they're back."

"Great. You know, I've been thinking, Al, that I'd be very grateful if you took the lead on the interview with Mrs. Grisham. I think I do better if I listen and react. You're better at settling people down and getting them to talk."

"I don't know if I agree with your assessment, Charlie, but if you want me to lead off, okay. That means, though, that you will have to take notes on what is said and your observations of the goings on. You all right with that?"

"Absolutely."

As they entered Hazard on Highway 82, Al drove down the main street, then turned left to get to the Simmons's house. As they neared the property, they saw two trucks in front of the house and two cars in the driveway.

"Wow, that's a crowd—wonder if that's a good thing, but I s'pose there's nothing we can do about it now."

"It is what it is, Charlie. Let's see what happens."

Al made a U-turn and parked in front of the house across the street from Simmons' two-story brick bungalow.

"Great house, don't you think?" Al was walking up the sidewalk to the house when the door opened and Bart Simmons stepped out and waved to them.

"Hi, gentlemen, how y'all doin'? Good to see you again."

The three shook hands and Bart held the door open for them. When they entered the house, Al saw Martha Simmons and two others sitting at the table in the dining room. There were three chairs waiting.

Bart followed them into the room, then said, "Beth, Bill … this is Al Rouse, and this is Charlie Berzinski. I can vouch for them. They're good guys."

"Hi," said Al as he shook hands, followed by Charlie. "And thank you so much for agreeing to talk to us. We know that we are asking you to recall a very hurtful time in your lives and we want to be sensitive to that. At the same time, we would like to get as much information as you are willing to share. If we stray into an area that bothers you, please just let us know and we'll stop."

Bill Grisham's smile was friendly. His wife was obviously nervous, tending to hide behind the handkerchief she held in her right hand.

"We've been quiet about Molly's disappearance for too long, detective. This is the first real chance, we feel, to receive some help, to find some closure. If we can help, we will."

His wife nodded her head, almost imperceptibly, and Martha Simmons reached over to hold her friend's hand.

"Let's start at the beginning, but before you begin, do you mind if the session is recorded? It may help us later." As Al offered this, both he and Charlie opened notebooks.

"Recording is fine," said Bill Grisham, nodding at his wife.

"So, tell us about Molly … about her childhood … and how she was brought up."

"We were too strict … or at least I was." As her husband began to speak Beth Grisham began to sniffle, but she spoke up in her soft voice: "Detective, we tried to be good parents. We wanted the best for Molly. We knew she was the only child we would have … she was a miracle, the doctors said, and we were very protective … yes, perhaps, overprotective. But we just wanted her to be and have the best."

After she had spoken, the woman retreated behind the hanky and stifled a sob.

"Call it overprotective or whatever you want, detective," said Bill. "I cracked the whip. Molly grew up a spirited child … always testing me … always trying to step over the line. I suppose the fact that I was too strict is one of the reasons she disappeared. It was obvious as she grew to be a teenager that she resented my discipline. If do-overs were possible, I'd sure ask for one."

Tears slipped down Bill's cheeks as he talked. His face reddened and he retreated into his coffee cup, taking several gulps as he tried to recover his composure. The heaviness in the air was formidable, and Charlie sought to defuse it. "You know Martha, I guess I would have a cup of that coffee."

Martha looked at Al as she rose. When he nodded, she took two cups from the counter and filled them from the nearby pot. "Cream or sugar?" Both officers shook their heads and Martha delivered the steaming cups as they were.

"Bill, we aren't here to assess any blame in this," Al continued. "We are simply trying to understand Molly better in the hope that we can find her."

The last works hung in the air until her father whispered, "Or her body."

"Well, we are certainly going to hope that is not the result. How long ago did Molly disappear?"

"Eighteen years ago, detective, when she was 15. She ran from the house one Saturday evening screaming that she hated me because I never cut her any slack. That was the last we saw or heard of her."

Grisham's last sentence came out in the midst of spasms that overtook him and seemed to strangle his words.

Al patted the man gently on the hand. "Bill, we're parents, too. We understand the aspirations we have for our kids and how it hurts when they seem disinclined to share our vision. We appreciate your candor—it's vital to our efforts to find her."

"She didn't like me, either." Beth was speaking now, so softly that the officers had to listen intently. "She and I had a terrible argument the day she left. So, Bill, honey, please don't blame yourself. I was responsible, too—perhaps even moreso.

"I never told you this, Bill, but … as I was making up her bed that morning … I knocked her purse off the bed, and the contents spilled on the floor. I'll never get over that moment, because, as I picked it all up, I found a partially used container of birth control pills. I was horrified at realizing what that meant. I just sat on the floor and cried. And as I was sitting there crying and holding them, Molly came out of the bathroom in her robe, looking so young and beautiful, and vulnerable … my little girl. When she saw what I was holding, she screamed at me. Accused me of spying on her and searching her room. I was so horrified by the situation, I couldn't speak." It was Bill's turn to reach over and put his hand on his wife's arm as her shoulders shook, as she relived her private nightmare.

Beth bravely continued, still shaky, but determined to finish the story. "She yelled at me and said, 'I guess you might as well see the rest, too.' And that's when she ran to her dresser and dumped out a drawer. I couldn't believe what I saw. Underwear of the sleaziest kind and of every color … and things that looked like … sex toys …"

Now she was openly sobbing. Martha Simmons pulled her friend to her feet, put her arm around her, and walked her from the room.

Bill shook his head, dazed. "Well … I guess there are secrets in every marriage, right?" He took a long breath. "But I can't say I'm surprised. Beth was more sheltered than me … and she hadn't heard the stories and whispers that I had, or perhaps she had and just couldn't bring herself to say so. I tried one time to talk to her about the rumors going around, but she refused to listen or even to talk about it. Now I guess I know why."

There was a respectful silence at the table. Al could hear the clock ticking on the mantel in the adjacent living room.

After it felt like things had settled, Al gently asked, "Do you have any guesses about what happened to Molly?"

"Yes … I do, Al. Yes, I do. She was always hanging around with a crowd of girls that sort of staked out the Dairy Queen parking lot, and waited for guys to come along. It could have looked innocent to others, I guess, just teenagers hanging out. But I saw her there several times and wondered if she wasn't … looking available. I even talked to Deputy Amos Brickner about it, because, often as not, he seemed to notice them, too. Or at least he was close by. Now I wonder if he was involved. He was young, nice-looking, and it later was revealed that he was dismissed for making improper advances to several women.

"I think somehow she may have been involved with him. Much as I hate to say it, he either killed her or she ran off to live the life she wanted. I'd like to think she's alive, but after this much time …"

Bill's voice trailed off as Martha and Beth walked back into the room. Beth was composed.

"Are you able to answer just a few more short questions, Beth?"

"I think so."

"Beth, is there anything else you can tell us about the day she left?"

Her voice was soft but steady. "Well, she was really upset, that's for sure. She stormed around the house, breaking anything she could get her hands on. She ripped all of the beautiful old china plates off the wall—family heirlooms—and, one by one, threw them against the brick fireplace. They shattered into a thousand pieces. I thought about that later. It was as if she was literally throwing away her family, her heritage. Then she stormed out the front door, saying she never wanted to see me again. I should have called Bill, but I was just too overwhelmed … and ashamed. She came back later because Bill saw her, but I wasn't there, I went to sit in a pew at the church. I don't know how long I sat there."

Al let the response linger for a time, then gently said, "What do you think might have happened to her?"

"I … I … don't think she's alive." She seemed to wilt, momentarily, and let out a sigh. Then, straightening her shoulders, she quietly summed up her private conclusions for the lawmen who had finally inquired, after all these years, what she thought. "I think she got in with a bad crowd, and either died of drugs or was killed. I think she left here and went to a big city, Milwaukee or Chicago." She paused, then said, "I'll tell you this—a friend of mine a few years ago said she saw someone who looked like Molly in downtown Chicago. It could have been her, I suppose. I wish it was, because that would mean she's alive. But, detective, I'm afraid to believe that. All this time, if she's been in Chicago, selling her body or doing whatever she had to do to keep herself together, how could she not have called, at some point, just to let us know she was alive?"

Taken altogether for a "sheltered" woman who was not given to talking about such things, she seemed to gain strength from speaking her truth.

"Would you give us the name of the woman who thought she saw Molly?"

"Of course. But let me talk to her first. It's Maude Henderson. Husband works for Organic Valley. He's in charge there. He travels for business and Maude often goes along."

Al was visibly relieved. "Thank you. Please call her tonight or tomorrow. We won't contact her until Friday."

"You've both been very helpful." Al and Charlie were both standing now and preparing to leave. Al was just finishing up. "If you think of anything else, no matter how trivial, please call us, you have our cards. Sometimes it is the most minor things that prove helpful."

Charlie added his own thanks, shaking their hands. "Beth, Bill … you have been generous with your time and your thoughts, too. Martha, Bart, thank you for opening your home to us." He turned and made his way toward the door. "If we learn anything, you will be the first to know."

Al followed Charlie, then paused, and turned back. "There is one more thing. A photo of Molly would be helpful—"

"—Or a negative," Charlie interrupted. "In fact a negative would be even better."

"He's right," said Al. "A negative would allow our artists to age the photo to how Molly might look today. Well, time for us to leave."

"Great thought on the negative." Al patted Charlie on the back as they got back to the car.

"Lots to do now," observed Charlie. "Several leads there that need follow-up. Gotta find out where Amos Brickner is. Gotta follow-up on Maude Henderson. Also gotta check out Molly's friends, if any are still around."

"And once we get the photo and have it aged, we need to circulate it in Milwaukee and Chicago."

13

Seated at his desk the next morning, Al was just finishing off a doughnut and drinking coffee when his phone rang.

"Detective Rouse? This is Beth … Beth Grisham. I have the negative you want. It's from her last school photo, near as I can tell, a good likeness of her when she disappeared. Would you like me to mail it to you?"

"Beth, I think it's important enough that we pick it up. I'm going to call Charlie and see where he is. He lives out Highway 14, so maybe I can get him to swing by before work. Will you be home? You will, good. Richland Center, right?"

"I'll be here this morning, but this afternoon I have a hair appointment. Oh, I almost forgot, I also got ahold of Maude Henderson. She said she will be home all week. She's expecting your call."

"Great work, Beth, that's very helpful. We couldn't ask for more. I will see if Charlie can stop by this morning and I will give Maude Henderson a ring. Do you have her number, by the way?"

Beth supplied the number along with her address. Al wrote them down, then thanked her again before hanging up. He quickly dialed Charlie's cell. The deputy answered on the first ring.

"I'll bet you're at work, right, Al?"

"I am. I just talked to Beth Grisham, in fact, and she has the negative we need. I was wondering…"

"Sure, I just got in the car to come to work, I'll call in and then head to Richland Center to pick it up. Anything else?"

"Not really. Beth gave me Maude Henderson's number. She talked to Maude last night and says she expects our call. I'm going to give her a call now. Why don't you come straight here after picking up the negative. We'll give it to our artists and have them age it. We can start looking for Amos Brickner. Let's see if we can run down that one today. Maybe Maude will have information that will help us with the Chicago police, too."

"Great. Sounds like a plan. I'm on the road now. I'll get the negative and see you in an hour. Gimme the address, if you have it?"

Al supplied it and after hanging up, he sipped at his coffee, disappointed that in the time he had talked to Beth and Charlie it had cooled considerably. He walked to the credenza, poured most of the coffee into an unused glass and brewed another cup of hazelnut. Returning to his desk with the coffee, he placed the cup carefully on a crisply folded paper towel and dialed Maude Henderson.

"Mrs. Henderson. Al Rouse. I'm with the La Crosse Police Department. Beth Grisham said she talked to you about my calling."

The woman's pleasant voice acknowledged the talk with Beth, said she hoped she could help, then waited for Al to ask her what he wanted to know.

"Beth said you think you saw someone who looked like Molly in Chicago. Before you respond, Mrs. Henderson, do you mind if I record our session? It likely will help me later as we continue our investigation."

When Maude assented, Al plugged the tape recorder into the phone, then placed the receiver on speaker.

"Okay, the recorder is running. Mrs. Henderson, could you please tell me about the woman you saw in Chicago?"

"Detective, Molly has been gone for a long time. She was a beautiful child … big blue eyes and a head full of blonde curls. The woman I saw had the same features … the eyes … the hair. But the thing that really set me off was the way this woman walked. Molly had a very distinctive walk … a bit of a shuffled limp … something left over from a bout with Guillain-Barre when she was little. That illness was the first we heard of the disease. No one else has ever had it, either, that I'm aware of. In any event, this woman walked with the same imperfect stride. I actually yelled after her, she turned and saw me and then took off running. Detective, I'd bet it was her."

"Sounds very much as if it could have been," agreed Al. "Where were you when you saw her? Do you remember?"

"I sure do. My husband, Leslie, was speaking at an organic growers' convention that day. I've heard that speech so many times I could deliver it. I thought it would be a great time to see the Field Museum. I'd never been. I had just gotten out of the cab in front of the museum, when I saw this woman talking to a man near the steps to the museum. When I yelled at her, she fled."

"Anything else you remember, mam?"

"No...not really. She was dressed in a coat...gray, as I recall. It was a chilly day. The wind was blowing off the lake. No...no, detective, that's it."

"You've been very helpful, mam. Thanks a million. Do you mind, if we have more questions, if we call again?"

No, not at all. Good-bye, detective."

Al replaced the receiver, then sat down and wrote thorough notes on the conversation. Just as he was finishing, Charlie walked in, an envelope in his hand.

"That the negative?" Al gestured to the envelope and when Charlie nodded in affirmation the deputy handed the envelope to Al.

"I'll be back in a minute," he told Charlie. "I'm gonna get this to the art department. I'll be back to tell you about my visit with Maude Henderson."

Rouse vanished out the door and down the hall. Charlie looked around, smiled, helped himself to coffee, took two doughnuts from the box after making certain there would be at least one left then settled into the chair in front of Al's desk. He was just brushing the powdered sugar from his uniform when Al returned.

"Found the doughnuts, I see."

"Damnit, Al, I was gonna go to Ma's for breakfast, but your call shelved that plan. I'm hungry enough to eat the butt out of a skunk. I thought you wouldn't mind my having a little snack. There's still one left."

Al laughed, shaking his head. "Charlie, I figured you'd find the doughnuts and help yourself. It's pretty much routine. I appreciate your saving me one."

"Well, it's almost lunchtime, Al. I didn't want to spoil my dinner."

Al laughed, shook his head, then turned to Charlie. "Well, before we take care of the empty spot in your stomach, how about we give this investigation a little attention?"

"Sure, what can I do?"

"I'm gonna call the Chicago P.D. – see if I can get a detective from the downtown precinct on line. How about you see what you can find out about Amos Brickner. Might start with Vernon County."

While Al busied himself with a directory, trying to find the right place to call in Chicago, Charlie walked across the hall to the conference room to make a call to Vernon County. When the two reconvened at noon, each had news.

"Did you find out anything?" Al wanted to know.

"Well, I found Amos Brickner, and that's quite a story. How about you?"

"I spoke to a detective in Chicago's First District. He said if she's doing street work in downtown, he'll find her for us. As soon as the photo is ready, I'll fax it to him and see what he can do with it. What about Brickner?"

"He's in prison. In Florida. Can you believe it?"

"What's he in for?"

"Sex trafficking. The guys in Walton County told me he was caught bringing a Chilean girl into their county on a boat. She didn't speak English. They saw the arrival but let it play for a couple of days, then arrested both of them, plus a guy Brickner had paired her with. They were at it when the cops walked in. Brickner was watching."

"Well that sort of confirms what we were told. Al remembered him being told Brickner was a sleazy guy. "I guess this proves it."

"I'm running his record now. I'll be interested to see what comes back."

Both officers refreshed after lunch, hustled back to the police department.

"You know, Charlie," said Al as the two paused at the doors to

Al's office and the conference room, "I'm not sure what this might have to do with the disappearance of Shirley Sovereign, but I have a feeling there is a connection…it's a pretty strong feeling."

"Your hunches are always good, Al, don't put 'em down. I'm gonna look at Brickner's record, then see if I can get on the phone with him."

"Good luck with that. I'm gonna check with the artists and see what they have for me. Hopefully they will be done and I can get the photo off to Chicago."

In his office, Al dialed the lab, asked for the staff artist and confirmed that she had finished with the photo. She invited him to come down and see if he thought it accurate. Walking down the stairs, he thought that no matter the look, he'd have to accept it. He had no idea what Molly Grisham might look like today.

When he saw the finished work, he was stunned. It seemed to him that Molly had taken a step forward in time. All the prominent features of her teen-age years were there, some even more prominent, others subdued. It was like looking at a cross between Molly and her mother. In fact, the resemblance to Beth Grisham was remarkable.

"You've done a fantastic job, Jenny. I don't know this person, but I know her mother and this looks like a great cross between the two." Al was holding the photo as he spoke to Jenny Hertzfeldt, the staff artist. "How about making me 20 copies? Can I take this one? I need to get it to Chicago ASAP."

"Sure there's nothing you want me to change? Usually you have me re-do photos three or four times. Do you suppose I'm getting better in my old age?"

"You were always fantastic, Jenny, and you know it. But can I take this with me?"

"Sure, take it. I'll enlarge the computer image I have and make the copies you want."

Excited by what he had, Al bounded up the back stairs and moved through the bullpen to his office, loaded his scanner with the information his Chicago counterpart had given him, and pressed "send."

Then he walked across the hall to find Charlie deep in conversation.

"So he will talk to me, you're sure about that? Okay, can we set it up for tomorrow morning at 8 your time?"

"Great." Charlie hung up phone, leaned back in the chair and looked at Al. "Well, we get to talk to Brickner at 7 our time tomorrow. We got the rest of the day to figure out what we're gonna ask him."

"Terrific," praised Al. "I just sent this to Chicago, what do you think?"

Charlie picked up the photo Al had sailed his way, studied it, then said, "Jenny did a great job, huh? She's exceptional, that gal."

"She is. Hopefully by tomorrow we'll have some leads."

14

"Hello, Amos. This is Charlie Berzinski up in La Crosse County, Wisconsin." Charlie had been surprised to find out the day before that Amos Brickner, imprisoned in Florida, would talk to him. He had just begun the dialog, hoping that he would be able to get the prisoner to provide some useful information. Brickner was being held on a sex trafficking conviction.

Charlie was pumped – and nervous. He had rehearsed his lines over and over last night. But now it was showtime and he had Brickner on the line.

"I and my partner Al Rouse of the La Crosse P.D. have a few questions for you this morning. We're hoping you can help us with an investigation we're doing, continued Charlie, reaching for the speaker phone button. "We're looking into a kidnapping that happened years ago. In the process of that investigation, we bumped into something down in Vernon County that we want to ask you about. I was told you're okay with that."

Charlie looked at Al and nodded. "Say hello to Al, Amos." Those greetings made, he continued, "We were visiting with people down in Hazard on Tuesday. Bill and Beth Grisham thought you might have information that would be helpful to us. They say you know their daughter, Molly. That right?"

"It is, Officer Berzinski, and I guess you want to know about Molly's disappearance?"

"That's right, Amos. If you have information it would be very helpful."

"First of all, I want to be sure if I help you that it won't lead to more time down here? The conditions here are terrible…and the food is inedible."

"I can't promise anything, Amos, but what I can tell you is if there are things that might suggest a return here would be helpful, we will try and make that happen. Do you still have roots up this way?"

"My mom and dad … my whole family, officer. It would be great to be home, even if I was still in jail."

"Okay, let's get on with it, then we will talk about favors. Tell us about Molly."

"Not sure what her folks told you, but she was the hottest thing I ever met. She'd jump in the squad car, grab me and plead with me to take her somewhere to make out. Man, I never knew anyone like her."

"Did you do what she wanted?"

"Officer, I held out for a time, but she grew into quite a woman. Big boobs, choice ass, the whole package, and she wasn't particular about who she favored. So the answer to your question is yes. We got to be quite friendly. Got together several times a week when I was on duty. I was scared as hell she would get pregnant but she assured me she was on the pill."

"Amos, did you have anything to do with her disappearance?" Al had asked the question after a nod from Charlie. Now he was hunched over the phone as Charlie repositioned the recorder, then reached for a pastry. There was a long silence, before Amos began to speak.

"Officer…Al…what I want you to know is that I only did what she asked…and if I hadn't done it, she would have found someone else. I swear she was screwing about seven or eight boys, in addition to me."

"So how did you help?" Charlie asked.

"She wanted to go to Milwaukee or Chicago to start whoring. She pleaded with me every time she saw me. After a couple weeks, I gave in. I took her to Milwaukee. She had an older friend there who took her in. I think the friend was selling, too."

"Sex or drugs?" Charlie wanted to know.

"Sex for sure. Prob'ly drugs, too, but I don't know about that."

"Is that the last you saw of her?"

"No, Charlie, I made several trips to Milwaukee on my day off. She never charged me, but the last time I went, she wasn't there. Her friend said she had moved to Chicago. Said she found a pimp there and took off. I never saw her after that. Never went to Chicago. Didn't want to fight with a pimp about free service."

"Anything else you want to tell us?"

"Can't think…oh, wait a minute. Her friend told me that she was known as Princess Goldie…because of her blonde hair. I never tried to find her. Anything here that might get me back to Wisconsin?"

Both Charlie and Al through for a few minutes, then Al said, "How old was she when you took her to Milwaukee?"

"Not real sure, but I'd say sixteen or so. All her friends were sophomores in high school."

"Trafficking of a minor. Charges could be brought up here, I suppose," said Charlie. "How much time you got left down there?"

"About four months, if I get out for good behavior, and I think I will."

"I think you better stay where you are. Up here you'd wind up doing a couple of years, I think."

"But, hey, guys, Molly wasn't the only girl I helped escape the boring lifestyle in Hazard. There were others, too."

"Any chance you remember who they were, Amos?" asked Charlie.

There was silence on the line. Finally Brickner spoke up. "I'll never forget the first two. God, what a mess that was. Abraham Svendson, the sheriff of Vernon County told me about these two girls, Helga Meyers and Jodie Olson. Meyers was being sexually and physically abused by her stepdad and she was scared to death to press charges. The sheriff said they had relatives … or, maybe, friends … in Milwaukee. I took 'em there, dropped 'em off. Never saw 'em again. Will that help?"

"If we could find them that might help, but you'd still do more time in Wisconsin than you're going to do down there," Al had spoken now after listening in to the conversation.

"Well, maybe you can find 'em. Meyers' stepdad and I had a big fight. He was one mean, mother, I'll tell you that. He went and found 'em after beatin' the snot out of me. Brought 'em home. Last I heard, both of 'em had gone overseas somewhere. France, maybe," responded Bickner.

The three men talked for a few more minutes, then Amos was thanked for his help. He told them that when he got out of prison he was going to return to Wisconsin.

"When I do, I'll look you guys up."

The call ended, Al said to Charlie, "It would appear that Mrs. Henderson might be right about seeing Molly in Chicago. Guess I'd better call my contact down there."

15

While Charlie rocked back in his chair, Al pulled the phone closer to him, took out his phone, looked up the number and dialed.

"Steve Scranton, please," he asked when his call was answered.

"Hi, Steve, Al Rouse here. Hope all is well. I'm here with my partner, Deputy Charlie Berzinski. I'm gonna put you on speaker phone."

"Hi, Charlie." The voice boomed from the phone, startling Charlie and causing him to back up. "Oops," said Al, "my bad. Steve, I had the phone on loud and your voice just about blew Charlie out the window. It's better now."

"Hope you got the photo I sent you yesterday. We took a negative from her mother and our artist aged it to what she might look like today," claimed Al.

"Your artist is fantastic," reported Steve. "I showed it around the office here and four detectives immediately recognized the girl in the photo. They said with the exception of the hair style and color it's a perfect likeness. Apparently she keeps her hair platinum blonde and goes by the name of Platinum Princess. We've had her in here four or five times on soliciting charges, but she's always back on the street as soon as her pimp bails her out."

"You know of her … that's great news. When is the last time you folks had any contact?"

"I looked that up, Al, once I got the name she goes by. The last time we had her in here is about 13 months ago. But before you lament that, let me tell you that our guys know she's still working… still in the central city area here."

"Tell us more about that."

"Well, one of my colleagues says he sees her every now and then. His theory is that she got a better pimp—if you can call a service a pimp—and moved from streetwalker to escort. There's a lot of that going on down here. If a girl is good and is a looker, the escort services make deals with pimps to buy the girl and list them."

"What are the chances of finding her so we can talk to her?" asked Al.

"Very good," answered Steve. "We've got the entire force on alert now. My guess is that we'll find her in no more than a few days. Our guys say they know where she hangs out. We'll have her for you soon, Al."

"Great, but how do we get her to sit down and talk to us?"

"I'll guarantee an audience, but I can't guarantee that she will talk. We'll bring her in on a soliciting charge and try for a 72-hour hold, but if I were you, I'd plan to get down here on a moment's notice, because once the service finds out what happened, they are going to try and bail her out."

"We'll be on the road the moment we hear," promised Al, looking as if he wanted to climb through the phone line. "It'll take us about five hours to get there. That's the best we can do. Hope it's quick enough."

"That will be fine. We can hold her without booking her for that long. In fact, we'd do that anyway in a case like this. That way she can just sit in a cell for the time it takes for you to get here."

"That would be wonderful, Steve. When you have her, give us a ring."

Al pressed a button on the phone to break the connection, then turned to Charlie, smiling.

"Won't it be wonderful to tell the Grishams that we've found their daughter?"

Charlie rose from his seat, stretched and walked to the window. Then, staring at the cars passing by outside, he stood with his hands on his hips. He replied without turning to face Al.

"It will be good, won't it? But there's a downside, too, Al: what if she won't talk to us? Or what if she talks to us but won't talk to her folks."

"Any of that's possible, but it doesn't overshadow the news that we know she's alive, where she is and have people looking for her… people who are confident they can find her."

"Still, she can refuse to talk to us or her parents."

"C'mon, Charlie, where's the happy, bubbly, confident man I've known. He needs to appear now, so he can use all his charm on Ms. Grisham to get her to both talk and to agree to see her folks."

Charlie stood there, continuing to gaze out the window. Finally, he turned to face Al. "You're right. The news is great. I never thought we'd have something on her this fast. We just have to do all we can to bring her back."

"Or at least get her to talk," agreed Al. "That will be the first step. What say we get some lunch and pick this up after we eat? We can talk over lunch about what to say to the Grishams. Or whether we say anything at all."

Walking back into the Law Enforcement Center an hour later, both men were upbeat. As Charlie pointed out, "Can't be down on a day like this." He was right. The sky was cloudless, the temperatures soaring into the 80s, seeming to make everything in the world right. The birds were singing, the streets of downtown were teeming with people, and the people they passed were smiling.

They arrived at Al's office to find a note pasted to his phone. The message was marked urgent and asked him to call Steve Scranton.

Al made the call, hit the speaker button and they listened to three rings before Scranton answered.

"Figured it would be you guys. I've been waiting for your call." After Al explained that they had been out for a sandwich, Steve continued: "One of our guys stopped in a bar-restaurant where he's seen her before. Apparently, he has talked to her often. He's brought her in twice, so they know each other. He explained what was going on, that you guys wanted to talk to her and gave her a choice of doing that voluntarily or being brought in on charges sufficient to keep her here until you could arrive. She quickly agreed to talk. Our guy said she even seemed anxious. We don't have her, but we have her cell phone and we know where she lives. When can you get here?"

"Well, if we leave now," said Al looking at his watch, "we can be down there by 8 tonight."

"How about tomorrow? Would that be better?"

"It would," said Al, looking at Charlie who was nodding. "If we left at, say five or six, we'd be down there before lunch. Would that work?"

"Sure would," agreed Scranton. "Why don't I set the meet up at the little bar-restaurant where she hangs out? That'll be comfortable for her and just off Lakeshore Drive for you guys. I'll meet you there to make sure the meet happens, then leave you to talk."

After Al and Charlie thanked him profusely and asked him to make sure his colleagues knew how pleased they were, the call ended.

"Probably better clear the trip with Brent and Dwight. "I'll go see Brent now. You can use the phone to call Dwight. I'll be back in a second."

Al found the chief in his office, told him about the progress they were making in the case that had taken a sudden turn from where they started.

"But, Al, if there is or was a sex trafficking operation in this area, it needs to be broken up. So by all means, go and see this woman in Chicago. If at all possible try to reunite her with her folks. Look, we both have kids. If this were us, think of how we'd feel to know that a missing daughter is alive, reasonably well…and think of how much we would want to talk to her."

"You're right, Chief. We plan to leave bright and early tomorrow, see her about 10 or so and then, depending upon the circumstances, get back here tomorrow night."

"Sounds good. Then I'll either see or hear from you some time tomorrow?"

"Or, depending upon how things go, maybe day after tomorrow. But we'll for sure try to give you an update tomorrow," said Al, lounging in the door of the Chief's office.

When Al returned, Charlie was just finishing up his call.

"Dwight's fully supportive," he reported. "Do we take clothes for an overnight stay?"

"Prob'ly a good idea, but I'm hoping we will be back tomorrow night. What vehicle do you want to take?"

"'Spose it's technically my investigation, given the location." Charlie was thinking as he talked. "Probably could be yours, too. Yours is unmarked. That important?"

"Not really. Besides, yours is more comfortable. You mind taking yours?"

"Heck no, but will you drive to my place, so I don't have to come back into the city to get you."

Plans made, the two men agreed Al would be at Charlie's by 5 a.m. They would take clothes for an overnight stay.

16

"Sure is a nice day." Charlie was driving as he spoke. They had gotten to Tomah before the sun rose and Charlie was right, it was a nice day. As fields of tall corn and green soybeans spread out on both sides of the SUV, traffic was picking up as they passed the junction with I-94 and continued south, passing over the Wisconsin River south of the Wisconsin Dells at about 8 o'clock.

"Sure hope the traffic stays like this for the rest of the trip," said Al, sipping on his coffee from a thermos that Charlie had brought.

"I've had 'er at a steady 75 since we got on the freeway," Charlie noted. "Haven't taken it off cruise once."

Charlie adeptly piloted the Ford Escape southeastward as the two La Crosse lawmen headed toward Chicago and a hoped-for meeting with Molly Grisham, also known as the Platinum Princess.

Traffic was relatively light as they skirted Madison and continued down I-90 toward the Chicago First District headquarters at 1718 South State Street.

"So Al," began Charlie as they moved through the Windy City's outer suburbs, "the bottom-line is to bring her home, right?"

"Well that would be nice, but the real reason I'm going is to find out what she can tell us about the mysterious disappearances of young women from Hazard."

"God, how could I forget that? Sometimes I amaze myself by the apparent things that I forget. Did it again, didn't I?"

"Well, I'm not sure it's anything you over..."

"B.S., Al, don't humor me; help me. You're a great detective. The real advantage in our relationship is the opportunity to learn from you. So when I screw up, say so. I learn best that way…by getting it beat into my head."

Al was still chuckling as Charlie piloted the cruiser up to the First District building on a quiet tree-lined street near downtown.

"Here we are," he said, "expert transport by Charlie Berzinski. Now it's yours, Al. Turn on the old Rouse charm and get that girl to fess up and maybe even make the trip back with us."

"We will do that." Al was opening the door as he spoke. He looked around for signs that prohibited parking at the front door. Finding none, he leaned back into the SUV. "Looks like we can let 'er here, Charlie. I don't see any signs suggesting parking here is taboo. Let's go."

They walked across the checkerboard-patterned sidewalk and into the door marked "PUBLIC" in the modern plate-glass fronted building.

The receptionist smiled as they walked up to the desk. "Hi, gentlemen. How can I help?"

"We're looking for Steve Scranton." Al returned the woman's smile as he answered her question, removed his handkerchief from his pocket and mopped his forehead.

"A hot one out there?"

"Yes it is," agreed Charlie, moving closer to the desk.

"You must be the officers from La Crosse, right?"

"Does our small-town image show like that? By the way, mam, I'm Al Rouse and this is Charlie Berzinski."

"I'm Melanie Nichols." The woman got to her feet, then pointed to a door down the hall. You'll find Detective Scranton in the first office on the left."

As they pushed through the door, Al first, followed by Charlie, they heard Scranton before they saw him.

"Been waitin' for you guys." The voice was friendly and when its owner emerged, he looked friendly, too. Steve Scranton was a big man, well over 300 pounds packed onto a frame that measured 6-feet-2 or -3. His round, reddish face was pulled into grin that made him look a little like a large version of the Pillsbury Doughboy.

"The Platinum Princess is looking forward to meeting you, too. She just told me that. She's having doughnuts with the boys. They're in the cafeteria and she's spinning stories. We thought we would have you meet her in the little bar that she hangs out at, she would rather meet here. Probably has something to do with her employers being too near. Let me show you the way to the cafeteria."

After they wound through a maze of hallways and desk cubicles, Steve led them down a bright hallway, at the end of which was the break room or cafeteria. As they neared the room, they could hear chatter and laughter. Then they entered the room. All conversation stopped. The room went silent.

Then Steve spoke to the wondering faces. "I'd like you to meet Al Rouse and Charlie Berzinski. They've come to see you (he nodded to a woman dressed scantily with a heavily painted face). I hope the visit is productive."

A female officer rose, gestured the La Crosse lawmen to come closer, then said, "Al, Charlie, I'm Donna Rice, and this is Molly Grisham, also known as the Platinum Princess. Welcome."

While the other officers in the room came forward to greet the visiting lawmen, the woman with the painted face remained seated, nervously twisting her hands and squirming in her chair. Then Charlie walked forward, held out his hand and smiled. "Young lady, we know some people who are mighty interested in finding you. They love you deeply."

Charlie reached out his hand, the young woman stood and they embraced. Al, standing near his friend but just behind him, marveled at the man's ability to size up a situation and do exactly the right thing to put everyone at ease. Charlie was a rough-cut gem, he thought, a great partner.

The young woman left Charlie's embrace, tears rolling down her cheeks. She clung to his hand as she sobbed. Before anyone else could react, Charlie took the seat beside her, his hand gently caressing her head as she cried. He bent toward her and in a voice so quiet that it couldn't be heard talked to her. Gradually the sobs quieted, then stopped and the woman reached for the handkerchief that Charlie offered.

As the sobbing ended, the Chicago officers stood and noiselessly left the room. Al took a chair beside Charlie and the three of them sat there silently. At last, Molly sat back from the table and managed a weak smile as she now dried tears, leaving streaks in her makeup mask.

Finally, making a last sob, she sniffled, blew her nose and looked at them.

I am so sorry," she said, gesturing at her clothing. "These are my work clothes. I had just come off a busy night when the guys stopped by to pick me up."

She looked both of them in the eye, although hers were brimming with tears. She looked frightened and inquisitive. Then she said:

"And what now?"

17

Sensing that the time was right, Al moved his chair so she could see him better. He placed his arms on the table and looked at her. "Molly, we have been talking to your parents and if they knew – rather than hoped – you are alive, they would be overjoyed. Obviously, Charlie and I are interested in your story and reuniting you with your parents, but we didn't know about you when we started our investigation."

"Investigation?"

"Yes, Molly … a few weeks ago we took on a cold-case assignment, hoping to finally solve the mystery surrounding the disappearance of Shirley Sovereign of La Crosse in 1979. Our search led us to Hazard and that led us to you. So if you thought we were hunting for you, that is a very recent development."

The woman looked at Al, then at Charlie. She was pretty, probably even beautiful, thought Al, but made up like she was, wearing what he suspected was a platinum wig and a get-up that looked like a cross between high school harlot and European gypsy, she was anything but attractive.

"Why," he said finally, breaking the silence, "did you leave?"

"It's a very … long story … officer." She looked as if she was about to cry again when Charlie broke in.

"Molly, we want to hear that story and both Al and I are here to help you in any way we can, assuming you want our help. You were brought in because we requested it. You have no obligation to be here, none to stay. But we hope you will. We hope you will tell us your story and we hope you will let us help you."

Again, Al was impressed by the big, gruff man's ability to

soften his voice until it had the soothing impact of an experienced psychologist.

Molly looked at Charlie. "I didn't want to leave … not really. But mom and me had a terrible fight about the things I was doing, things I wish now I had never done. I also had a friend—a police officer—who had helped other girls leave Hazard for the big city and bright lights. You know, Mr. Berzinski, the lights here are not all that bright."

A tear slid down her cheek. Charlie wiped it away with his handkerchief, leaving another streak on her cheek. "Tell us more, Molly." Charlie was stroking her shoulder, then bent to look her in the eye.

"Well, when I left the house that day, I headed downtown to find the cop. He was right where I suspected he would be and he said he was willing to help."

"Was that officer Amos Brickner?" asked Al.

"Yes, yes it was. How did you know? Oh, I suppose everyone knows about how he helped young women. Is he well? He was nice to me."

"He is well, Molly, but he's in prison." Al was talking again from his position at the end of the table. "His help got him in trouble and he's finishing a sentence in Florida."

"What's he in for?"

"The charge was sex trafficking. He was caught bringing a Chilean woman into Florida for solicitation purposes."

The woman bent her head, and fiddled with Charlie's handkerchief that she had in her lap.

"I guess I'm not surprised, but he was a good friend. He was my first. In his squad car—that excited me. Then things got really heated. I tried to please him and my mother found all the evidence of that the morning I left. I'm so sorry now … so very sorry … I just don't know …"

She was sobbing again now, the handkerchief held over her face. Eventually she stopped, sat up straighter and composed herself.

"How are my folks? I think of them all the time … wish I could see them … wish I …"

"Molly, if you dream of being at home, I think they would love that," Charlie told her. "They would be the happiest people in the world if they had you back home."

"Really … you really believe that? How could they? After all I have done … all I have become …"

"I am absolutely sure," said Al. "They pray for that each day."

Charlie drew Al's anger when he jumped in. "Molly, we'd be happy to give you a ride home, if you'd like."

The upset was quickly erased when the young woman brightened. "Would you—really?" Then her expression darkened. "But how could I go home. After all this time … and the scene I created when leaving. And then not calling. I bet mom hates me … and dad, too. I think dad knew what I was doing. He was furious."

Both Al and Charlie smiled. Then Al said, "Molly, I won't pretend they weren't upset. But Charlie and I are parents, too. And when people have kids, I can tell you it's like a marriage ceremony: for better or worse. Regardless of the mistakes you make, we still love you. And that love, Molly, is unconditional. I promise you."

Charlie, looking on, now re-entered the conversation. "Molly, you can't imagine how happy your parents were when we told them we would look for you. For every one of the days since you left, your mom and dad have prayed that you are alive and that you will return to them. It's their greatest hope … their absolutely greatest hope."

"I just can't believe you are serious. How could they forgive me? They have to hate me. I bet they do."

"Absolutely not," said Al with conviction. "They love you, Molly, very much and, as I said, unconditionally."

"They do, Molly," agreed Charlie. "Please believe us. They want you home."

"I want to go back … have dreamt of going back … but how can I? What if they ask me what I have done for a living? They are such good people, they could never forgive someone like me. Dad would be livid."

"Molly," said Al, gently, "you have to trust us. Yes, your mother and father were upset with you when you were 16. They knew you were making bad choices and they didn't know how to talk to you … how to make you understand."

"You know, Molly," followed up Charlie, "we parents are not always right. We want to be but we make mistakes, too. You parents saw you as a little angel and tried to make you that. They know now that what they did caused you to rebel. They know that was a mistake. They want to tell you that. They want to tell you how much they love you and want you back. It's their fondest wish. I wish you would give them that."

It was a timeless moment as the three sat there looking at each other, lost in thought.

Molly broke the silence. "Do they really want me home? Really?"

"Yes really," replied Al, a soft smile on his face.

"More than you could ever know," was Charlie's follow-up.

"I want to believe you. Want to. But look at me. To them, I'm just a whore. The things I've done are unbelievable. And, probably for them, unforgivable."

"They are not." Charlie's voice was soft but firm.

"The long and short of it, Molly, is they want you home. How about we give you a ride?"

"Would you? And would you help me?" Both officers nodded, smiling. "And would you help me with my folks, too?"

The officers were smiling now. "We would be delighted," said Al, "in fact you can sit up front with Charlie and worry about his driving. I've had enough of that for one day."

It was exactly the mood lightener that was needed. Molly dried her eyes, handed the hanky back to Charlie and squared her shoulders. Then she looked both of them in the eye.

"Officers, I accept your offer. Let's get me home."

"Great idea," exclaimed Charlie, giving her a hand and leading her out to his SUV and opening the front door on the rider's side while Al got in the back.

"You probably need to stop at your place to pick up some things," suggested Charlie. Molly agreed, then gave Charlie directions to her place. I live upstairs over a bar—the bar where they found me this morning. I usually stop for a soda after a long night."

As Charlie navigated the police vehicle to the bar and pulled up in front, Molly looked like she might be losing her confidence.

Hoping to break that feeling, Charlie asked, "How long will it take you to get ready?"

Molly stammered as she began to answer.

"None of the clothes I have—except maybe jeans and a sweat-shirt—are going to work. I sure don't want to go home looking like this. I will have to shower, re-do my hair—it needs washing—pack the few things I have that are suitable … I would guess, ummm, maybe an hour."

Al was incredulous. "You can just walk away? What about friends? You must have some. Can you really just leave without a word to anyone?"

"Al, I get the idea you don't really like me. You know, in this business, you develop pretty sharp-edged perceptions … and I'm getting all the wrong vibes from you."

As she finished, she crossed her arms, a defiant scowl on her face. "You know, we should just forget the whole thing. It was a bad idea from the start."

Al leaned over the seat and grasped her shoulder. The stern look had left his face. He was in his "parenting" mode.

"Molly, you are a perceptive woman. I must admit that your lifestyle—what you have done to your parents, your general lack of caring—have me wondering about your sincerity. About whether you really want to go home, or are doing it just to get a break from the life you have chosen. I am skeptical, yes. But you should also know that deep in my heart I hope you are leveling with us … that you really want to see your parents. Because if you are doing this only as a break, well then, you are just going to hurt them more. I don't want that. And I don't want you to do that to them."

Al had continued to move closer to Molly, until only inches separated them.

"Do you understand what I am saying?"

Molly returned Al's gaze. Then, without flinching, she said, "Al, are you always this quick to judge? Do you think you have some divine ability to judge someone's heart when you have only just met them?"

While the comeback surprised Al, he was not deterred. "Molly, you have for more than 15 years now made your parents miserable. You mother is old before her time—your father is a beaten man. They blame themselves for your running away. And they probably should, but they are not the only ones responsible for your running away. You are to blame, too. And, yes, you're right, I don't much like people who willfully make others miserable and keep them in suspense for years, wondering what they could have done differently. It's despicable, in my mind, and if you're looking for sympathy from me, you're not going to get it."

Staring at Al, Molly's face took on a new look, one of sadness and despair. She looked as if she would cry, then straightened, folded her hands in her lap, and just sat there for a minute.

"I know, Al, that you don't like me ... don't like what I have become ... don't like that I have been out of touch with my parents. I don't like any of those things, either. I really don't, believe it or not. Were I not so ashamed, I would have been in touch long ago. But once you're in this life, breaking free of it is virtually impossible. You have someone watching you 24/7, every hour, and every day.

"I'm not going to alibi. It's my life—I made it and I will own it. But I am also very glad that you came along—both of you—and I am happy to be going home with you, even though I am scared to death. You can't understand, I know that. But I hope you will believe me when I say that, at 16, thinking you know all there is to know, once you make a decision like I did, there is no way to reverse it ... to just walk away."

Molly was all business now, Al realized, and he enjoyed seeing her this way. She was a force, he sensed, a force that could now go where she wanted. And if he and Charlie were her ticket home, then he was happy with that.

Molly dabbed at her eyes, took a deep breath and started again.

"Al, you and Charlie have a stake in this, too, believe it or not. You are taking me back. I think that obligates you to protect me, because I will need protection … I definitely will."

"Who will want to hurt you?" asked Al, certain he knew the answer.

"Everyone in the business has a pimp—at least in Chicago. That person owns you, Al … makes a good living off of you … and doesn't tolerate anyone who runs away. Someone paid to get me, and that person will want me back … will want what I can do for them. I can make him or her several thousand a night. Yes, several thousand. My guy will miss that—you can bet on it. And he'll track me down to bring me back. Failing that, he'll kill me. That's how it works in this business. But I'm not a dumb broad, Al. I have a degree in finance from Northwestern and an MBA from the University of Chicago."

Now Al was incredulous. An undergraduate degree from Northwestern and an MBA from Chicago. Wow, impressive, if true.

"So, if you went back to school and got an MBA …" he began, as they sat there, car idling, in front of the bar, "Why are you doing what you do? Is it that good a living?"

"It's a long story, but the bottom line is they never let you quit the business. The real winner is the pimp … the manager. He gets 80 percent—the girl, 20. But the pimp manages everything … everything. He gets the appointments, collects, deposits, schedules exams, pays the bills—everything."

"Even at 20 percent I was doing well … and all I had to do was …"

Her statement tailed off. She sat there looking vulnerable, Al thought, almost like a little girl.

"Molly, if you miss your folks, why have you not made contact with them?"

"Would you want to see your daughter like this, Al? C'mon, you know it would be terrible. I've put my folks through enough already without that, too. I have wanted to go home, but I didn't want them to see me like this. Do you understand?"

"I think so, yes. So why now?"

"Because I am hoping that being dragged away by cops may at

least have some impact on my boss … might keep him away. But if that doesn't work, I'm in real trouble. Life-ending trouble."

Charlie had been listening to the exchange. Now he broke in.

"Molly, we didn't come to get you just so your folks would see you get killed. We have an obligation to see to it that you are safe. We will do that, too."

"We will," agreed Al. "You can count on it."

"If you can do that, you're miracle workers," she said. "But I am going to believe in this miracle. Give me an hour." She jumped from the car, walked up the steps on the side of the old brick building and disappeared through the door.

Less than fifty minutes later she was back—transformed. Gone was the platinum wig, exposing a short, blonde, and attractive hair-cut. The made-up face had been replaced by minimal makeup and she now looked sweet and pretty. And she was wearing stylish skinny jeans and a white blouse. She was, altogether, an extremely attractive young woman on the threshold of middle-age.

"Wow, you look great," praised Charlie. Al nodded and smiled.

"You think I look okay? Will my folks think I look okay?"

"They'd like you any way at all," said Al, "but I think you look great, Molly. It's nice to know that there was a real, down-to-earth person under all that makeup and the wig."

On the way home, discussion centered on Molly's parents, what their reaction would be, and what she could expect from the towns-people in Hazard. The closer they got to home, the greater her stress level. They stopped for burgers at Monk's in the Wisconsin Dells and Molly was noticeably nervous.

Finally, Al said, "Molly, when we are back in the car, why don't we call your parents to tell them you are coming home? They are older now, and we probably shouldn't just surprise them. They may need that couple of hours to get ready to see you, too."

"Oh, God, that scares me to death. Do you have any idea how frightening that is? Do either of you even have a clue?" Then she stopped, and got a grip on her nerves. "But … of course, you're right, they should know. However, could you call them and be the one to tell them I'm coming home? And then maybe we can see how they take it ... maybe we'll see if they want to talk to me."

"Molly, I can assure you that you will be welcomed with open arms," Al told her, squeezing her on the arm, sensing that she was sincerely alarmed at the prospect of facing her parents. "You need not worry about whether they want to see you. They will be very pleased to have you back."

Molly was sniffling. Charlie again handed her his hanky. "C'mon, Molly. Let's have a burger, and get back on the road. Then we can give your folks a ring."

On the road again, heading north on I-90/94, Charlie punched in the numbers on the SUV's Bluetooth as Al read them off. It rang once, then twice, but before the third ring concluded, the phone was answered.

"Hello, this is Beth."

"Mrs. Grisham, this is Al Rouse. Charlie and I on our way back to Hazard, and I think you're going to be pleased at what we have to tell you. Actually, there's someone here who wants to say hello."

He was taking a chance, but he nodded at Molly, smiled and pointed to the dashboard phone, then to her lips. Molly was tentative, but then she surprised him and did exactly what she needed to do.

"Mother ... mom. It's Molly."

Beth let out a small shriek, "Oh my God!" Then she was heard to shout away from the phone, "Bill, come here, it's Molly!" Then the tears started, on both ends of the line—Molly was sobbing, as was Beth.

Then Beth said in a gentle voice, "Oh Molly, honey ... is it really you?"

"Yes, mom, it's me. It's so good to hear your voice. I am so sorry ... so terribly sorry."

Molly was about to give in to fresh tears, but Beth hurriedly asked, "When will you be here? Are you coming now? Tonight?"

Charlie checked his watch and cut in, "Mrs. Grisham, this is Charlie. We should be at your house by seven ... 7:15 at the latest."

"Wonderful. What a miracle." Beth sounded like a completely

different person. "Charlie, I don't know how you two did this but please get her here safely. And, Molly, dad and I love you so!"

"I love you, too, mom … I do… I am just so … so terribly sorry. Is dad going to be okay with my coming home? I made him so angry …"

Beth cut in with a soothing tone. "Oh, honey, don't worry about that. It's water under the bridge, and a long, long time ago. You just get home, now. We can't wait to hug you. And that means dad, too."

18

I t was three minutes past seven when Charlie stopped the SUV in front of the well-kept rambler on East Highland Street. Although the sun had slipped away, the lights glowed brightly through the windows at the front of the house. Molly studied the house for a minute, then reached for the overnight bag that held her belongings. Al's hand stopped her. "Molly, why don't you just go in. Charlie and I will bring your things."

But Molly hung back, still uncertain. "Please come with me," she asked. "I just need you with me … okay?"

"Okay, Molly, we'll go with you." Charlie edged his substantial girth out from under the wheel and walked around the vehicle to the passenger side, opened the door, helped Molly out, then put his arm around her and escorted her up the sidewalk. Al retrieved Mollie's bag from the storage area and followed them.

Before they had taken two steps up the walk, the front door burst open and Beth and Bill Grisham hurried down the walk and together took their daughter in their arms. Al and Charlie stood back, watching the reunion unfold, happy that they were able to make all three of the Grishams' dreams come true.

Twenty minutes later they were back in the car and on their way to La Crosse. They would return to Hazard the next afternoon, it was agreed, to talk to Molly more about her disappearance and what she knew about other girls from the area who had gone missing.

"Makes you feel awfully good, doesn't it?"

"Sure does, Charlie. It's not often that we get a happy ending like this one. And even though it's far from over, we have to celebrate small victories as they come along."

"Amen to that."

Half an hour later, Charlie dropped Al off, telling him, "I'll be by for you tomorrow at one. Sound okay?"

"Perfect, buddy. See you then. Hi to Kelly."

"And Jo Anne. Get some rest."

The next afternoon, promptly at one o'clock, Charlie pulled the SUV into the Rouse driveway and gently tooted the horn.

Al came out, anxious and prepared. As they drove the now familiar road to Hazard, they talked about what they might encounter when they met with Molly and her parents.

When they walked up the sidewalk to the Grisham home, the door opened and Bill waved them in, saying, "Molly and Beth are sleeping. We talked all night. They just laid down about two hours ago. It is so great to have her home. It's a true miracle."

Bill ushered them into the house and asked if they'd like some coffee. Both agreed and Bill went into the kitchen. As they were waiting, Molly stuck her head around the corner from the other side of the house, smiled at them and walked into the living room.

She looked beautiful, glowingly so. She was dressed in jeans and a University of Chicago sweatshirt, her short blonde hair was clean and swept back, and her face radiated happiness. She walked into the room, slipped into an easy chair across from them, tucked her right leg under her and said, "I'm not sure how to thank you for rescuing me from that life back there, but I am so happy to be home. Last night was wonderful. I would've never believed in a million years that I could come back home and be welcomed with open arms, but mom and dad are beautiful. We talked all night." Then she proudly announced, "And you will be glad to know that I am officially all cried out."

Al and Charlie laughed. "That's really good to hear," Al replied with a smile. "It's not every day that dreams come true, so I guess you could be granted at least one or two Niagara moments. Your dad's getting some coffee, do you want some?"

"I'd love some, Al. Want me to go?"

"No, I'll go. Just relax."

Al walked into the kitchen and Molly smiled at Charlie and said, "Deputy Berzinski, how can I help you? What do you want to know?"

"Let's wait for Al, but you can start thinking about the people you knew from this area that may have gone the same way you did. Were there others? And do you know where they are? We also want to know who helped them get wherever they are."

"Okay, that's a good place to start."

Just then Al and Bill walked back into the room, each carrying two cups of coffee.

"Cream? Sugar?" asked Bill. "Something to eat. I think we might have some cookies."

"You know, dad, all the way home last night I was dreaming about your buckwheat pancakes. Do you still make those? And you were the best at frying up bacon, too."

The pleased grin on Bill's face was wide with pride. "Of *course* I still make them … and we have some of your favorite bacon, too. Just got it yesterday. How about you, officers? Hungry?"

Although Al started to decline, Charlie cut him off, saying, "Bill, I think, if it's not too much trouble, we'd love some."

"No trouble at all. It's been a long time since I have been able to cook for a whole platoon. I'd love it. You visit, breakfast in a minute." He turned toward the kitchen, then looked at his watch. "Oops, a late lunch, perhaps."

While sounds and smells from the kitchen tickled their ears and nostrils, Al and Charlie visited with Molly. She was of uncommon help. And her story was more coherent than what they'd been able to piece together during the emotional journey bringing her home last night.

Molly took a deep breath and started from the beginning. "By the time I got to Chicago, I had learned there was a regular parade of young women from this area to Chicago and other big cities—Indianapolis, Columbus, Cincinnati, St. Louis … and I heard about some from cities in Florida and Texas, too, although I don't know much about that. Back then, Amos was the recruiter from this area. He was good looking and easy to talk to. He'd get to know girls, let them ride in the squad car, even drive it sometimes. When he was re-cruiting me, it was a thrilling introduction to sex and living the fan-tasy of a grown-up world. And sometimes we'd wind up at the dump or at a landing field or somewhere off the beaten path late at night. Amos was a skilled lover and he made me think I was the greatest woman on the earth. He always picked out what he'd call "his lost puppies"—those of us who he expected had a rocky home life.

"I had a good life here, even though I didn't know it until later. Back then, everyone wanted more freedom. I began to run with a wild crowd … although we thought we were pretty cool. Then with Amos sweet-talking me and teaching me how to please a man, I was just one step from being handed off to someone in a big city. And that's what I wanted. Or so I thought.

"I knew almost at once what a mistake I had made and tried to come back, but there was no way that was going to happen. If I'd wanted to go home, the trip would have been made in a body bag. That's how it was. And eventually the booze and drugs took over and things seemed good … until I woke up one morning when I was about 20 and realized I wanted more than just sex and parties and good times. I wanted to go to school and get a degree, and feel like I had accomplished something.

"The thing was, I knew I was smart, at least book-wise, and one of my regular clients was on the board of trustees with the University of Chicago. He offered to set me up in a condo and get me in school, and he fixed it with my manager to buy an exclusive contract with me for five years. So, I quit the booze and drugs, and had something almost like a normal life that actually lasted for about eight years. But when Max died suddenly two years ago, all of that came to an end."

Molly stopped to take a breath, then plowed on.

"I mistakenly thought I could ease out into the world and get a job at a bank. But that wasn't to be—my old life returned with a threat from my old manager who knew just how to pull me back into the underworld of the sex trade. He made sure I understood why no bank or business would ever hire me, because he would guarantee they'd hear about my "real" story. So, I was trapped. And as I was now a little older, the tricks weren't so plentiful or tips so lavish. Early on, back when I had just started out, there were all sorts of great perks … money, gifts, trips. But now, when 30 came along, it all sort of began to slide.

"I always knew the life wasn't great, but the money had made it livable—at least until the last year or so when I was bringing in less than a thousand a night. That's a benchmark in the trade at the higher end. And so, just a few months ago, my manager started talking about selling me to the trade in the islands. He stood to make a bundle off of some deal with the business down there. I was terrified. So, when one of the policemen I knew found me at the bar day before yesterday, and told me what was up, I jumped at the chance to leave. But still, the risks were high that I wouldn't be able to make it out alive."

Al had moved to the front of his chair, and he asked the question that was his most immediate concern. "Molly, did you know lots of women from around here who were involved?"

"Not lots, I guess … but some. There were at least two others from Hazard. They had left before me, though. There was a girl from Viroqua that I saw in Florida … at a party. There was one girl from Bangor that I saw in Chicago one night. She was with someone from West Salem—a younger girl that I didn't know."

"Was this area a regular recruitment area?" This time Charlie asked the question.

"Not regular, no. But as time went on, I learned that about once a year a guy or two from Chicago would come through here looking for girls. I think Amos knew all of them. I think he worked with all of them." She paused. "As I think about it now, he was the nicest of the bunch. Once I left here, there was nothing but trouble."

The three of them sat there in thoughtful silence. Bill Grisham, coming in from the kitchen, broke in and announced, "Brunch is on—come and get it."

Bill herded them into the dining room. "You folks sit down over here … Molly, you here … in your old place. I'll go and get Beth."

Soon he was back, leading Beth by the hand to her chair at the table. Even though she'd had only a few hours of sleep, she radiated calm with a shy smile.

"Hi, Al—hi, Charlie … great to see you. We are so grateful to you for bringing our Molly home. Aren't we, Bill?"

"We sure are," said her husband. "And we will always be grateful. Now you all dig in."

For the next several minutes, the five of them filled their plates and ate in companionable silence—feasting on mounds of buckwheat pancakes, crisply fried bacon, and fresh fruit that Bill had piled high on old fashioned serving platters. It looked as if he'd cooked up enough for a whole brigade.

A few minutes later, having cleaned her plate—holding her cup of coffee in both hands with her elbows on the table—Molly said, matter-of-factly, "So, I've been thinking about what comes next. I know the guys from Chicago will likely be coming after me. And I'm afraid we're all in danger here … mom … dad … me. Is there anything that can be done to protect us?"

Al considered the grim prospect as he forked the last bite of apple on his plate. "We can't stop them from coming after you," Al told them, his jaw set. "But I can guarantee you that if they do show up, they will get more than they asked for. I have a daughter … so does Charlie. I don't think they want to be messing with us."

"Oh, but Al, they are so dangerous." She pressed her case. "Their livelihood depends on a stream of fresh, young girls. It's a multibillion-dollar business, and they will stop at nothing to maintain it and to protect it. They won't stop coming."

Al held out his cup as Bill came around with the pot of coffee. Then he took a different tack with a question he'd waited awhile to ask. "Did you ever run across a woman by the name of Shirley Sovereign?"

"I heard of her. She was the big earner when I was first recruited. She must have been quite a bit older, though. I heard of her soon after I got to Chicago, but after a couple of years, not so much. Since she was marketed at the high end of the trade, she might have gone to the islands."

Charlie had been thinking about that since the first time she had brought it up. He helped himself to another stack of pancakes and said, "Tell us more about this islands business."

Molly answered in an informed, businesslike tone, as if discussing statistics. "The Bahamas, Cuba, the Virgins. That's where they shipped some of the older 'quality' sex workers. Apparently, some of the wealthy older clients living there liked older women. And it was a way the sex managers could extend the pipeline—they could get more value out of their 'merch' in a single sale than a year's worth of daily managing and overhead costs in the escort service. I learned that if a woman was considered high value, she could be sold to a wealthy client who would pay as much as half a million. But, of course, there were horror stories that filtered back about what happened to the women who were sold down there."

After a sobering minute, considering the implications of Molly's depth of knowledge about the business, Al returned to the local area of immediate concern. "So, there's a regular channel for women who are enticed away from home. And this syndicate comes through this area on an annual basis, looking for young women … girls really … who possibly have been recruited by some local contact, who has led them to believe there's better life away from here. Is that the picture?"

"That's it, Al. It's highly organized. To an outsider it might seem as if things happen randomly, but that's not it at all. They know exactly what they are doing … know exactly how to attract young women with the promise of a better life. It's insidious, and it's a lie, but it's the way the business works."

Taking his role as host seriously, Bill Grisham had fussed over his guests as they demolished the pancakes and freshly sliced summer fruit from local orchards. After Charlie finished polishing off three platefuls, he finally declared a truce. "Bill, I have to get that pancake recipe. Those cakes were outstanding—as was everything else—but your pancakes are exceptional … I know because I like food."

"He does know," laughed Al, "because when he says he likes food, that's a considerable understatement." Then Al pushed back from the table, stood, coffee cup in hand, and asked, "Do you mind, Molly, if we ask just a few more questions?"

"Gosh, no. Fifteen years ago, I would have reacted differently, I suppose." A soft chuckle punctuated her statement. "Can't we just keep talking here at the table? I don't have anything I want to keep from mom and dad. It's just so good to be home, and we have a whole new open relationship."

As Al and Charlie settled back into their places, Bill Grisham made yet another trip around the table with the coffee pot, refilled all the cups, then took his place, carefully positioning the coffee pot on a cloth napkin.

Then the interrogation began anew, Al and Charlie peppering Molly with questions about her life in Chicago and, more importantly, about every detail she knew about the group that recruited girls from Western Wisconsin for the sex trades.

Finally, several additional cups of coffee later, Molly looked up, smiled wryly at her inquisitors and said, "I think that's it, gentlemen. I don't think there is one thing we haven't been over. I'm glad to help … I hope you know that. You're my heroes. I will do anything I can to help you stop the trade in this area."

"You've been great, Molly. We can't thank you enough." As he spoke, Al rose from the table, then drained his coffee cup and put it carefully back on its saucer. "We want you to think about the Sovereign woman. She'd be older now … in her mid-fifties, and if you can think of anything useful, please call us."

"I will, Al … you can count on it. I owe you guys big-time."

ack in the La Crosse County SUV, Charlie behind the wheel, he steered them out of Hazard and back toward La Crosse. "What's next?"

"Lots to do … lots," answered Al. "I think we need to start by having a talk with Steve Scranton. Maybe he'll put us in touch with his vice guys so we can talk through this trafficking thing. You agree?"

"I do."

"Then that's a job for first thing tomorrow. I think I'll message him tonight and ask if we can call in the morning. I want to find out what the Chicago cops know about this syndicate of sorts, and what information they might have about girls who have aged beyond usefulness in this country being sent to the islands to spend the rest of their life with older men."

"Man, Al, if she's right about that and we could somehow bring about a crackdown, that would really be something, wouldn't it?"

"It sure would, it sure as heck would," agreed Al as the SUV swept past the "Welcome to La Crosse" sign.

"Ya know, Al, normally I'd be suggesting a beer, but tonight I just wanna get home and put my feet up. Know what I mean?"

"I do. I'm still full of those wonderful pancakes that Bill cooked. Sure seems like Molly's homecoming has been a good one, doesn't it?"

"Sure does. They all seem happy. Well, here we are pal. See you tomorrow."

Charlie pulled the SUV into Al's driveway, waited until his

passenger got out, then backed out and sped away with a wave of his hand.

Al and Jo Anne spent a relaxing evening. Jo Anne had made pot roast, boiled potatoes and a banana cream pie for dessert. Afterwards, Al helped her clean up the dishes, they watched a little TV and then turned in.

When they were in bed, Jo Anne rolled toward him, put her hand on his chest and said, "Something's bothering you, Al. I know it. Want to talk about it?"

Al told her about their talk with Molly, was careful to give her all the facts of the syndicate Molly talked about, spoke about the older women being sent to the islands when they were no longer producing high levels of revenue.

"Do you think that's where Shirley is?" Jo Anne wanted to know.

"I don't know, Jo Anne, I really don't. We have to learn a lot more. That will happen, starting tomorrow."

The next morning dawned with promise. Both Al and Charlie were up early, and it was just a few minutes after six when their vehicles nosed up to the curb in front of Ma's Café. Ma had coffee on the table waiting for them as they shrugged out of their jackets, hung them carefully on the backs of their chairs, and got ready to order.

Charlie was uncommonly reserved ("Still dieting," he told Ma) and Al had his usual two eggs, bacon and hash browns with rye toast. It seemed they had just ordered when the food was on the table. They talked as they ate.

"We really have to press Scranton hard," said Al between mouthfuls. "We need to visit with the vice cops in the First District. It suddenly looks as if we are dealing with a much bigger deal than Molly Grisham and Shirley Sovereign. Sounds like there's a lot of women from this area that have been recruited."

"Sure does," said Charlie, his mouth full of eggs and toast. "Sounds like it's widespread, too."

Forty-five minutes later, the two officers were hunched over the table in the conference room across from Al's office talking to Steve Scranton in Chicago.

"Steve, Molly Grisham has been a remarkable source of information … and by the way, thank you for your help in bringing all of this about—wish you could have attended the reunion. Anyway, Molly sat down with us yesterday and told us a horror story of a sex trafficking ring that makes regular trips through our area to recruit women and spirit them away. Sounds like some of these women are under age, too. Do you think your guys could help us?"

"You know, Al, we've been trying to get a handle on this situation for a long time, but every time we think we have a promising lead, it dries up as quickly as we get to work on it. Do you think Molly would help us?"

"I'm not sure." Al was scratching his head as he spoke to his Chicago friend. "She was very willing to talk yesterday. What do you think, Charlie?"

"I think she might." Charlie leaned closer to the phone as he spoke. "She was very serious when she talked to us about the group making regular trips through this area."

"You know, Charlie's right. She was pretty adamant."

"Tell you what," said Scranton, "why don't I talk to the vice guys and maybe we can all get on the phone together and hatch a plan. If Molly is willing to meet with us that would be wonderful."

"I know, if she'd be willing, that the meeting would have to be held up here. She'd be afraid of going back to Chicago for any reason. She's frightened enough as it is," explained Al.

"Give me a couple of hours to talk with our guys here and I'll be back to you before noon."

"Sounds great," chorused Al and Charlie. The three officers laughed at the synchronized response, then concluded their call.

"How do you think we go about putting Molly at ease?" Charlie wanted to know.

"I'm not totally sure, Charlie, but she was very willing to talk to us. I think if Bill and Beth were willing to have us meet at their house that might be enough to make it happen. Let's hear back from Steve and then I can give Bill a ring on his cell."

"Great idea. So now we wait."

"Yes, but why don't we go over the files on Shirley again, just to see if there is anything there that might be helpful, in light of the new information from Molly." Al was already digging through a box on the table as he spoke. A row of them were still on the end of the table. With Al exploring one, Charlie grabbed another and began sorting through the contents.

"There's a report here that says Shirley and her friends used to take rides to Hazard and other places to do some underage drinking. Wonder if any of her friends are still around and would be willing to help?"

"Let me see that." Al was focused now on the document Charlie was holding. He took it, looked it over, then said, "There was that one friend of Shirley's that still lived here ... at least she did on the 39th anniversary of their La Crosse Central class. Her names in here somewhere ... let me look for it."

Charlie went back to his box of contents while Al searched for the name he was looking for. Half an hour later, he sat back, a document in his hand. "Aha, here it is. The *Tribune* ran a story on Shirley's unsolved case when the class met for its 35th reunion a few years ago. Their main source was a Linda Williamson. Wonder if she's still living here."

Al began to search their databases for a Linda Williamson while Charlie went back to work on his box of materials.

"Got her," exclaimed Al. "Tom and Linda Williamson live on Losey Boulevard. The address is near the campus. Wonder if that's where she lived when she was running around with Shirley?"

"Does she have a phone?" Charlie asked while looking through the papers surrounding him.

"You look like a librarian ... or some sort of researcher," said Al, chuckling. "The look becomes you, Charlie."

"Go back to work, Al. I don't need the stress."

Al laughed heartily, then looked up Tom and Linda Williamson in the phone book. "They're listed," he said suddenly. "I'll give 'em a call."

He picked up the phone and dialed. Charlie watched.

"Hi, Linda? This is Al Rouse, La Crosse Police Department. Deputy Charlie Berzinski and I are doing some work on the Shirley Sovereign disappearance. Would you have a few minutes to answer some questions? Great. Can I put you on speaker? Thanks."

Al punched the magic button. "There, can everyone hear okay?" Linda said she could hear fine.

"Linda, Charlie and I are looking into the Shirley Sovereign case, as I said, and we'd like to bring that to closure, if we can. We're thinking this might be the charm, since we have many more tools available now than in 1979 ... in fact, more tools than just a few years ago. But let me get right to the point.

"We know that one of Shirley's friends or acquaintances said something about trips to communities near La Crosse where alcoholic beverages might have been available to under-age kids. We'd like to talk to you about that, if you wouldn't mind?"

"No, go ahead. I hope I can help." Linda's voice was calm and she seemed collected.

"Thanks ... let me continue then. What can you tell us about trips ... say, to Hazard or Viroqua ... to go drinking?"

Linda Williamson paused for a moment, then said, "Yes, officer, we did make such trips. Shirley was always the adventurous one. I don't want to besmirch her reputation, but when we turned 15, we met some older men at the La Crosse County Fair. We flirted with them and we thought we were pretty hot stuff when they paid attention to us. I only went to the fair once that year, but Shirley went several times. They told her they could take us to a place where we could drink beer and dance ... and so, once after the fair, I went along on a night we planned to go to a movie and a sleepover. Instead, we went to Hazard ... to a country-western bar there. We had a great time. We danced and drank several beers, enjoying the high life ... and ... frankly ... we came home looped. We sneaked into a girlfriend's house where we were staying and crept down to the basement where we were sleeping. We all felt crappy the next day."

"Was that the only time you went?"

"Me? Yes. But not Shirley. She and other friends went quite often that year. My parents were so strict I was afraid they would find out and put me on lockdown, so I didn't go again. But the girls who went had quite a few tales to tell. Until you mentioned it, I had forgotten about it. They had stories about some pretty wild parties."

"Were there others involved?"

"Oh, yes, the whole crowd we ran around with. Shirley was always the leader, but the rest of us were willing followers. Don't think I didn't want to go to these parties, because I did, but I was fearful of getting caught."

"So, you don't know the names of any of the men involved?"

"Well, there was an Amos, he was a cop. There were two or three others, but I don't know their names. Ruth Clauson Weber might know. I'm pretty sure she was along on all of them. There were others, too, but they have all moved away from La Crosse, and I have no idea where they are. None of them was at the reunion a few years ago."

"Tell you what, Linda, you have been of great help. I'm gonna try Ruth Weber, and if I need those other names, I will call you back, okay?

"That would be fine, Detective. I'd really like help. Seems awful that there has never been anything found in all this time since Shirley's disappearance."

The call concluded, Charlie held up the phone book and pointed. "Here it is, Al—Roy and Ruth Weber, 1486 S. 32nd Street. Want the number?"

When Charlie read it to him, Al dialed. It rang twice, then was picked up.

"Mr. Weber? This is Detective Al Rouse, La Crosse P.D. How are you today, sir? Great. I wonder if your wife is home? She is ... could I talk to her, please?

"Trouble, oh, absolutely not. I just want to talk to her about an old friend of hers."

Roy Weber called for his wife and Al heard him say, "It's the La Crosse Police Department. A detective wants to talk to you about an old friend of yours."

"Yes?" Ruth Weber's voice was soft but sweet.

"Mrs. Weber, Detective Al Rouse calling. I'd like to ask you a few questions about Shirley Sovereign, if you don't mind? … Fine, can I put you on speaker so my colleague, Deputy Charlie Berzinski can hear? … Good, thanks.

"Mrs. Weber, I just finished speaking with Linda Williamson about parties you folks might have attended with Shirley when you were in high school."

Ruth said, "Oh, you're talking about when we'd go out on Friday nights, those parties."

"Yes, and in particular, the times there would be a group of you girls who would go down to Hazard. I am interested in the men who took you there. We think they could be of help in trying to track down Shirley."

Al and Charlie could almost hear Ruth Weber thinking, but the phone was silent. Then she spoke. "Well, there was a Johnny … Arnold, I think. And a Glen Siefert. And the one I knew best was Orvin Lechler. I dated him for a while. But, gosh, officer, I haven't heard of any of them for years and years."

Al assured her that the names could be of help and the conversation concluded.

"More names," said Al. "Let's both check the La Crosse City Directory. It has county and area names in the back. All the directories are on line. Why don't you take Vernon County and I will do La Crosse."

"Sounds good. Then maybe lunch?" Charlie stretched then returned to his computer. Across the table, Al was studying his screen, too.

Al was the next to speak. "I have a John Arnold in La Crosse County."

"And I have an Orvin Lechler in rural Hazard," said Charlie a short time later. "Two names to follow up on after lunch then?"

20

Refreshed after Chicken Pad Thai at Four Sisters near the La Crosse riverfront, the two officers settled back into their chairs at the La Crosse P.D. and prepared to make calls to John Arnold and Orvin Lechler, hoping they would learn something of interest.

Al placed the first call to the residence of John Arnold. The phone rang a few times and a woman answered. "Are you Mrs. Arnold?" Al wanted to know. "You are? Good. Ma'am, we are looking for the John Arnold that grew up in Hazard and likely is in his 60s. You don't sound that old.

"Oh, you're from Mississippi? … Moved here four years ago … Your husband teaches at UWL? Mrs. Arnold, thanks for your help, but your husband is not the man we are looking to talk to. Thanks for your time."

The call concluded, Al smiled at Charlie and offered, "She didn't even ask who I was. Must be used to those kinds of calls. Oh, well, you want to try the next one?" When Charlie nodded, Al slid the phone over toward him and soon Charlie was speaking to someone in rural Hazard.

"Ma'am, this is Charlie Berzinski from the La Crosse County Sheriff's Department. If Orvin is neaby, could I speak to him?"

Charlie heard some rustling and squeaks in the background, then a man's voice came over the speaker. "This is Orvin. What can I do for you?"

"Mr. Lechler, Charlie Berzinski with the La Crosse Sheriff's Department. Sir, I'm here with Detective Al Rouse on the speaker phone, and we were visiting with Ruth Clauson Weber this morning and she said she dated an Orvin Lechler a few times back in high school. Was that you?"

After an extended pause, Lechler said, "Well, I'll be damned … Ruth Clauson. Sure, I remember her. Great looking little blonde who liked to party. She was quite a girl. I haven't seen her for … must be forty years now … where is she?"

"She lives in La Crosse, Orvin. After talking to her, we're hoping you might help us. I wonder sir, if we drove out to see you if you would meet with us. We're looking into the disappearance of Shirley Sovereign and maybe you might remember something that would be helpful to us."

Lechler invited them to "come on out," then gave them directions to his farm, which Al wrote down. "In the meantime," Lechler told them, "I'll try and remember something that might be helpful to you guys. That's a long, long time ago, you know?"

An hour later, with Charlie at the wheel, the SUV he was driving turned off Highway 82 after passing through Hazard and onto County Road D, then followed that for a time, finally turning left onto County Road P. A half mile later, Charlie turned left onto a gravel road that, another quarter mile later, led to a well-kept farmstead.

A raw-boned man with a weather-tanned face and a slim body, that rose about six-foot-five, waved at the two lawmen from the steps of the house. He met them as they entered the yard and pointed to a picnic table under a giant oak tree that shaded the lawn and house.

"Let's sit out here," he suggested. "Nicer than the house today. Janet has coffee, lemonade and some cookies coming out in a minute."

Shortly, an attractive middle-age lady came out of the house, coffee pot in one hand and a pitcher of lemonade in the other. When Charlie went to take the containers from her, she wiped her hands on her apron and quickly disappeared back into the house.

She re-emerged with Styrofoam cups under one arm, a bunch of napkins in one hand, and a plate filled with cookies in the other.

Again, wiping her hands on her apron, she nodded at the visitors and smiled. "Not sure what Orvin did back forty years, but he's been a pretty good boy now for a long time. Farming will do that to you, you know?"

"So, you're still farmin?" asked Charlie, his arm sweeping around the fields visible behind the barn buildings.

"Sure are," she told them, "and milkin' forty cows twice a day, too. Darn good thing Orvin was blessed with great knees. Most others have given up the milkin', but not my Orvin. He loves farmin', that's for sure. Me, I'd be livin' in town, if he'd listen to me. But farm life is a good life … just lotsa work."

"Now, Janet, better head back inside and let us guys visit, okay. These folks ain't got all day."

Janet disappeared and Charlie said, helping himself to an oatmeal raisin cookie, "She sure could stay, Orvin. Nothing we have to talk about is very private, I don't think."

"Prob'ly not, but we got our great-grandson in there and he's just a little shaver. Might need a bottle or something. Now, how can I help you?"

"We're looking into the disappearance of Shirley Sovereign a long time ago. When we talked with Ruth Clauson Weber, she told us their crowd partied with you folks once in a while."

"Sure did." Lechler slid his cap back to scratch his head, then smiled, "Yessir, we sure as hell did. Those La Crosse girls were something. Thought they were going to teach us a thing or two, but I think it was the other way around. I think they got a little more than they expected from the Hazard hayseeds."

"How so?"

Lechler tilted his head back, thinking, then said, "Deputy Berzinski, they come down here, swingin' their asses and acting smart by drinkin' beer. We thought they were older, 'til that Sovereign girl disappeared and we found out she was only 15. Damn, scared the heck out of me. I was dating Ruthie and she admitted she was only 15, too. Coulda knocked me over with a feather. I mean they were big girls, know what I mean? They were filled out like nobody's business. And when it came to makin' out, they was like firecrackers—hotter'n hell."

"Any idea what happened to the Sovereign girl?"

"Not really, but I always kinda thought she linked up with Amos Brickner and left town with him." Lechler paused to wet his whistle with some lemonade. "She was always complaining about being stifled at home. Her folks were really strict. We only got to see her when she could convince her folks she was stayin' at Ruthie's house.

"She come down one night with a different girl. A Donna somebody, I think. Both of them wound up with Brickner. It was his night off, and they took off toward Viroqua or somewhere. That was the last night we saw Shirley. It ended my times with Ruthie, too. I was afraid to call her for fear someone would think I got rid of Shirley."

Lechler stopped and thought a minute, then continued, "If you really want to find out what happened to her, I think you gotta track down Amos. I think he would know."

The men sat and talked for a while longer, munching on the cookies that were as good as Al had eaten, and drinking coffee and lemonade. As they got ready to leave, Lechler walked to the SUV with them, then leaned in and said, "Sure glad you was willing to meet in the yard. Janet and I been married damn near forty years now. She's a keeper and I didn't want her stirred up about my past, not that I done nothin' wrong, you understand."

"We do understand," said Al.

Charlie started the SUV and Lechler leaned back in for a moment. "If you get a hold of Brickner, say hi to him, will you? We was close back then, but after Shirley disappeared, he left, too, and we ain't seen him since."

"We'll do that," Al assured him as Charlie began to ease the SUV out of the drive and back toward La Crosse.

"I think we better figure out a way to visit with Brickner again," said Charlie. "Sounds like he has more information than he's given us. What do you think?"

"Absolutely. And we know how to get a hold of him, too. We can call when we get back to the office."

A quick call to the Florida Department of Corrections led to another conversation with Brickner that afternoon.

"Amos, this is Al Rouse in La Crosse. We have some more questions for you. We visited with Orvin Lechler this morning and he thought you might be able to help us track down Shirley Sovereign. Remember her?"

"I do, of course, detective. Shirley was really unhappy. She thought her folks were stifling her. All she talked about was leaving La Crosse, and she loved to party. We'd bring her down to Hazard, give her a couple of beers, and she'd do anything anyone wanted. One night, we were sitting in my squad car talking when she asked me point-blank if I could help her escape the area. Told me she'd give me anything I wanted if I helped her. Even gave me a little sample. I was taken by her, that's for sure."

"So, you helped her?"

"I did, Al. There were these guys that came through the area every couple of months or so, looking for girls. I think they took 'em to Chicago. I told Shirley about 'em and she wanted me to help her meet them."

Al and Charlie shook their heads, then Al said, "And did you?"

"Detective, I was young. I'd had some bad times at home myself. I felt sorry for her. Did I help her?" Amos waited a beat, gave a long sigh, then spilled his part in the infamous "kidnapping" of Shirley Sovereign. "I never told anybody how it happened, and you've got to believe me when I say she deserved a break, and so, yes, I helped her. I was out patrolling the road between La Crosse and Hazard late that night of the football game in September, and my headlights picked out a half-naked woman stumbling along the side of the road. It was Shirley, and she was a terrible mess. She told me she had been raped over and over by the Overland boys." Brickner paused and, when it seemed he was finished, Al jumped in.

"Amos, you can't just leave us hanging. Then what happened?"

"Welllll … I explained that the Overland boys were two bad cats and I said that while she could sign a complaint that they would probably kill her. She quickly said she didn't want to press charges because that wouldn't go well with her folks. She was afraid stories of the trips to Hazard would come out. We talked until two in the morning and she told me her folks were tough. She said she just wanted to run away. When she said that, I told her about the group from Chicago. Even after I told her what they would want her for, she wanted to go with them.

"I didn't know what to do, so I took her over to Richland Center … to Veronica Stone."

When Brickner stopped talking again, Al prompted him once more. "Then what? What happened next?"

"She stayed with Veronica for a few days and then, as luck would have it, we got word that the Chicago boys were gonna be here. Both Veronica and I talked to Shirley and she insisted she wanted to go with them … said she didn't mind that they would want to make her a prostitute."

Both Al and Charlie were on the edges of their chairs. Charlie just couldn't wait. "So then what, Amos?"

"Well, Veronica and me introduced her to the group from Chicago over at Viroqua."

"Did she go with 'em?" asked Charlie.

"I left before they did, Charlie, but I think so. She told me to take off, 'cause she knew I wasn't supposed to be in Viroqua, and she didn't want to get me in trouble. So, yeah, I guess I helped her, but I've done almost ten years down here and I'm really counting on being out for Christmas this year. Is this going to set that back?"

"It could," said Al seriously. "But we're grateful for the help and will put in a good word for you, okay?"

"Sure would appreciate that. If there's anything else you need, you know how to reach me." Al ended the call.

"Do you think he's learned his lesson?" Charlie kept his eye on Al as he talked to him.

"I think he has learned, but, as a law officer, he was aiding and abetting a minor on a runaway deal—across state lines, yet. It's a pretty serious crime. We're gonna have to think about this one."

"I kinda feel sorry for the guy," said Charlie. "Besides, we gotta shake him down for names of those guys."

"Absolutely. Starting tomorrow."

21

The next morning—fueled by a sensible breakfast from Ma's that had Charlie frowning—the big fella sat hunched over the table, his face resting on his hands. Al dialed the phone, waited for it to be answered, then told the guard at the Northwest Florida Reception Center that he had an appointment to speak to Amos Brickner, a prisoner scheduled for release in two months.

"He's waitin', ah believe," drawled the guard. "Just one minute, pleeze."

There were a few seconds of static, then the voice of Amos Brickner filled the room. "Hi, folks, how can I help you today? Happy to do what I can. The warden told me just a few minutes ago that if I provide 'significant material assistance'—his words—that I might be out in two weeks."

"Good news for both you and us," said Al. "We are calling this morning to get a line on the group from Chicago that makes recruiting trips through West Central Wisconsin. If you can give us some hard leads to follow, we'll be all over your warden to get you out of there."

"So, what do you want to know?"

"Names, if you have them, of course. Leaders, if you know them. What kinds of women were recruited, from where, and where they were going."

While Al was ready to continue, Amos broke in, saying, "Well, let's take those one at a time for openers. Okay with you?"

"Absolutely," chorused Al and Charlie.

"Okay, there were several groups from the same organization, and I dealt with all of them at one time or another—even down here."

"Before you start, were they all from Chicago?" asked Al.

"I think so, yes, but now that you ask, I can't say for sure."

"Okay, give us your best shot."

"Okay, here's what I know. I'll give you that first and then supply some things I think but don't know for sure. So here goes. I never met the big boss. The guys I knew referred to him only as 'The Guy.' That was it: 'The Guy.' Everyone I knew worked for him. And they were all afraid of him, too. Mainly I worked with a guy named Sonny Sebastian. I think his first name was LeRoy, but I only heard it once. He was the main guy for Wisconsin … or at least our part of Wisconsin.

"The deal was, when we had a girl—or sometimes two—we'd call Sonny and he'd arrange for the pickup. Most of the time he came himself, but once or twice I dealt with a guy by the name of Lipper Lipinski. He had a bad stutter. I liked Sonny better but both were fine to work with."

"Did you recruit the women?" Al wanted to know.

"Either me or my guys. I really don't want to talk about them because they are all good guys. They're out of it now, and I want to leave them out of it. I'm paying the bill for them and me, and I'm fine with that."

"So where did you recruit from?" asked Charlie.

"Our territory ran along the river from Pepin County down through Grant County. We also had Eau Claire, Jackson, Monroe, Richaland, and La Fayette—although we didn't work the southern part of the territory nearly as hard as the northern part. You'd be surprised how many girls want to get away from home—or, in some cases, their old man."

"Can you give us the process?" Al had moved nearer the phone until he looked as if he was going to climb into it.

"When we had a girl, we'd call Sonny's cell phone and leave a message. He'd call us back to get the details. He'd wanna know age, hair color, measurements, and circumstances. Sometimes he or his guys would pick 'em up the same day—sometimes we had to wait a few days. I always assumed he had people he recruited for. If the girl's description fit a need, he'd be right up to get 'em. But, sometimes, I got the idea he had to find a place to put 'em. Blondes were really popular. And a big-boobed blonde was the best. There were never enough of those."

"How did you get paid?" Charlie broke in now. He had been listening intently and making lots of notes.

"We got paid by the girl. The flat fee was $7,500, but sometimes we got more, depending upon the quality of the girl. Blondes brought more, and we once got $12,000 for a blonde who was about 16 and was built like the proverbial brick …"

"Did you ever know where these women went?"

"Not very often—only once in a great, great while. Like the blonde that netted us twelve grand. She was going to Mexico, Sonny told me. He let slip that the folks down there might pay as much as $100,000. That made me mad. He knew it, and he upped the rates a bit. But we never really knew where anyone went … except we knew that the older women ultimately went to the islands. There was big market for them down there—from Cuba down through Grenada, we was told."

"So, Amos, what makes you think that Shirley Sovereign is down there?" asked Al.

"Well, right before I got sent up, I was up in Chicago visiting with Sonny. I had moved to Florida cause I liked the warmer weather, and recruiting was good there, too. In any event, I was up in Chicago talking to Sonny, and he got a call from someone in his network. They talked for a long time … about a woman, I was pretty sure, so I kept my ears perked.

"When Sonny hung up, he looked at me and said, 'That was about one of yours.' 'One of mine?' I asked, 'Whaddaya mean?' He told me that the woman was Shirley Sovereign. He said he had placed her with a guy in Montserrat. Said the guy was overjoyed. Hoped Sonny could find others like 'er."

"So, is that the last you heard about her?"

"Heck, Al, it was about the *only* time I heard about a girl I had sent to him. We just almost never talked about it. That was just by accident."

"How long ago was this?" Al was relaxed now, thinking the interview was about over.

"Well, I been in here damn near 10 years. And I s'pose it was a year or so before that, so maybe about 11 years ago, give or take a few months."

Charlie too had relaxed into his interview ending mode. Now he said, "Anything else?"

"Gosh, I think that's about it. Can't think of anything I haven't told you. I'm sure hopin' you'll go to bat for me with the warden. I'm sick of this place … and I get sicker of it every day. If you can put in a good word for me, that would be much appreciated."

"We'll do that, Amos," Al assured him. "Any idea if the pipeline is still in place?"

"I'd bet on it. I heard Sonny is doin' time, but someone would have stepped in. There's always a market for young women. But I really want nothing to do with it when I get out … so don't even ask me about trying to find out more information for you after that."

"We won't, Amos, I promise. And we will put in a good word for you with the warden. In fact, we'll do that when we hang up. Oh, one more thing, any idea who the man in Montserrat is?"

"Nope—never heard a name."

The call finished, Al and Charlie talked over their notes to make sure they had everything, then Al called the warden in Florida to praise Amos Brickner's cooperation. When he finished that task, he looked at Charlie. "It's been a good day, buddy, don't you think? I think our next stop is with the chief and sheriff. How about a trip to the islands?"

"How d'ya think I'd look in a grass skirt?"

22

The next morning when the familiar shadow fell across his desk, Al was prepared. A few blocks away, the scene was being repeated in another police administrative office, where Charlie was waiting for his boss, too. The two officers had planned their strategy well, determining they would mount a two-pronged strategy designed to get their bosses up to speed and ready to cooperate on a trip to the Caribbean.

"Hey, boss, c'mon in." Al was straightening up some paperwork on his desk and as Brent Whigg, the chief of police walked in, he reached for a white paper bag on the credenza behind his desk. "How about a doughnut?"

"Doughnut'd be good." The chief accepted the offered cup of coffee, placed the doughnut on the napkin that accompanied it and prepared for a first bite.

"How's the travel budget?" Al was smiling as he made the comment, because he knew that his boss watched all line items like a hawk, making sure no dime was spent in a manner that could be misconstrued as frivolous.

"What, you and Charlie need a vacation?"

"Well, ummm, no, but time in the sun would be nice."

"Tell me more."

Al carefully laid out the story for the chief, telling him about the return of Molly Grisham to her home in Hazard, the relationship he and Charlie had developed with Amos Brickner, and what Brickner had to say about the case of the missing Shirley Sovereign he and Charlie were working on.

Whigg listened with great interest, interrupting from time to time so Al could flesh out a fact. When the story ended, he took a last bite of his doughnut, tidied up the sprinkles of powdered sugar that drifted to the desk top. When he'd wiped the new protective glass covering clean, he made sure the sugar was gone from his fingers. "So you think this lead is solid enough that you believe the Sovereign woman is alive and living somewhere in the islands?"

"Yes, chief, I do. I think Amos is trying to be as helpful as he can, because he has an even earlier release riding on his helpfulness."

"But was he making up the story just to get you guys to put in a good word for him?"

"I don't think so, chief. 'Course we couldn't look him in the eye, but I believe he was being as honest as he could possibly be. I don't think he would have much to gain by being dishonest, because it could land him back in the pokey for another stay."

"You're probably right, but turning you two guys loose to travel to the tropics to chase a woman missing for more than forty years seems a waste of good money... at least until some other steps are taken."

"I agree." Al was looking into his boss' eyes, an imploring look on his face. "And I think those steps should be taken as soon as possible. Here's what I'm thinking: First, we have to test the story through our friends in Chicago. If they have any snitches they can use to try for some additional proof, that would be good. Second, I don't know anything about the police in Montserrat. We should find out about that and either use them or someone else—haven't yet thought about that piece—to see if any leads ... good solid leads, that is ... can be developed. What have I missed, chief?"

"Your thinking is on track," agreed the chief, "but you might consider involving the FBI and, through them, Interpol."

"Do you really think involving the FBI now is a good idea?"

"Al, the FBI is just another useful tool. I like to use every tool available. Why wouldn't we?"

"You're right, chief, it's just that ..."

"That you want to be in the middle of anything that happens, right?"

"Yea, I guess you're right about that."

"I was just like you." The chief's eyes were twinkling now and his face broke into a smile as he spoke. "I always wanted to keep everything in front of me in a tight little box. Then came the day, on an important case, I screwed up, and the FBI picked up the pieces, solved the puzzle, and made me feel like an idiot. I learned then that they have great tools and that using them makes incredibly good sense. Did I like the lesson? Of course not. But when I thought about the end game, involving them left me defenseless when it came to ensuring that the job got done."

"Yeah, you make a good point chief. I'll call Charlie and we'll talk it through. We'll get hold of Steve Scranton in Chicago and, through him, we'll get the vice cops to test the story. And we'll also call the FBI, bring them up to speed and see what they can find out."

"And, Al, what else…"

Al looked at the now frowning Brent Whigg and sensed immediately what he was looking for.

"And, yes, chief, I will do it in a friendly way and be on my best behavior when I go through our evidence."

"There, that's all I can ask." Whigg stood, crumpled the napkin, tossed it in the wastebasket, picked up the cup, drained it, then walked to the credenza where he placed it back where it belonged, grabbed his hat and jacket, and turned to exit. When he was halfway out the door, he looked back over his shoulder. "And make sure Charlie gets the message, too, okay?"

"Sure will."

After Whigg had departed, Al made some notes on the ever-present legal pad and then, smiling to himself, dialed the number for Charlie.

"Berzinski. Yeah, before you say a word, Dwight chewed my ass, too."

"Really?"

"Well, maybe not quite that, but he let me know there were more steps to be taken before I can don my grass skirt and coconuts."

The image Charlie had improvised by adding the coconuts

caused Al to laugh. "Now just what the hell is so funny," began Charlie. Then, realizing the image he imagined Al was seeing, he laughed, too.

"Okay, so baggy shorts and flip-flops would be more appropriate, I guess."

They both laughed heartily again, then Al said, "Well, I guess you got the same lecture I got … even if the boss didn't see it as a lecture."

"Yeah, I got it. Guess we better deal in the Fibbies, right?"

"Yessir. Want to come over and help start the message to them?"

"Be there in 15 minutes. Better stop at Fayze's and get some doughnuts."

"No need to stop, Charlie. For one thing, doughnuts are not—definitely not—on your diet. Second, I have a bag on my desk and if you're really good, I may let you steal one and I promise not to tell Kelly."

"Deal. See you soon, man."

Five minutes later, Charlie walked in, picked up the doughnut bag, inspected its contents thoroughly, and frowned. "No powdered sugar?"

"Oops, sorry. Guess Brent and I ate those. But you like the chocolate-covered ones, too, don't ya?"

"Oh, I guess that'll do, but powdered sugar are my faves … really, really like 'em."

"Well, have one of the other ones and let's get to work."

Al already had his notebook and pens and was headed out the door as he spoke. Charlie grabbed a doughnut, not bothering with a napkin, grabbed his computer case, and followed across the hall.

"Okay," said Al, after pulling up a chair in front of the desktop on the table, "where do we start."

He looked at Charlie and chuckled. His friend's cheeks bulged with the contents of a doughnut that must've been devoured whole.

"Some help you're going to be." Then he began typing, carefully picking his way through the notes from his discussion with the chief. In a few minutes, he looked at Charlie. "Get your laptop out so I can send this to you."

His larger companion struggled with his laptop, but soon had it in front of him and was looking at the memo Al had written to the FBI. "Two things. Shouldn't we talk to the Chicago boys before we send this off? And I think we should strengthen the part about Interpol."

Noticing the frown on Al's face, he conceded, saying, "Let me explain, first of all I think Interpol will be more helpful than the FBI. They have jurisdiction in Montserrat, as well as the other islands, and if she's been moved somewhere else—like Europe or Asia—their network has the best chance of locating her."

"I wasn't frowning about your suggestion … I think it was just a look. Want to take a shot at strengthening it?"

"Hell, no. Man, you're the wordsmith, not I. I just had the idea."

Al, grinning, shook his head. "You just had the idea…and I get the work—that's how it goes?"

"Hell, yes, you're the man with the brains."

"I see." Al's wry smile faded as he pulled the keyboard over to him and then began to type. He finished up, turned the monitor around so Charlie could see it. "Like this better?"

"It's great. Terrific work."

"Okay." Al returned the monitor to where he could see it, addressed one memo to the FBI chief in Madison, Wisconsin, and sent the other to Interpol headquarters in Lyon, France, marked for the Caribbean director's attention.

"Done. Prob'ly won't hear anything today. Good time to get lunch anyway, don't you think?"

"Awww, I'm not really very hungry, Al."

The look on his friend's face was one of incredulity … so incredulous, in fact, that Charlie lost it and had to laugh.

"Hell, man, I ain't dead yet. I may be on a diet but I still like to eat. Lunch? Hell, yes, where do you want to go? I'm buyin', and don't you dare give me that look."

"Who me?"

"C'mon, let's go … it'll be twenty-four hours until we hear from anyone anyway."

"You're right. And if you're paying, we'll go where you want to."

"Ummm, if you want me to drive, we're gonna have to hike back over to my office. I walked over."

"Okay, I'll drive. Just tell me where to go."

As they drove back from lunch at Rocky's in Stoddard—Charlie wanted to go somewhere different … and the food was extraordinary—they talked about the search for Shirley.

"I just think," said Al, "how tragic it will be even if we do find her—of course, she will considerably older by now."

"Well, maybe not so old by today's standards. Think about it. She was 15 when she went missing in 1979. So 41 plus 15 is 56. That takes us to 2020. Fifty-six sure isn't old. My guess is she's still sexy as she can be."

"Yeah, I guess you're right. Think about Genevieve. She was 83 when she died and she had just gotten married. Not only did she act spry, she looked about 55 or so.

"So, I see what you mean." Al turned from 4th Street into the LEC parking lot, shut off the engine and released his seat belt. "Well, wanna bet that we haven't heard anything?"

"Why the heck would I bet you on that? It'd be like throwing away money."

"Yeah, like that insurance commercial. You see it, yet? Guy is lamenting how the insurance companies rip off auto owners who have an accident by giving them only what the car was worth when the accident happened. The guy says they should pay replacement and says insurance is like throwing money in the ocean—and he pitches his wallet into the water. It's funny as hell. When it dawns on him what he has done, he says, 'I think I'll regret that.'"

"Nope, haven't seen it, but I'm still not betting."

When they walked into Al's office, they were greeted by a thick stack of papers.

"What the heck …" Al took off his coat, laid it over his chair then picked up the papers and began to page through them. "I should have taken the bet, Charlie. We have reports back from both the FBI and Interpol. Can you believe it?"

"That's flat amazing. Well, let's get at 'em. what do they say?"

"Let's go over to the conference room. I'll take one stack, and, Charlie, you can take the other."

Al tossed the Interpol report to Charlie then began to study the FBI memo.

Al was the first to speak. "Whoa, says here that the FBI has been aware of Sonny Sebastian for years now but has been unable to get enough evidence to convict him of trafficking. They say the guy he works for is a Johnny Antonelli, who lives in one of Chicago's western suburbs. They'd like nothing better than to nail both of them. Wonder if Amos would talk to them?"

"Well, if we're gonna ask him, we should do it before we talk to the Feds. If he doesn't wanna talk, I'd let it be."

"I think you're right, Charlie. Amos has been helpful and I don't want to get him in any more trouble—not when he's on the verge of getting out."

"Why don't you call him?"

Al dialed the prison, talked to the chief guard and soon Brickner was on the phone.

"Hey, Al, thanks a million for your help." Even though Al couldn't see him, he sensed that Brickner was smiling and in an upbeat mood. "What's up?"

"Well, as you know, we're looking for the Sovereign woman and, after talking to you, we filed reports with the FBI and Interpol. We've heard back from both, but the FBI would prob'ly like to talk to you. They say they have been trying to nail Sonny Sebastian and his boss Johnny Antonelli for a long time."

"Geez, Al, I don't know. I get out tomorrow, and I'm worried enough about where to go to make sure I stay alive."

"You know, Amos, maybe the FBI would put you in their witness protection program."

"Ya think so, Al?"

"Won't hurt to ask."

"Would you do that for me?"

"Sure would—you've been very helpful."

"If we can work that out, I'll sing like a bird."

"Let me talk to them and see what I can do. More later."

"Crap, now we gotta go back to the Feds and ask for something else—that's disgusting … makes us look like we've always got our hand out … and it maybe dooming."

"C'mon, Charlie, we have pretty much gotten what we wanted—at least for now. Molly is home and happy. We have some idea where Shirley is and we're on her trail. Let's trust that we can get what we want from the Feds. No sense being petty obstructionists."

Al's words seemed to fall on deaf ears as Charlie sat there, unmoving for what seemed like several minutes but, in reality, was only a few seconds.

"Ya know, Al, I think those guys are jerks. How many times have we done the work, only to have them take the credit? It's made me damn mad to be honest. But if we have to have their help, we do, I guess. I guess we gotta go through them."

"Yes, we do. And we likely will have more luck if we're nice rather than if we're snippy. Let's try it the sugary way before we get out the hammer."

Charlie nodded and Al picked up the phone and dialed the FBI office in Madison. As expected, the agent in charge quickly said any protection deal was above his pay grade and he transferred them to the office in Washington. The Washington official he talked to was, as always, officious and guarded, but Al was assured he would get a call back before the end of the day.

"So now we wait?"

"Yes, Charlie, now we wait. Not sure about you, but I have a mound of paperwork on my desk that needs attention."

"You go ahead, I think I'll just stay here and sort through the Sovereign file to see if I can come up with any helpful information."

The rest of the afternoon slipped past without a call. Al was disappointed. Charlie adopted a "told-you-so" attitude.

As they headed out the door, Charlie slapped Al on the back. "Well, old buddy, I told you they're slower than molasses in January.

No need getting fussed up. Hell, we'll still be waitin' a month from now, I suspect."

Al mumbled a retort under his breath, then straightened up and smiled at his friend. "I'd bet it won't be a month, if you're up to a wager."

"Sure. How about lunch. At the place of the winner's choice. Work for you?"

"You're on. See you tomorrow?"

"You bet … if there's anything to do."

23

The rest of the week passed as quietly as the day they made the bet. Charlie was growing smugger by the day. Al worried—not about the bet, but about the lack of response. His concern was fueled by the fact that Amos was due for release, and he was afraid that when that happened, if there was no place hosted by the FBI waiting for him, he would just disappear, and whatever information he had would disappear with him.

On the thirteenth day after Al sent the message, he walked into his office to find a memo waiting. And when he read it, he was overjoyed. It said:

> *Dear Detective Rouse: Please be advised that we have been in touch with your friend and he is now safely ensconced in the Federal Witness Protection Program. His whereabouts will remain unknown to all but his handlers. Should you need to be in touch with him for any reason, please call or text 202-594-8600. Your message will be sent to your friend. With sincere thanks for providing a great helping hand!*

The memo was signed by Agent John Grimsley, Federal Bureau of Investigation, Washington, D.C.

But what about Shirley Sovereign? he wondered. *We'd sure like to know something about her.*

He stood at his desk and called Charlie on the speaker phone so he could pace while he talked. "The good news is," he said when his friend answered, "you lost the bet. The bad news is that I have no news about Shirley."

"Did they get Amos taken care of?" Charlie wanted to know.

"Yes, they did. He's in the witness program. If we have to reach him, we have a number we can call to get a message relayed to him. The memo was short and sweet. That's about what it said. They did thank us for helping them out, though."

"Nice of 'em. Well, that's better'n a poke in the eye with a sharp stick, I guess. So whadda we do now?"

"Well, they said our message was delivered to Amos, so maybe we just wait for a while. You okay with that?"

"Have to be, I guess. If we don't like it, what else are we going to do? If we pester the Feds, we just wind up with nothing, don't you think?"

"That is what I think, Charlie. Yes, waiting is the best strategy. Heck, it's the only strategy. In the meantime, we have other things to do, don't you think? We have to worry about Molly, and we have to try and crack this sex trafficking ring, if it still exists … I'd say we have plenty to do."

"Plenty to do but our hands are tied. That's a helluva predicament, isn't it? Is there anything we can actually *do* now?"

"Well, I guess not … at least for a while. No sense bothering Molly again right now. I think she's told us everything she knows, don't you?"

"Absolutely. She's been of great help. I think we need to let her settle in with her folks and begin to think of what's next for her. She's a nice lady. And tough as she's had it, she's still soft. I didn't detect any hard edges, did you?"

"No, she's had a helluva life, that's for sure. But she's still sweet as sugar. Now that she's back home, I hope she can get it all together." Al was still going back and forth in front of his desk, hands in his pockets. *The waiting is the worst,* he thought as he paced. "Ya know, Charlie, my mind's racing with things we could do and there isn't a single good idea among them. I think I'm just gonna hunker down and try and take care of the things on my desk that have been collecting dust." Then he stopped pacing as he thought of something. "Except there's at least one interesting item in the mix."

"Oh, yeah? What's that?" Charlie dropped his legs from his desk and sat up straight in his chair, waiting for Al's answer.

"Some tip about a large wooden box that was uncovered in the backwaters near Alma and sent down here for testing. Apparently, there were some gold coins in the bottom of the box, but what's of most interest are a collection of bones that were stuffed in with the coins. About all we know right now is that they're human. I'm gonna go look all the stuff over. The Chief said there was no urgency attached, but at least it will take my mind off the immediate issues."

"Wish I had one like that. Well, I guess I kinda have one like that. Some folks in the Middle Ridge area reported some strange goings on at a mobile home they rent near their farmhouse. Guess I'll take a run out there to see what it's all about. Family's name is Hoffstetter. I know one of our guys stopped at the trailer but didn't find anything amiss. At least it'll give me something to do while we wait. Let's me know if anything happens."

"Sure will. Bye, Charlie."

Al clicked the phone off, then settled down at his desk to study the notes of the mysterious chest that had been found by a couple of youths in the backwaters across the river from Alma. He quickly discerned that the information triggered many more questions than answers.

As he was studying the inventory of items found in the old box, his phone rang.

"Al Rouse."

"Hi, Al, this is Agent John Grimsley. I have a message from your friend."

"Well, this is a welcome call," Al told him. "I've been stewing about what to do, wondering when I might hear from Am ... er, my friend, as you put it. What can you tell me?"

"Your friend wants to be helpful," Grimsley told him. "He thinks the best way to approach the situation is for you to send me a list of your questions. I'll relay them to him and then get you his answers."

"No chance of talking to him directly?"

"Not right now, I'm afraid, detective. We just got him settled and we want his whereabouts to be as secret as they can be. That means any direct contact will have to wait until we're sure that any spying ears have given up."

"I guess that makes sense, sir. Let me get with Deputy Berzinski and put together the list. We should be able to get it for you tomorrow. Will that be okay?"

Grimsley assured him the next day would be fine, then they concluded the call with the formality of two law enforcement officers who have not met.

The minute he left the call, Al dialed Charlie. "Just heard from the FBI," he told his friend. "Grimsley suggests we use him to relay our questions to Amos. You still at the office?"

"Yup, was just getting ready to leave. I'll be over in a minute."

Just a few minutes later, Charlie huffed into the office, his face red and his breath labored.

"Did you run over here?" Al wanted to know.

Charlie, shrugging out of his leather jacket, said, "Well, you said to get over here and I thought I'd better hurry it up. Guess I'm not in as good a shape as I thought I was. I jogged from the parking lot. Better get back to working out. Damn, I hate it, though."

"Well, I'd love to have you around for a while longer, and even though you're dieting, it might be good to do a little tone job, too, don't you think?"

"What I think and what I want to do are definitely two different things. But right now, I ain't got workin' out on my mind, that's for sure."

"Okay, have a seat and we'll get at the questions."

Charlie positioned himself in the chair in front of Al's desk, his elbows on the glass expanse atop Al's desk that was, as usual, clean and neat.

"Okay, what do we want to know?" Al was poised in front of the keyboard, as if ready to take dictation.

Charlie stared at him for a moment. "Well, we sure as heck want to know how that trafficking ring operates, don't we?"

"Absolutely, but is that where we want to start? I was thinking that a first question might ask who Amos called when he had a girl that needed to be moved. What do you think?"

"Probably a good place to start—put it down."

Al tapped his keyboard for a few seconds, then stopped and looked up.

"I think, after that, we should ask about what happened next … you know, how long it took for the boys in Chicago—if that was headquarters—to respond. And, along with the time factor, let's find out if his contacts were in Chicago or somewhere else."

"Good suggestions." Al's keys were flying over the keyboard now.

"Damn, how'd you get that good?" Charlie wanted to know. "If I tried to type that fast, you couldn't read the result."

"Didn't you take keyboard touch typing in 7th grade, Charlie?"

"Typing, are you kidding me? That was for girls and sissies. I majored in P.E. in middle school, with a double minor: football and basketball."

"You were damn good, too, weren't you?"

"Nah, not that good … just bigger and stronger in football and a lot taller in basketball. Tallest man in the conference, I think."

"Well, let's get back to this, okay? So, we have an original contact, a timeline once the first call was made, and other contacts in Chicago or somewhere else. What else?"

"I'd really like to know who else was involved up here. I think Amos took the fall for a gang. I'd just like to know who those people are."

Al's keyboard clattered, then he looked up again. "And?"

"Let's find out more about the pay. I'd also like to find out how the money was divided. I'm guessin' someone made a pretty penny and I'd like to know if they hung out around here."

"Good idea. Not sure he'll answer, but we can try it. I also think we should ask if the folks up here got reports about where the girls went after leaving. Oh, man, we almost forgot. We've gotta try and find out how many other girls were recruited from around here, if Amos can tell us. It would be great if we could get the names and towns."

"That's great, too. I think we're closing in. Let's think for a while. Is there anything else?"

Both Charlie and Al stared at the desk. Finally, Al broke the silence.

"I'm assuming drugs were involved. We need to find out if that was true here, too, or restricted to the big cities."

"Okay, sounds good Al. Tell you what, I'll keep thinking while you get what we have to date in order to send."

Al bowed his head over the keyboard while Charlie looked on in amazement as Al's fingers rapidly tapped the keyboard. A few minutes later, he straightened, pushed a couple of keys, and the printer whirred to life and dropped out two pieces of paper. Al handed one to Charlie, kept one for himself, and sat back and began to read.

1. *How did the recruiting process work?*
2. *How many people were involved in this area?*
3. *Who was Amos' contact when a girl was identified?*
4. *Did they pick up individual girls or wait for a group?*
5. *How many people were involved in recruitment in the Coulee region?*
6. *How many girls were recruited in Amos' time up here?*
7. *Where were they from?*
8. *Were the women taken directly to Chicago or was there an interim stop?*
9. *Were drugs involved in the recruitment process here ... or later?*
10. *How were recruiters compensated and by whom?*
11. *Were there reports back on where the women were?*

Charlie read for a while, then looked up to find Al staring at him.

"What? Did you even read it? I'm about halfway finished. Gimme some time to finish."

A couple minutes later, Charlie straightened and said, "Looks pretty good to me. I'm fine with it, Al."

"Let's take a couple of minutes to think about it. If we still think it's okay, we'll send it to Grimsley."

Charlie went back to studying the paper. Al got up, took the paper and walked out of the office. He went to Chief Whigg's office, found his boss there, cleared his throat and asked for a minute of the Chief's time.

The chief studied the sheet. "I think it looks good, Al. Amos was a cop when he was involved up here, right?"

When Al nodded, the Chief said, "As much as I fear the answer, we should find out if there were any other cops involved, don't you think?

"Absolutely. Good catch, Chief. I'll add that before sending this. Anything else?"

"What about geography? We should know how much of our area was involved, don't you think?"

"I sure do. Thanks a million for your help."

Returning to his office, Charlie had finished his study and told Al, "I think it looks great."

"The chief added a couple of points. Let me add 'em and I'll print a copy."

A bit more clattering and the printer again whirred to life.

"Here you go." Al handed the paper to Charlie, kept one for himself and sat back to read.

1. *How did the recruiting process work?*
2. *How many people involved in this area?*
3. *Were there any other area officers involved?*
4. *Who was Amos' contact when a girl was identified?*
5. *Did they pick up individual girls or wait for a group?*
6. *How many people were involved in recruitment in the Coulee region?*
7. *How much area geography was involved?*
8. *How many girls were recruited in Amos's time up here?*

9. *Where were they from?*
10. *Were the women taken directly to Chicago or was there an interim stop?*
11. *Were drugs involved in the recruitment process here … or later?*
12. *How were recruiters compensated and by whom?*
13. *Were there reports sent back on where the women were?*

"Looks thorough to me. The Chief thought of a couple of really good points. Glad you decided to show it to him. Mind if I show a copy to Dwight?"

"Heck, no. The Sheriff should see it. Why don't you take it over—here, I'll print another copy. Show it to him, if he's in, get his feedback, and give me a ring. Once that's done, I'll send it off to Grimsley."

Charlie grabbed the sheet of paper from the printer, wrestled into his jacket, and disappeared out the door. Not ten minutes later, Al's phone rang. "The Sheriff likes it. Let 'er go."

Al thanked his pal, typed a quick cover note to Agent John Grimsley, attached the list of questions, and hit send. Then he tapped out a quick note to Charlie. "Questions are sent."

24

The next four days passed with agonizing slowness. No matter how hard Al tried to get into new things, or to tend to paperwork on his desk, the mental image of Shirley Sovereign haunted his memory. When he came to work on the fifth day, it was with a promise to himself that today would be different—that he would, somehow, find the energy and the focus to at least rid his desk of the accumulating paperwork.

As he stepped into his office, he noticed that the red voice mail light on his phone was blinking, but he went about his morning ritual as usual—hung his hat and coat on the hall tree someone unknown years ago had deposited in his office, stopped at the Keurig to brew a cup of Green Mountain hazelnut, and then, seated at the desk, he reached for the phone.

He listened to FBI Agent John Grimsley tell him that Amos (no last name given) had provided answers to his questions. Grimsley urged Al to call him when he was at work so he could transport the message to Al's office computer.

Glancing at his watch, he noted the time was 7:45 in the morning where Grimsley worked in Washington, D.C. Deciding Grimsley was unlikely to be at work yet, he decided to try Charlie's cell to invite his pal and colleague to join him to examine the document.

As expected, he reached Charlie at Ma's. "Hey, Al, what's up?" When Al told him, Charlie said, "Here comes my breakfast now. Won't take me long to eat it, either. Ya know, Al, I'd give anything to have one of those old breakfasts."

"Sure you would. And then when you'd get here I would listen to the sound of your arteries closing behind the weight of four eggs, bacon, ham, sausage, pancakes, and a waffle for dessert."

"Yea, you make a point. Guess Kelly's way has some merit. And guess what? When I stepped on the scale this morning I was under 300 pounds—the first time that's happened since I was a sophomore at Aquinas. I tell ya, Al, I'm just wastin' away."

"Ummm … Charlie, I don't think there's much chance of that—at least for a little while."

"S'pose you're right. Well, give me 20 minutes and I'll be by."

That done, Al concentrated on straightening up his desk, although in reality there was little to straighten. Nonetheless, he didn't look up until a large shadow fell over his desk accompanied by the customary "How ya doin'?" Charlie had arrived.

"Good morning. Good to see you, Your Slimness," said Al in reference to their earlier conversation.

"Aww, c'mon, Al, just a slight acknowledgement that I'm losin' weight would be good enough."

"And you are, Charlie, that's for sure." Al looked his friend up and down, concluding that his friend had, indeed, lost enough weight for it to be visible. "You're looking good … and the weight loss does show."

If a 299-pound hulk could swoon, Al was certain that his pal was swooning before settling into the chair across from Al, leaning on his desk, chin on his hands, seemingly ready for action.

"Well, since you're set, let's get a hold of Agent Grimsley and see what he has for us."

Al picked up a piece of paper and studied it while dialing his phone. Two rings later, they heard: "Grimsley. How can I help?"

"Hi, Agent Grimsley. Charlie and I are here and anxious to see the document you have for us."

"Oh, hi Al … Charlie. Yup, I have it right here waiting to be sent to you. Are you at your computer?"

"I am … and anxious to see it, too."

"I just hit send. Should be in your inbox right about now."

As Grimsley spoke, a ding sounded, signaling the arrival of a new message.

"I think it's here." Al opened his in-box, confirmed the message had arrived and told Grimsley they had it.

"Good," was the response. "Just let me know when there is anything else I can do."

Al and Charlie thanked the agent, then Al activated his printer and when it was done spitting out several sheets of paper, he divided the two copies, handed one to Charlie, and sat back to study his. This is what they saw, typed in red:

1. *How did the recruiting process work?*

   We'd hang out with women in the little towns around La Crosse, listening to hear if anyone was upset with their life. When we found that situation, we'd sort of cozy up to them and begin to cultivate their friendship. We'd buy them things, treat them to dinner and drinks, generally look out for them. When we thought they were ready, we'd begin to talk about a good life somewhere else. Then, when a woman had committed, we'd get in touch with our contacts.

2. *How many people involved in this area?*

   Not sure, but there were two I worked with—a guy from Prairie du Chien in Crawford County, and a woman from Richland Center. I think there were others, but I didn't know them. The fellow from Prairie was young, in his 20s, I think. The Richland Center woman was in her forties. She was a mother type.

3. *Were there any other area officers involved?*

   I think the Prairie guy might have been a deputy. He never said that, but it was the way he acted. However, I think the Prairie guy, the chief contact in this area, was in the Crawford County Sheriff's office. Might have been the Sheriff, although I don't know that for sure. But from the way people talked, he might have been the Sheriff.

4. *Who was Amos' contact when a girl was identified?*

When I first identified someone I thought might be a candidate, I talked with the woman from Richland Center. Her name was Veronica Stone. She was very nice—the kind of person you wouldn't mind spilling your guts to. She would provide advice and would even meet with the woman, if things were going slow. I would also let her know when a woman had committed and she would keep them at her house prior to pick-up if there was a special circumstance. Then I'd call Sonny. I guess that's different than what I said earlier. This is the correct version.

5. *Did they pick up individual girls or wait for a group?*
   It could be one or more than one, it just depended upon the circumstance. There was no set formula.

6. *How many people were involved in recruitment in the Coulee region?*
   There were a number of people, although I know only the name of Veronica. They were very careful not to share the names of other people involved. I only know this one because she was a direct contact.

7. *How much area geography was involved?*
   Again, I don't really know, but I think it was Crawford, Richland, Vernon, Monroe, La Crosse, Trempealeau, Jackson and Buffalo. I know the state was divided into regions and this area was known as West Central.

8. *How many girls were recruited in your time up here?*
   I really have no idea, but I do know that I recruited six myself. The guy from Prairie once told me he had sent 12 women to the folks in the southeast.

9. *Where were they from?*
   Of the women I sent, two were from La Crosse, two from Hazard, one from Sparta, and one from Tomah. Those are the only ones I know.

10. *Were the women taken directly to Chicago, or was there an interim stop?*

I'm not sure. I think they went directly to Chicago, but there could have been some who went to Milwaukee, too.

11. *Were drugs involved in the recruitment process here … or later?*
    We had whatever we needed to make the catch. If we needed drugs, they were supplied. Whatever we needed was available: weed, cocaine, heroin … anything. But I almost always stayed away from drugs because of being a deputy and not wanting to get caught with anything like that.

12. *How were recruiters compensated and by whom?*
    The payment was always in cash. I was paid $7,500 for each girl I sent, but sometimes I got more, like I told you. Whoever came to get the girl always had the payment in an envelope. It almost always was Sonny. Once it was that Lipinski guy. He was a piece of work. I didn't like him at all.

13. *Were there reports back on where the women were?*
    No. The only one I ever found out about was Shirley, and that's because, as I said before, I was sitting there when my contact got a call, and he told me she was in Montserrat.

Al finished first and waited for Charlie to finish. He kept turning over the information in his mind and was about to burst when Charlie finally looked up.

"Sounds like a pretty disciplined effort, doesn't it?"

"Sure does," Al agreed. "I'm just grateful that he heard about Shirley, and at least got a little information. That news was from long ago, though, so she could be anywhere by now."

"Or dead," finished Charlie, echoing a thought that had been running through Al's head, too.

"Yes, or dead."

25

The next morning, as Al set the little bell atop the door at Ma's Café in south La Crosse ting-a-linging, Charlie was already seated in his customary place and intently studying the menu.

"Anything new and interesting?" Al approached the table while shrugging out of his jacket.

"Nothing new, but everything is interesting," was Charlie's glum response, uttered without looking up. "You know, Al, Kelly seems to think that every starving man should have enough willpower to say no when someone passes a tray of food around."

"So the diet has you down on this fine day?"

"And starving."

Al slid into his chair opposite Charlie, looked at his friend and smiled. "Now, Charlie, there's no way you're starving. You may miss those 10,000-calorie breakfasts of not long ago, but you're definitely not in danger of dying of starvation."

"Guess you're right." Charlie looked up, stretched, and sipped at his coffee. "Let's talk about something else. Unless we do, the thought of food will just nibble me to death." Charlie smirked at his own pun. "So where do we go from here?"

Assuming he was talking about the case they were working on, Al poured himself coffee from the carafe left on the table, then said, "Well, I think the best leads we have center on Veronica Stone in Richland Center and a guy named Olaf Torgerson in Prairie du Chien."

"Where'd you get that name?" Charlie wanted to know.

"After we quit last night, the fact that someone from Prairie du Chien was involved and we didn't have a name just nagged at me. I finally got so irritated, I called Grimsley. Lo and behold, there was a text from him this morning that said Amos thinks it's a guy named Torgerson, first name Olaf."

"Hmmph, seems he could have told us the first time," said Charlie.

"What's worse," said Al, "is that it means both Stone and Torgerson operate in jurisdictions outside ours. I think we oughta get Brent and Dwight involved."

"I think so, too. We need them to tell us how to proceed and also how to go about it. You know, Al, we're lucky. Both our bosses have great contacts and both always want to be helpful. I think we should see if we can set up a meeting for today."

"I can talk to Brent when I get in. Can you do the same with Dwight?"

"Sure can. Should the goal be to get them together today?"

"I think that's a great goal. How about we shoot for 2 p.m."

Arrangements were made swiftly after Al and Charlie got back to the office, and the four met in Chief Whigg's office at two o'clock sharp. Al and Charlie carefully laid out their case.

"So, our question to you is," began Al, "what is the best way for us to make contact with Veronica Stone in Richland Center and Olaf Torgerson in Prairie?"

The Chief and Sheriff considered the matter for a minute, then Sheriff Hooper said, "I know the sheriffs in Richland and Crawford counties. How about I contact them and see what, if anything, they know about the people we are talking about here? If they do, perhaps they will have some insight on how best to approach them."

Chief Whigg leaned back in his chair, stretched, tipped forward and put his elbows on the desk. "I was hoping you'd say that Dwight. I don't know the sheriffs in those areas—may have met one of them some time ago, but I really can't remember. And I don't know the people. It would be good if you looked into it."

"I'll try them this afternoon. Once I've spoken to them, I'll be in touch." The sheriff reached for his jacket and hat and prepared to leave. He leaned over the desk to shake the Chief's hand, did the same with Al, then took Charlie by the arm and the two county officers headed out.

The next morning the Chief stopped by Al's office to say that Dwight and Charlie would be in at 1 p.m. to report on calls the Sheriff had made to Richland and Crawford counties.

As the four men later that day assembled in Chief Whigg's office, Sheriff Dwight Hooper startled them by saying, "When I made those calls, I got a reaction, all right. But it sure as heck wasn't the one I expected."

With looks of surprise on the faces of the Chief and the detective, he continued, "First of all, Sheriff Betty Rowekamp in Richland County was great. She said she knew Veronica Stone personally and had long suspected there was more to the social worker than there appeared. She told me Stone has worked for the county for more than 20 years and has always lived beyond her means. When I told her why I was asking, she quickly opened up and filled in a number of blanks.

"George Carsten in Crawford County was exactly the opposite. In fact, he blew me away—screaming at me after I asked if he knew an Olaf Torgerson." Al looked wide-eyed at Charlie, and Charlie confirmed with a shrug, while Hooper backed up to the beginning of the story. "The conversation began innocently enough. I quickly found out that Torgerson is a veteran deputy and is considered a pillar of the department and the Prairie du Chien community. When I told him why I was asking, Carsten went ballistic. He told me that he doesn't understand where this 'crap' comes from, told me Torgerson is a decorated deputy twice honored by the state for valor, and suggested I should concentrate on La Crosse County and forget about Crawford. Then he hung up on me."

"Wow, sounds like you struck a nerve." Al was all business as he leaned across the table toward Hooper.

"I sure as hell did," agreed the Sheriff. "And I've been trying to figure out why ever since. George is a good guy, that much I do know. And he must have really been distraught to fire back like he did. I did a little checking, and I did pick up a clue or two. Apparently last election, George was nearly unseated by his chief deputy, who alleged the department was frequently operating on the side of the county's criminal element. The deputy apparently said that Torgerson was operating a drug and sex trafficking ring."

"Where's the deputy now?" the Chief wanted to know. "Is he still with the department?"

"I don't believe so," said the Sheriff. "I looked up the department roster and I did not find his name on the list. It's Roy Whorton, by the way. Know anyone by that name?"

"I do," said the Chief. "There's a new officer in La Crescent by that name. Started a few months back. You know him, don't you Al? Didn't you cooperate on a case?"

"Oh, that George," responded Al. "Yes, we worked on those stolen autos together. He's a good guy—a very serious cop. Do you think that's him?"

"I do." The Chief was standing now and smiling at his three guests. "You know, Sheriff, I think we ought to have Al and Charlie call on George and see what he might be willing to tell them. What do you think?"

"I agree." Sheriff Hooper had risen, too, a sure sign that the meeting was coming to an end. "I had no idea you might know this officer, but the fact that Al has worked with him tells me that he might be willing to open up to you guys. It's surely worth a try."

"I agree," replied the Chief. As he looked at Al and gestured toward Charlie, he said, "I think the two of you ought to get over to La Crescent and have a talk with Officer Whorton. If he is the man we think he is, you could have an interesting chat."

Not ten minutes later, Al and Charlie walked outside. It was a beautiful day—one of those spring days when you knew that summer was right around the corner. Temperatures hovered near 70, and a steady but gentle breeze floated the scents of flowers under their noses.

"I think we better take our time on this one, Al. It's too damn nice to spend any time in the office at the end of the day."

"You'll get no argument from me. C'mon, I'll drive."

"Yer gonna have to—I rode over here with the Sheriff, and he left me with you."

Not 15 minutes later they pulled into the lot of the La Crescent Police Department and walked into the office, telling the receptionist they had an appointment with Officer Whorton.

A few seconds later a tall, raw-boned man in his forties appeared in the outer office, greeted Al warmly, then said, "And this must be the famous Charlie Berzinski. Man, I've been looking forward to meeting you. I've heard stories about your prodigious appetite, so it's a good thing you're here at midafternoon, although I'd be happy to buy you coffee. There's a great little shop just around the corner."

They began their walk, warmed by the springtime sun, chatting about weather and other non-business things.

"They got pie at this place?"

"You're in luck, Charlie," said Whorton. "This place is a darn good small-town bakery. I think they have pies, although I've never had one of those. Their doughnuts are incredible, that much I do know."

"I like this guy," said Charlie, smiling. "He must know that I have a weakness for doughnuts."

"Charlie," offered Al, amused, "you have a weakness for anything that looks and smells edible ... and sometimes things that you consider edible confuse me."

"Now that," said Whorton, setting the bell over the door of the nearby bakery jingling, "is the Charlie I've heard about. Gentlemen ..."

The bakery had display cases arranged in an "L" along the east and south walls of the area, with four tables staggered at random in the open area.

"Hi, Roy," said the attendant, wiping her hands on her apron. "I see you brought some muscle with you today." She looked Charlie up and down, then said, "Big guy, you look hungry. What'll it be?"

"What kind of pies today?" Charlie wanted to know.

"We got 23 kinds. It'll be easier for you to tell me what you want than for me to try and repeat all 23 varieties."

"Fair enough. How about lemon meringue and sour cream raisin?"

"Yup—we got both. Which one?"

"Oh, c'mon now … what'd Roy say your name was? Belle?"

"It's Isabelle … or Belle, yes."

"Okay, c'mon, Belle, do I look like a one-piece-a-pie guy—even if I'm on a diet?"

She stood there, hands on hips and looked him up and down. "No, m' man, you don't. How many can I get ya?"

"Let's start with the lemon and raisin and then we'll go from there. I'll get these guys, too." As Charlie ordered he nodded over his shoulder to where Al and Roy were waiting.

With doughnuts in front of Roy and Al, two pieces of pie for Charlie, and coffee for all, the three lawmen hunched over the table.

"Now, what brings you to La Crescent?"

"Well, Roy, Sheriff Dwight Hooper talked to your former boss in Prairie, and …"

"Stop! Say no more." Roy was frowning now, deep creases topping his eyebrows as he studied his companions. "I'm pretty sure old George had nothing good to say about me, right?"

"Well," began Charlie, "I guess you could say it started that way, but then your former boss got angry and hung up on Dwight."

"Oh-oh, lemme guess. Your boss mentioned Olaf Torgerson and that was it."

"That's what the sheriff said," agreed Al.

"Thought so. Well, let's finish our pie and head back to the office. I'd like to ask my chief to sit in on our talk if yer okay with that?"

Both Al and Charlie nodded in agreement and for the rest of the time the talk centered on things other than law enforcement.

26

Back at the office, Whorton took his two La Crosse acquaintances to a conference room, then left to see if his chief could join them. Not two minutes later, Whorton was back with a youthful looking man with graying hair. Whorton introduced Chief Patrick Timm. With Whorton seated beside Al and Timm next to Charlie, the mood turned serious.

"Chief, Al and Charlie came over today to visit with me after my former boss hung up on La Crosse County Sheriff Dwight Hooper."

When Whorton talked about the circumstances leading to the visit, Gray moved closer to the table and his intensity seemed to increase.

"You'll remember, Chief, when I interviewed, I told you I was leaving Prairie du Chien because of a disagreement with the Crawford County Sheriff. I didn't say much about the circumstances but when Al and Charlie wanted to talk, I thought you should be here, too."

Having set the stage, Whorton launched into a dialogue detailing the things that caused him to seek employment outside Wisconsin.

"It was apparent to me—I was the chief deputy, by the way—that one of the deputies, a guy by the name of Olaf Torgerson, was involved in some illegal activities that involved sex trafficking. I took my concerns to Sheriff Carsten … George. He's a really good guy, by the way, but when I talked to him about Torgerson, he went ballistic. Told me there was a group around the county who wanted to get rid of him and would stop at nothing to get it done. Told me Torgerson was a good guy, a great deputy and to mind my own business when it came to him. I'm not sure why the Sheriff had blinders on, but he sure did."

Whorton paused, took a drink of water, then began again. "I thought about everything I had heard, did some snooping—on my own time, mind you. And I found that Torgerson was about as dirty as they come. But he also had a very long nose … and I don't think I have to tell you where he had it most of the time. In fact, it got so bad, I decided to run against the Sheriff in the next election. I came damn close, too, but I lost. And rather than face the music that I feared, I resigned and began to look for a job. I landed here, and I'm really happy. Crawford County, because of Torgerson and the Sheriff, was a really toxic environment. The only thing I feel badly about is leaving without bringing anything to resolution."

"Well, maybe we can help you on that score," offered Al. "Roy, Sheriff, Charlie and I are here because we agreed to take on a case that had been cold for more than forty years. In fact, Charlie and I only know what we read in the case files. It concerns a young woman who vanished from a place where she was babysitting. The case generated a good deal of interest and lots of publicity, but few solid leads. And as of today, we are still seeking resolution."

"Aha, Shirley Sovereign, right?" Chief Timm offered, a glazed look in his eyes as he rocked back in his chair, his hands behind his head.

"Wow," said Timm, straightening up, "what a coup it would be to bring the Sovereign case to conclusion. I can't say I remember it all that well. I was a young boy in Alma, Wisconsin, at the time and the Sovereign case scared the bejeesus out of everyone in this area."

"That's the one," agreed Al, "and we think that her disappearance might be linked to the kind of activity that Roy felt existed in Crawford County. Recently, we found a young woman who had been missing from our area for years. She was in Chicago, working as a prostitute. She has lent great credibility to Roy's suspicions, confirming that she was taken by a group from this area, then moved to Chicago and put to work as a sex slave. Our informant on that case was a former deputy from our area who was serving time for sex trafficking crimes in Florida. He's in witness protection now, and we communicate with him through an FBI agent in D.C."

"Amazing," said the Chief. "Roy, I hope you tell them everything you know that you think can help them."

"I will, Chief. You can be sure of that."

The officer thought for a while, then said, "You know guys, Carsten, was a good guy—a prince of a guy. But he had blinders when it came to Torgerson and it's going to hurt him when the truth begins to come out. Everyone in the department knew Olaf was doing some bad things, but because Carsten had labeled him untouchable, no one said anything. There were also people in the county who were upset.

"A county resident in the know convinced me to run for sheriff and made sure it didn't cost me a dime. But George is a popular guy, and even though we outspent him by a considerable margin, his friends and reputation kept him in office. That's when I knew I had to leave."

Al, Charlie, and the Chief looked at Roy with understanding. It was Al, who broke the silence. "The woman we just returned home suggested there were people in Richland and Crawford counties that were involved when she decided to run away."

"Well, Torgerson was involved for sure, that much I know," said Whorton. "Olaf was frequently in the east part of the county and was always meeting with a woman over in Richland Center."

"That makes sense, given what we have learned," said Al. "But we are still trying to bring the trafficking ring—especially those around here—to justice, and we are also trying to find Shirley. We have information suggesting she is in the Caribbean somewhere, maybe Montserrat."

"I think Torgerson would be a darn good source," said Whorton, "assuming you could get past Carsten and get him to talk. But that's a real long shot."

"If we decide to go after him, could we count on your help?" Charlie leaned forward as he made the comment, his eyes moving from Whorton to Timm and back again.

Timm didn't hesitate, rapping his knuckles on the table as he spoke. "Of course you can count on us. I'm more than happy to make Roy available to you 24-7, if that will be of help."

"I think a full-time assignment is a great offer," replied Al, "but probably more generous than is needed. If you, Chief, are willing to let us have him from time to time to help plan and execute our moves, that would meet our needs perfectly."

Whorton was nodding as Timm rose from his chair, looked from man to man and said, "Whenever you need him, he's yours. If a 24-hour notice is possible, it will be helpful, but it's not a deal breaker. We'll make whatever you need work."

"Except for one thing," said Whorton, holding up his hand. "I will provide whatever information I have, but I don't want to be directly involved in any way. Behind the scenes, absolutely. Out front, no way. Understood?"

Al and Charlie nodded and then, the meeting over, Al and Charlie checked signals with Whorton, donned their jackets and left the station.

"Pretty darn generous, if you ask me."

"Al, you can say that again. Those two are really good guys."

They drove back to La Crosse anxious to talk to their respective bosses of help offered by the La Crescent officers.

27

The sun was shining brightly the next morning when Charlie walked into the La Crosse Police Department headquarters, his stomach warmed with one of Ma's breakfasts, frugal though it was. He was looking for his boss, Sheriff Dwight Hooper. When he found the Sheriff, they headed immediately to the La Crosse P.D. and Chief Brent Whigg's office.

As they reached the glassed cubicle in the corner of the building, they found Al and the Chief waiting for them. Both men were munching on doughnuts and, his mouth filled with pastry, Whigg simply pointed to a box on the table in the corner and waved his hand, indicating they were to take their pick. Charlie opened the box, then peered in cautiously. His shoulders slumped a bit as he observed the display of Fayze's goodies. As his boss reached for a bearclaw, Charlie shook his head, turned and took a chair in front of the desk next to Al.

"What, no doughnut?" asked Al as his larger friend dropped into the chair.

"Nah, dieting. Kelly is really on my ass about taking off some weight, and I'm trying really hard to stay on her good side. Conjugal favors, you know?"

"Conjugal? Did I hear that right?" said the Sheriff, who was making his pastry selection. "That's a pretty big word."

"Aw, come on, you guys, cut me some slack. Let's have a good day."

"Yes, let's," agreed Al, beginning to take over the conversation. "We wanted to let you, Sheriff, and you, Chief, know about our meeting with Roy Whorton over in La Crescent."

"And what did Whorton have to say?" the Sheriff wanted to know.

"He gave us a full update on his problems down in Crawford County," began Al. "And let me first clear up one thing. He really likes Sheriff George Carsten as a person, but it was pretty apparent that he considers him a lousy administrator in that he has blinders on when it comes to Olaf Torgerson. As a result, he said Carsten and Torgerson had created a toxic environment in the county. He went to the Sheriff with evidence against Torgerson and practically got thrown out of Carsten's office."

Both the Sheriff and Chief were now leaning forward and looking intensely at Al as he prepared to continue.

"Well, apparently, Whorton thought he had conclusive evidence that Torgerson was involved with sex trafficking and other crimes. He said he had him cold." Al stopped for a sip of coffee and a bit of doughnut, wiped his lips with a napkin and sat back, then continued. "Then Carsten apparently told him to mind his own business and to let Torgerson alone. In fact, the Sheriff praised Torgerson for the job he was doing."

Another sip of coffee, a final bite of the pastry, and then, "So, Whorton decided to try and change the situation by running against Carsten. He apparently ran a good campaign, but he lost. He said he knew then that he had to move, and landed in La Crescent."

Al looked at Charlie. "What did I miss?"

"Not much," replied the big deputy, "but he did tell us that he'd help us in any way he could, but that he wouldn't be directly involved. I got the idea that he'd give us everything he has if we want to pursue it."

"Yeah, he was pretty open about that, but he was also adamant about not wanting to be directly involved." Al jumped back in, his elbows on the Chief's desk as he talked. "The question for us is what our next step would be. Frankly, Charlie and I could care less about Crawford County's problems, but we need to get this sex trafficking ring stopped."

Stopping there, Al and Charlie searched the eyes of La Crosse County's two top lawmen, waiting for them to speak.

"Seems to me—" said the Chief, "and, Dwight, you'd know best—that if we take this one on we might be asking for trouble."

"Absolutely." The Sheriff's face twisted into a grimace and frown as he replied, then sat back, thought for a minute and said, "Brent, we have no jurisdiction there. If we aren't going to work with authorities in Crawford and Richland counties, we have to find someone who can, right?"

"Right." The chief studied the sheriff, then eyed Al and Charlie as he continued. "Best bet—no screams, now—is the FBI. They are the organization for a number of reasons. First, this ring operates across state lines. Second, they have authority in Wisconsin. Third, ultimately, this amounts to kidnapping. And, fourth, this is what they do. I know they can be pushy, authoritative, and arrogant, but they are the best for this. I think we get them involved, but we wait until we can talk with exactly the right person. The Milwaukee office has a really good agent: Gloria Miller. I think she's the right person, because she's both a great communicator and a great collaborator."

Both Al and Charlie were nodding as the chief spoke. "We talked to her on the moonshine case," said Al. "She was great. Do you agree, Charlie?"

"Damn, right, we haven't met her, but she was great help. Get her!"

"Good enough for me," agreed the Sheriff. "Brent, you make the call. Sounds like you know her."

The chief was rummaging in his center desk drawer as he listened. "I have her information on her card here somewhere. If I can find it, let's call her now and see what she has to say."

The rummaging continued for several minutes—to the amazement of the three officers who were watching the steady stream of materials hitting the desk.

"Ah." The chief lifted his head and his arm, his hand waving a card. "Found it right where I thought it would be."

That brought a roar of laughter from the Sheriff, Al, and Charlie.

"We all knew where it would be, Chief." Al was using Charlie as a shield as he spoke, "because everything important that you own is in that desk drawer. It's what allows you to keep your desktop clean."

This time the Chief laughed, too. "Guess you got me there." As the laughter quieted, the Chief looked from face to face, the card in his hand. "Should we give her a call?"

Three nods later, the Chief was dialing and putting the phone on speaker. The three stared at the phone as it rang three ... four ... five times. "Agent Miller."

Gloria's voice startled the three men, but Whigg recovered in time to pick up the conversation.

"Agent Miller. Good morning. This is Brent Whigg in La Crosse, how are you?"

"Great, Chief. Hope you're the same. What's up?"

"Gloria, I'm here with Sheriff Dwight Hooper, Chief Deputy Charlie Berzinski, and Chief Detective Al Rouse."

"Gentlemen, good morning. I'm honored," said Gloria over the telephone. "And I'm wondering what brings you to me."

"Well, to be honest, Agent, I suggested we call you for several specific reasons, not the least of which is your willingness to cooperate and communicate. Al and Charlie have been working on a case up here and we've taken it about as far as we can."

"Well, thank you for the compliments, Chief. Al, Charlie, what's going on?"

Charlie nodded at Al. "Agent Miller, Charlie and I are working a cold case—a kidnapping that occurred in 1979. The victim has not been seen or heard from since her apparent abduction on a night in September of that year. Her name is Shirley Sovereign. We have reason to believe she might be in the Caribbean—on an island."

"What makes you believe that, Al? Oh, sorry, do you folks mind if we continue on a first-name basis? I hate the formality of titles and all."

Assured that would be fine, Al continued. Forty-five minutes later, he thought he had covered it thoroughly and both he and Charlie had answered questions from Agent Miller.

"Wow, that's quite a story," said the FBI officer. "It's not totally surprising though. We've been looking into sex trafficking problems across Wisconsin for more than a year now. To be honest, though, we haven't been very lucky. This might be the information needed to break this thing up."

When Al and Charlie leaped in with questions, Miller was quick to assure them. "Gentlemen, let me be clear. This investigation will be conducted with your participation, and any information uncovered by the FBI will be immediately shared with you. The only way we are going to get this done right is if we all participate … all play key roles. Does that make it clear where I stand?"

Again, Miller was given assurances from Al and Charlie. Now, with the clock approaching noon, Miller, Al, and Charlie agreed to talk more following lunch in the hope of developing a path forward before the day was over.

28

An hour and fifteen minutes later, Al and Charlie were back in the detective's office and ready to dial the FBI agent in Milwaukee. Just as Al began to dial the phone, Charlie said, "Hold on just a minute." Al paused and the noise made by a loud fart echoed through the office. Charlie grinned, stood for a moment, returned to his chair and nodded to Al. "Go ahead."

"Damn it, Charlie, I told you eating that fried cabbage was a bad idea," said Al, seething, and then, getting wind of the result of the emission, fleeing the office. Realizing what had happened, Al's co-workers in the bullpen were roaring as Charlie's face took on the color of sunset.

"Dammit, Al, get back in here; it wasn't that bad." Charlie's exclamation resulted in a wide grin as he moved to sit in his chair. Al approached the office, stuck his head into the enclosure and backed away again. "I'll be back in a few minutes, I have something I need to check on."

Irked by his friend's lack of manners, Al walked through the bullpen and stopped at the Chief's office.

"Hey, Al, what's up?" Chief Brent Whigg waved Al in.

"Just killin' time, Chief. My office currently is not inhabitable."

"Not, inh…oh!" A grin bathed the Chief's face. "What did Charlie have for lunch?"

"You got it, boss … that's just it. Charlie is on this diet, and he chose liver and onions and fried cabbage for lunch. I'm taking a few-minute hiatus to let the aroma clear."

The Chief grinned, got up from his desk and took Al by the shoulder. Deftly turning him back toward his office, Al was guided back toward the scene of the indiscretion. When they reached the office, he looked in, Charlie saw him and brightened.

"Sorry, Al … really. Oh, hi, Chief. It's safe. C'mon in."

The two strode into Al's office, Al walked to behind his desk, while Charlie pulled up another wooden chair for the Chief.

"So what's going on here … have you made the phone call to Miller yet?"

"That's it, Chief. Charlie and I want to do as you suggested and get back to her, because we're at an end to what we can do without having some entry into Crawford and Richland counties."

"So call her back." The Chief dug in his pocket, took out his bill-fold and soon was holding a card. "Here's her number: four-one-four, two-nine-seven, seventeen hundred—if you didn't write it down."

Al dialed as the chief spoke, put the phone on speaker, and the three officers listened to the phone ring until answered by a female voice. "Federal Bureau of Investigation, Eastern Wisconsin District. How might we help?"

"This is Brent Whigg, La Crosse, Wisconsin, police chief. Could we speak with Agent Miller, please?"

"She's in and free, Chief Whigg, would you like to talk to her?"

"Please."

The phone rang again. "AIC Miller."

"Hi, Gloria. Chief Brent Whigg calling. I'm here with Chief Detective Al and Charlie. I'll let them explain the help we need."

"I'm all ears," said Miller. "Then I'll see what we can do."

Charlie nodded at Al, who picked up the conversation. "Gloria, Al Rouse here."

"How are you, sir?"

"Doing well. Just got back from lunch. As you know, Charlie and I are working on a cold case—a cold, cold case—and we have made some progress, but now we need your help to move ahead."

"Let's hear it."

So, Al sat back in his chair, lounging as he began to tell Miller about the case and the dilemma. He moved through the story briefly but effectively, skipping the pieces she already had been told and explaining the case to her, focusing on the return home of Molly Grisham, her disclosures about the ring that operated in rural Wisconsin— sending girls to Milwaukee and Chicago—and ending with the report that Shirley Sovereign was reported to be living on a Caribbean island, because that's where women who outlive their usefulness as prostitutes in the states were reportedly sent.

When he finished, the three men sat there. Charlie fidgeted in his seat, Al turned to make a cup of coffee. When he turned back around, the Chief extended a hand, requesting a cup, too. As Al brewed the Chief's cup in his Keurig, Miller began to speak.

"We've heard rumors about that, but until your comments just now, we didn't have anything specific to peg it to—like Crawford and Richland counties. This is a very big development, from my point of view. Yes … you bet … we'd like to help any way we can. If I send two agents up there, are you willing to share what you have with them and help organize the actions that they suggest?"

"There will be no territorial arguments, Gloria." Chief Whigg looked at both Charlie and Al as he made the comment, pleased that they nodded in return. "We have much bigger fish to fry than worrying about whether this is our case or yours. It's got to be yours for a number of reasons … the most important of which are our lack of jurisdiction and the need to preserve the relations we have with officers in those counties. Damn right we'll help. Send those agents up here so we can get going."

"If they arrive tomorrow is that too soon?" Miller wanted to know.

"Really, that soon? Al, Charlie … what do you think."

"We're ready today," replied Al. Then, looking at the phone, "Things must be quiet in your office."

A chuckle was heard and Miller responded. "They are slow. We had so many resources assigned to the Jayme Closs case north of you that, when that fiasco ended, we were looking for things to do. I'm pretty sure neither Jerry Fender—that's Jerry as in Jerome—nor Tim Mueller are working on things so urgent they can't be up there tomorrow. But I'll confirm that with an email to the three of you, if you'll give me those addresses."

The addresses supplied, the conversation ended. Whigg drained his cup and handed it back to Rouse. Then he stood and prepared to leave.

"If I were the two of you, I'd get the hell out of here and head for home. You're gonna be very busy, starting tomorrow, and that will include weekends. This would be a good time to break the news to your spouses and do some honey-do chores."

He laughed at the honey-do comment, then slapped Charlie on the back, smiled at Al and headed back toward his office.

"Ya know, Al, I could really use a beer, but it's probably not a good idea for either one of us to be seen drinking beer at three in the afternoon. I think the chief's right. Making nice with the women is a good thought."

Charlie rose from his chair, hitched up his pants, straightened his gun belt and grabbed his jacket. "Let's see, did I drive or did you?"

Al shook his head and smiled. "I drove, you big lug … is your memory that bad? Tell you what, let me make a call to Whorton over in La Crescent and tell him where we are on this. We'll want him here tomorrow, won't we?"

Charlie nodded as Al took the phone, opened his middle desk drawer and began to dial.

"Is Roy Whorton in?"

Soon he was talking to the La Crescent officer, explaining that the FBI was sending two agents to La Crosse. "They will arrive tomorrow. I'm sure the first thing they're gonna want is a thorough briefing. Roy, I know it's a lot to ask, but can we call you when they get here, and will you high-tail it over here to help with the briefing?"

Whorton put Al on hold for a minute and went to talk to his boss about the request. When he rejoined the call a few minutes later, it was apparent from his voice that he had succeeded in getting what he wanted.

"The chief says whatever you need from me, you can have. So, do want me just to come over there right away in the morning?"

Al looked at Charlie, who nodded. "Tell you what, don't know if you've ever been to Ma's Café on the south side of La Crosse, but if you want to meet us there at seven, I'll pop for breakfast."

"Guess they pay you more in Wisconsin than over here in Minnesota," joked Whorton. "No, I don't know Ma's, but I'll find it, and meet you there at seven."

That done, Al dropped Charlie at his office and headed home. He walked in at 3:20 and yelled to his wife as he entered.

"Jo Anne, it's me."

His wife, a petite lady, who stood five-foot-three and was slight of build, also pretty and blonde, came out of the kitchen, wiping her hands on an apron. "What are you doing home so early?"

"I heard a rumor you were entertaining men while I was at work. Just wanted to check on it."

She picked up a magazine and playfully threw it at him, hitting him in the knee. He stooped, picked up the missile from the floor and smiled. "Nah, nothin' like that. I trust you, ya know. The Chief sent me home to help you."

"You're crazy. Why would Brent do that?"

"I'm not crazy. We're working on the Sovereign case, you know, and we think we may have found some things out that can help us. Eastern Wisconsin FBI is sending two agents here tomorrow to help us, and the chief thinks we'll be working long hours, including weekends."

"So, in other words, he's trying to butter me up because you're going to be gone, right?"

"Something like that, I guess."

"Great. I have just the job. The dog pen needs cleaning. I was going to do it later, but as long as you are home ..."

"Geez, Jo Anne, you know how I hate that damn job." He paused to take off his jacket and hang it, then looked at his wife. Seeing the look on her face, he quickly reconsidered. "Oh, all right, I'll change and get at it. But you damn well better be making something great for dinner."

"I'm making pot roast."

"Wow. That's special. Okay, I'll get the dog pen. Just gotta change first."

29

Hgh-powered topics began to hit the table the next morning at 11—one hour after Agents Fender and Mueller arrived in La Crosse. Noting they'd been on the road since six, the agents said they'd like to get down to work. Charlie and Roy Whorton arrived at 10:15, Chief Whigg stopped by at 10:30 to get a cup of coffee, welcome the agents, and tell them his office would cooperate in every way it could.

"This is your case now," he told them. "No one in this room disputes that. At the same time, the people in this room know as much or more about the case than you do, so we are looking for outstanding cooperation."

"That's exactly what AIC Miller told us," said Fender. "We are looking forward to working with everyone around this table."

That squared away, it took only 20 minutes for the first burning topic to surface.

"How dangerous are the cop and the social worker." Mueller was looking over some printed information on Deputy Olaf Torgerson and Social Worker Veronica Stone.

"I'd put the deputy down as very dangerous." Mueller raised his eyebrows when Whorton responded to his question.

"Why do you say that?"

"Because I saw him go ballistic on four or five occasions, and the last encounter I had with him, he was reaching for his weapon until the sheriff grabbed his arm. He's hot-headed and sometimes uncontrollable."

"Pretty harsh." Fender has been facing out the conference room window. Now he turned and joined the discussion.

"I know it seems harsh, Agent Mueller, but you haven't met the guy. I worked with him and fought with him too. He's not a nice guy."

"I get it, Roy. Sorry if I ruffled your feathers, but I wanted to make sure your opinion was as strong as your words. There's no doubt in my mind now."

"What about Stone?" Mueller seemed satisfied that Torgerson was someone to take seriously. He also seemed edgy, as if he wanted to move things along.

"Stone is a pussy cat. She's calm as can be, has a reputation as a good social worker, and has taken in and mothered more than one abused woman." Whorton seemed totally sympathetic to Stone. Fender immediately sensed it.

"Sounds like you admire her." He was looking out the window again, his hands clasped behind his back.

"Yea, I guess you could say that. My opinion always was that if she sent women on their way to a job in the bigger cities, it was because she found their situation in this area hopeless."

"I have a hard time agreeing with that," piped up Rouse. "Seems to me that Molly Grisham had an ideal home life. She was a wayward child, yes, but it wasn't because of the lack of love at home, in my opinion."

"I don't know Molly," agreed Whorton. "And I don't know her folks. If Stone sent her down the road, I guess I see why you questioned my statement. You know the situation better than I do."

As Whorton talked, the clock moved past noon. Charlie rubbed his stomach, which had emitted a mournful groan. "Sorry. It's been a while since breakfast, and my wife has me on such a damn strict diet that when mealtime rolls around I'm hungry as a horse."

"No need to apologize. Except for a Rice Krispie treat on the road and two cups of coffee since we arrived, I'm pretty darn hungry myself." As Mueller spoke, Fender turned back from the window. "I'm hungry, too, and looking at all that sun out there, it might be great to get outta here for awhile and continue this over lunch. AIC Miller gave us a pretty lavish expense account for this trip, so we'll buy."

Mueller and the others reached for their jackets. Fender stopped them. "I think that sun is damn hot. Why don't we enjoy the spring air? Is there any place near the river we can enjoy a bite and soak up some sun?"

Al and Charlie looked at each other. "How about Four Sisters, Al? That'd be good, wouldn't it?"

"They serve small plate lunches, but they have good sandwiches, too," agreed Al. "It's got a nice, laid back ambience. It's a wine bar, too, but drinking is optional."

"Miller isn't going to pay for any alcohol." Fender was firm in his statement.

"And none of us will be drinking," seconded Rouse. "It's about a four-block walk from here. Do we walk or ride?"

"I'll be drivin'," said Charlie.

"I'm riding with Charlie," replied Mueller. The other three agreed to walk.

When they got to the 4th Street bar, they grabbed a round corner booth that sat three and pulled up two chairs for the others. Fender ordered a selection of small plates, the group deciding that sharing would be a good way to spend lunch. Charlie wrinkled up his nose a bit at the prospect of small plates, but settled down when Al reminded him of his diet.

The food arrived, the four dug in, enjoying the sun that flooded through the windows. Soon, though, the conversation got back to business.

"So how do we get this Torgerson in position to question him?" Fender wanted to know.

Whorton suggested he had some friends in the Crawford County department that he might lean on for information.

"Wouldn't it be great to sting him a bit?" Charlie was at the edge of his seat and even seemed to forget his food for a moment. "Like how, Charlie?" Fender wanted to know.

"Well," Charlie was almost preening now, "what if we could find out where he will be tomorrow and then set up a deal to have you guys go speeding past him—you have an unmarked, right?" Fender nodded and Charlie continued. "Say you whiz past going about 65 or 70. He pulls you over and, bingo, you badge him and tell him he's just the guy you want to talk to. Then Al and I—and Roy here, if he wants to—will pull up behind you and participate."

Everyone except Charlie exploded into laughter. The La Crosse deputy's face reddened. "So, what don't you like about it?" Charlie was half on his feet now and Fender and Al realized the big guy was offended.

"Whoa … settle back, big guy, settle back." Al, sitting next to him, had a hand on his shoulder as if to coax him back into his seat.

"Well just what the hell is wrong with that idea?"

"There isn't a thing wrong with it. If you were offended by our laughing, we were only laughing because the idea is ingenious … absolutely great," praised Fender.

"Ya …you … you mean you liked it?" Charlie was really enjoying himself now. On his feet, he bowed to the table, then to the bartender before he sat down.

"Do you think, Roy, that you can find out if he will be on patrol?" Fender wanted to know.

"Sure can. My best friend down there is the dispatcher and I know for a fact that he's working tomorrow. I'm sure I can get him to keep track of our friend. But what grounds are we going to badge him on?"

"Suspicion of trafficking sounds pretty good to me. I bet Miller can get us what we need to make the stop."

"Wonderful to have a cooperative boss, isn't it?" asked Al. "Charlie and I both have great bosses, and you seem to, too, Roy."

"Sure do, Chief Timm is a fantastic guy and a great boss—tough as nails, but with a heart made of pure gold."

"Tell you what," said Fender, "when we finish here, I'll call the office and get Miller to find out what we'd need to pull over Torgerson and question him on suspicion of trafficking women and minors. Sound good?"

They all nodded, then went back to eating. When every one of the 12 plates Fender had ordered was picked clean, the FBI agent paid the bill and they walked outside, stopping to admire the river, swollen now with spring runoff and brown with mud flowing into the big river from its tributaries.

"It's an angry river." Al pointed to debris in the form of tree trunks and branches floating offshore and cruising on a quick current.

They watched the flowing water for a time, then reluctantly decided it was time to get back to work. As the walkers moved from the riverfront into downtown, Fender fell back to talk with his boss. When they got to the station, he told the group Miller would have anything they needed by the time they assembled in the morning.

"Anybody here worried about working Saturday?" Fender wanted to know. Everyone shook their heads, indicating they expected to spend the weekend at work.

"Great, Tim and I have been at it since about four this morning," reported Fender. "We need to find a place to stay—recommendations, anyone?—and then get a nap."

"Lots of good places nearby," Rouse told him, pulling out a map. "I'd recommend the Radisson, it's right down the way we came. We're right here," he pointed at the map, "and the hotel is right here."

"Looks like a left from where we're parked, then a quick right, down to the river and left and we're there. If we meet here tomorrow at eight, will that be early enough?" Fender wanted to know.

"Perfect. I'll stop at Fayze's, our favorite bakery, pick up some goodies and juice. I've got coffee in my office. Sound good?" Al wanted to know.

"Perfect," said Fender. "Get some rest, everyone, and everybody show up armed tomorrow—you, too, Roy, we'll cover you. Never know what we might run into."

30

By noon the next day, the sting operation was set. Whorton had found out from his Crawford County dispatcher friend that Torgerson was going to be staked out at a section of roadway near the intersection of State Highway 27 and County Road E. The area had been the scene of a number of fatal accidents.

Fender and Mueller were parked along County Road E, about two miles east of Highway 27. Al, Charlie, and Whorton were parked on County S, four miles north of the stakeout point.

"Heading east." The message crackled across the police radio on a rarely-used frequency, chosen for that reason. "On alert and ready to roll." Al sent the message across the airways, then placed the microphone back on the dash unit. He looked at Charlie, then at Whorton in the backseat. "Everyone ready?" When both nodded, he put the car in gear, stopped at the sign off Highway 27 and waited for the next communication.

"Highway in sight," came the message at 12:10. "Have decided to blow the stop sign. County car parked a few yards from intersection."

As Fender prepared to accelerate to speed through the intersection, Al turned south on 27 and moved along at 50 miles an hour. Five minutes later, they observed two cars, one a county sheriff's car, parked east of Highway 27. The lights on the sheriff's car were flashing. Al activated his signal light and pulled up behind the officer's car to effectively block him in.

Al and Charlie got out of the car. Whorton, as agreed, hung back. As the two La Crosse officers approached the Crawford County deputy, Al heard him say, "Hey, what the hell is going on, I'll ..."

"I don't think so." Fender reached in his vest pocket, pulled out his badge and said, "Olaf Torgerson you are under arrest for trafficking women and under-age women. Hands on your head, please."

Torgerson made a move toward the gun holstered at his side.

"I wouldn't," snapped Al, leveling his Glock 22 at Torgerson. Charlie took up a position opposite Torgerson and beside the FBI agents' car. Mueller got out of the FBI car, slipped around the front of the sedan and took Togerson's gun out of the suspect's holster.

When Mueller had stepped back out of Torgerson's reach, Al said, "Safe to search him."

Fender exited the car, stepped behind Torgerson and began to pat him down. He pulled a knife from a pocket, then bent to do the legs. "Aha," he exclaimed, pulling a small handgun from an ankle holster. He handed the gun to Al, then continued the search.

When he finished, he turned Torgerson toward the car, ordered him to place his hands on the roof, then said to Al, "Cuff him, will you, Al?"

"Gladly." Rouse took the handcuffs from his belt, then ordered, "Hands behind your back." When Torgerson complied, Al read him his rights as he hooked the cuffs over Torgerson's wrists. An ominous clank sounded as they snapped closed.

That done, Al turned to look back at his car and nodded to Whorton. "How about you do the honors, Roy, and drive this one back to Prairie du Chien? We do plan to hold him there, don't we?"

"Not on your life." Fender was all business now, grimacing as he opened the rear door of his car and pushed Torgerson into the back seat. "We'll stop in Prairie du Chien to drop the car and make our arrest official, but we are going to hold him in La Crosse. Do you see any problem with that?"

"None. We house our prisoners in the La Crosse Law Enforcement Center. It'll be a good place for this guy."

Fender smiled at his colleagues. "Charlie, how about you ride with Roy and the prisoner? Roy, you take the lead, we'll follow you, and Al will bring up the rear. I want the lights on all three vehicles. Might as well create the biggest spectacle we can."

Whorton got into the Crawford County squad car. Al backed up his Prius so Whorton could exit, at the same time snapping on his grill lights. The lights on the Crawford County car were already on. Whorton eased onto the County Road and drove east until finding a spot to turn around. Fender followed, and Al came last.

The caravan drove into Prairie du Chien at 2:15 and Whorton led the procession to the Crawford County Sheriff's Office.

"Want to take the keys in and tell them what's happened to their guy?" Fender was giving Whorton the pleasure of conveying the message he had once tried to make the sheriff understand. "It'll be a pleasure." He waved at Al to come along with him.

Once inside, a young female officer was seated at the desk.

"Roy, it's great to see you. What brings you our way?" She rose, straightening her jacket and checking the crease in her trousers.

"Official business, Megan." Whorton's voice was soft and gentle. "Is the sheriff in?"

"No, it's Saturday, you know?"

"We do, but you'd better call him and tell him to come in. We have some information he needs to hear."

She looked at him questioningly. "Call him at home? You know how he hates that!"

"I do, but trust me, he'll want to hear this."

A worried look on her face, she dialed the phone. "Sheriff, Roy Whorton and another man are here. They asked me to call you to tell you that they have information for you that you are going to want to hear in person." Then, after a long pause during which they could hear Sheriff George Carsten talking in an angry voice but, because he was speaking so fast, they couldn't pick up. "I'll tell them, Sheriff."

Covering the handset, the officer said, "The Sheriff says anything you need to tell him can wait until Monday."

Al motioned for the phone. "Sheriff, Detective Al Rouse, La Crosse P.D. I think, sir, you are going to want to get over here as quickly as you can. You see, we have one of your officers in federal custody and we are taking him to La Crosse, where he will be imprisoned until he is scheduled to appear in court."

Al held the phone away from his ear, and both Whorton and

Megan could hear the Sheriff cursing and vowing he "will have your ass for this." The conversation ended when the Sheriff slammed down his phone.

"Guess he's coming." Al was grinning at Whorton.

"It better be good. He's not happy. He was watching a baseball game," Megan said. "Roy, you know what a Brewers' fan he is. Not sure I want to be here when he arrives."

"You'll be fine." The soothing comment came from Whorton, who now was leaning on the counter while talking to Megan.

"Which one of our guys do you have … let me guess," said Megan smiling. "I'm betting on Olaf Torgerson. Am I right?"

Whorton looked at Al, who nodded. "You're right," Whorton told her, "but what made you choose him?"

"It's a pretty well-known fact around here that you and the Sheriff didn't agree on Olaf's effectiveness. I can also tell you it's a view—yours, that is—shared by all the other deputies."

As she finished, they heard the sound of a siren screeching and growing louder by the second.

"He's here—wish I wasn't."

"Relax, Megan, it's our show." Al turned toward the door as Fender walked in. A minute later a red-faced and obviously angry George Carsten stormed into the office, the door slamming loudly behind him.

He strode to the counter and then, hands on hips, looked at the three men waiting for him. He quickly acknowledged Whorton. "You … might have known it'd be you. Why the hell aren't you up in Minnesota where you belong?"

Stepping forward, Fender held out his badge. "Agent Jerry Fender, FBI, Milwaukee Office."

The sheriff looked at the badge, wrinkled his nose. "What the hell does the FBI want in my county?"

The look on the Sheriff's face indicated he thought whatever it was wasn't necessary.

"Bad news, I'm afraid, Sheriff. Do you want to talk about it in your office?"

"What's the matter with here? I'm in a hurry."

"Yes, sir, as you wish." Fender reached in the vest pocket and brought out a folded paper. He handed it to the Sheriff. "A warrant, Sheriff, for the arrest of Olaf Torgerson on the suspicion of trafficking women and underaged females for the purpose of illicit sex. We have taken Officer …"

"Just hold on a goddamn minute." The Sheriff was really angry now. His face was red and veins in his neck pulsed as he talked. "Whorton here has been on a witch hunt against Torgerson. And we were damn glad to get rid of him. There's no basis for this."

As the sheriff prepared for more of his tirade, Fender stepped closer to him. "Sheriff, calm down. If you continue this diatribe I will be forced to arrest you, too, for obstruction of justice."

Although it was obvious he didn't like it, Carsten quieted. After a moment passed, Fender picked up the conversation. "As I was saying, we have taken Officer Torgerson into custody. We have stopped here to return his car to you. You may check it and confirm it was returned in good condition, after which we are taking Officer Torgerson to La Crosse, where he will be held until his court appearance, likely Monday."

Carsten's face convulsed as if he had been slapped. He stepped back, slumping into the counter, which appeared to hold him up as he studied his visitors.

Finally, he straightened and, with hands on hips, snorted, "I can assure you that Crawford County will fight this injustice all the way to the Supreme Court, if necessary. Just what makes you think you can waltz into my county and arrest one of my employees? You have no authority here."

"Sheriff, you're wrong." Fender's tone was gentle and even, and his comments delivered smoothly. "I can assure you we have every right to be here. Let me reference Title 28, Section 533 of the U.S. Code."

"Don't give me that kind of bullshit," sputtered the Sheriff. "Just talk English."

"I was, Sheriff." Fender appeared unruffled by the Sheriff's spunk. "As I was telling you, Title 28, Section 533 of the U.S. Code, gives me authority to make arrests in your county if I suspect that the person or persons arrested have broken federal laws. And transporting women across state lines against their will, sir, is illegal under federal law."

The sheriff, struggling to regain his composure, failed. He began to curse, ending with, "If you don't get the hell out of my jail, I'm going to throw you into a cell and throw away the key. You goddamn FBI guys think you walk on water. Around here we treat people like you the way we treat unwanted animals … by putting them in a sack with a boulder and tossing them in the river, you hear?"

"Stop right there." Fender was offended now. "If I hear one more word out of you, I am arresting you and taking you with us to La Crosse, where you, sir, will be imprisoned."

At that point the sheriff came totally unglued. Shouting and making threatening comments, he strode toward the back of the room, entered a room and came back brandishing a handgun. Approaching the counter, he began to raise the hand holding the gun. "Now, you hear me, you jackass! You get the hell out of here. If I ever see you in …"

Megan, who had been cowering behind her desk, had gotten up and headed for the door, disappearing just as the trouble began. With Megan out of the way, Fender moved like lightning through the opening in the counter. He grabbed the Sheriff's gun hand—the weapon discharging in the process—and took the gun away from Carsten in what seemed a seamless move. Al and Whorton entered, too, and held the Sheriff as Fender cuffed him and read him his rights, ending with "you are under arrest for obstructing justice and threatening an agent of the United States government and a law officer from La Crosse, Wisconsin."

As Rouse and Whorton pushed the Sheriff toward the entrance Megan peeked in, saw what was happening and returned to the room. Fender turned to her and smiled.

"I am sorry, ma'am, for disrupting your afternoon. Not sure how these things are handled in Wisconsin, but if I were you, I would contact the Sheriff's supervisor and inform him. It is my opinion a temporary sheriff will have to be named, but that's up to Sheriff Carsten's supervisor or the county."

Then, as he moved to join Rouse and Carsten, he turned back, smiled again and said, "We'll be going now. I suspect we have created enough turmoil for today."

31

Carsten sputtered all the way to La Crosse. Riding in the same car with Whorton seemed to bring out the worst in the Sheriff, erasing in Rouse's mind the reputation that the Sheriff was a kindly man … a good guy.

"You gotta lotta guts coming into my county, accusing a trusted deputy of sex trafficking, and then—as if that wasn't enough—arresting me for obstruction of justice. I should have fired your ass, Whorton, long before you left. You were nothing but trouble from the beginning."

The badgering continued, Rouse and Whorton remaining quiet for the first 25 miles. Eventually Whorton's patience wore thin.

"You know, George, you're a really good guy. I admired you. I thought you liked me, too. You gave me commendations two years in a row, if you remember. But when it came to Olaf, you had blinders on. He was anything but a good guy … anything but someone who deserved your trust and support, but you just wouldn't listen. Why?"

Carsten remained silent. After another 15 miles, he sighed, "You know, Roy, I'm a stubborn old guy. Sometimes I don't see the forest for the trees. But then I guess you know that. What you don't know is that Olaf is my sister Edith's youngest son. He's been a problem almost from the day he was born. I thought I could straighten him out. I guess my trust was misplaced."

The ride continued in silence until the sheriff spoke again. "Roy, I want to apologize to you. I am a stubborn old goat. I should have listened."

Another long silence, then, "I knew you were right, but my pride just wouldn't let me acknowledge that I'd failed. I regret that now, but I know it's too late."

Whorton turned to look at Carsten. Outside, the gray of the day matched the spirits inside. None of the three occupants in the car were happy with the outcome, even though Rouse and Whorton—and now likely Carsten, too—realized the arrest of Torgerson was warranted.

Whorton stared out the window, failing to notice the new-growth beauty of the bluffs that spread majestically into the waters of the Mississippi, and missing as well the roiling waters of the great river that boiled into whitecaps under the brisk wind from the south that faced off against the current.

Finally, he looked up, turned and smiled at Carsten. "George that's kind of you. I accept your apology. Had I known about the relationship, I would have handled things differently."

"I should have handled it differently, too." The Sheriff also was staring out the window at the hill as he spoke. "I was sensitive to what might have been called nepotism by many. Edith moved away from Prairie years ago. She raised Olaf in Iowa—Ames. That's where he went to school. He's got a degree in law enforcement, and the Crawford County panel recommended him for the post. But no one knew he was my nephew."

After Carsten's information, the car got very silent. It stayed that way until Rouse pulled his Prius up in front of the La Crosse LEC. Torgerson was quickly booked into the jail. When the jailer led Torgerson to his cell, Rouse asked Fender if he might have a word.

Quickly the La Crosse detective explained what had transpired in his car on the ride to La Crosse. He ended with, "Jerry, I think the sheriff understands exactly what he did wrong, beginning with failing to admit his relationship to Torgerson at the time Olaf was hired. I'm not sure I think that one indiscretion—compounded, admittedly—deserves to end what has been a distinguished law enforcement career."

For a long moment, Fender stared at him, then looked down and studied his shoes.

"He was pretty unruly, Al."

"I know. I was there. But don't you think, Jerry, that it was more a case of frustration with everything going on, and his pride not letting him admit his wrongdoing? He was pretty contrite on the way back."

Fender—making a mental note of the scuff on the toe of the left oxford—finally looked up at Al and said, "I guess I've got a reputation as a hardass when it comes to these kinds of things. Normally, I wouldn't even think of backing off. But I appreciate working with you, Al. And I trust you. How about we get George and me in a room for a little talk?"

Al was delighted. "Take my office. You know where it is." He pointed down the hall. I'll go get George. No reason to keep him cuffed, is there?"

"You're asking for some pretty diametric changes in my behavior, Al," Fender pointed out with a half-smile. "But if you think he's trustworthy, that's good enough for me."

The two parted, Fender to Al's office, and Al to the bullpen to find Carsten. When he got there, the jailer was anxious to carry out his duties.

"You bookin' this guy, Al?" he asked.

"Not quite yet." Questioning looks came over the faces of the group in the bullpen. "George, why don't you come with me for a moment. Agent Fender wants to have a word with you."

Al walked Carsten to his office, showed him inside, then closed the door and walked back to the bullpen.

The jailer and the group that had brought the two prisoners back from Prairie du Chien were relaxing in the bullpen. Charlie stuffed a cookie into his mouth, then quickly handed the package back to the jailer. "What's going on, Al?" Agent Tim Mueller wanted to know.

Al sat down in one of the desk chairs and leaned back on the swivel, looking from one officer to the next. "Did Roy tell you anything about our ride home?"

When he saw the negative nods, he straightened up. "Well, we had a short but good talk with the Sheriff," Al began, looking from one face to the next. "Roy and I learned some things that allowed us to understand the Sheriff's testiness. He told us some things that don't excuse his conduct, but that raised our understanding. He apologized to Roy."

He looked at the La Crescent officer, "Right, Roy?"

"Sure did. I felt sorry for the guy … and I am sorry his actions led to the arrest."

"I feel the same way, Roy," agreed Al. "He did some mighty dumb things, but given what we now know, I guess we could agree those things are more understandable. I told Agent Fender about the talk, and he wanted to have a word with the Sheriff. They're meeting in my office."

"Sure hope that goes well," stated Whorton. "George is really a good guy … a good cop, too. We all make mistakes."

As Whorton finished talking, Sheriff Carsten came back into the area, trailed by Fender.

Fender walked to the center of the group. "The Sheriff and I have had a little meeting. We've concluded that the two of us—and, by association, some of you, too—had a bit of a misunderstanding. George was a little fired up. I was a little feisty after events earlier in the day. We let it get out of control, something for which I think both of us feel badly. In any event, we're not going to let a misunderstanding ruin anyone's day. George will not be charged with anything, and I am going to drive him back to Prairie du Chien. Any questions?"

No one spoke. Whorton stood, walked to Carsten, and shook his hand. Then the others followed. That done, Carsten and Fender grabbed their jackets to get on their way. Just as they were starting for the door, the jailer rushed into the room.

"I need some help. The new prisoner has gone berserk—I can't calm him down." As everyone jumped up, Sheriff Carsten turned around, dropped his jacket on the desk and said, "Let me take care of this."

The other officers stood aside as Carsten and the jailer hurried to the area where the cells were located. Fender looked at Al and said, "It might be good if you went, too, Al."

"Good idea." Rouse was on his feet and walking after the jailer and Carsten.

When Al reached the cell, he was amazed to see blood spatters on the floor and wall. Torgerson, looking like a wild man, was bleeding from cuts on the head and face. His fists were scratched raw, apparently from hitting the concrete block walls of his cell. He was screaming obscenities at the top of his voice. Four other prisoners held in the area were contributing to the commotion.

"Olaf. OLAF! Calm down."

Togerson grasped the bars of his cell, his face twisted in a deranged look, and screamed invectives at the Sheriff. He saw Rouse and began screaming at him, too. Then he retreated to the rear of his cell, slamming first his fists and then his head against the concrete blocks. Blood spurted from his nose and began to stain the floor the cell.

Recognizing the man was out of control—and likely to remain that way—Al turned to the jailer. "Quick, get me a taser—we have to get this guy under control before he kills himself."

The jailer was back in a flash. He handed the taser to Al, who pointed the weapon just as Torgerson, a wild look on his face, charged the front of the cell. Al fired the weapon, the two small darts flying with uncanny accuracy just as Torgerson reached the cell, grasped it, then fell to the floor writhing.

"Open the cell. Now." Al had dropped the weapon and now waited helplessly to get into the cell to aid Torgerson, who had taken a direct hit to the chest at point-blank range.

The cell door swung open, Al rushed to Torgerson, knelt to assist him—and suddenly found himself in the firm grasp of a maddened prisoner. Al felt fingers reach for and grasp his throat and soon he was fighting for his life. As they rolled on the floor, Al fought to free the fingers at his throat—feeling his own panic rise when he couldn't breathe.

As they rolled over—Torgerson now on top of Al—the voice of Sheriff George Carsten thundered through the cellblock—"Olaf! Stop now or I'll fire!" The Sheriff had grabbed the jailer's gun and had it pointed at Torgerson's shoulder. Torgerson, snarling, suddenly released Al and lunged for Carsten, who took a step back and fired the weapon, striking the deputy in the chest.

Al rolled over, gasping for breath, got to his knees and crawled over to where Torgerson lay sprawled on his back. Feeling for the man's pulse, he found it faint and thready. "Quick," he yelled, "get an ambulance, this guy needs to go to the hospital!"

In what seemed only seconds, two paramedics rushed in pushing a gurney. One of them tended to the wound, applying a fast-pack dressing. In less than a minute, they had lifted Torgerson onto the gurney and were out the door with the wounded prisoner on their way to the Gundersen Lutheran emergency room.

Al gathered in the bullpen with the rest of the group that had returned from Prairie du Chien. "We're going to need to post an officer with Torgerson, assuming he lives."

"He's our prisoner, but we'd be grateful for any help that you guys might give us, or whatever you suggest," said Fender.

"I'll take the first shift. I'll head over there now." Charlie was shrugging into his jacket as he stood.

"Charlie, I'll get to Brent, have him call Dwight, and we'll get a schedule set up. You should have relief soon."

Charlie rushed out the door, uncertain of what he might find when he got to Gundersen. The group left at the La Crosse LEC began to post-mortem the incident to determine what, if anything, might have been done differently.

That done, Al made a call to Police Chief Brent Whigg, informed him of events at the LEC, and asked if he would call Sheriff Dwight Hooper to arrange a schedule of room guards for Gundersen to relieve Charlie from his post.

32

Charlie raced from the LEC to Gundersen, siren wailing, and lights flashing. He pulled through the E.R. sheltered entrance to the law enforcement parking spot just beyond and screeched to a stop. The big guy then demonstrated he could move pretty fast when motivated, hurrying into the receiving room of the E.R., where he found a familiar face manning the desk.

Donna Ramirez had been staffing the E.R. for nearly 20 years. A still attractive woman of 48, she had packed a few additional pounds onto a slight frame over the years. She was, as always, dressed in a freshly starched white uniform. And the smile on her face seemed to add additional light to the pastel walls and bright lighting.

"Charlie Berzinski, haven't seen you in a while." She rose to her feet. "Do you always hafta send 'em in here nearly beyond repair? This last guy is pretty badly shot up, and the whole team is working on him now. Good thing it's a quiet afternoon."

The nurse pointed toward chairs along the wall, saying, "Might as well have a seat. Unless you want to see blood and gore, no sense going in there now. Everyone's too busy to talk anyway. And the guy you sent here isn't going to be escaping anywhere except, maybe, to heaven."

Charlie eased his big frame into a chair built for someone smaller, turning it toward the reception desk as he eased back.

"How's the family, Donna?"

"Oh Charlie, you're so nice—the kids are all fine."

"That's right, you've got two of 'em right? One or two by your first husband? Sure was a shame when he died. How many with…with…"

"Juan," she supplied. "I had two girls with Claude." She paused.

193

"Yes, his cancer was a tragedy that had me down-and-out for a while. And now I have three boys with Juan. You know, Charlie, I've had two great men, and I'm blessed to have two sets of kids that get along famously. The girls look like perfect Norwegians—blonde and blue-eyed. And the boys are all handsome little señors—black hair and coal-black eyes."

Charlie conjured up a mental image of her family. "Must be quite a sight when the seven of you go out to eat."

"Well, at today's prices, there isn't much of that—but, yes, we get more than a few looks from other diners when we do. You know, Charlie, I've really been lucky. Both Claude and Juan ... wonderful ... and the girls love their half-brothers. Life couldn't be better."

Just as Charlie was getting ready to respond, the door into the E.R. proper opened and Dr. Jamie Gundersen came out, looked around, spotted Charlie and headed over, stripping off synthetic gloves as she walked.

Donna held out a waste basket marked "Sterile Waste." Jamie deposited the gloves and shook Charlie's hand. "You know, Charlie, it sure would be nice if you sent us an easy case now and then."

"I understand, doc. This one is a dandy. Was choking Al Rouse until being shot by his boss. Boss's a cop."

"A cop? Sounds like a story I want to hear, but I don't have time right now. As luck would have it, we believe the bullet missed everything vital, but he lost a lot of blood. They're taking him into the O.R. right now, and I'm needed in there. I just wanted you to know that we think he'll make it, but he's a long way from out of the woods."

She gave the deputy a friendly salute, turned and headed back the way she'd come.

"Good thing Jamie is here. We don't have a better trauma surgeon. If she says she thinks he'll make it, he'll make it." Donna seemed very confident, punctuating her statements slapping her palms on the desk.

"She is good, that's for sure. We've brought her plenty of rough ones and they're all still alive," agreed Charlie.

For the next hour, the two sat there visiting. It was a quiet night, and eventually Charlie propped his chair up on two legs, tipped his hat over his eyes, and was soon asleep. Just as he was slipping into a dream involving a giant slice of lemon meringue pie, he was shaken awake.

Wha…what?" He came out of his slumber disoriented. He tipped the chair down, pushed up the hat and found himself staring into the blue eyes of Jamie Gundersen.

"Charlie, sorry to disturb your rest." The surgeon's eyes twinkled as she talked. "Just wanted you to know I patched up your friend, and we provided him with a couple units of blood. We're just moving him to the ICU. He should be up there in the next half hour." She pushed up the sleeve of her gown and looked at her watch. "I don't think he's gonna be out of lala land for another hour, so you have plenty of time to get up there. Might want to get a cup of coffee." Then the petite blonde trauma surgeon straightened, grabbed the surgical cap from her head, lobbed it and another pair of gloves into Donna's wastebasket and shook out her hair, which fell messily around her face.

"God, it's been a long day, Donna. Nothing else right now, right?"

"Right. You look like you could use a long, hot shower. If I were you, I'd do that now and then head home for some rest."

"Gonna be a short night." The surgeon was untying the straps on her gown, then pulled it off, compacted it into a blue ball and tossed it in the basket. "Important meeting with the brass tomorrow, but a few hours will be better than none."

She took a few steps toward the E.R. door, then turned back toward Charlie. "What the heck did the guy do to get himself shot up like that?"

The question was directed at Charlie, who had arisen from his chair and grabbed his jacket.

"Just your run-of-the-mill jailhouse scuffle." He stretched now, then smiled at the pretty surgeon. "Got a little rowdy."

"I guess it did." Her tone was sharp but her smile was warm. "He was leaking like a sprinkling can when he arrived. Good thing he didn't have far to go or we might have lost him. He should be ready for questions in about six or eight hours, I'm guessing. Night, Charlie … see you soon, Donna."

Then she was gone, disappearing through the door into the E.R. Charlie stretched again, hitched up his pants and looked at Donna. "Thanks, Donna. I enjoyed our visit."

"I don't think it was as exciting as your nap, though, Charlie. You talked about food the whole time you were out."

"Really? Well, I guess I was hungry and dreamin' about Ma's."

"You'd probably have time to run over there for breakfast." Her eyes sparkled as she teased him.

"Thanks for your hospitality." Charlie picked up his hat and moved toward the door, trying to reorient himself as he went.

"Out the door and left," she told him. "Elevators to the fourth floor. Right when you get off. ICU is dead ahead."

Five hours later, Charlie, who had been joined by Al Rouse, waited in the room off the ICU for the word that Olaf Torgerson was awake and talking.

"How's Carsten?" Charlie was worried about the Crawford County Sheriff who had shot his own deputy—his own nephew, it turned out—after the imprisoned deputy had threatened to strangle Al.

"Pretty broken up." Both men were seated in recliners. They were the only souls in the waiting room. Charlie had his recliner back and was stretched out. Al was on the edge of his chair, facing Charlie with his elbows on his knees and his chin in his hands. "The guy's like a son to him. He did what he had to do, but when it was over, the enormity of having shot his nephew hit him like a ton of bricks."

"How *you* feelin'?"

"I'm fine. A little embarrassed for getting myself into that fix." Al was on his feet now. "Want some water?"

"Nah, I'm fine."

Al returned from the water cooler at the other end of the room, then sat and sipped from the small plastic container.

The door opened, a nurse in scrubs entered. Charlie slammed his recliner into its upright position. "Is the prisoner awake?"

"He is. He's asking lots of questions, so we're ready for you. He's in 12, at the far end of the unit."

"Thanks." The two officers were on their feet and moving to the door. Holding the door for Al, Charlie followed his partner into the ICU. Al moved assertively through the area, peered around the curtains, and then held the cloth barrier aside to admit Charlie. He followed the deputy into the room.

Torgerson's right wrist and left ankle were shackled to the bed, his face was pale, and they could see—beneath the hospital gown—his abdomen and shoulder were swathed in bandages.

In spite of his pallid condition, his face looked like a gathering thunderstorm as the two officers entered the room. When he spoke, he leaned forward like he wanted to leap off the bed as he snarled, "Did you shoot me? You gotta lotta guts showing up after doing this to me."

The tenacity of his diatribe overexerted him, causing him to slump back onto the bed, gasping for air.

"Olaf, if I were you I'd get rid of the 'tude." Charlie had gone straight to the side of the bed and was leaning over the man to talk. "Neither of us shot you, but you were trying to kill Al, here."

"Yeah, another 30 seconds and the job would have been done. Damn twerp … world would be better off without 'im," Torgerson sneered in Al's direction.

"Let me warn you, this session is being recorded and anything you say may be used against you." Charlie turned and set the small recorder on the stand at the foot of the bed, the arm of which projected over the bed at Torgerson's ankles. Then he pulled over a chair to sit nearby.

"Whadda I care if you record it or not? I ain't done nothing."

"We don't think that's true, and neither does your boss. In fact, it was Sheriff Carsten who shot you when he saw you choking Al," gesturing toward the detective. "You're damn lucky the docs were able to patch you up. Don't make me angry that they did that. It would be best if you answered our questions … being honest and forthright might help you in the long run."

Torgerson's breath came in pants as he considered the message, and then his face reddened. "George shot me? I don't believe it. He's my uncle."

"And I think what he now knows about you has him reconsidering that designation. But, yes, he did the shooting. He's not very proud of you, that much I know. The only way you're going to earn back any points is to tell us everything you know." The recorder beeped. Charlie got up from his bedside seat, picked up the recorder, reactivated the device, and returned to his chair.

Just then the Crawford County Sheriff entered the room. When he did, Al rose from his chair, and extended his arm to the Sheriff, urging him to take the seat.

"Uncle George." Torgerson seemed pleased to see the Sheriff, but the reverse wasn't true.

"Olaf, I'm ashamed to say I wish I'd never hired you. You're a disgrace to the badge. What a damn fool I've been." Carsten paused, then continued in a low growl, "You made a fool of the whole damn department, you jerk. You're going away for a very long time. I will make it my personal job to make sure you get the book thrown at you."

"Wha...what did I do, uncle?"

"Don't you dare 'uncle' me! You and your little sex trafficking scheme ... what a blind idiot I was. I am just so grateful your mother is gone." Carsten shook his head. "What a mess ... what a damn mess. You are a fool, Olaf, and I have been one, too. Thankfully, your nasty little game is over."

The Sheriff turned and stalked from the room. Ringing behind him were the words, "I'm going to do everything I can to make certain you get your reward."

The prisoner seemed to slink down in his bed. Then Charlie interrupted. "You, know, Olaf, you could help your situation and your uncle by coming clean on this trafficking deal. You could help us break this thing up."

Torgerson scowled up at Charlie and Al, then tried to roll on his side.

"Forget it." The words were more mumble than statement, but the occupants of the room picked them up, clear as crystal.

Charlie got up, gestured to Al, and prepared to leave.

"Okay, then, we've tried to help you … tried to get you to help your uncle … but, apparently, you're just the little sniveling brat he thinks you are," Charlie rebuked him. "You're going to get what's coming to you, that's for sure."

33

Outside the room, Al stopped Charlie. "What the hell was that about? Usually you're the good cop—but this time you were on the attack."

"You know, Al, the guy just pisses me off. There's nothing about him that I like. Anyone who would do that to an uncle, who was just trying to help him out, makes me mad."

"And you were." Al was smiling now. "It's good to see that side of you. Once in a while, it's a relief that I don't always have to be the bad guy."

"You're not a bad guy, Al, you're just a pragmatist. I try to see the good in people. This time I saw no good at all."

"Charlie, the philosopher. By gosh, this is a whole new side of you, my man."

"All sorts of new things, right?" Charlie was grinning like a Cheshire cat. "I ain't just a marshmallow, you know, even if that's what you think I am most of the time."

Al had to smile at that, then returned to the matter at hand. "I say we let this guy stew for the night, and maybe tomorrow, too. I think we should warn the jailer assigned here to say nothing—not a word. My fear is that Torgerson will try to bribe someone to get him out of here when he feels up to it. We also need to warn the nurses."

Just then a tall, broad-shouldered man wearing the uniform of a La Crosse County Deputy came around the corner and walked toward them.

"Hi, Ron. Good to see you. Al, you remember Ron Ryder, right?"

"Sure do. Welcome, Ron. Charlie, why don't you brief Ron, and I'll go talk to the head ICU nurse."

"Sounds like a plan."

Al walked back into the ICU and strolled to the nurses' station. Smiling, he asked, "Who's in charge here?"

A big-boned woman with graying hair rolled into a bun, stood and smiled at him. "That would be me. I'm Cheryl Lawrence. How can I help you?"

"Cheryl, I'm Detective Chief Al Rouse, La Crosse P.D."

"Detective Rouse, I recognize you from your photos in the paper, although you are much more handsome in the skin, I must say."

A tinge of pink lit Al's cheeks. He smiled back at the woman. "Why, thank you. Not sure I have ever been called handsome before, but it's nice of you to say."

"What can I do for you?" Cheryl had moved nearer to where Al was standing to make sure their conversation was not overheard by the patients.

"We have a prisoner in Unit 12," began Al. Cheryl nodded in understanding. "He's considered dangerous, as you know, and we have him shackled to his bed. We would rather none of you speak a word to him, if that's possible."

"Detective Rouse, that's something we can't do." She was shaking her head in disapproval. "We have to have at least limited communication, but we can limit it to only those things that are essential."

"Yes, of course, Cheryl, I understand. But if you can limit your communication to only business, that would be great. We will have a jailer posted in his room at all times. He will try to be as unobtrusive as possible, but if he's in the way, just explain what you want him to do. His name is Ron Ryder. He's a good guy."

"Pretty good lookin', too, I see." She glanced into the hallway and saw the deputy standing there. "We'll make him feel right at home. Show him in."

The introductions made, Ryder stepped into Unit 12, and took up his post on a chair propped against the wall.

Five minutes later, Al and Charlie were headed home. "What do you think? Will Torgerson decide to do the right thing?"

"I don't know, Al. He didn't flinch one bit when his uncle came in. He's a pretty cool customer. I'm not sure I can see him saying anything. He's a guy who's darn easy to dislike."

They drove through the south side of La Crosse in silence, then the radio crackled.

"10-78 ... all units respond, Gundersen-Lutheran ICU."

"Damn," said Al, looking behind, then wheeling the car into a U-turn and activating the lights and sirens. "Must be something going on with Torgerson. There goes a night at home."

Four minutes later, the Prius pulled into the police parking area. Two other cars were already present, lights flashing. No officers were visible.

"Let's get up there," urged Al, leaving the lights activated but taking the keys. "No telling what we're going to find."

As they ran breathlessly into the ICU, police and health care personnel were seen in Unit 12.

Al and Charlie joined the group, Al saying, "What's going on here?"

Ron Ryder was seated in his chair, but blood was running down his face and pooling in a crease in his shirt. Two other officers were wrestling with Torgerson, trying to get him to calm down.

A nurse rushed into the room, pushing a cart laden with towels and an assortment of medical items. She began attending to Ryder, mopping the blood from his face, applying ointment to the wound and bandaging it with a large bandage. Then Ryder addressed the blood stain on his shirt, mopping it up with some material taken from the cart. The deputy tended to, the nurse moved to the patient, where the officers had wrestled Torgerson back onto the bed where he belonged. He too was bleeding. His face wore a sullen look and he spit at the nurse as she tended to his wounds. She backed away from him, a furious look on her face.

"Look, buster, I've been a nurse longer than you've been alive. You're just a snot-nosed kid to me, and if you want to play rough, I can assure you I'll beat the crap out of you. Now settle down or I'll make good on that promise."

The look on Torgerson's face melted as the nurse censured him. Unexpectedly, the prisoner began to sniffle.

"I am so sorry … for everything. I feel like hell. I hurt … it's like fire in my gut. I took it out on you and that's unfair. Forgive me, will you, please?" Torgerson was suddenly uncharacteristically compliant.

The nurse didn't seem terribly affected by the apology, but she did acknowledge it.

"Mr. Torgerson, I have here a pain shot, but I'm not going to attempt to give it to you unless you promise to behave. Is that clear?"

The prisoner nodded his agreement, the nurse filled the needle from a vial on the nearby table, then injected the drug into the intravenous drip attached to Torgerson's arm.

"You're gonna get sleepy now. Don't fight it. When you wake up, we'll plan on a chat, okay?"

When the prisoner nodded, the nurse swept out of the ICU cube, her crisply starched white dress uniform rustling as she went.

"What the hell just happened?" Charlie asked Al.

"I think you just saw the iron hand of authority descend on our prisoner." Al was shaking his head in wonderment at the nurse's masterful effectiveness in shutting down Torgerson. "I think we can learn a thing or two from her, don't you?"

"Damn right. That was something to see."

In a couple of minutes, Torgerson was snoring. The nurse walked back in, looked at the prisoner, adjusted his covers, and stopped to visit with the lawmen.

"Sometimes tough love is the best medicine. I've perfected my delivery over the years until I can make almost anyone behave."

"I was just telling Charlie, here, that we can learn a thing or two from you. And if we weren't so damn tired, I'd start right now."

"Well, detective, I don't know about that, but the lesson can wait. The prisoner is going to be out for at least four hours, maybe longer. It looks as if Officer Ryder here can handle his duty watching over him for a few hours. If I were you, I'd head home to bed."

Given permission, Al and Charlie shrugged into their jackets, then left the ICU and headed for the parking lot.

As Al parked the car in Charlie's driveway and waited for his friend to grab his things, he remained pensive. "You know, Charlie, something feels ominous, like something big is going to happen, and it's going to happen soon. Not sure what's causing it … just a gut feeling."

Twenty minutes later, he was home, and, after kissing Jo Anne hello, he fumbled his way up the stairs, shed his clothes, and crawled into bed. Ten minutes later, Jo Anne came up and tidied the room, with Al none the wiser. He was sound asleep.

34

Two hours later, as Al was just settling into a dream about bringing into custody the kidnappers who took Shirley Sovereign, something or someone was shaking the bed. He fought off the attack for a few seconds, but when it persisted, he opened one eye. "Jo Anne … wha … what are you doing here …?"

Then realizing where he was and that he had been dreaming, he quickly shifted into focus. "Oh, hi, I was dreaming. What time is it?"

"It's 5:30 a.m., Al. You've only been asleep for a couple of hours but Brent is on the phone for you. I told him you were trying to rest but he insisted I wake you."

"Chief, hi, what's up? … Yes, got home about 3. I've gotten about two hours, I guess … Oh, really? Who called?… Cheryl. Yup, she's in charge of the ICU. What's up? … He is? Really? You bet. I'll be on my way in a minute."

When he hung up, Jo Anne walked in with suit pants, shirt, and coat. "Better take a shower, Al, you'll feel better. What's so important they need you back there right now?"

"Apparently our prisoner has decided to talk." Al, naked now, was heading for the bathroom and a shower. "Brent thinks I'd better get there quick before he changes his mind." He grabbed a towel and headed for the shower. Then he stopped. "Do me a favor, will you? Call Charlie. Tell him if he wants to go along, I'll pick him up in 15 minutes." Then the shower door slammed.

Ten minutes later Al was showered, had run the razor over his face, and was ready to head out. "Charlie will be waiting for you." Jo Anne stood on her tiptoes, kissed her husband, then watched him walk down the stairs to his car.

Twenty-five minutes later, Al and Charlie were back in the ICU. Cheryl waved at them, then motioned for them to follow her. She took them into an unused room and closed the door.

"Torgerson woke up about a half hour ago and he was still acting like a little kid." She smiled evilly as she made the report. "I leaned on him pretty hard, told him how things were going to go down hard for him, and suggested he might want to think about cooperating and seeing if he could work some sort of deal. I figured if it loosened his lips, you might be willing to cut him a little slack. In any event, I went to get him some ice water, and when I came back, he said to call and tell you he was ready to talk."

She smiled at the two officers, obviously proud at having brought the prisoner to the point of cooperation. "I called the Police Chief, thinking you had only gotten out of here a couple hours ago. But here you are anyway."

When she had finished her briefing, she opened the door, walked out of the room and gestured them toward Unit 12.

Pushing aside the curtain, Al and Charlie were greeted by the sight of Torgerson sitting up in bed, the table tray was extended over the bed, and he and Ryder were playing cards. When he saw them, Torgerson smiled and waved them toward the bed with his free hand, which was also holding his playing cards.

"Let's put this aside, Ron. We can pick it up again when I finish with Detective Rouse and Deputy Berzinski."

The prisoner's tone was one of friendliness. Al looked back at Charlie with amazement, then turned and walked on into the room. "Mr. Torgerson, you wanted to see us?"

"I did. Yes, I did. I got to thinking about what the nurse had to say—you know, the tough one with the white dress. She thought if I straightened up and helped you guys, maybe you'd figure out a way to help me."

"We don't make the deals," said Al, looking now at Charlie for support. "But we can help, that's for sure."

"Al's right," began Charlie. "The prosecutors always come to us for advice and we usually try to help out the people who have been cooperative."

"So, you think you could help me out … if I help you?"

"Absolutely." Al was totally focused on the situation now and anxious to get some information.

"Can you get the prosecutor to sign an agreement?"

"I don't think that's a very good idea, Mr. Torgerson. I think a request like that would cause the prosecutor to back away. You'd be asking more than any prosecutor would be willing to provide, I'm quite sure." Al was now deadly serious and his face displayed a worried look.

Torgerson got it immediately and backed away. "Okay, I understand. Just thought I'd ask. But you will try to get me a deal?"

"I guarantee you that Charlie and I will do our best to try and get you a deal. But you have to help us, too."

"Okay, what do you need from me?"

"First, can we tape your responses to our questions?" As Al asked the question, he brought a small digital recorder out of his coat pocket and showed it to Torgerson.

"If you allow us to record the session, we will have something to show them that demonstrates your good faith."

"Okay. Let's do it. If that's what you need, it's fine."

With Charlie looking on, Al quickly queued up the recorder, then introduced the subject, recording the date, time, and participants.

"Mr. Torgerson, tell us about your involvement in the Western Wisconsin sex trafficking operation."

Torgerson had organized his thoughts and was ready to tell his story. "I had been working for the Crawford County Sheriff's Department for about a year. I had made quite a few friends in the area, socializing during off hours and bumping into them when on duty from time to time. Then one day a woman—Veronica Stone, a social worker from Richland County—was talking to me about a case I was investigating. Eventually, she asked me how I liked my job. We talked some more and she asked if I had a hard time making ends meet.

"I told her a deputy's pay wasn't great—she agreed with that, and asked if I would like to make some additional money. I told her if I could work it in, it would be great to earn some extra. I assumed it was a legitimate venture. I didn't think another thing of it, until one day I got a call from her. She told me she understood there was a girl from Hazard who wanted to make it in the big city. She said she needed someone to pick her up and bring her to Richland Center. I got the details and went and did the job. Picked up the girl one evening at a bar, and drove her to Veronica's house. Got paid $5,000. Man, I thought, that's great way to make some extra money. Little did I know.

"The first few jobs were easy ... like that first one. They sorta just reeled me in like a trout. It was about the seventh job, I think, when things began to change. By that time, I had picked up $25,000 or $30,000, and I was getting dependent on the money. Then one day, Veronica sat down with me and began to explain what was going on. She told me these were all kids who had broken home lives and they were trying to escape for something better. She told me she placed them in homes of wealthy people as nannies or maids. She said they made good money, got to continue their education, and for the first time in their lives had places to be where people cared about them.

"She told me the real money was in the recruitment. She said transport fees of $5,000 were small change compared to the money she made—ten or 20 times that—for recruiting young women. She wanted to know if I'd like to get into that phase of the game. She had me hooked. Totally."

By this time Torgerson was getting hoarse and seemed as if he was struggling to maintain the conversation. His face had paled, and he was breathing in gulps.

"Let's take a break, Olaf. Looks like you could use a rest." Al walked to the nurses' station and suggested someone check on the prisoner. Cheryl bustled away from her station and entered Unit 12. She was there for more than 15 minutes. When she returned, he face wore a worried frown.

"I think he overexerted," she told Al and Charlie. "He's totally worn out, and he's having trouble breathing. I turned the oxygen on. I think you're going to have to let him rest now."

"Can we say good-bye?" Al was thinking that he had left his cassette device in the room and needed to retrieve it.

"I'd prefer you just leave him alone. Perhaps tomorrow he will be able to spend some more time with you."

"I left my recorder on the table. May I go and get it?"

"How about I do it for you. I really think Mr. Torgerson has to be left completely alone so he can rest. I fear he tried to do too much."

She went into the unit, returned with the recorder and announced, "He's sound asleep. Maybe just tired."

"Tell you what, maybe Charlie and I will go down to the cafeteria and grab some dinner. We'll stop back and see how the prisoner is doing. If he's awake and wants to talk – and it's okay with you – we'll continue the discussion. Are you all right with that?"

"Yes, Detective, as long as you listen to me and stop when I say so, we'll get along just fine."

Several minutes later, seated in the cafeteria, trays of food in front of them, Al took a moment to marvel at the dramatic cutback in Charlie's consumption. "Kelly really is working wonders on you, Charlie. There was a time, not so long ago, when that would not even have been an appetizer for you."

"You know, Al, I'm kinda enjoying the result of it, too. Getting rid of the paunch has been a big deal. It was tough, but now that it's gone, I'm happy."

After finishing what for each was a very light dinner, they headed back to the fourth floor.

"You were prophetic," Cheryl told them. "He awoke about five minutes ago and asked for you. Said he was anxious to continue the discussion."

Al and Charlie slipped through the curtain and were greeted by smiles from Torgerson. Al took out the recorder, set it on the table and activated the machine. "Ready to continue?"

"I am," the prisoner told Al.

Al sat in the chair at bedside. Charlie left and returned momentarily with a chair and also sat to listen.

"When we stopped," said Al, "you were telling us about being totally hooked on the easy money and you were talking about how Veronica hooked you on a bigger role."

"She talked with me about taking on more responsibility. She told me that I could make at least $50,000 for each woman I recruited. Not sure, Detective, but that really made me sit up and pay attention. Because I knew a lot of young women from the Hazard area who had been recruited, I started hanging around there during off hours. I quickly found out, I was good at the game. Once I hooked the first one, it go easier and easier and, I think, I got sloppier and sloppier."

"Was all of your work with Veronica?"

"No, after the second or third recruit, she suggested I should work directly with her contact. A couple weeks later I got a call from her, asking me to come over to Richland Center that evening for dinner. When I got there, I met two guys from Chicago. Moe Larkin was one, as I remember, but the one I worked for directly was Scarface Frenetti. He was a tough guy, about 6-feet-2 and 200 pounds. He didn't take nothing from no one. I was with him one night, having a coupla beers in Prairie and some snot-nosed kid came up and challenged him. Scarface didn't even get up, just swiveled around and popped the guy in the temple, and down he went. Just like that any sign of trouble ended. Frenetti was a cool guy…well connected, for sure. I think he worked directly for the mob boss in Chicago. He also worked the mob in Milwaukee. He loved what I did for him. He paid me well."

"How much extra money did you make?" Al checked the recorder. It was working fine. He turned it back toward Torgerson in time for the response.

"I got $50,000 per recruit. Cash. I no longer had a financial worry. I turned over five women in four years."

"When did you send the last one with Frenetti." Charlie was

really interested now and pressing for more information pertinent to their investigation.

"Not quite two months ago. That was a really happy one. Maisie Evans was a beautiful woman. Her father was black and her mother was, I'm pretty sure, Norwegian. She had this honey-tone skin and the most compelling features ever. She was beautiful. And she was abused – by her uncle…her mother's sister's husband. She wanted out, and I helped her. I understand she's now one of the top women in New York."

"So, this group you work with supplies women to all parts of the country?" Al had reached into the pocket of his suitcoat hanging on the chair. He made several notes as Torgerson began to respond.

"The bulk of the women worked in Chicago—some in Milwaukee. But if there was an exceptionally beautiful recruit, they might be sent to bigger venues. Maisie is one of the really lucky ones. She's got a great boss, I'm told, and is making big money."

"Great boss? Pimp, you mean?"

"Well, Al, you can call it what you want, but I think of this case as him being her boss, because she has a lot of say in what she does, and she makes really big money."

"How do you know this?"

"Scarface keeps me posted. He makes a trip through here each month to meet with people like me. We exchange notes about past business deals."

"Did it ever occur to you that what you were doing was wrong?"

"I … guess, but you didn't know the circumstances. Maisie was horribly abused—sexually. By an evil uncle. I like to think I saved her."

As Al was considering the last response, Nurse Cheryl Lawrence bustled into the cube. "Time for vitals, gentlemen. Could I ask you to please step out? I'll be with you in a moment."

When the lawmen left, the nurse pulled the curtain behind them. Al and Charlie lounged against the counter in front of the nurses' station. Al reviewed his notes and checked the recorder while Charlie engaged one of the nurses in small talk.

About five minutes later, Lawrence returned, a rather grim look on her face. "I believe the prisoner is exhausted, gentlemen, so I am going to have to end the interrogation. I hope you'll understand. Torgerson shows signs of needing rest. His blood pressure is elevated—not dangerously, but higher than normal. He is running a low-grade fever and his pulse is thready. I just think it best if we stop for now."

Al pocketed the recorder and grabbed his coat from the counter. "Nurse, we're at your order. If you say Torgerson needs rest, we'll be going. By the way, Officer Ryder will be relieved at 11 p.m. tonight. I'm not sure who the replacement is … but another sheriff's officer, I'm sure."

With that, Al and Charlie turned to leave. As they exited the unit, Al stopped and looked at Charlie.

"Not sure what it is, pal, but I still just have a creepy feeling about tonight … as if something bad is going to happen. I've tried to shrug it off, but it just won't stop."

"The famous Rouse premonition, right?" Charlie wasn't either kidding or smiling as he made his statement. "Do you think I should call Dwight and have him beef up enforcement?"

"I know the Sheriff won't like it, but I'd feel better if you did that, Charlie. This place is full of holes, and I'm worried about someone slipping in and deep-sixing Olaf. I know it doesn't make sense, but …"

"Not to worry. Dwight and Brent are well aware of your perceptive genes. I don't think there will be a problem."

Charlie already had his phone out and was calling his boss. A short talk later, he returned the phone to its pouch and looked up.

"Brent is going to send some additional personnel. We'll double up on the guards in the ICU, and also station another officer outside the door to the unit. I think you can rest easy, Al."

"I hope so … I really hope so."

But the tone of his response made it seem eerily insufficient.

35

Al dropped Charlie, drove home, kissed Jo Anne, and stumbled up the steps to their bedroom—where he dropped his clothes on a chair, almost without knowing it, and was virtually asleep before hitting the bed. Jo Anne came up two hours later and, careful not to disturb Al, slipped into bed, then laid there listening to him breathe and snore gently. Sometime after midnight, she fell asleep.

A few minutes later the police radio in Al's pants pocket crackled to life, directing all officers to report to Gundersen Lutheran ICU to quell a disturbance.

Al was instantly awake, leapt from the bed, dressed, and was on his way downstairs even before Jo Anne was awake. The door slammed, and that was when she knew Al had gone. In his car, he called Charlie, who told him he was already en route and to drive directly to the southside hospital.

With no traffic at this time of night, Al made record time, steering the car into an open parking space near the hospital's visitor entrance, running into the building, and boarding the elevator for a trip to the fourth floor.

He ran from the elevator to the ICU. When the doors opened, he was greeted by a disturbing sight. Two nurses were being freed from tape that held them to chairs, and Unit 12 was ablaze with lights.

"What the hell happened?" Al had stopped short of the counter when he saw the officers on the floor.

"Nasty visitors." This came from a nurse in scrubs who was on her feet but still had remnants of tape hanging from her wrists. "Walked in here a half hour ago, guns drawn, and said they were here to get Olaf Torgerson. They began to go unit to unit until Judith—Judith

Sorenson, the night charge nurse—braced them and asked just what the hell they thought they were doing. The one guy got really nasty with her. Banged her on her head with his gun and knocked out her cold. The next unit they came to was Torgerson's. The first thing they did was disarm the guard who was with him. Apparently, he had fallen asleep. Then they tried to get Torgerson out of bed, but he was shackled. They roughed him up pretty good, then took off in a hurry when they heard sirens approaching. Both Torgerson and Judith are down in the E.R. getting patched up. Your guy is down there, too."

"Only one?" Al was confused, thinking there were several people on duty guarding the prisoner.

"I think only one. There were two others here, but when it hit 10 p.m. and it was real quiet, the guy in with Torgerson told them they could go home since nothing was happening."

Al, the red rising from his neck, looked at Charlie, who resembled a volcano about to erupt.

Before Charlie could let loose, Al took him by the arm and led him outside the ICU and into a vacant room off the exit.

Charlie was sputtering, his face as red as a cherry. "What the hell was that about! The guard told those other two they could go? That's crap, Al—just plain crap. I wanna talk to Dwight and I want to do that right now."

"Charlie, just settle down a little will you … no sense busting a gasket getting yourself in a sweat over what's done. We can't change that. All we can do is make sure whatever hole there was is plugged and won't happen again. I'm just wondering if someone got to the guard and bought him off."

"I'm wondering about that, too, and you can damn well bet I'm gonna find out."

Charlie wrestled his phone out of his jacket and punched in a speed dial number. "Dwight … Dwight, you there? This is Charlie. You hear what happened here at the hospital?"

Charlie's face was red again and he was shaking his head. "One of the guys who came over to babysit our prisoner decided he didn't need any help. He told the other two guards to take off. After they left, a couple guys walked in and roughed up the ICU staff and our prisoner. I think we gotta problem on our hands. Either you're gonna take care of it or I am!"

Al could hear Dwight Hooper from where he was standing. The Sheriff was composed but loud. The conversation continued for several minutes before Charlie seemed appeased and concluded the discussion. He turned to Al, wiping his brow as he began to speak.

"The blame rests with the Sheriff, but at least I understand the situation."

"What happened?"

Charlie flushed, leaned against the wall and thought for a time, brows deeply furrowed. Then he said, "The Sheriff told the lead guy that if, in his estimation, things had quieted and were likely to stay that way, he could dismiss the other two volunteer officers and let them go home for the night. The Sheriff said he also made a bad choice for a lead guard, because the volunteer—Dick Johnson—had been out on assignment most of the night before. He was probably so tired, he just nodded off when things quieted down, and Torgerson went to sleep. Sorry, Al, but I have to call it a total C.F. and it's all our fault."

"Look, it is what it is, Charlie. We can't change it, so we have to deal with it. First job is to make sure that everyone who was injured in the invasion is all right. That includes Torgerson. Although the threat may have passed, we have to reinstitute the watch with folks who are more vigilant and alert."

"Makes sense, Al, but why aren't you as mad as I am? We really screwed up, and you act calm as an old maid at bedtime."

"Well, Charlie, what do you want me to do … throw a fit? Who the heck would benefit from that? Besides, like I told you, I could feel something was coming, and at least my premonition has proved out. I think we just correct what we have to and move on. We need to get back to talking to Torgerson as soon as the docs say he's able."

"Al, we screwed up, plain and simple. No question about it. I'd like a chance to make it up to you, if you're willing."

"No need to make anything up. But, yes, if you want to post new guards, I know that Brent would appreciate it. Our budget is damn tight. Then we need to get back to work with Torgerson. Want to call the Sheriff and see what he says about posting guards?"

Al and Charlie were visiting in ICU Unit 12, the unit that Torgerson had been in before the attack occurred. As they visited, two nurses came in to straighten things up. The taller of the two—a young, shapely brunette with radiant blue eyes—smiled when she saw them.

"Brenda Svendsen," she said by way of introduction. "I just came in to relieve Judith. She got a pretty serious rap on the head. They admitted her for observation, so I am filling in. We are going to move the prisoner to Unit 16. It's a lot more secure. Has a heavy door that can be locked, too. Not sure why he wasn't put there right away. Are you sending guards again?"

"Yes … as a matter of fact, we certainly are." Charlie had a look on his face that suggested all the fault for the problems were his. "There will be four guards. Not sure who, though. We'll put one in the room with Torgerson, station one outside the door, if that's okay with you. Put one at the doors to the ICU and one at the nurses' station to protect everyone working. How does that sound?"

"Sounds perfect, but would you please instruct them that their job will be to stay as inconspicuous as possible? I know it's a boring job, and they like to visit, but I would appreciate it if they were reminded that the nurses are here to work—not to be company for the guards."

"Got it, ma'am. I will personally instruct them that they are not to be socializing with medical personnel. It will be a firm message, I promise."

"Well, let's not make it totally anti-social." The nurse was leaning on her elbows at the counter. They should feel free to talk as long as they recognize the reason these people are here is to work, and it would be best if they stay out of their way."

"Yes, ma'am, got it. I will make sure they understand."

As they were finishing up with the nurse supervisor, the double doors swung open and a bed was wheeled through. As the male in scrubs pushed the bed even with the law officers, they saw it was Torgerson. His head was swathed in bandages and his right arm appeared to be heavily bandaged.

He lifted his arm, gave Al and Charlie a sort of smile and nodded. Al walked closer to the bed and placed his hand on Torgerson's shoulder. "Olaf, it looks like they were pretty rough on you."

The prisoner shifted in his bed a bit, turning toward Al. "They were here to make sure I didn't talk. They were supposed to take care of that any way they could … with death being the primary solution. I'm scared, you guys. I'm not sure this is the safest place for me to be."

"I agree with you," Al told him, "but unfortunately you need to be where the doctors are—and that's here. We're going to make sure you have a more secure room and we're also going to vet the guards who are sent here to make sure they are fit, alert, and able to watch over you properly."

"Al, you'll make sure of that, will you?"

"Charlie and I pledge that to you, Olaf. We're very embarrassed by what happened. We'll make sure it doesn't happen again. And as soon as you've recovered enough to be moved, we'll get you out of here. Promise."

"That sounds better, but the last group was supposed to take care of that, too."

"You have a right to be skeptical, but we have communicated the same concerns to the Sheriff, who says he will make sure the people he assigns are prepared to do a better job."

"Look, Olaf," said Al, "we need you to get some rest now. We're going to make sure that no one interrupts you until at least mid-morning tomorrow. Then, if you're feeling up to it, Charlie and I will come back to continue our visit. Is that okay with you?"

"It is … I feel much better when the two of you are with me. I trust you guys and I want to help all I can. I really let my uncle down and I'd like to try to make it up."

"The best thing you can do now is rest. We'll see you tomorrow."

"See you, Al."

The male nurse then continued to push the bed toward the

waiting cube in the corner where they believed Torgerson would be more secure.

After checking in the new four-person guard team—two women and two men—Al and Charlie assigned them to their places after briefing them thoroughly. That done, and the area and Torgerson's cube as secure as they could be made, Al and Charlie decided to try and get some more rest.

"Home or here?" asked Charlie as they prepared to leave the ICU.

"Best to go home, I think. We'll rest more securely and comfortably in our own beds, don't you think?"

"Sure do, Al. What time do you want me back?"

"Let's plan on 11 a.m., unless we get called earlier."

36

Settled in Torgerson's new cube the next morning at eleven, Al had the recorder on the table, Olaf looked as if he was feeling better, and Al and Charlie had both had a great night's sleep. The mood was lighter than the night before, and everyone in the cube benefitted from the bright sunlight that streamed into the room setting the dust motes dancing. Al had been worried by the corner widows until finding out they were a form of Plexiglas that was bullet-proof.

Now he looked at Torgerson and asked, "All set?"

Getting a nod from the prisoner, he opened by saying, "Olaf, when we ended our session yesterday, you were talking about Maisie Evans, a young woman from the Hazard area, who you said was abused. As I recall, I think you said you like to think that you saved her. Is that right?"

"Exactly. She was in a horrible situation. Both her cousin and his father—her uncle—were abusing her, and her mother wouldn't listen to her when she tried to talk to her about it. Maisie said her mother told her she should keep her mouth shut, because her uncle was a good man who was providing well for his family. She felt she had no alternative other than to flee, so she sought me out."

"What I want to know is, did these girls know what was going to happen to them when they reached Chicago or Milwaukee?"

"Absolutely. Yes sir, they did, Al. We had very frank conversations with them when they were recruited about everything and anything they might be asked to do. They'd kinda shrug their shoulders and say, 'We do it now for free … and there are a lot of "icks," too.

Could it be worse than that?' It boggled my mind, but it's a different world out there."

"So, you're saying these recruits embraced prostitution?" Al's comment inflected disbelief.

"You don't believe me, do you, Al? I can understand. I didn't believe it, either, until I saw and heard it."

"But prostitution is hard, often rough, and sometimes lethal, isn't it?"

"It is, but do you think the life for these women around here is any better? If you do, get over it. It's not like you think. There are no cozy homes, no warm blankets, no loving arms. And most of these women are basically selling themselves every night without any safety net or compensation. The medical care they are provided with and the money they can make in Chicago … or other cities … is at least a way of living that is on their own terms, as difficult as it is."

Al shook his head. This interview was not anything like he expected. "You know, Olaf, if what you say is true, you think you're recruiting these women to a better life. Is that your opinion?"

"It's just not my opinion, Al. It's a fact. Life for them here was terrible—in most cases a heckuva lot worse than in Chicago or Milwaukee. Most come home to visit, and if they see me, they thank me."

Al stared at Charlie, then looked back at Torgerson and shook his head. "Unbelievable. Totally unbelievable."

"I understand." The prisoner, unshackled, rolled on his side and propped his head on an elbow. "I didn't believe it, either. Sometimes I still don't. Don't think I haven't had second thoughts … don't think I haven't agonized over what I was doing. And even though I know it will sound self-serving, I actually began to think of the process as potentially beneficial to the women I recruited."

"It does sound self-serving, even though your actions suggest you do believe you were helping." Al rubbed his chin, looked at Charlie then back at the prisoner.

"When you get out of here, would you be willing to introduce us to one of your recruits?" The tone suggested Al didn't expect any help.

"Happy to do that." Torgerson's comment surprised both officers.

"Like I said, I don't think you believe me. Tell you what I'll do. Tonight, I'll write down the names of all nine people I recruited and the names they go by now. Then you can pick the one or two you want to interview. That way I can't just choose my favorites."

"Sounds fair." Al was nodding, "but I'd also like to know how to contact them, if you know."

"I can give you names of contacts in this area, but I don't know how to contact them in Chicago or Milwaukee. Some also may have been sent to other places."

"Are you willing to make the list now?"

"Sure, give me your notebook and pen. It'll take me a little while … hard to write with this arm the way it is."

The prisoner took the notebook and pen, then turned on his back and activated his bed control to get into a sitting position. With the notebook propped on his knees, and pen at the ready, he began to think before writing.

At last he began to write. Al tipped his chair forward and nodded at Charlie. "How about a cup of coffee?"

"Sounds great." The big officer got up and looked at Torgerson. "Anything from the caf', Olaf?"

"Nope, fine."

Seated over coffee, Al looked at Charlie. "Do you think this is for real? He seems almost too cooperative—like he's one of us rather than a prisoner."

"No." Charlie was shaking his head. "I absolutely think he's shooting us straight. Why? That's a good question. Could be having disappointed his uncle is really stinging him. Or maybe he wants to make a deal. Not sure."

As they visited over coffee, suddenly alarm bells sounded. When the whooping sounds stopped, a nasal voice blasted from the speaker system: "Emergency medical personnel report to ICU, STAT. Emergency medical personnel report to ICU, STAT." Three whoops followed the announcement, then the cafeteria again grew quiet, although a group in scrubs near the exit hurried from the room.

"I have a bad feeling about that announcement." Al was already on his feet and tugging on Charlie's arm.

They too hurried from the room and raced to the elevator.

"C'mon. C'mon." Al's words were directed to the elevator. It seemed to have the desired effect because the doors in front of them slid open. They rushed into the car, Al pushed 4 and the doors slid shut.

37

When the elevator doors opened onto the fourth floor, Al was nearly tripped by Charlie as they scrambled to get to the ICU. Reaching the area, they were surprised to find the doors locked. Rebuffed in his attempt to enter, Al stepped back, shook his head, and gestured to Charlie to go to the waiting room just off to the side.

In the comfortably furnished room, Charlie slumped into a recliner while Al paced. Eventually the detective stopped in front of the phone on a wooden stand. He read the posting on the wall, then picked up the phone.

Connected with the ICU, a recorded message told him: "Currently all personnel are busy attending to important ICU matters. When these are resolved, a message will be posted to alert anyone waiting for the reopening of the unit."

"Damn, this is frustrating." Al had continued pacing. Now he stopped in front of Charlie, hands on his hips. "I sure as hell hope it has nothing to do with Olaf. We really need him to provide information on this case. We haven't even gotten around to asking about Shirley Sovereign. Doubt that he'd know anything first-hand, but he might have heard the name."

The pacing continued. After another five minutes of watching him walking back and forth, Charlie spoke up. "Al, how about sitting down. You're making me nervous."

"I'm nervous, too." Al had stopped in front of an easy chair next to Charlie's recliner. He eased his way into it, crossed his legs and folded his arms across his chest.

Two minutes later, he was on his feet again. "I can't handle this.

I just bet something is wrong with Olaf. This thing has a fishy smell to it."

A few minutes later a woman in scrubs entered the room—empty except for the two officers. She wore a worried look and seemed nervous as she looked around. Spotting them she hurried over.

"Detective Rouse, Deputy Berzinski?"

When the officers nodded, she said, "Please come with me."

She led them into the ICU, locked the door behind them, then moved toward the unit in the corner of the room.

"I knew it." Al made the comment intended for Charlie over his shoulder.

"If you'll please wait here, Nurse Lawrence wants to visit with you." She left them and disappeared into the unit occupied by Torgerson.

The head of the unit came out and joined them. She was not the confident, super-in-charge personality she had been on previous occasions. Even her customary crisp white uniform somehow seemed wilted.

"We've had a bit of a problem, I'm afraid. Shortly after you left, Mr. Torgerson began to gasp for air. Thankfully we reached him immediately, even though his monitor had been turned off. Had Joliene Olson—one of our best nurses—not been with him, we would have lost him for sure. As it was, Dr. Turner had to perform an emergency cricothyrotomy, which you probably know better by the term tracheostomy. Mr. Torgerson is in the E.R. now, where he is doing better. They are also doing tests to see what might have caused the attack. Was he fine when you left?"

"He was. He had just asked for a notebook and pen. I gave him mine and we left him as he started to write."

"These are yours, then." The nurse was holding up a notebook and pen. Al quickly nodded, confirming those were the objects.

"He only has one full name and a second first name written. Would you mind if we sent these to pathology for testing?" the nurse asked.

"Not at all … in fact, I'd prefer it. I'd feel terrible if either of those things were responsible for the problem." Al stood with his hands on his hips as he talked to the nurse. Charlie was peering into Unit No. 12. "Do you mind if we have a look?"

"Not at all, Deputy Berzinski. You two are probably much more familiar with things suspicious than we are. It would be good if you did take a close look."

Al and Charlie began a systematic check of the ICU unit. In one corner of the area, Al found a rag. He took a plastic evidence bag out of his pocket, picked it up with the point of a pencil, and bagged it. Other than the rag, the unit was spotless.

As they walked out of the unit, Al turned to the nurses, who were congregated at the central station. "Was anyone in here after Charlie and I left?"

Cheryl Lawrence shook her head, but Joliene Olson spoke up. "That third officer who was with you popped in for a moment and then left to find you."

Al was instantly alert. "Third officer? What third officer? We didn't have anyone with us."

"Really? He was dressed just like you." She pointed at Charlie. "He said he was with you and asked where you had gone. The prisoner told him where you had gone. He said he'd catch up with you, but then he stayed for a while. Feeling Mr. Torgerson was in safe hands, I stepped out for a few minutes to check on other patients. As I was returning, the officer came out and said he was leaving. After he left, I didn't hear any of the normal monitor noises and went to check. I found him turning blue and gasping for air. That's when we called for help."

"I'm guessing that we are going to find that this rag is covered with some chemical that caused that condition," said Al. "We'll get it to our lab as soon as we get back. In the meantime, you'll keep us posted as to what you find, right?"

"Of course." Nurse Lawrence seemed highly distressed as she responded. "I sure wonder who that other guy was who walked in here looking for you. We are going to have to be more alert."

Al and Charlie left the unit. In the lead, Al was actually marching, his head down.

"Hey, Al, hold on, will ya?"

Al stopped and turned and Charlie huffed up, breathing hard.

"I am so damn mad. I should have known better than to leave him alone." Al's face was flushed and his fists were clenched. "The guy waltzed right in—probably saw us go—and almost killed the prisoner. In broad daylight. We're damn lucky we didn't lose him."

As Al turned to leave, Charlie tapped him on the shoulder, and when Al turned said, "Hate to mention it, but aren't we doing the same thing right now? Maybe I should stay behind until we can get a guard in here. I'm thinkin' we should have posted guards around the clock, not just during the night hours."

"Damn good catch … and damn good idea." Al clenched and unclenched his fists. If you take over for a little while, I'll have Brent send someone over here in a few minutes. And when you go back in there, make sure you instruct them to look for a badge—an authentic one."

Then he stomped off, obviously angry at himself.

38

Al was at work before six the next morning and his mood matched the weather: stormy. Outside, thunderheads boiled across the sky, lightning bolts streaked the horizon, and thunder claps echoed through the community. Even after he got into his office—slamming the door that rarely was closed—he could both hear and feel the storm that was raging outside. He made coffee, slumped into his chair, elbows on his desk, and chin in his hands. That's the way Chief Brent Whigg found him forty minutes later.

"You look like hell." The chief had opened the door cautiously. "Thought you might have had someone in here, but it's just you. What's wrong?"

The scowl on Al's face deepened. The Chief backed up a step and held up his hand. "Excuse me. I just thought I'd say hi to my old buddy, but apparently he didn't make it this morning."

"Oh, sit the hell down, Chief. Don't mind me. I'm just in a bad mood. Still kicking myself for my stupidity. Damn near got Torgerson killed in the middle of the day yesterday. Carelessness, that's all it was … pure damn carelessness."

The Chief entered with exaggerated caution, carefully stepped around Al, and inserted a pod in the Keurig. His coffee cup filled, he returned to the chair on the other side of the desk and sat, the crease in his blue uniform pants so crisp Al was certain anyone touching it would get cut.

The chief was a broad-shouldered man of about six-foot-five. He towered over most of his officers, but he was gentle as a kitten and kind as a new puppy. And now, it was obvious, he was concerned about his chief of detectives.

"*Almost* got Torgerson killed? Tell me more."

"Charlie and I took a break yesterday, thinking all was well. We'd had a great, somewhat informative talk, and Olaf was going to write down the names of the women he had recruited. When we got downstairs to the caf' and ordered coffee, the alarm went off and, after we hustled back to the ICU, we found he'd been drugged by an imposter impersonating an officer who had come in just after us."

"Drugged? Is Torgerson okay? What was used?" the chief asked in rapid fire.

"Yes, he seems fine. And the cloth the imposter used is in the lab for testing. I called down here and had officers assigned to guard his cubicle during the day even when Charlie and I are there. I think you'll want to call Dwight today and get his department to participate."

Yes, yes I will." The sheriff was on the edge of his chair and getting ready to go. He stood, straightened his coat and took a step toward the door. "You know," he said turning, "you'd better get back there and get the rest of the story before something else happens."

"I agree. I'm picking Charlie up at 8."

When Al and Charlie walked into the ICU at ten minutes after eight, Torgerson was finishing breakfast. The two officers on duty—a sheriff's man at the ICU desk and one from Al's unit at Torgerson's door—both acknowledged their superior officers as they went in.

"How are you doing this morning, Olaf?" Al wanted to know.

"I'm okay. Look." His hand swept the area near his bed. "No monitors, no tubes."

"That's real progress," agreed Al, with Charlie, standing behind him, and nodding.

"Yup. Gonna be moved today. They haven't told me where, though. Hope it's okay if I plan to take the new guards with me."

Al gave Charlie a look that spoke volumes, then turned back to Olaf. "That's an affirmative," said Al.

Just as Al was about to ask for the list, Nurse Lawrence bustled in, saw the officers, and stopped. "Did he tell you we are sending him away today?"

Al winced at the choice of words. The nurse saw the look on his face, realized her faux pas and tried to recover. "Um … uh … I mean he's leaving the ICU. No, he's really not going anywhere. We're just sending him to med-surg."

"He must be making real progress."

"Miraculous progress," corrected the nurse. "Never seen anything like it. He was in terrible shape when we got him, and only a few days later, he's making a remarkable recovery."

"When do you expect the transfer to occur?"

The nurse looked at her watch. "Hmm, it's about eight-thirty. I would expect he would be moved before ten—as soon as they have a room ready for him."

"Thanks," said Al, nodding. "Thanks also for everything you did yesterday after we'd left."

"That was something, wasn't it?" Lawrence had picked up the tray and was about to leave with it. "Scary as can be, but he was in the right place."

"Sure was," agreed Al as Charlie stepped to move the table from over Torgerson's bed.

The nurse poked her head back in, saw that the table had been moved and thanked Al and Charlie. "He's had his shower, so he's ready to go whenever they are ready. I'll let you know as soon as I hear."

The nurse gone and the curtain pulled away to provide a view of the unit, Al and Charlie settled into their chairs. Torgerson activated the control, moving his bed into a sitting position.

"There," he said. "Much better."

"Getting back to business, did you have time to finish our list?"

"Sure did, Al. Charlie, pull that drawer open there. You should find the notebook on top. It should be open to the information you asked for."

Charlie got the book, looked it over, then handed it to Al.

Al flipped through the pages, then let the notebook rest in his lap. "Mind if we talk about this, Olaf?"

The prisoner nodded as he shifted in his bed so he was on his side and facing the officers.

"When did you start recruiting women for this group?" Al asked the question. Charlie nodded.

The prisoner closed his eyes for a moment, then opened them and said, "Sometime in mid-2008, I think. I started working for the Sheriff's Office in 2006, and it was about a year or so after that, like I told you. In any event, it was after all of that historic flooding on the Kickapoo, when they moved the entire town of Gays Mills—which was just down the road—and rebuilt it on higher ground. Not sure why I remember that, but I do."

"Okay" confirmed Al. "Let's switch signals. The first name you list is Carolyn Nelson. Was that in 2008?"

"No ... she was definitely later. I worked with an officer from Richland County—Nate Oddam. He died a few years ago. I think I recruited Carolyn—she was from Genoa—in 2010 or so. Nice girl. Came from an abusive home. I managed to convince myself I was doing her a favor."

"Have you seen her since?"

"I haven't, but every once in a while I ask about her. She's still working, I'm pretty sure."

"That was at ten years ago. How old was she?"

"Just turned 18. She went with us just as soon as she graduated.

"So she's nearly 30 years old now ... and still working. Is there still a demand for women that age?" Al had Molly's story in the back of his mind, and was looking for corroborating data.

"Dunno. Not really familiar with that part of the business. I imagine if she's good enough and there's demand, she can keep working. Johns get old, too, you know."

And so they started through the list, one by one. Al and Charlie pursued the questioning with meticulous attention until Nurse Lawrence came in to say Torgerson was ready to be moved.

When the orderlies came into the room and moved the prisoner in his bed, Al and Charlie went along, not letting Torgerson out of sight.

On the second floor and in the med-surge room, the charge nurse asked Al and Charlie for a few minutes to get the patient settled. She showed them to the waiting room.

"How do you think it's going?" Al asked Charlie.

"So far, so good. We just got started."

"I know, but are we on the right track?"

"I think so, but we can't forget that our real interest is trying to find Shirley Sovereign or find out about her."

"Agreed. But we want to smash this ring, too."

Just as Al finished, a young nurse stuck her head in the door. "Mr. Torgerson is settled and waiting for you."

The room in which they found Torgerson was much more pleasant and less technology-driven than the one he had just left. The pale yellow walls and blue trim seemed dressier, somehow, and the absence of wall monitors and other beeping techno-equipment made the place seem more homelike.

"Wow, I like the new digs."

"I agree … now if the food is better, too, I'll be real happy."

Al and Charlie sat in the room's two chairs, Al with his notebook and pen ready.

"Let's get back to it then. You had just given us an updated list through Maisie Evans. We have names, addresses, aliases, and where you think they are now, right?"

"That's right, Al. I only included information that I was certain of—that I know to be the most recent. With some of the earlier women, they may have moved, and if they did, I wouldn't know about that."

"Okay, let's move on to a few other questions. Did you ever hear of Molly Grisham, Olaf?"

"Umm, yeah, that name is familiar. Was she one of the recruits from my area, maybe?"

Al and Charlie sat without answering, waiting for more from the prisoner.

"I think she was one of the recruits. Yes, I'm pretty sure she was. She was recruited before my time, I think. Was she from Hazard?"

"So you *do* remember her?" Al was hyped up now.

"I don't know her, if that's what you mean, but I do remember her being talked about. She was said to be an exceptional beauty. If I had to guess, it would have been maybe a couple or three years before I got into the business—2005 or so."

Al was surprised at the accuracy of his recollection. "It was 2004. She's back home with her parents now. When we talked to her in Chicago, she was anxious to leave the sex trade behind and return home. She was still afraid the Chicago crowd could find her, but she's really happy to be out of it."

"You know, Al, every girl has a different story. Maybe I am a bad guy, but like I told you, the girls I recruited were living in abusive situations, and if they had a chance to get out, I thought maybe it was a choice they ought to be able to make. But I never liked it, the recruiting of young women. In fact, I knew that, on the face of it, it looked like trading one bad situation for another. However, the girls I helped, that I've heard from, have been happier where they are now. But, to be honest, I liked the money, and after you've got it, it's hard to let go."

"Okay, Olaf, we believe you, and you're doing well here." Al was writing as Charlie kept track of the recorder. Torgerson took advantage of the lull to straighten up in his bed and take a sip of water.

"How about Shirley Sovereign? Ever hear that name?"

"Who hasn't? Isn't that the girl who was kidnapped in La Crosse a long time ago?"

"It is. She was 15 at the time. She was taken in 1979."

"She was the daughter of the professor, right?" When Al nodded, Torgerson said, "Yeah, I've heard of her. And she was kidnapped … or at least kind of. From what I heard, she'd been in Hazard plenty of times with the men who took her that night. She was the really young one—she convinced 'em she was 18. She was talked about as the cautionary tale—too young—and I was advised to not seek out anyone younger than 17. So hers is a story that was retold as a situation to be avoided.

As he made it through the last sentence he started to cough.

Charlie immediately jumped up, handed him the glass of water and knocked the recorder onto the floor.

"Damn, hope I didn't break it."

He held it up, looked at it, shook it and held it to his ear.

"You know, Charlie, if you keep shaking it, it *is* going to break. If it's still recording, just put it down."

Charlie set the small digital recorder onto the table with exaggerated care, and sat back in his chair. Torgerson held onto the water even though he leaned back on the bed.

"Okay to continue?" asked Al

"Yeah, fine. Just a little tickle."

"So are you saying that this wasn't really a kidnapping?" asked Al, frowning.

"No, no, I'm not saying that exactly. They said she was babysitting, and when they came by, and wanted either to take her down the road or have a little fun with her there, she got upset and told 'em to get lost. That didn't go over well. They left, according to what I've heard, and then decided to go back and get what they came for. When she refused, they decided to take her."

Again he paused for a sip of water, straightened his covers and moved the bed up a bit.

"So then what happened?"

"Well, the story goes that she fought like a banshee, all the way to Hazard. One of the guys was in the backseat with her and tried to undress her. Got her blouse, bra, and panties off, and threw them out the window. After they got her to Hazard and had their fun, they didn't know what to do with her—so someone took her to a woman who worked with the mob down in Richland Center. She took her in, calmed her down, and took advantage of how scared she was to talk her into going to work. Like I said, she was exceptionally beautiful, apparently, so there was big money to be made."

"Sounds like it was not exactly saving her from an abusive situation." But Al thought it was a fair outline of the contours of the story from the tape, and he looked at Charlie for his assessment. Charlie gave a small nod.

"Al, that's what I've been told. Fact is, that story is told every time we take on a new recruiter. It's told to illustrate the wrong way to recruit."

Just then the lights in the hallway began to flash and P.A. was activated. "Lockdown! Lockdown! All visitors are asked to leave immediately."

The charge nurse rushed in. "You've gotta leave," she shrieked. "We've got intruders and everyone has been ordered out."

"Ma'am," said Al, reaching into his coat and withdrawing his badge. "We're police officers. This is our prisoner. Didn't you know that?" Only now did Al realize that the officers from ICU hadn't followed them to the new room. *Where were they?* "There were supposed to be two officers outside this door." Al looked at Charlie, who had launched from his chair in full attack mode, ready for action. "In any event, we're not going anywhere. Understood?"

She glared at him, then whirled and left, saying something about "we'll see about that" and "my supervisor."

Charlie said, "I've got the outside, you've got the inside," and immediately drew his pistol. His arm cocked, aiming the gun at the ceiling, Charlie took his position outside the door to Torgerson's room. Al closed the door, locked it and placed a chair under the handle. Then he moved the prisoner's bed away from the door, slid the second chair into place opposite the door, drew his pistol, and sat down, ordering Torgerson to "stay put."

39

As Charlie took up his position in the hallway, he was on high alert. The floor was still. Nothing moved. Even the air circulating system seemed to have gone on alert, growing silent. In no time, Charlie's large frame was heating up, due to the lack of cooling. Sweat broke out on his head and soaked the armpits of his uniform. Gun up, his eyes constantly swept the unit—from the nurse's station ten feet away on his left to the fifty feet of hallway to his right. All doors were closed.

Then, he noticed a shadow slide across the floor from a stairwell near the end of the hall. He gripped the Glock with both hands, arms straight out from his shoulders. The Glock 17 was a large, black weapon that delivered a kill at fifty-five yards. It would take down an elephant, he had been told, but he had never had to fire it except on the firing range. He hoped that would still be the case when the day was over.

He melted back into the door frame—as best a large man of 6-foot-5 and nearly 300 pounds could melt into a tiny space. He steadied his aim with his right shoulder against the door frame.

As he watched, the shadow grew—first in length and then in girth—until a man emerged, dressed all in black, carrying an odd-looking machine pistol. Charlie recognized it—a Besa, manufactured by Mauser. It was nothing more than a pistol with an elongated barrel.

The gunman, wearing a mask, stepped cautiously into the hall—then took another step. He stopped abruptly as his eyes found Charlie—in full isosoles shooting stance—in the door frame, about forty feet away. The invader immediately raised the Besa to his shoulder—he and Charlie fired simultaneously. With the advantage of preparation, Charlie's bullet found its target. The gunman fell to the floor in a heap. The bullet his assailant had fired—Charlie looked around, then up—had lodged in the ceiling above his head.

Close but no cigar, you bastard.

Charlie began moving forward in a crouch, moving stealthily, taking a step toward the gunman. There was no movement. From his position, Charlie could not discern breathing, but he fantasized that the gunman was alive. Charlie took a second step, then a third.

As his right foot moved forward again, another masked figure crept from the stairwell and, prepared by the misfortune of his partner, fired twice down the hall before he was fully visible. One shot whined past Charlie, ricocheting off the tile wall as it continued its journey toward the nurse's station.

Distracted by the ricochet, Charlie felt a terrible burning sensation in his chest. He went to the floor, realizing he'd been shot. As he fell back, he got off a shot as the second assailant emerged from behind the wall.

The last sensation Charlie had was of oddly shaped pink clouds floating into view. Then everything went black.

***

Inside the room, Al was now crouched behind the bed, pistol drawn. He had locked Torgerson in the bathroom as shots were fired, and then had called headquarters on the private line reserved for emergency use. After the second round of shots were fired, Al silently prayed that his buddy was all right. His vigilance was heightened, his arms tensed. When all went quiet, he watched carefully as a minute passed, then two … three.

As three minutes stretched to four, he could stand it no longer. He moved to the door, taking great care to soundlessly disengage the lock, then, praying it would move silently, he pulled it toward him. Able to see little but a view across the hall and toward the nurse's station, he kept moving the door until he had to give up his cover and move around the door so he could access the hallway.

The first thing he saw was Charlie lying on the floor, a puddle of blood spreading outward from his body.

Resisting the temptation to both call out and rush, Al first studied the hallway, starting with the nurse's station, which was quiet and appeared unscathed. He slowly shifted his gaze to his right. He saw one person dressed in black spreadeagled on the floor, a gun lying near his right hand. As his eyes moved further, he realized there was a second body, also clad in black, lying at the top of the stairs. This person did not move—although, from his vantage point, Al could only see the head and part of the torso.

Crouching against the wall, Al duck-walked to Charlie. Although his friend's face was pale, he felt the pulse on Charlie's neck. Thready but steady. Charlie was lying on his back. With controlled panic Al realized he'd been shot in the chest. The left side of his uniform was soaked in blood that was steadily pooling out on the tile floor.

Silently praying that help might come swiftly to save his friend, Al continued his duck-walk down the hallway toward the other two bodies. When he reached the first body, he checked for a pulse. There was none. He removed the ski mask—it was a long, thin face crowned by stringy gray hair. The man was not breathing.

Al moved on quickly to the next figure. Removing the mask, he found a much younger male. This man was breathing and his pulse was strong and steady. At that point, Al stood and ran toward the nurse station. When he got there, he called out, "Anyone here?"

The charge nurse crawled out from a desk well, and two more nurses crept from under the desks where they were hiding.

Al quickly briefed the three on the situation, emphasizing that he could not say for certain that the danger was past. He told them there were two wounded men among the three lying on the floor of the unit, and the nearest one was a priority.

"I'll go with you," said the charge nurse. "You two stay here until we know that the danger is past."

Then she nodded and moved out from behind the counter, cautiously following Al to where Charlie was lying. She knelt, took his pulse, shook her head, and then, with Al standing guard, she ran to the nurse's station to grab bandages. When she came back, she quickly cut away Charlie's uniform shirt as Al watched—keeping an eye down the hall. The nurse then packed his chest with bandages to staunch the bleeding, nodded at Al and began to follow him toward the other two bodies.

Again, she knelt beside the first man, checked his pulse and shook her head. She moved swiftly to the second man, assessed the situation and again cut away his shirt. Ugly black blood was oozing from his lower abdomen.

"Gut shot," she said. "Not good." As she again pushed bandages against the wound, she looked up at Al. "Both these guys need to be in the E.R. We need help up here, but I'm not sure what the situation is."

Al helped her to her feet, and as they prepared to return to the nurse's station, footfalls echoed up the stairwell. Al pushed the nurse behind the wall, then took up a shooter's stance atop the stairs.

Suddenly, a shot shield moved into view on the landing, and behind it armed men in camo uniforms—the La Crosse County SWAT team. The second man in line recognized Al and ordered, "Stand down. Everything clear up there?"

"Near as I can tell, this area of the second floor is clear, but we have two men down—Charlie Berzinski and one of the assailants. Another assailant is dead. We need help to get Charlie and the other man to the E.R. while your team clears the other floors."

The SWAT leader ordered a man back to the E.R. to summon help, then the unit moved up the stairs and down the hall, clearing the second floor before moving on.

In what seemed seconds, the elevator door opened and several orderlies pushing gurneys moved onto the floor, and, with crisp directions from the charge nurse, quickly loaded Charlie onto a gurney. After two orderlies had swiftly moved the lawman to the elevator and disappeared, two more loaded the second wounded man for a trip to the E.R. The nurse then called for a third gurney to remove the dead man.

Slowly the floor began to return to normal. After hearing and observing what had gone on, Al was reasonably certain that the gunmen were looking for Torgerson. He returned to the room, knocked on the bathroom door, and told Torgerson it was safe to come out. Al then called Sheriff Dwight Hooper to tell him about Charlie and to ask for relief so he could go to be with his friend.

"I'll get someone there right away, Al. Just hold tight until the guard arrives, and I will meet you in the E.R.

After what seemed hours, but in reality was less than twenty minutes, the relief guard arrived. Al briefed him quickly then raced down the steps to the emergency room. As he burst into the E.R. waiting room, Sheriff Hooper held up his hand.

"He's in surgery, Al. That's all I know. They said they'd let me know when there was something to report."

The two officers sat side by side. Al silently prayed that his friend would recover. Finally breaking the silence, Al turned to the sheriff and said, "Dwight, I'm really sorry. When the alarm went off, I locked the prisoner in the bathroom and Charlie went outside to stand guard while I took up a post inside the room. If only I'd known. I'd gladly have changed places with …"

A tear slipped down Al's cheek, and the Sheriff put a hand on his shoulder. "Al, I know that. Had I been here, I would have, too. But we couldn't and we didn't. We can't change that. All we can do is wait and hope that he's going to be okay."

Tears streaming silently, Al summoned up the strength to say, "But Dwight, he took a bullet to the chest … near his heart. It didn't look good."

"Then we'll pray harder."

Al wiped at his face as the Sheriff settled back to wait, his hand still on Al's shoulder.

Two hours later, one of the young Drs. Gundersen pushed out of the treatment room, wiping his hands with a paper towel. His green operating room mask hung loosely around his neck, his hair was covered in a surgical cap, and his gown was splotched with blood. *Charlie's blood,* Al realized with fresh misery.

"Gentlemen, I'm Iver Gundersen. Your friend is alive, but that's all I can say. The bullet went through his chest. It nicked the epicardium on the left side and also scratched the aortic valve. He's far from out of the woods, but he's also one enormously fortunate man. If that bullet had been a hair to the right or left, it would have killed him. As it is, he'll be fighting for his life for the next couple of days, but he looks like a strong man, a fighter. Am I right about that?"

Al nodded at the Sheriff. "He's one of the toughest men I know. As for being a fighter, yes, he's that all right."

"Good. He's going to need every bit of that strength and fight to survive."

The doctor tossed the towel into a wastebasket, then turned to leave. As he reached the door, he turned back. "Gentlemen, if I were you, I'd go get some rest. There's nothing for you to do here. It will be several hours until we know anything definitive."

"I'm not leaving." Al had folded his arms over his chest as if daring anyone to dispute his intention.

"I'm not gonna argue with you," replied the Sheriff. "But I think I had better go and tell Kelly."

"God, yes, Kelly. How could I forget? If you'll bring me back, Sheriff, I'd like to go along, if it's okay with you."

Two lawmen, bearing the weight of the world on their shoulders, walked out of the hospital, headed for a meeting that would be heartbreaking.

40

Haggard and sleep-starved, Al Rouse held fast to the hand of Kelly Berzinski as they continued their vigil in the waiting room of the intensive care unit at Gundersen Lutheran Hospital. It had been forty-eight hours since Sheriff Dwight Hooper had dropped the two of them off at the hospital after the Sheriff and Al had delivered the message to his wife that Charlie had been shot. Since entering the ICU that afternoon, Charlie had been in a coma. During the last two days, the only trips that either of them had made from the room were to fetch coffee and an occasional sandwich.

As Kelly dozed, her head bobbing against Al's shoulder, he straightened, waking her, in spite of intentions to the contrary. "Is something new?" she asked, her voice tinged by drowsiness. "Not a thing. Go ahead, nap."

She placed her hand on his arm, rubbing it gently as she sat up. "Al, you need to get some rest. Why don't you go on home, have dinner with Jo Anne. Come back in the morning."

A wry smile touched his lips. "I smell that bad, do I?"

"Of course not, but you've been here and awake for forty-eight hours with me, Al, and you were here the full day before that, too. You need to get some sleep, have a meal, take a shower. It would do you good."

"Kelly, do you really think I could leave? Charlie's fighting for his life in there. I am not leaving, and that's final."

"Oh, Al, I'm sorry, I didn't want to sound mean about it. I just think you look so, so tired …"

Her voice faded as the smile on his lips spread, wrinkles appearing around his eyes. "I should sleep? I look tired? Kelly, you'd better take a look at yourself in a mirror. You've aged twenty years in the two days we've been here. Well, maybe only ten years." Kelly lightly punched him on the shoulder for that.

They had tried to buoy each other's spirits as Kelly's husband and Al's partner—and best friend—tenaciously held on to life in the very unit that, only the week before, was occupied by Olaf Torgerson.

As they sat there quietly, Kelly's head on Al's shoulder, fingers entwined, a nurse walked in and told them that Charlie was giving signs of awakening. She suggested they might want to be with him.

As wife and friend hurried into Cubicle 12, it seemed to Al that little had changed. The sterile room was a collection of tubes and wires, all leading to the lump in the quilts of the bed. Some burbled, others beeped, still others blipped. As they stood there, they watched the steady rise and fall of the shoulders under the covers—he was breathing deeply, but he was lying on his side, faced away from them. The ICU paraphernalia was everywhere. Tubes provided liquid channels of fluid in, and fluid out. Still other lines measured pulse and blood pressure, charted on a computer screen on a post beside the bed—evidence of the electrical activity of Charlie's heart. It was showing strong and regular rhythms, a good sign—but otherwise, nothing had seemed to change.

As they stood there, lost in thought, a tear trickled down Kelly's check. Although she quickly brushed it away, Al wrapped his arm around her shoulder. The ICU head nurse bustled in, checked the monitors, straightened the covers and, moving around to the other side of the bed, said, "Why, good morning, Deputy Berzinski. You're being a bit antisocial this morning. You have visitors and you've turned your back to them." She motioned Kelly and Al to join her.

When they moved to the other side of the bed, they found Charlie's eyes were open. They tracked them as Al and Kelly moved into view. When he comprehended it was Kelly, he tried to smile, struggled to turn his head a little, and then mumbled, "Hi, Babe ... sorry about all this."

As the nurse nodded, Kelly bent over, rubbed her husband's cheek, then touched his nose with hers. "You big lug—don't you 'sorry' me. You've been gone for a while, and I'm just grateful you're back. No need to talk. Just stay with me."

The nurse pushed a vinyl covered chair to the side of the bed. Kelly slumped into it and took Charlie's hand. Charlie mumbled something that sounded like "I'm still here ... gonna be here awhile, huh? ..."

The "huh" was punctuated with a yawn. Charlie's eyes fluttered. He yawned again. Then his eyes closed. This time they didn't reopen.

"I just started some pretty heavy drugs in the IV," the nurse told them. "It's important for him to rest, and sleep is the best kind of rest. I expect he'll be out for at least four hours. The good news is that the docs this morning said he is out of the woods. He's gonna get better, Mrs. Berzinski, but it's going to take a while."

Kelly took a deep breath and looked at the nurse. "Did they ... did they say how long he might be in here, and how long before he comes home?"

"No, far too early for that. I suspect they will keep him here with us for the next week or so before they transfer him to a regular room. He has a slightly enlarged heart, and a very serious wound. The problem with wounds like his is that infection is a real danger. We have him on an ultra-high dose of antibiotics."

Tears brimmed Kelly's eyes, but she kept herself composed, "I feel like I haven't cleaned up for days and days. I just really need a shower and a change of clothes."

"Honey, you need to take a break." The nurse was smiling and rubbing Kelly's arm as she responded. "Look, both of you, he's going to be sleeping for at least four hours. Why don't you head home and get cleaned up if you want to?"

Al looked at Kelly. "You know, Kelly, you could take my car and go home and clean up. I'll stay here with Charlie. Then when you're back, I'll go home for a shower. How does that sound?"

"Sounds like a plan," replied Kelly. "I just don't want him to be alone. You're sure you're okay with staying while I clean up?" She managed a brave smile, but tears threatened.

"Of course, it's okay."

Kelly looked down a minute, shook her head, then said, "Actually, Al, on second thought, I don't want to take your car. I should take a cab. I'm not sure I'd be a safe driver out there."

"Okay, here's what we'll do. I'll call the department and get a ride home for you. It's the least we can do. Then when you're done, you can call and they'll give you a ride back here. Sound good?"

"Do you think they'll mind? I don't want to be an imposition."

Within a few minutes, the arrangements had been made, and, ten minutes later, Officer John Fraser appeared at the ICU nurse's station.

Three hours later, Kelly and Al had made their separate trips home and back. Jo Anne, Al's wife, returned with him, bringing a basket of blueberry muffins for the ICU staff. They had all crowded together in Cubicle 12 for a few minutes before the head nurse came in and suggested they would be more comfortable in the waiting room.

"Trust me, I will come get you the second he's awake. But right now, there's coffee in the waiting room, and the muffins from Mrs. Rouse are wonderful—there are enough for you, too."

Enjoying one of Jo Anne's prize-winning muffins, Al called Chief Brent Whigg. "Any I.D. on the guy Charlie killed, Chief?"

"There is." Brent's voice boomed through the phone, loud enough for both Kelly and Jo Anne to hear. "He was a minor hood from Chicago. And the other guy, the one wounded, is singing like a cardinal in spring. The mob sent them to get rid of Torgerson, of course. Charlie was never the target. They just didn't expect him to greet them when they reached the second floor. It's a damn good thing they were focused on looking for Torgerson. Otherwise, a whole lot of people might have been killed." Then, changing subjects, the Chief asked, "How's the big guy doing, Al? Heard he woke up this morning."

"Sure did, but he's sleeping again. John Whorton stopped and picked up Kelly this morning—gave her a ride home and then a lift back. When I went home, Jo Anne came back with me. You're missing her blueberry muffins."

"Damn, wish I were there."

"There's plenty, Chief." Al laughed. "C'mon over."

"I'd love to Al, but I better pass. There's a lot going on this morning. But nothing you need to bother about—you take care of Charlie. But I'd better stay here."

"Sure, Chief. Thanks for letting me stay with Charlie, too."

"Can't have it any other way. You take good care of him, hear?"

"Yes sir, Chief."

"And Al, when you're sure he's out of the woods, I need to visit with you. Something big that I don't want to discuss over the phone, and nothing that needs attention today. But when the big fella is on the road to recovery, I need an hour of your time."

"Sure, Chief. Let me see what tomorrow brings."

"No, rush. I'll be here when you're ready to visit."

41

Wondering in the back of his mind about the Chief's request for a "visit," Al finally felt Charlie had sufficiently recovered by Friday afternoon to call Whigg and ask if he'd be free for breakfast the next day.

"Just so happens, you've got perfect timing. My wife's out of town with friends, and I'm batching it this weekend. And, it so happens, I've never been to Ma's. So how about I buy you breakfast there?"

The date made, Al left the hospital at six that Friday and headed home to spend a night in his own bed. Jo Anne suggested he had time to take a shower. "Dinner'll be ready when you are."

Al stood in a hot shower for half an hour, then finished off with two minutes of icy water, and appeared to be a new man at the dinner table, dressed in a T-shirt and freshly pressed jeans.

"You look like yourself again," Jo Anne told him. "I left a slow cooker on this morning when we left, so your favorite pot roast and potatoes are ready to dish up."

The next morning, Al was up at five. He poked around the house after dressing, read the paper, checked his email three times, and finally left for Ma's at quarter to seven.

When he arrived, the Chief was already there—a towering presence in his uniform, four stars on the collar of his shirt, and, as always, a box-cutter crease in his trousers. He saluted Al as his detective chief walked in the door, then clasped the arriving officer in a bear hug. Al directed the Chief to a table and said, "Welcome to Ma's, Brent. I think you're gonna like it here."

"I'm sure I will. I'm hungry as a bear and I have lots to share."

"And you're a poet, too." Ma hustled into the picture, wiping her hands on her apron and extracting an order pad from its pocket. "My goodness, rarely get royalty in here and never on a Saturday, that's for sure. Welcome."

"You must be Ma?" The Chief smiled warmly and extended his hand. Ma shook it, then gestured to a chair. "And you're Chief Whigg. I know from the pictures in the newspaper and on TV. What brings you in this morning?"

"My buddy, Al, has been crowing about this place for years, and I finally decided I had to experience it for myself. I must say, the smells are nearly hypnotizing. What are you baking up in the kitchen this morning, dear lady?"

Without hesitation, Ma told him, "Cinnamon rolls, my new friend. You'd better have one. But a big man like you needs more than that, much more. Eggs? Bacon? Biscuits and gravy? What can I get you?"

"A cinnamon roll for sure. But I think I'll also have a couple eggs, over easy, with toast and hash browns, too, if you have 'em."

"We do," Ma told him. "And they are the best, too, if I do say so myself."

"I'll bet they are. I just bet they are." The Chief took the chair at the left of the table and Al sat on the right, nodding and saying, "The usual, Ma."

"Sure you don't want a cinnamon roll, too?"

"Why not? I'll have one in Charlie's honor, and take one to go for him, too."

"How is that dear man?" Ma wanted to know. "Is he getting better?"

"He regained consciousness earlier this week. He's out of the weeds, the docs say. So that's good news."

"And the cinnamon roll to go will be on me," declared Ma. "And you tell him I said I want him well enough to come in and order one for himself."

"I sure will." Al tipped his cup in salute, then sipped the steaming liquid.

"Great coffee. Maybe even better than the brew you make." The chief raised his cup in Al's direction, then took a second sip, wiping his lips as he set the cup down.

"So," began Al, leaning toward his boss, "what is so important that you would meet me here early on a Saturday?"

The Chief smiled, then grew sober. He wiped his mouth again. "Lots to tell you. Important stuff, too."

"Talk now or wait for our food?"

The Chief leaned back and looked Al in the eye. "If you don't mind, I'd kinda like to just enjoy all of this for a moment or two." He looked around, taking in the lunch counter and it's six round-top stools from another century. The pale blue walls above a backsplash of red and royal blue, the six red and blue formica-topped tables for two and four showing the nicks and stains of time and heavy use.

Ma stood behind the counter, expertly watching the grill but occasionally casting an eye on her customers, exchanging wisecracks and witticisms as she flipped flapjacks with practiced artistry, and cracked eggs with the easy touch of someone who has done it for years.

"It ain't fancy," she said, noticing the Chief's eyes. "But the breakfast fare is the best in town … heck, best in La Crosse County."

"I've heard that," acknowledged the Chief, "and I'm hoping that my failure to get here sooner will not be held against me."

"Ignorance ain't no reason for retaliation," Ma asserted. "After this morning, you'll be a helluva lot smarter."

"Touché. I'm sure I will. I may be a slow starter, but I finish fast."

"Then you'll soon be a regular." Ma worked two eggs onto each of two plates, added hash browns from the grill, lathered four pieces of toast with butter, then picked up two smaller plates filled with cinnamon rolls topped with frosting oozing down the sides. She loaded it all up on a large tray and then bustled over to Al and the Chief. "There you go. Eat hearty." Then she was back at the grill, popping off to the new diners at the counter.

For the next five minutes the only sounds heard from Al's table were chewing and lip-smacking.

Ma returned with the coffee pot, surveyed the attack going on at the table, and declared, "Edible, right?"

"Exquisite," corrected the Chief. "Without question, the best in La Crosse.'

"That's my man." She topped off both cups and returned to the grill.

"Now I see why you and Charlie are regulars. What I don't see is how you manage to stay slim after breakfasts like these."

"We rarely eat like this, trust me. And, Charlie's gonna love the cinnamon roll. He's been on a diet for two months, but I think he's earned this treat."

"He surely has." Suddenly the Chief was serious, so serious the room even seemed to shrink. "So, here's the thing I wanted to talk to you about. Dwight has been talking to the docs, Al. They tell him that Charlie won't be going back to regular duty as a sheriff's deputy. His heart, the Sheriff says, won't allow it. His job will have to be a heckuva lot lighter, and less filled with action."

Al, studied the Chief's face, looking for signs of a joke. The look was deadly serious and unwavering. "You're not kidding, are you?"

"No, I'm afraid not. Kelly knows, and she's extremely worried. Says the lack of activity will kill him if his heart condition doesn't."

Al pondered the news, at first refusing to believe that his pal's days as an active officer were over. "What're we going to do? This is awful. Charlie's gonna feel like he got hit by a ton of bricks."

"We're afraid of that," agreed the Chief. "And that won't be good for him, either. So, we've come up with a plan."

Al looked the Chief in the eye. He said nothing as he waited for his boss to tell him what he and Sheriff had concocted.

"Al, at the end of October, I will have served in this office for twenty-five years. In November, I will be sixty-five. I've had a good run … heck, I've had a *great* run. I've enjoyed all of it—the good and the bad. But my wife and I have things we want to do. The kids are scattered—one in Massachusetts, one in Alabama, and one out in Oregon. What I really want to do now is buy a motorhome like the one you have sitting in your neighbor's garage. What I'm getting at here is that, when I hit my silver anniversary with the department, I want to retire. And Al, I want you to replace me. And we want Charlie to be your assistant chief."

Al was stunned. It was a lot to take in. He stared at Whigg, shook his head, and said, "Wait … wait, did I just hear you say you're retiring?" Al stopped. Then went on, "I guess that has to come sometime, but … you want *me* to be chief? Did I hear you right?"

The kind, fatherly smile that Al had seen repeatedly over the time he had served with Whigg spread over the Chief's face. "I think you heard me just fine, Al."

"But, Chief," argued Al, "You're too young to retire. You're in your prime, you're a great leader … and a great boss. Why would you think about stepping down now? You're not that old."

The Chief chuckled at Al's remark, then he shook his head. "Al, I am far past my prime. And I don't feel old, true, but that's also why I want to step down. I've had a good career—you've had a great deal to do with that, you know. I want to leave while I still have the energy to do the things I dream about. This *is* the right time."

"Is" was emphasized as the chief stabbed another bite of eggs and hash browns. "And you know Al," he said as he chewed, "I want you to take over. You're just the right person. And with Charlie, you'd be an unstoppable team."

Al sat there, dazed, thinking about what he had just heard. It was impossible to concentrate as his mind reeled, filled with thoughts about how it could change everything—and it was hard to believe the Chief was really serious and not just playing one of his pranks. Finally, he looked up, found the Chief's gaze and said, "You're really not kidding, are you?"

"No sir, I'm not. Completely serious. No need to respond right now, I know I've caught you by surprise. We'll have plenty of time to talk about this, and taking over the department, before October rolls around. But for now, I'd like to tackle that cinnamon roll. This place is as good as you have said … or, better yet, as Charlie has said. On that note, were you there when he woke up yesterday?"

"Just briefly. I thought he should spend the time with Kelly. She's really handling a lot. It was important that she have the chance to visit with him. His first conscious moments were pretty much filled with comments that were a little garbled. I'm hoping he did better the second time. I'm heading there after we eat."

"Good deal. Spend as much time as you want with him. Help with the situation. He'll listen to you. When the Sheriff tells him what the docs have said, you need to be there. You need to pick him up. This plan will take his mind off that message and give him something to think about."

As they finished, the Chief insisted on paying the bill. Ma let him know his next visit better be soon, and Whigg promised it would be. As they prepared to leave, the Chief put his hand on Al's shoulder. Opening the door with his other hand, he guided Al out the door.

"Now you give this some thought. The weekend will give you some time. Go over it withJo Anne. We'll talk next week."

Al was still a bit dazed as he got into his car, automatically going through the process of starting it and driving toward the hospital.

Crazy. Just plain crazy. That thought was going through his mind as he parked, then began his walk to the hospital and to the ICU on the fourth floor.

42

With dizzying speed, the weekend flew by. Al headed to work on Monday uneasy about the future and uncertain of his role in it. Charlie was improving, for which he was grateful, allowing Al to head back to a desk piled high with reports, most of them updating the many pieces of the investigation relating to sex-trafficking, and investigations that other officers had worked on. *I've never seen it this bad.* That thought filtered through his head as he surveyed the desk that looked as if a tornado had torn through it.

But with customary, systematic discipline, he began to work his way through the tidy stack of papers organized from the maelstrom. By noon, things requiring attention had been attended to. The rest could wait. He was worrying about Charlie and decided it was time to make a visit.

But, before departing for the hospital, he paid an important visit to Chief Whigg. "Brent, have you got a second?" he asked as he arrived at the office.

"Of course, c'mon in. How are you doing? And better yet, how was your weekend?"

"Confusing, to be honest. I'm still wrapping my head around why you think I have the tools to take over your job."

A broad smile wrinkled the Chief's face and he shook his head before responding. "Al, there is no doubt in my mind that you are eminently qualified to do this job. You're a great detective, you grew up in La Crosse, your colleagues respect you, and they listen to you without question. All of those are great reasons why you are my choice to succeed me. How about you stop doubting yourself and just agree that this move makes sense?"

"I'm still not sure you're right, Chief, but okay, let's for a moment agree that I'll take the job. Will Dwight want to lose his chief deputy?"

"Al, Dwight's nine years younger than I am. He knows that Charlie cannot continue in his current job because of the injury he just suffered. We have talked about this for several hours and both of us agree that you as Chief and Charlie as your assistant make for an unbeatable combination."

"So, let's say you convince me of that. Is it okay if I go ahead and talk to Charlie about this idea?"

"Dwight and I hoped you might want to do that. Yes, it's perfectly fine. But you two need to agree that you keep it between you and your spouses until Dwight and I have a chance to move it through the process, okay?"

"Sure, no problem with that. And you're not leaving until October, right?" After the chief nodded, Al continued. "Charlie and I still have to clean up the Shirley Sovereign case, you know. We are close. I think we can be done by October."

Al walked out of the LEC still mulling it over at a deep level. Although the birds were singing, he didn't hear them. Although the sky was blue and the sun bright, he didn't feel it. His mind was occupied with thoughts about what Charlie would say. *Will he be happy? Will he be angry? Will he ask about his current job? And what will I say if he does?*

Ten minutes later he walked into the hospital, went up to the fourth floor, and breezed into the ICU like it was a second home. He greeted the staff and saw that his friend was alone. "Is Kelly here somewhere?"

"I haven't seen her this morning. No, I don't think she is."

"Hi, buddy." He greeted his friend with a handshake and was pleased to feel the bone-crushing strength of Charlie's normal grip. "How're you doing this morning?"

"You know, Al, I feel pretty good. Better than I should, they tell me. Guess I escaped the devil by a hair. Guess God wasn't done with me here yet."

"Well, I don't know about God, but I sure as heck know *I'm* not done with you, that's a fact. And if you'd get your lazy butt outta bed, we've got work to do."

"You think I don't know? Well, get another thought. If they'll just let me out of bed, I'll be ready to go."

"You might think so, but you'd better listen to the docs and nurses—they're still in charge."

"That's what everyone says. Well … at least Kelly and you. But I'm getting antsy. Not much to do in here. You ever watched daytime TV? It ain't much fun."

"I imagine not, but while you're healing up, you can still help me out with the case we're working on. And when you get out of here, I have another job for you."

Charlie activated his bed, moving it into a sitting position. He pushed himself up a little in the bed, wincing as he did, causing Al to say, "Guess that won't be today, huh?"

"Guess not." Charlie's face was screwed into a grimace. He held that pose for a few seconds, then said, "It only hurts a little when I move."

"I can see that. There's no hurry, you know—you can work from here until you're given the green light."

Charlie stared at him, his face relaxing, then he growled, "I may not be ready today, but I just might be tomorrow. By the way, what'd they do with Olaf?"

"He went upstairs. I haven't seen him since you were sh … I mean since you became a patient. I think I'll go up and see him later."

"Yeah, he was spilling it pretty good, last I remember," affirmed Charlie

"Say, Charlie, I've got something to ask you."

Charlie scrunched a pillow up a bit higher, then straightened. "Well, ask away."

Al moved a chair over closer to the bed, sat down, and hunched forward with a steady look at his friend, "I've been asked to consider becoming the next chief of police."

The statement hung there, Al trying to figure out where to go next, but he thought he'd wait for Charlie to answer.

"Well, geez, that ain't news. Who else they gonna get when Brent steps down? Who else is as qualified? Hell, Al, no one's got more savvy than you. Of course, they're gonna ask you. You're a natural."

For Charlie it was a pretty long speech, delivered with his customary spunk, but he seemed to lose a little steam as he finished. Al let him rest for a moment. "I wish I were as certain as you are about that. Seems like a darn big step to me. Not sure I'm cut out for a desk job."

"Well, hell, Al, that's what assistant chiefs are for." This response was a little softer, and it left Al at a loss for how to break the news on that score.

Leaning forward in his chair, scooting it a little closer to the bed, he said, "Well, that's kind of the point. Not sure how to say this, but I told the Chief the only person I'd want in that job is you."

A wry smile moved across the patient's lips. "Figured that was coming. You're about as subtle as a ton of bricks … you and your co-conspirators."

Shocked, Al sat back and stared at his friend. "Oh, come on." Charlie was ready for him, and let it come out slowly and thoughtfully. "You know, Al, every nurse I have … and Kelly … and the Sheriff … all of them 'been talking at me all weekend … all of them talking about the future and what it might be like for me. It's pretty obvious that I'm not gonna be allowed to go back to full-time duty in my old job." His voice was still strong, and he kept going. "So, it seems to me that I'm either gonna captain a desk or find a new career. I been thinkin' about the options, and they ain't too numerous."

Al took that in, Charlie's having sorted it all out. "Well, then, teaming up with me should be on your list of options." Al gazed at his friend, trying to gauge the look on Charlie's face. Wheels in his friend's head were turning at high speed. Al got up and walked to the window and watched the traffic passing on South Avenue, his arms folded behind his back.

"And I guess, while you're thinking about that," he began looking back over his shoulder, "maybe we should also think about next steps in finding Shirley Sovereign and how we're going to break up this sex trafficking ring."

"Now that's a helluva fine idea." Charlie waited a beat, and then said, casually, but with a firm undertone, "Besides, I don't need to think about the other thing. If that was a formal offer, I'm in."

Al turned around and gave Charlie a relieved smile, and a look of deep regard. "You honor me with that, Charlie Berzinski. Best thing you could have ever said," affirmed Al. In the long look that passed between them, the two lawmen made a silent pact, sealing the deal.

"Tell you what, I'll be by tomorrow, but we'll plan on you getting mostly a lot of rest through the weekend—to get you healed up. Come next Monday, I'll try and have all the details pulled together, and we'll talk about what we want to do about breaking up the sex ring, and then plan out our search for Shirley. Sound good to you?"

"Sounds great … partner."

43

"How're ya doin', pal?"

Charlie's voice boomed through the ICU as Al stuck his head into Cubicle 12 on Monday morning. The big chief deputy was sitting up in a chair, and the smile on his face was reminiscent of the "old Charlie," as was his voice—full and low, with a special richness of timbre.

"My goodness, what's happened to you? You look like you're ready to go home. Where's the guy who inhabited this room who was knocking at death's door?"

Charlie's face suddenly broke into a brilliant smile—crinkling his face from ear to ear and across his forehead. There was a ruddiness to his cheeks that wasn't there the day before, and it appeared to Al that his good friend had, indeed, made it all the way back.

"Had a great night. Bless 'em, they didn't even wake me for pills. Been waitin' for you. Anxious to get to work."

"Great, then that's just what we'll do. But I gotta head out about ten. Want to catch Brent after his news conference so he can talk to Dwight, and they can begin to plan the transition. They said anything to you about when you're getting out of here?"

"I'm leavin' here today or tomorrow. Should be home before the weekend, they say. That's progress, ain't it?"

"It sure is," said Al, who couldn't help hugging his friend.

"Easy, easy, don't want anyone asking questions, do we?"

"Let 'em, I don't care."

Al pulled up a chair, grabbed a notebook from his backpack. For the next two hours, the two officers explored together every aspect they knew about the Shirley Sovereign case, as well as the suppositions formed during their investigation. Charlie stayed with it the whole time, not once wavering or asking to rest. To Al, it was as if his pal had changed bodies, exchanging the wounded one for a newer model that was healthy and vibrant and ready to act.

Finally, as they worked through the action plan for the third time, Al asked, "We've been at this for a long time. Sure you want to continue?"

"Damn right, I'm sure. I'm so damn sick of that bed over there, it's about time they got me up." Then sobering, he told Al, "You know, this is a great day. Not one tinge of pain. I feel great."

Finally, Al put down his pen. Charlie leaned back in his chair but he made no claim of weariness, nor did he look as if he was spent. In fact, he looked more like he was ready to race from the hospital and apprehend a bunch of bad guys.

"This is some transformation," acknowledged Al as he shrugged into his jacket. "I am very impressed with your improvement from yesterday to today, even."

Charlie smiled at him. "Last night, just before bedtime, I began to feel like a million bucks. It was like some magic potion had kicked in and stamped out all the bugs. Felt that way when I woke up, too. Best part is, the nurses noticed. Can't wait for the docs to come in. Gonna put the arm on 'em. Get 'em to release me."

"Well, just don't push it, okay? We don't need a relapse because you did too much too soon."

"Al, for God's sake, I been in this place … what … eleven days? Seems like half a lifetime. I'm ready to get outta here. Trust me."

"Okay, but do what they tell you, please. That's gonna get you out of here a whole lot quicker."

As Al moved to the door, he turned back and waved to his buddy. "See you later, pal."

"Yup, but check when you come in. I'll be in a new room. I'm sure of it."

As Al walked to the elevator, he caught himself whistling. *Charlie's high spirits were contagious*, he thought to himself with a smile.

Later, at work, he met with Chief Brent Whigg to report on his work with Charlie that morning and on the remarkable recovery his friend had made over the weekend.

"Honestly, Chief, it's like a miracle. He looks and sounds like the old Charlie. He thinks he's getting out—and I won't be surprised if he does."

The Chief greeted the news with a nod of the head and a grin, then looked up at Al, his grin widening to a wide smile of genuine satisfaction. "So, looks like Dwight and I have work to do. I'll talk to him this afternoon."

"And I have lots to do getting ready to go after these sex traffickers—and then, ultimately, we'll see if that roundup can lead us to Shirley Sovereign."

Fifteen minutes later, Al was talking to Detective Steve Scranton in Chicago, briefing him on the work he and Charlie had done earlier, and bringing him up to speed on what Olaf Torgerson had reported.

"So, do you know this Scarface Frenetti?"

"Oh, we know him all right," reported Scranton, "but he's as elusive as a ghost. In fact, some of my colleagues call him "Phantom" Frenetti. He's hard to catch … and even harder to find."

"Do you think you could pick him up on a warrant from Wisconsin?"

"Well, Al, Wisconsin warrants are good in Illinois. You know that. I'd be happy to lead the effort, but I can't promise anything. Maybe if we put out an APB on him we'll get lucky."

"I'll have the warrant to you as quickly as I can find a judge," promised Al. "Keep your eye on your inbox."

"I sure will, pal. While I wait for the warrant, I'll get the word out that we may want him, and see if we can get something on his location."

"Back to you soon."

44

A l scrambled to put the warrant together—seeking one Albert "Scarface" Frenetti on suspicion of sex trafficking—then talked to Chief Whigg. Al got Whigg to sign off, then went to the La Crosse Courthouse looking for a judge. As he was walking up the steps to the building, he bumped into Judge A.L. Twesme, a circuit judge from Trempealeau County.

"Just the guy I'm looking for." Al shook hands with Twesme who greeted him warmly. Al told the judge briefly about his quest for a signature on the warrant he carried. Twesme agreed to sign it, but suggested it would be better if John Pzytarski, a La Crosse County judge, could be located.

They entered the Courthouse together and Judge Twesme led Al around turns in two corridors before opening an unmarked door. "Well, there you are, just as I suspected." Twesme led the way into a large well-furnished room that held a tufted red leather sofa, a large legal bookcase along one wall, a table with two casebooks spread open for study, two wingback leather easy chairs, and a TV tuned to the local news station that Judge Pzytarski had been watching. Twesme sat down in the wingback near Pzytarski, then said, "Al's looking for a signature on a warrant, John. Told him I'd sign it, but that it would be better if we could find you. And here you are."

Al smiled as he glanced around the handsome room before his attention returned to Pzytarski. He pulled the warrant out of his pocket. "We're hot on the trail of a sex trafficker, Judge. We need to question him about a number of things, including the Shirley Sovereign kidnapping."

The judge extended his hand, took the warrant, opened it and began to read. "Says here you and Charlie want to talk to this guy. Thought Charlie got shot." The Judge looked up at Al, waiting for an answer.

"Yes, sir, Charlie's still in the hospital, but he's out of intensive care and making a remarkable recovery. The Chief, the Sheriff, and I conceived a plot to keep him busy and relatively quiet while he convalesces. But he's worked this case with me from the beginning. Didn't want to leave him out now, not after what he's been through."

"Glad to hear he's recovering. Well, how about you two have a cup of coffee with me—just help yourself over there—and then we'll head up to my office in a few minutes and get this thing signed."

Not wanting to appear to impatient, he followed Twesme to the coffee urn, dispensed a cup for himself, turned back to survey his options, and decided to try out the sofa.

He sat down, took a sip, and then winced as the coffee seared his lips and tongue.

"Oops, forgot to tell you about that," said Pzytarski, shaking his head. "That urn produces the hottest coffee on the planet. Shoulda warned you."

The three watched the news for a while as Al and Twesme carefully sipped their coffee, averting further disaster. Finally, Pzytarski said, "This sex trafficking thing? Sounds pretty interesting, especially when you mention the name Shirley Sovereign. I was new to the bench when that happened, but it sure shook up the people of La Crosse. They never found her body, did they?"

"No, Judge, they didn't," replied Al. "In fact, we have reason to believe she is alive and being kept somewhere in the Caribbean."

"Now that's a story I'd love to hear," said Pzytarski, "but we better stop there. Don't want to ruin my chance of presiding over that case if it comes to court in La Crosse County. Well, gentlemen, let's head to my office and get this thing signed."

Ten minutes later, Al was finally on his way back to his office to fax the warrant to Scranton in Chicago. That done, he popped his head into the Chief's office, told him about Judge Pzytarski and faxing the warrant to Chicago, then said, "I think I'll head to the hospital to bring Charlie up to date, and then maybe I'll take an early lunch."

"Say hi to Charlie for me. Tell him I will be up to see him one day this week."

As he had been talking to Al, the Chief was shuffling through several papers before finding what he was looking for, then picking up the telephone and dialing a number. Chief was clearly busy. "See you later, Chief," Al said as he turned and retraced his steps to his office, grabbed his coat and hat, and headed out of the building to see his friend.

Al found Charlie strolling the halls of the ICU, pushing the mast that held his IV bag. When he saw Al, he waved.

"You supposed to be doing that without a nurse helping you?"

"Ya know, Al, you're as bad as the rest of them. You all think I'm helpless. Well, I got a message for you: I am a helluva lot better and stronger than you think. So just get the hell out of my way."

Al and the nurses were laughing now. Al raised his hands in self-defense. "Okay, okay, big guy, just relax. Just finish taking your walk."

Settling into a chair in Charlie's corner cubicle, Al tilted his head back, closed his eyes, and began to think of all that lay ahead. Just as he was forming a plan, he heard the muffled din of metal scraping across the floor.

"Lost a wheel, dammit," as his friend came into the cubicle. "Ya know, Al, they just don't make stuff like they used to."

Al was laughing again as two nurses rushed into the room, one pulling a new standard—this one with four wheels.

"Here, let me change that," said the nurse with the new standard.

"Don't have to change it on my account. I don't plan to be here long. And that's defined as in minutes … maybe seconds."

"So, just what's going on here?" The speaker was a tall man. He wore a white jacket with the Gundersen Lutheran insignia on the pocket. He had a shock of snowy white hair that fell in gentle waves across his forehead. His blue eyes twinkled. All in all, he looked like a guy you'd want to go fishing with.

"Oh, hi, doc." Charlie, sitting on the edge of the bed, struggled to present a more modest view to his visitor.

"Never mind, Charlie. I'm pretty sure nothing you expose will shock me."

Charlie's face flushed, but, never caught off guard, he quipped, "Yeah, but what about the nurses? Don't want 'em all twitterpated, now do we?"

"I'm pretty sure, Charlie, you aren't going to shock them either."

Charlie looked ready to retort, then, thinking better of it, said instead, "Doc, I'm fine as can be. Can't you let me out of here? My wife's a nurse. How about we let her take me off your hands?"

The doctor studied his patient for a moment, hand on his chin. Then he picked up the chart from its saddle at the end of the bed and studied it.

"Says here you are doing well. Looks like all your vital signs are right where they should be."

"Well, heck, I coulda told ya that. So how about it? Let me go home."

The argument went back and forth for several minutes, the doctor talking about the severity of Charlie's wound, the danger of infection, and the fact that it wasn't his practice to transfer patients directly from the ICU to home.

Charlie's counter-arguments were just as forceful. "Now doc, we both know that there's far more chance of me getting an infection here than at home. We also know that there's better use of this space than me hanging out in it. The nurses here are great, but they're already overworked. Why not lessen the burden by sending me home?"

"You make a compelling argument," admitted the doctor, "but let's take a look at the wound and see how that's going. Roll over on your side, will you, please?"

Charlie quickly complied and the doctor took a pair of surgical scissors from his jacket pocket and gently snipped away at the gauze covering the wound, then deftly stripped back the bandage and ripped away the tape in a quick action.

"Hey. That hurt." Charlie was resting on his elbows and looking back at the doctor, a grimace on his face.

"A big, strong guy like you bothered by a little owie? Really?"

"Doc, a little owie? A wound from an AK-47 is not a little owie … it's a big, bad hole, and you know it."

"You're right, Charlie. It is a big, bad hole. And although it's looking good, you have sort of made my case for keeping you here a few more days."

Charlie was incensed. "That's entrapment, Doc. You led me into that. That's not fair … not fair at all. You should let me out of here on that basis alone."

"That basis alone? You must be kidding. You said it, Charlie. You made the point better than I could have."

"Awww, Doc," said Charlie as he started to roll onto his back.

"Cut that out, Charlie. I have to pack and rebandage that wound. You're not being very cooperative."

"Okay, okay, I get it. Sorta like good-cop-bad-cop and I was my own bad-cop foil. Now my plan to go home is screwed, right?"

"Right."

45

wo days later, Al rushed into Charlie's new room on the main medical floor at Lutheran Hospital. "Damn, I wish you were out of here," the detective told his wounded colleague. "I just heard from Steve Scranton and they took Scarface Frenetti into custody last night with our warrant. I'm gonna head down there tomorrow."

"Well, just what the hell makes you think I'm not fit enough to go along?"

The big deputy was wrestling with his covers and attempting to sit up in his hospital bed. As Al watched, Charlie raised the head of his bed until he could sit on his own, whipped his legs out from under the covers and over the side of the bed, then, lowered the head of the bed.

"No sense lettin' 'em know I need a little crutch to sit up. You see Dr. Gundersen on your way in here?"

"No sign of him," admitted Al, "But don't you think you'd be better off staying here through the weekend and then thinking about going home Monday?"

"You know, Al, you still sound like a damn nurse." There was a rustle at the door, and Charlie looked up to find a tall, gray-haired lady in a stiffly starched white uniform standing there. "Ooh, sorry nurse." Charlie was grimacing now and the nurse, who had turned toward Al, seemed amused to have caught out her patient not only with a wise crack, but also clearly in the act of mutiny.

"Deputy Berzinski, you know you are supposed to call when you want to move in any way from your bed ... and that includes hanging your legs over the edge."

"I know, I know, Nurse Stedman, but I'm feeling so damn ... er, so darn good that I just forget calling for help. I feel so good, I was just thinking I'd call Kelly and tell her I'm ready for her to come take me home."

"You were thinking that, were you?" she said in a sweet, teasing voice. "Well, *I* was just thinking what would happen if I accidentally bumped into that big ol' bandage on your side as you went out the door. How 'good' do you think you would be feeling *then*?"

"Now that would be nasty, wouldn't it? But you wouldn't do that, would you?"

The nurse just smiled, then shook her head and turned to leave, winking as Al as she did.

As Al looked up, Charlie was also shaking his head. "You know, Al. This strategy isn't working."

"And what strategy would that be?"

"Well, for a few days, I was really nice. That didn't work. They were just as crabby and just as tough as ever. Then I tried being just as crabby as they were. That didn't work, either. So now I'm just being me. Don't seem to work, either, does it? What the hell do I gotta do to get outta here? I miss Kelly like crazy, and they don't allow no conjugal visits in here, either. You know that?"

"Well, Charlie, what the heck do you expect? You think they want you breaking your stitches? Especially in some kind of 'conjugal' recreation? Seems to me that would make a really big mess."

"That's the whole point. If they let me outta here, any mess we make would be at home. That would be better, wouldn't it?"

"I suppose it would," agreed Al, chuckling, "but Kelly might not appreciate having to do all of the cleaning up."

"Heck, Al, she's horny as me. Neither one of us can hardly stand to be in the same room, the way it is now."

"Well, buddy, I don't think I can help you with that problem, but how about we chat a bit about my trip to Chicago?"

"How about *'our'* trip, Al? I'd like that better."

"So would I," agreed Al, "but even if that were the case and they discharged you today, do you really think they'd approve a drive to

Chicago tomorrow? If you even mention it, it might land you a few extra days here."

"Well, who the hell would be stupid enough to tell 'em about a trip? I'm a helluva lot smarter than that, Al."

"Charlie, I'd like to get down to business here. And let's just agree that you won't be going. I think it would be much better if we just left it at that."

"It might be, but I wanna hear the guy. I wanna ask him my questions."

"I know that, Charlie." Then suddenly Al had an idea. "What about …" he began, "what if we put you on a speaker phone so you can participate that way?"

Charlie shot Al a look of pure gratitude. "Al, that's a terrific idea … great. Yes, let's do it that way."

The two friends and fellow officers spent an hour and a half strategizing. About halfway through their planning session, Dr. Gundersen arrived to check on Charlie. He "oohed" and "aahed," poked and prodded the patient, then said, "Charlie, you're doing great. Let's see, today's Thursday. I think we might be able to let you go home on Saturday."

Charlie's face took on a sour look. "I was hopin' it might be today, doc."

"Makes sense. Yesterday you hoped it would be today. And two days ago you hoped it would be day before yesterday. And I think you're just about ready. I think Saturday is a great day to send you home. And around here, Charlie, I have the badge," pointing to the hospital logo on his pocket. Then relenting a little with a half-smile, "Well, maybe not exactly, but my word *is* the law, you know."

"Yeah, guess it is." Charlie looked crestfallen. Then he brightened. "But doc, me and Al are working on a really important case … a really big one. Al's going to Chicago tomorrow to interview a guy we need to talk to. He needs me to participate. He said so. Think we could get a speaker phone in here?"

"I think you have one in here already, Charlie." The doctor

pointed at the phone on Charlie's bedside table. "And if Al needs you on the call, well then, you folks can use that."

Having issued all necessary declarations to his satisfaction, the doctor strode from the room—then poked his head back in and looked at Al. "Just don't get him too riled up, okay?"

"Absolutely," promised Al.

Suddenly Charlie seemed to have forgotten going home and was focused on the call the next day. He made Al stay as they finished up strategizing and planning the questions they would ask.

Finally, that task done, Al prepared to leave. As he stood, Charlie shifted his legs back into the bed and lowered the bed a bit.

"Now, Al, remember, you don't start without me."

"Got it."

46

J ust after 10:30 a.m. the next morning, Al was seated at a table before a glass window in the Police Control Detention facility at 1718 State Street. The weather outside was cool and when Al sat down, he shivered just a bit after experiencing the cold wind that blew off Lake Michigan giving rise to Chicago's nickname: The Windy City. At both his left and right hands were telephones. Al had called ahead to make sure there would be a way to dial Charlie into the interrogation.

The door on the opposite side of the room beyond the glass opened and two guards led a man in shackles into the area. The prisoner shuffled across the room. He slumped into a chair, then waited as the guards fastened his chains into brackets in the concrete floor. Now fully secured, he sat back in the chair and glowered at Al. The reason for his nickname was obvious. A scar ran from the corner of his right eye to just below his bottom lip. His jet-black hair was unkempt and the smile on his face might have qualified as a sneer.

As the prisoner gazed at him, Al picked up the phone near his right hand and introduced himself. That done, he told the prisoner, "Mr. Frenetti, I have a partner recovering from a gunshot wound. I am going to dial him into our discussion. Any objection?"

Frenetti shifted in his chair, sitting up a bit straighter. Then he nodded slightly.

That done, Al dialed the number he had brought with him. Charlie answered on the first ring, sounding as if he was next to Al. Al made the introductions. "Mr. Frenetti, on the phone is La Crosse County Chief Deputy Charlie Berzinski. Charlie?"

"I'm here. Let's get goin'."

Now Al leaned forward, moved the microphone closer to him, and said, "Mr. Frenetti, you are being held on suspicion of sex trafficking. You know that, right?"

"Yeah, but I don't know nothin' about that. And let's skip the Mr. Frenetti shit. Call me Scarface."

"Okay, Scarface, why don't you give us your full name and we'll get started."

"Carl Franetti." The prisoner's response bordered on brashness.

Al quickly interrupted. "Mr. Baldelli ... Scarface ... you realize that your cooperation may have a lot to do with how your case is handled, right?"

"Yeah, that's what you cops always say. But it don't make no difference. I don't got nothin' to hide."

"Scarface, Deputy Berzinski and I are investigating a series of cases in the La Crosse area. We have one young woman we picked up in Chicago a few months ago who says she was brought from our area to Chicago and forced into prostitution. Her name is Molly Grisham, but you know her as the Platinum Princess. Do you recognize those names?"

Frenetti immediately started to respond, but sensing what he was about to say, Al held up his hand. "Scarface, think carefully about your answer. If you try to play dumb and refuse to cooperate, I think the authorities here will throw the proverbial book at you. Conversely, if you cooperate, it will help you a lot. Now, you were about to say?"

"I was gonna say, yah, I know that name. She disappeared last winter."

"That's right." Charlie was talking now. "And she has told us all about you and your operation. So, as Al said, your cooperation is not only requested but it will be helpful to you, too."

Scarface contemplated what he had just heard, then looked up at Al. "She used to work with me. She was a good girl and a great friend. I hope she's okay?"

"She is," reported Al, "and when we talked to her a couple of days ago to ask her about a specific woman who disappeared from La Crosse, she said she was sure you could help us."

"Her name," broke in Charlie, "is Shirley Sovereign. Remember her?"

Scarface grimaced, tilted his head from side to side … seemed to be thinking intently.

"Well?" Charlie's voice echoed out of the speaker.

"I'm thinkin', goddammit, gimme a minute." The response was in the form of a short, snappy, sarcastic remark.

After several minutes, Frenetti straightened in the chair, leaned forward and pulled the microphone toward him. "Yah, I knew her. Went with her for a while, too. We dated on the side. Good girl. Beautiful. Pleasant. A great piece of ass."

"Do you know what happened to her?" asked Al.

"Well, she got too old for Chicago. Her regular Johns started dying. Even the mayor partied with her a few times. Then there were none of her guys left. The younger guys wanted younger chicks."

Frenetti sat back, and began to examine his finger nails. He didn't look up, nor did he say anything.

"And then," prompted Al.

Frenetti slowly leaned forward into the microphone. "Well, the syndicate did with her what they do with all the aging hookers." He stopped, appeared somewhat startled, and looked Al in the eyes. "Forget I said that, okay? If anyone knew I did, I'd be in deep shit. Understand?"

"Forgotten." Al paused. Frenetti continued to stare into his eyes, as if wanting to continue.

"So, then what happened to her? Any idea?"

"Well …" Frenetti paused, again looked down at his hands and again contemplated his finger nails.

"Well?" Al was growing impatient.

"Well, if ya promise to keep this between us, I'll tell ya."

"You know I can't make that promise. But I can assure you I won't tell anyone in Chicago. How's that?"

"I guess … good enough."

Again he paused, again studied his hands, then lifted his head.

"Yah know, Rouse, you seem like a straight shooter. Can't see your partner … can't look him in the eye. He as straight as you?"

"You damn right." Charlie's voice echoed from the speaker. It was sharp and forceful.

"Okay, then, I'll help, but ya gotta promise to try an' make it count for somethin' here, okay?"

"You know we will," pledged Al.

Frenetti began to tell the story on Shirley Sovereign. "Shirley—we called her Sweet Momma—was a great gal. Told us she'd had a helluva life in La Crosse. Folks too strict. She had a wild hair, too, I can tell ya. Great in the sack, know what I mean?"

Al nodded, Charlie grunted and Frenetti was off again, "Made us a lotta money, that one. For years, she was a steady $10,000-a-week-girl. Johns loved her. I'm guessin' she made that much in tips, too. Girls are supposed to turn over tips, but I don't think we ever get the full amount. She was a smart one, too. I imagine she left here a rich gal."

"Smart … how?" Al was interested in what would come next.

"Well, we're supposed to split 50-50 with the woman, see. But most of 'em put all their share up their noses. Coke. Some need heroin. Even more, speed. It's a racket … and a good one. Sweet Momma was different. She tried drugs at first, then quit cold turkey. So she prob'ly left here with lots of cash in the bank."

"Left here for where?" asked Charlie.

"When women's stipends fade, we send 'em to the islands. In the South Atlantic. Lots of retired mob bosses down there—Cuba, Virgins, even Costa Rica. It's a great deal. We get a big payday and the retired John gets a housegirl. It's not a bad deal for 'em—or at least it can be a good deal."

"How's that?" Al wanted to know.

"If the woman's been good to us, she goes away with the ability to select her John. If she's high all the time or tries to cheat, she gets the trash. Shirley, I'm sure, got to pick."

"You don't know where she went?" queried Al.

"I don't. I coulda found out, I just never asked," the mobster told Al.

"Any chance you can find out now?"

"Al—it's Al, right?" Al nodded. "Al, I can prob'ly find out some-thin'. But no one is gonna tell me a thing while I'm in here. And if they knew I talked, the chances of me gettin' any information would be as good as me stealin' all the gold in Fort Knox, know what I mean?"

"Okay, makes sense," said Al. "Charlie, any other questions?"

The three men then talked about general issues, without pushing the Shirley topic.

Looking at his watch, Al realized ninety minutes had passed. He leaned forward and said, "Look Scarface, you've been helpful. We'll make sure to put in a good word for you."

"How about gettin' me outta here?"

"Not sure I can do that," Al told him, "but let me see what I can do."

Al rose from his chair, tapped the window two times in a gesture that meant "good talk." Frenetti, unable to reach the window, tapped the microphone twice on the desk.

Moments later, Al was in his car and talking to Charlie. "Charlie, I gotta go over and see Steve Scranton. Any reason I shouldn't tell him Frenetti was very helpful?"

"Hell, no," replied Charlie, "he was very helpful … cooperative as he can be. Don't suppose we can spring him, can we?"

"Don't know. That's what I'm going to talk to Steve about."

With Charlie's "good luck" echoing in his ears, Al started the car and headed for Scranton's office in the same building.

He walked into the brick building and was recognized by the receptionist—who told him Scranton was waiting for him.

"You know where the lounge is, right?"

He assured her that he did, then opened the swinging gate and walked toward the back of the building. Scranton had coffee poured for him and Al quickly briefed him on the discussion, emphasizing

Frenetti's boast about being able to find out where Shirley Sovereign was if he was out of jail.

"Any possibility of making that happen?" Al wanted to know.

"I think so." Scranton was smiling conspiratorially. "We've got him in on a 72-hour hold, so, unless we charge him, we have to let him go. I was surprised when we picked him up that he didn't immediately call the lawyers. We even told him he could, but he said he didn't need to. I'd like to emphasize, though, that he's getting out because of you. I'd like to tell him that if he fails to get us the information you requested we're gonna pick him up again."

"What if he runs?"

"Al, if he runs, he becomes somebody else's problem, and that's just fine with me."

"If you're just gonna let him go, can I go along when you do it?"

"Sure, we can do it now. Let's go."

***

Back in front of Frenetti a few moments later, Al referred to Scranton, nodding in Scranton's direction, and telling the mobster he had good news.

"Detective Rouse tells me that you were uncommonly helpful," Scranton said. "He tells me that you will be even more helpful if you are out of here. That true?"

Frenetti nodded his head vigorously. "Yes sir."

"Okay, Frenetti, here's what I'm gonna do. I'm gonna go to the judge and see what I can do. If you get out and don't help, though, we're gonna come get you again, got it?"

"Yes sir."

"Okay, I'll see what I can do."

As they walked out the door, Scranton said, "I'll let him stew for an hour or two, then come over and let him out."

"That'd be great. Can you emphasize that he needs to come back to you with any message for me? Maybe that'll help."

"Great idea, Al. Yup, that's what I'll do."

***

The two men shook hands, Al got into his car, headed away from Lake Michigan, and picked up I-90 West. When the traffic cleared, he dialed Charlie's number.

"I think we've got a good plan," he told Charlie. "In about two hours, Frenetti's going to be a free man. Scranton's gonna let him go with a stern message that if he fails to produce in short order, he'll be back in jail.

"Hallelujah." Al could almost see Charlie smiling. "Now all I gotta do is get outta here and we can get ready to go get her."

"Charlie, it may not be that simple," Al told him. "Let's see what happens before we head for the islands, okay?"

"Sure, Al, that's fine. But you've given me something to dream about."

47

Three days later, Al was getting anxious. He had heard nothing from Chicago. He decided a visit to Charlie was in order. The big guy had gotten out of the hospital the day before and was home with his wife, Kelly. Al decided she might need a break, and told the Chief he was heading out to pay a visit to Charlie.

"Think he'll be ready to travel if you get the information you're hoping for?"

"Not sure that I know the answer to that one, boss, but I'm pretty sure *he* will think he's ready. Guess we'll just have to see."

"Well, say hi to him from me, will you, Al? Tell him I will stop by sometime this week."

As Al drove to Charlie's house, he dialed Scranton in Chicago.

"Morning, Steve, how are you?"

"Al, I'm great. Thought I might hear from you this morning. Let me quickly bring you up to date. I'm on my way to a murder scene on the south side, but I have a few moments to talk."

"Please, fill me in."

"Earlier this morning I had a visit with your pal. I told him that you were responsible for him being freed and that, if it were up to me, he'd be going up the river for a long time. He sneered at me. Then he said, and I quote: 'Why don't you guys learn to be as nice as the cops in Wisconsin? You'd get a lot farther.' Then he told me he'd have information for you as early as this afternoon. He asked for your contact information and I gave it to him. Hope that's okay?"

"Yes, yes, it is. Glad you gave it to him. Did you give him my cell?"

"Sure did. And then I let him have it good—told him that if he didn't produce, I'd find him, and throw him back in jail. I said you had hornswoggled the judge into letting him go and that I was pissed as hell. I think I scared him good. If you don't hear from him by the end of the day tomorrow, let me know. Come to think of it, let me know either way, will you?"

"Sure will, Steve. Thanks a million."

"No problem. Well, gotta go. Gotta see if I can find a murderer."

Al concluded the call by wishing his Chicago friend good luck. Then, he turned into Charlie's driveway, and headed up the steps to see his friend.

An hour and a half later, Al was on his way back to headquarters. He found Charlie doing well. Although his friend had told him he was perfectly able to get up and sit in a chair, Kelly was insisting he stay in bed—at least for the day. She was doting on him and had hovered over the two of them as they visited. Al thought how good it was that his friend had found love in middle-age. His first wife had been a shrew, and Charlie was glad to be rid of her. The kids, Charlie found, were glad their mother was gone, too. They spent most of their time with Charlie and Kelly and loved their stepmom. Al caught Charlie up on his last conversation with Scranton.

Returning to work an hour later, Al was whistling as he walked into the building that housed his office. He checked in first at the Chief's office to fill him in, then went back to his desk, brewed a fresh cup, something unusual for him in the afternoon, and settled down to complete some paper work.

As the time passed, Al lost himself in the work, and didn't look up until his cell phone rang precisely at 4:30 p.m.

He picked up his cell, but before he could get his name out the caller interrupted. "Al, it's Carl Frenetti ... Scarface ... in Chicago. Got what ya want."

"Great, I'm ready anytime you're ready. Mind if I record the call?"

"Rather you not. Paranoid ya know. But if it'll keep me out of jail, I guess it's okay. Just wouldn't want the guys down here to know I snitched, okay?"

"Whatever you tell me is safe," Al assured him. "And if you need a good word from a cop, I'm it."

"Okay, then here goes ... ready?"

Assured he was set, Al listened as Scarface began by telling him that Shirley Sovereign, also known as Sweet Momma in Chicago, had retired from active prostitution in the Windy City at age fifty-one. Al did the math in his head, then said, "So that woulda been 2015?"

"Yea, about then, I guess. I wasn't good at math. I was just told she was fifty-one. I musta heard that wrong. She was still a very beautiful woman, I was told. She asked to be relocated to somewhere warm where she could live a good life and not be known. According to my boss, she went to Costa Rica to work for a guy down there name a' Frank Russo. Not long ago, they moved to Panama."

"Like 'R-U-S-S-O'?"

"Didn't ask, but I'm pretty sure that's it. Yah ... yah, that's it."

"So, she retired down there?"

"Um ... well, not exactly. She's workin'—or at least *was* workin'. Her new name is Mandy Russo. She is now livin' in a place called La Chorrera in Panama—in an area named La Mitra. I'm told she lives on a private road down near the ocean and surrounded by a big fence and a high gate."

"Is there anything more you can tell me?"

"There is only one thing more, Al. And when I tell you, I hope you will agree that I have kept my end of this bargain. La Chorrera is about twenty-five miles southwest of Panama City. I was told it is a very beautiful place about six miles from the Pacific Ocean. Russo's house is more like a stockade, up in the hills in the northwest part of the city, and heavily guarded. That is all I know, Al."

"You've been very helpful, Scarface. I will tell Detective Scranton that you have kept your end of the bargain. Try to keep your nose clean now, and you'll stay out of jail, okay?"

"I will try, Al. I surely will try. Thank you for everything you did for me. I owe you."

"You've paid your bill, and I think I have paid mine. So, I will leave you now and wish you the best."

"You, too, Al. Be careful, though. I'm told Russo is a tough guy who often shoots first and asks questions later."

Al thanked him for the information and ended the call, anxious to talk to the Chief about what he'd learned.

48

The next morning, Al was ready when Chief Brent Whigg came into his office for his morning cup of coffee.

"Here's what I have, Chief," Al said. "Scarface Frenetti called late yesterday to say Shirley Sovereign decided to leave Chicago when she turned fifty-one. She was sent to Costa Rica to be with a Frank Russo—a former mob boss from the U.S. Later they moved to Panama, to a place called La Chorrera. She now goes by the name Mandy Russo, although Scarface didn't know if she actually married Russo. I'd like to go talk to her, boss. See if this is the missing woman who was kidnapped in 1979. Put this case to rest."

The chief sat there thinking. Then he smiled. "Panama, huh? Charlie going, too?"

"Don't know. Haven't asked him … or told him about the talk with Frenetti. Wanted to talk to you first. No sense getting him all stirred up unless you think it's worth making the trip."

Whigg rubbed his chin, tilted his chair back against the wall and closed his eyes. A minute later, his eyes snapped open with the look of having come to a decision. He dropped the chair back onto four legs, leaned forward, and said, "Charlie should go, too. Here's what I think. We put a clamp on this. Keep it to you, me, Dwight, and Charlie. We let Charlie heal up for a couple of weeks so he'll be ready. In the meantime, you use the time to find out all you can about Russo—what he does now, if anything, and exactly where he lives. Then, when we send you down there, you'll be ready to make some progress. How does that sound?"

Al thought for a minute. "Sounds like a good plan to me. Maybe we can stir up a lead or two before we go. Wish we knew someone there, but that's not likely. Maybe we know someone who knows someone, though. At least we'd have time to find out."

"I agree. Better let me talk to Dwight before we let Charlie in on the plan. I can try and do that this morning if you can wait to go out there."

"That would be great, Chief. I'd rather have the big issues tied up before I talk to Charlie. No sense giving him fits if the Sheriff doesn't want him to go."

"I'll give him a ring." The chief finished his coffee, set the cup next to the Keurig, and headed to his office. Al settled back to think about who might know someone in Panama. *I wonder if Amos Brickner might know someone? Before I can ask him, I'll have to find out where he is. FBI Agent John Grimsley. I need to get a hold of him.*

Al grabbed his old-fashioned Rolodex, flipped the "G" forward, and six card flips later was rewarded with the number of the agent in Washington, D.C. Two minutes later he was talking to Grimsley and asking about Amos Brickner.

"What is it you're looking for, Al. Maybe I can help."

"I need to find out a way to make contact with a Frank Russo, a retired mob boss living in Panama. Well, I guess first I need to find out if that's even a good idea."

"Tell me more," said Grimsley.

Al patiently explained why he was asking, concluding with, "If you have a better idea than Amos, I'd be grateful. I just don't know anyone that I could ask."

"Gimme a day, we may have some folks down there who have access to the mob. Let me see what I can find out. I'll call you the minute I have something, okay?"

"You bet, John, that will be terrific. If you don't find anyone, let me know that, too, will you, please?"

Grimsley agreed, and they rang off. Al immediately thought of Charlie, and felt he needed to go see his convalescing friend. He briefly checked in with Whigg, sticking his head in the door while the chief was on the phone, and got a thumbs up. Al drove to the rural site of Charlie's house, parked in the driveway, bounded up the steps, rang the bell and waited.

Two minutes went by. He rang the bell again. Still no answer, so he walked around the house to the back-yard patio, then peered through the back door. He thought he saw a foot, then moved a bit to get a better view. It was a foot. Also visible were two legs, but they weren't moving.

What the hell's going on? That's gotta be Charlie. Where's Kelly?

As the string of thoughts ran through his head, his hand was on the door knob. He turned it slowly and the door opened silently. Al drew his gun, then stepped cautiously into the kitchen. Moving stealthily, he covered the path to where his friend lay. As he reached Charlie, he saw blood pooling beneath him. His friend's eyes were shut. He knelt and grasped Charlie's wrist. He got a pulse, a strong pulse. But Charlie was not conscious. Al shook his pal gently. There was no reaction.

He stood up, reached for his cell, dialed 911, told the operator who he was, and that he needed an ambulance on the double. He gave them the address and hung up. Then he leaned back down to check on his buddy. Charlie's breathing was strong and steady, so Al quickly went into the living room, grabbed a pillow from the sofa, and brought it back to put it under his friend's head. Then he slowly lowered himself into a chair at the kitchen table and waited, dumbfounded.

What happened here? he wondered. He looked around the kitchen for signs of struggle. Nothing looked out of place. Nothing made sense.

Finally, he heard the dim sound of sirens growing stronger and coming closer—until they stopped. He had told the dispatcher to send them to the back door, so that's where he went to wait—anxiously counting the seconds.

Suddenly the storm door was flung open and Kelly Berzinski raced into the room, hair flying. Although she may have seen Al, she rushed to the spot where Charlie was lying and knelt beside him, cradling his head in her hand. "Charlie ... Charlie ..." When she realized he was unconscious, she looked up at Al with her mouth open and a look of horror.

"*What happened?*" she gasped.

"I don't know, Kelly, I got here just a couple of minutes ago and this is how I found him. When I saw his legs through the door, I came in, checked his pulse, and called 911… his pulse is strong, so I got pillow for his head and settled in to wait."

At that moment the ambulance crew walked in, hauling a gurney.

"What happened?" the first guy through the road wanted to know.

"No idea," Al told him. "This is how I found him." Al looked at his watch, then up again. "Got here about five minutes ago."

"Lots of blood," said the EMT as he knelt on the other side of Charlie. "Any idea where it's coming from? Hate to roll him over until I know."

With Kelly ashen-faced and seemingly paralyzed, Al said, "He's convalescing after suffering a gunshot wound a week ago at Lutheran Hospital."

"Oh, that one," said the attendant, recognition crossing his face. "Heard about that. We have to get the bleeding stopped, so I am going to roll him over to check."

Al nodded and the EMT rolled Charlie onto his stomach. His pajama top was soaked in blood from his shoulder to his waist. The EMT grabbed a pair of scissors out of his holster and carefully cut away the pajama top, exposing a wound that had reopened and was pumping blood. He immediately applied gauze and a pressure bandage, then quickly began examining Charlie, starting at his head—and found a significant lump.

He looked up at Kelly and Al. "This hematoma is obviously related to the unconsciousness. I'm going to see if we can revive him before we move him to the hospital."

When Kelly nodded, after looking at Al, the EMT opened his kit, took out a bottle and some gauze. "Whiff of this should help." Then he carefully eased Charlie onto his back and passed the gauze under his nose a couple of times.

Charlie's eyes fluttered, then opened wide, looking at Kelly and Al. "Wha … what happened?" he said. Awareness flooded his face as he realized where he was, and he tried to sit up. The EMT restrained him. "We're taking you to the hospital, Charlie. Please just wait until the gurney is readied. Should only be a sec."

Now Charlie became agitated, struggling to sit up. In spite of the EMT's restraining grasp, his face reddening, Charlie kept trying to get up. The EMT's hold was no match for him, and Charlie squirmed to a sitting position. "I wanna get up. And I wanna get up *now*. And I'm not going to any damn hospital."

Al finally stepped in, kneeling and looking his pal in the eye and speaking firmly. "Charlie, just settle down. No sense working yourself up. Just hold on."

Charlie eased his struggle a bit. "Now, dammit, Al, I'm not going to the hospital. That's where I draw the line and all of you better understand it."

"You know, Charlie, you're a helluva nice guy, but sometimes you're stubborn."

As Charlie made his plea, Kelly knelt on the other side of her husband. In a gentle, no-nonsense tone of voice, she said, "Charlie Berzinski, you're my life. And you better listen to me, because I'm as serious as you'll ever see me. You … need … to … go … to … the … hospital. And you are going. *Now!*"

That did it. Charlie stared at Kelly for a minute, then made a verbal retreat. "Damn, Kelly, I just got outta that place. I wanna be here with you."

"I know that, darling. And I want you here." Her voice softened and she stroked his cheek as she talked. "But the doctors need to check you out. You've been bleeding and you were unconscious. Don't you think being checked over is a good idea?"

Charlie melted. His expression wilted into a look of resignation. "Well … okay, 'spose that makes sense. But do I have to go in an ambulance?"

Al smiled at his buddy. "Charlie, if we were talking to an accident victim—bleeding from an open gunshot wound with a large, unexplained bump on the head—what do you think you'd tell him?"

Charlie's head slumped, his eyes closed, then opened. "Dammit, Al, you always know just what to say to get your way. Okay, okay, I'll go to the hospital, and I'll go by ambulance—but I ain't being rolled on a gurney. Just get me to my feet, will you?" He rolled on his side and began to struggle to his feet. Then, suddenly, he fell back and lay crumpled on the floor. As the EMT quickly bent over him, he found Charlie unresponsive, apparently having lost consciousness again.

"Get that gurney over here, now!" As he efficiently maneuvered Charlie onto his back, his partner laid the gurney in place. Quickly, the two EMTs, with Al's help, rolled the huge lawman on his side, slid the gurney under him, and rolled him back onto it—then hustled the gurney out the door and into the ambulance. Charlie was on his way back to Gundersen Lutheran.

Al and Kelly hurried after the ambulance in Al's car. Kelly now was furious, splotches of red anger on her cheeks. She railed at not knowing what or how it had happened—angry at herself for having left Charlie alone while she went to the store. Al used the time in transit to try and calm her down. When they reached the hospital, Charlie was already being treated in the E.R., so Al and Kelly made their way to the all-too-familiar waiting room.

An hour later, a white-coated man entered the room and introduced himself as Dr. Rothman. Kelly introduced herself, then Al, noting, "Al and Charlie are very close, so whatever you have to say to me, Al can surely hear."

The doctor thanked her, then told them, "He's a lucky guy he got here when he did. The loss of blood was severe. That was our first issue. We gave him four pints of blood. Then we began to work on the head trauma. That's a nasty wound on his head. I can't believe it didn't break the skin, but frankly it worries me. He's having an MRI now. I suspect we will have those results in half an hour or so. When I know more, I will let you know. Will I find you here?"

Both nodded numbly as the doctor turned and disappeared back into the emergency room.

49

Al comforted Kelly, then made calls to Sheriff Dwight Hooper, Police Chief Brent Whigg, and his wife, Jo Anne. All were worried about Charlie. Al promised to keep them updated as there was new information, but Jo Anne insisted that she was coming to the hospital. She arrived with a basket of sandwiches and fruit and made sure Kelly and Al were eating.

About forty-five minutes after the first update on Charlie, the doctor returned. Smiling down at Kelly, he said, "There's no fracture, and that's what really worried me. But he has a concussion. It's not the worst I've seen, but bad enough. I think, Mrs. Berzinski, that I am going to admit him for observation. I suspect tonight will be tough for him. He's likely to have a lot of pain, so it will be best for him to be here. If all goes well, maybe he can go home tomorrow. We'll have to see."

When the doctor made his report, Kelly slumped against Al and murmured a quiet prayer. "You know, Al, I'm not all that religious but I think that, given what you guys do, this might be a good time for us to find a church and get active."

"Great idea, Kelly. I've wanted to talk to Charlie about that for a long time but, you know how it is, I didn't want to make trouble, either. Jo Anne and I attend church regularly and every time I go, I feel so much better. Do it. This is a good time."

As they sat there, the door opened again and a nurse bustled out. Since they were the only people there, she came up to them and asked, "About Mr. Berzinski?" When Kelly nodded, she continued, "We are moving him to the ICU. He didn't want to go … said he just got out of there, but Dr. Rothman says it's the best place for him, so that's where he's going. The doctor said I should tell you to go easy on him because he has some gaps in his memory." After delivering the message, the nurse smiled at them, turned and made her way back into the E.R.

"Upstairs we go," said Al, taking Kelly by the hand and helping her to her feet.

When they arrived in the unit, they found Charlie already in a bed and looking none too happy.

Kelly ran to him and embraced him. "Oh, Charlie—I was afraid I'd lost you for sure this time." Kelly was blinking back tears, determined not to break down. "Please, please take care of yourself. You've got to be more careful."

Charlie stared at her with a blank look on his face. "What did I do, Kelly?"

Al quickly stepped in, remembering what the nurse had said about Charlie's memory. "I found you on the floor at your house, Charlie. You were near the door from the dining room into the kitchen, lying on your back in a pool of blood."

Charlie turned toward Al, seemingly trying to get his eyes to focus. "Oh. Hi, Al. I was on the floor?" He was still a little dazed. "Gosh, I don't remember a thing about that. Everything is a bit fuzzy. Doc said things may come back to me, and maybe not." Charlie winced as he leaned his head back on the pillow. "Damn, I have a heckuva headache. Guess I hit my head on something hard when I fell."

Sensing Kelly was about to break in, Al took her by the arm, squeezing it gently to prevent her from saying anything. Then he turned to Charlie. "I'm sure you wanted something in the kitchen, right? You and that appetite of yours. Probably tripped and fell as you were going to the fridge. It'll come to you. Best thing for you now is to get some rest. You've had kind of a bad day."

"Guess … guess I have at … that. Kinda sleepy, too. They musta put something in that stuff they fed me. Sorry, you guys, but I think I should …"

Before he could complete the sentence, Charlie was sound asleep.

Kelly looked at him, a single tear slipping down her cheek. "Oh, Al, what am I going to do? He's really hurt badly, isn't he?"

Al hugged her, then backed away, put both hands on her shoulders, and looked her in the eye. "Kelly, he got a knock on the head, most likely from a fall. He doesn't remember … maybe never will. And if he doesn't remember, we won't know. I think we should just stay calm. He was recovering nicely from his gunshot wound. I'm sure he's going to be fine. Let's just wait to hear what the doc has to say. We shouldn't presume the worst."

"You're right, Al. I know you're right, but lately, with the gunshot wound and now this, I'm beginning to lose my nerve, posing as a brave wife of a law officer. I say prayers all the time, but God doesn't seem to be listening, and I don't blame Him, given our record."

"Now, Kelly, I'm certain He hears you. We really are careful, you know. Sometimes bad things happen, and then it's our job to hunt down the bad guys. But, given what Charlie and I do, it isn't all that often."

Not sure what he was going to follow that with to reassure Kelly, Al was grateful when the curtain parted and Dr. Asmund Gundersen strode in, walked over to Kelly and hugged her, then shook Al's hand, and finally turned to look at Charlie. "Sleep is good for him. I was hoping he'd be sleeping." Then he moved around the bed, checking all the screens and looking closely at the readings.

"He's doing fine," he told them when he finished his tour. "All his signs are right where they should be. He's a strong man, this one. And he has a hard head. He's doing just fine."

"Did you give him something to make him sleepy?" Kelly wanted to know.

"Yep." The doctor was smiling at them. "I know how this guy is. If he was awake, he'd be wanting to go home. I think it best if he stays overnight. A good sedative will make sure that happens."

"That makes me feel better," Kelly told him. "I was afraid it was the effects of the fall, and that worried me."

Putting his arm around her shoulder, the doctor told her, "Now don't you be worrying. We're a lot smarter than when Charlie came in the last time. Lots of procedures were changed. He'll get a good rest tonight. And he'll be much better in the morning, just you wait and see."

The doctor left and, half an hour later, Al convinced Kelly that, after talking to the nurses, her staying through the night wasn't a good idea. "He's going to be out, they tell me, until eight or nine tomorrow. Let's get you home to a good night's rest. When we come in tomorrow, he'll be more like himself.

***

As it turned out, when Al and Kelly walked into Charlie's ICU cube the next morning, they found him sitting up in bed and eating breakfast. He was, best as Al could tell, the same old Charlie.

"Hey, Kelly, come here and give me a kiss, will you? Soon as I finish breakfast, you can get me out of here and back home." Kelly smiled and gave him a kiss on the cheek, and then turned back toward Al. Charlie realized what she was telling him. "Hey, Al, how are you?"

"Better than I was when I found you yesterday, that's for sure."

"It's funny. Don't remember much about that." Charlie forked the last piece of ham, shoved it in his mouth, and sat chewing, looking at his plate. "Just don't recall," he said, his mouth still full. "Some images flit in and out of my mind, but nothing sticks. I remember getting up from the couch when the doorbell rang. But that's about it."

Well, that's a start, Al thought. "No problem," Al told him, "what's important is that you are on the mend."

"And they're gonna let me go home, Al, right? Are they?"

"I don't know, Charlie," Al said, trying to keep it light. "I haven't seen the doctor. I take it you haven't either?"

"No, and that is not a good sign. I wanna go home, Al. You make sure that happens."

"I've no authority to make that decision, Charlie, You know that. We'll have to wait to see what the doc says."

For the next hour, conversation lagged as they watched the big man fidget in his bed. When he wasn't fidgeting, he was working on

Kelly and Al to make a break for it and take him home. Finally, when the two of them were near the point of exasperation, Dr. Gundersen walked in, an electronic medical note pad in his hand.

"How's the patient today?"

"Feelin' great, doc. Ready to go home."

"Oh, you are, are you? Well, let's see what the signs say this morning, then we'll talk about that."

The doctor worked his way around the bed, noting things on his electronic writing pad. Then he concentrated on the patient, asking Charlie to roll on his stomach. He removed the bandage from his shoulder area, examined the wound and then replaced the bandage with fresh gauze and adhesive. Once that was done, he sat on the edge of the bed, looked Charlie in the eye and said, "How do you feel? No B.S. now, I want the truth."

"Doc, I feel okay, but let me tell you that this is the worst place in the world to recover. People rushing in all hours of the day and night, poking and prodding. Taking your temp and doing all sorts of things that I don't understand and probably don't need. Know what I mean?

"Hell, doc, if I was on my death bed—and I ain't close to that—I'd want out … just to have some peace and quiet."

"Well that's about as eloquent a diatribe as I've heard about health care." The doctor chuckled, then laughed, then looked at Charlie. "I guess if you're well enough to tell me off like that you're well enough to go home."

"Aw, doc, c'mon, I wasn't telling you off, I was just tellin' like it is. You ever been in here? As a patient, I mean."

The doctor's eyes were twinkling as he gazed first at the clipboard and then at Charlie. "I had gallstone surgery four months ago, Charlie. Matter of fact, I had a number of things changed after that experience. Apparently not enough, huh?"

"C'mon, you're puttin' me on the spot. Just let me out, okay?"

"I got it. Have you eaten?" When Charlie nodded, the doc said, "Okay, I'll write the release order." Then he looked at Kelly. "You gonna be able to handle him?" She laughed, then nodded. "Okay, Charlie, go home. But take it easy … you got that?"

Charlie nodded. The doc then turned to Kelly and Al. "I think that nod was as good as my ability to carry an elephant." He turned back to the patient. "But Charlie, that's a serious wound. If you come back here again, you're in for a good long time. Do you hear?"

Then he was gone, and Charlie, with no regard for privacy, threw off the covers and sat up. "Kelly, get my clothes, I want out of this place."

Later, dressed and ready to go, the big man looked at his wife and said, "What car did you bring?"

There was a long pause. "Ummm, the Mustang. Guess that was a mistake?"

"Al, do you have your SUV?"

"I do, Charlie, and if the Mustang is too tight for you, I'll be happy to be your delivery service."

Once in the car and buckled in, Charlie looked at Al. "Don't drive too fast. I have something to tell you. I hoped Kelly would be in the Mustang so this discussion could occur."

Al looked across the front seat at his pal and nodded, encouraging him to continue.

"The day I came home from the hospital, Al, I got a call from a guy with a sinister voice, warning me to forget about pursuing the Sovereign case. About twenty minutes later, there was a knock at the front door. I could see two guys through the curtain. I didn't recognize them but they were tough-looking. I decided to get my gun before answering, so I crawled to the bedroom. But when I came out of the bedroom, they were already in the house … in the dining room … and the biggest one hit me with a baseball bat. I remember ducking, which is why I got hit in the back of the head. I didn't want Kelly to know because she is such a worry wart."

"So, there were two men. How old?"

Charlie paused and seemed to be digging into his memory for a response. "I guess in their late thirties or early forties."

"Any distinguishing marks?"

The bigger of the two—the guy with the bat—had a scar on his forehead. Looked like it hadn't been stitched right and had healed … like, puckered up. In fact, the scar made him look weird."

Al remained deep in thought for a couple of minutes. Finally, he turned to Charlie. "This is serious, Charlie. I'm guessing they were interested in just roughing you up, but the fact that you ducked may have saved you from greater harm. We need to be sure you and Kelly are protected."

"Aw, Al, I can take care of myself, and Kelly, too," whined Charlie. "I don't need muscle hanging around ogling my wife."

"I think you do. Just give me a few minutes to think it through, okay?"

As they neared Charlie's house, Al spoke again. "I think we can use Abe and Samantha. They're nice, they're effective, and they are happily married to each other. Does that satisfy you?"

"Yeah, I guess. Probably will put Kelly at ease, too, right?"

"Yes, and I'll handle that," said Al as he steered the vehicle up Charlie's driveway to the patio at the rear of the house.

50

After telling Kelly he was going to post a couple of plainclothes police at the house, just to be sure nothing further would happen, nor would Charlie be left alone, Al drove back to police headquarters. After checking his office and finding nothing of an urgent nature, he went looking for the Chief. Finding him alone in his office, he brought him up to date on Charlie's latest "accident."

"I know it happened, Chief, because Charlie's explanation was just too vivid to have been made up or dreamt. Now I'm concerned about what to do about Panama. Charlie's going to need at least two weeks to heal, and I'm anxious to get this thing wrapped up. Any advice?"

The Chief had risen from his desk, walked to the office's only window, and stood with his back to Al, his hands clasped behind his back.

"Charlie's earned the right to go, Al. He's been with you every step of the way, and now that you think you know where she is, he's suffered two injuries—it's a tough call. But I don't think it would be right to go without him—unless your information tells you that she's about to flee Panama."

Al thought about that for a few moments. "Chief, you're always so pragmatic ... so good about telling me the right thing to do. I admire that quality in you, that's for sure. I think I knew that was what I should do, but I am also anxious."

"Al, never let anxiousness trump right action—it just never turns out well. Charlie has been a good soldier on this one, just as he always is. It would not be right to cut him out. You know, thinking about it, maybe you should consider taking Rick Olson along. It would be an extra set of hands for you and he'd be able to keep a watchful eye on Charlie."

"Chief, that's a phenomenal idea. That way, Charlie would have his own personal physician and I would have someone to watch over Charlie. That would be a big relief for me."

The Chief smiled and Al went off to call Dr. Rick Olson, the La Crosse County coroner, to ask about him going along.

For the next two weeks, Al tried to learn as much as possible about La Chorrera, Panama, including talking to people he knew who had traveled to Central America. He also visited Charlie each day, and as week one turned to week two, his friend was doing admirably.

On Wednesday of the second week he found Charlie sitting on the patio behind his house, soaking in the sun. "You're looking pretty comfortable," he teased. "You must like this life of leisure."

"Up yours," was flung his way, along with a coaster that had been under Charlie's glass of lemonade. "I'm dyin' of inactivity. You damn well better have something for us when I get back to work next week."

"Well now, it's my responsibility, is that right?" Then looking at Charlie's glass, he asked, "Think Kelly would mind if I poured a glass for me?"

"Course not. You'll probably find her in the kitchen." He thought for a moment. "That's another thing—since I've been home, she spoils me. Forgot all about the diet she had me on. I'm getting fat, Al. Really fat. I gotta get back to work."

Al was laughing as he opened the screen door and then the main door into the house. Careful to close the door behind him to preserve the cool air, he found Kelly in the kitchen, mixing up what appeared to be a cake.

"Hey, Kelly, told Charlie I'd like some of that lemonade—but I really wanted to talk to you. We have a line on Shirley Sovereign that places her in Panama. I want to solve this case if I can. It's been open more than forty years and this is as close as we have been to finding her. Charlie has worked on this with me from the beginning, and he deserves to be with me when it's solved. But before asking him, I wanted to talk to you."

Kelly faced him, wiping her hands on her apron as she turned. Al was certain a tear was forming in the corner of her eye, "Well, Al, it scares me to death just thinking about it. But so does everything he does." She slumped into a chair, rested her head in her hands, finally looking up. "Al, I'd love to tell you not to mention it to him, but I don't think I can do that. If he ever found out, he'd be furious. He loves his job. I hate it. Worry about him whenever he's on duty. But if I kept him out of this, it'd break his heart. For me, there's no win. But I cannot say no. You have to ask him to go."

Sensing how torn she was, Al walked over to her and hugged her. "I will do everything I can to take good care of him, Kelly. I promise you that."

"Please do that, Al ... please." Then, taking a deep breath, and with the courage that comes with resolve, she got up from the table, squared her shoulders, and went back to cake making.

Al patted her shoulder before walking back to the patio with his lemonade.

"What the hell were you doing? Squeezing lemons?"

"No, I was talking to Kelly—about you. Now I need to talk to *you*."

A cloud swept across Charlie's face. "Am I in trouble? Please don't tell me my injuries are going to cost me my job. You're not, are you?"

"Oh, gosh no, Charlie. Put that out of your mind. That is absolutely not part of this."

Charlie brightened as he listened to Al. "Well, then what the hell's the problem?"

"The problem, Charlie, is you're a lawman." Al was chuckling as he spoke. "And you're also a very lucky man, Charlie. Your wife loves you with all of her heart, even though what we do scares her to death. And I knew she would have good reason to feel concerned about you taking on a dangerous assignment after all that's happened to you. So, I felt that meant I had to talk to her before talking to you."

Charlie took it all in. He looked perplexed. He shook his head. "You mean you thought you had to talk to her about my job before talking to me?"

"Well … yes … kinda."

"No matter what she said, you better talk to me, Al."

"She said, yes, Charlie. She didn't want to, but she did. Satisfied?"

"No, because I don't know what it is."

Al thought about his buddy's comment for a time, shifting from one foot to the other for support. At last he was ready. "Charlie, I have traced Shirley Sovereign to Panama. You remember Amos, of course. He was a great help. And so was Scarface Franetti. You remember him, too, right?"

When Charlie nodded, Al continued. "Well, Shirley … she's in Panama. A place called La Chorrera. It's near the west coast of Panama, pretty close to Panama City. Apparently, she's living in a fortress with a former mob boss down there named Russo. And Scarface made a point of letting me know that Russo is the kind who shoots first and asks questions later. So it's likely to be as dangerous a situation as it gets." He stopped to let that sink in.

"So, do you want to go with me, or do you want to stay here and let Kelly be your nursemaid?"

Charlie wasn't sure he heard him right. "What? What did ya say? Did you say go? If I heard that right, damn right I want to go." Charlie was already halfway out of his chair and Al had to restrain his pal to get him to sit back.

"Whoa. We aren't going today, Charlie, and it will take a couple of weeks to be sure we have a secure plan, and to get you healed up. We'll go as soon as the doc says you're ready."

51

The next two weeks sped by. Al visited Charlie every day and helped the big guy with his exercises. Most days Dr. Rick Olson was there, too, watching over the big guy's recovery. Every day when Al got to Charlie's house, his friend was ready to work out. Al even did a light workout with him most afternoons, and often didn't leave until they were both soaked with sweat.

"I just want to be back in top form." Charlie was panting as he rolled over on the floor after completing 100 sit-ups on this day in mid-June. He was wringing wet, and Kelly had brought both of them glasses of ice water.

"I have lemonade, too," she told Al, "but Charlie is trying to avoid everything with sugar in it these days. He's determined to be in prime shape for your next adventure."

"I think he's doing very well." Al was leaning on the door into the kitchen, waiting for Charlie to clean up, and talking with Kelly. "I'm thinking that maybe this is a good time to have Rick come and do a final assessment to see if Charlie is up for the trip."

Rick Olson was a good friend who traveled with them when they were working on the case that finally brought Genevieve Wangen to justice only to have her slip away and then die of wounds suffered during her re-capture.

At mention of the trip, Kelly tensed, giving Al an anxious glance, then looking away as she said, "You might as well give me a few details, Al. Even though you'd think it would make me even more nervous, it's actually better if I have an idea of what you expect to run into down there instead of letting my imagination run wild."

Al knew she was putting on a good face, but he also knew she was right. "You know I will do the very best I can, Kelly," he assured her. "And since you ask, I have to say we are going to be in a situation we have never been in before. Shirley is living with a mobster in a heavily fortified villa on the coast. Accomplishing our goal will neither be easy nor assured. It's a tough assignment."

Kelly blinked at that, but remained firm. "Just watch over him," she said quietly.

"Of course I will," he told her. Then, switching topics, "And will you call Rick or should I?"

"I'd be happy if you would do it, Al. I'm sure you have more things to discuss with him anyway." She turned back to finish glazing the fresh ham she was preparing for dinner—one of Charlie's favorites.

Al then walked back to the dining room, where Charlie was waiting.

"You know, big guy. You're in damn good shape. I think we oughta have Rick come out and check you over. He can tell us what else needs to be done before you can travel."

Charlie was pumped. "You think I'm ready?"

"I do. In fact, why don't I call Rick right now?"

Al dialed the number, Rick answered on the first ring and Al told him the reason for his call. Rick promised to come out that very afternoon to check on Charlie. "If Charlie's in shape, when will you leave?" Rick wanted to know.

"I'd like to go as soon as we can get everything together," said Al. "It will be great to have you along. You're great company, and second it would double the people there to look out for Charlie and handle any other medical needs that might pop up on this trip."

Rick did make his visit that afternoon and pronounced Charlie ready for action. "You can go back to work," he told the big guy as he sat buttoning up his shirt, "and you can also go to Panama, if you want to. You're up to it, that much I can tell you. But you also have to have the heart for it."

"Doc, I got the heart for it," was Charlie's quick comeback. "Believe me, I'm ready to go."

"Yes, Charlie, you are," said Rick as Kelly looked on. "I don't believe I have ever seen you as fit as you are now. You're as ready as you'll ever be."

Kelly came over, wrapped her arms around Charlie, held his head close to her breast, and gave him a big hug. "Baby, I'm happy for you. You know I don't want you to go, but you also know I will do nothing to stop you. I know how badly you want it. Guess we better start planning a trip."

"Yes ma'am," spouted Charlie. "What say we call Al and get him over here? You game for that, Rick?"

With Rick signaling his assent with a grin, Charlie grabbed his phone off the dining room table and dialed his buddy and paced the room while he talked. "Al, I'm signed off for going to Panama, Rick says. How 'bout you get over here so the three of us can talk about it? … You're free? Great. See you soon."

Charlie turned back around to report what Rick and Kelly already knew. "Better get out some beer, Kelly, we're gonna have a party," Charlie told her.

Al arrived ten minutes later, sweating from the early summer heat spell. He sat at the table with his two friends and Kelly brought them all bottles of beer and frosty glasses. "Just what you need on a warm summer day," she pronounced as she set the glasses and bottles down, then returned to the kitchen for bowls of pretzels and chips. "Charlie's been starving himself," she said, "so beer and chips should taste good to him." She stood for a moment with her hands on her hips, then turned to go busy herself elsewhere, telling them over her shoulder, "Well, I'm gonna let you guys alone to talk."

As she left, Rick said, "Okay, Al, tell us all you know about this place and what we are going to do."

Al poured beer into his mug as he laid out the situation for Rick. "My informants tell me that Shirley Sovereign, allegedly kidnapped in 1979, is now living with mobster Frank Russo in La Chorrera, Panama. Shirley, who became a prostitute in Chicago after her alleged kidnapping, moved to Central America when she turned fifty-one. They say she and Russo 'retired' to La Chorrera a couple of years ago."

"What do we know about this place?" Rick asked.

"We know that La Chorrera is a city of about 200,000 southwest of Panama City. The Russos live in a heavily fortified villa on the Pacific coast. They have several servants and bodyguards, and live a life of wealth and leisure on a 30-acre compound. The heavily-guarded compound is apparently near the ocean. In fact, I'm told only the highway separates the estate from the water. That may be the most vulnerable area. I'm determined to bring Shirley back … but at the very least, we are going to put the case to rest once and for all."

"Is this jungle?" Charlie wanted to know.

"I think the jungle is nearby," Rick told him, looking at his phone, "but this is a big city … the capital of a province in Panama. It is obviously a warm climate, with highs in the ninety-degree range this time of the year. Probably need to take light clothing."

Rick asked, "What about weapons? I assume we'll each be taking one or two types of guns."

"I'm gonna take care of that," Al told them. "We will need handguns but I'm gonna make sure we take a rifle or two also. From what I've been told, the people she's with are armed and dangerous. I don't think we should take any chances."

"Do we know anyone down there who can help us?" Rick was still looking at his phone as he spoke. Then he carefully put it into the carrying case on his belt.

"I have some feelers out," replied Al. "I want someone from the local area to be with us when we go there. Panama is apparently well policed with both a local force and a national force, in addition to a group of police detailed for tourists. From what I've been able to gather, the area was the scene of a major drug bust just a week ago—the cops seized eleven tons of drugs in and around La Chorrera and then destroyed them. I am hoping one or all three groups of law enforcement down there will be on hand to help."

"When will we know?" Charlie was totally focused on the

mission and apparently raring to go. He was half standing at his place at the table as he talked.

"First of next week at the latest," reported Al. "Rick, if we get the answers we need, do you think you could leave before the end of next week?"

Charlie interrupted, "Does Dwight know?"

"Chief Whigg has already taken care of that detail. You're cleared to go," Al told him.

"How certain is the time line?" Rick asked. "I need to arrange for vacation as soon as I can. In fact, it's a little late now."

"I think now that Charlie's ready, it's a go," Al said. "Go ahead and put in the scheduling request now."

Given that, Rick stepped into the living room to call his office. He returned a few minutes later, smiling and nodding his head. "I'm good to go. My colleagues at Gundersen are happy to cover for me. I had the trip approved a week ago, but I had to confirm the exact dates. I asked for two weeks. Is that enough?"

"I think we have to wrap it up in two weeks," said Al. "Our bosses aren't going to let us vacation in the tropics for longer than that. Yup, two weeks at the max."

And so the early plans were hatched for the trip starting the following week. When the next Wednesday rolled around, all three men were in the midst of packing for the trip that would begin the next day.

Al had gotten confirmation from all three branches of police in Panama, and a Lt. Miguel Cruz had been assigned to accompany them while they were in the country. Cruz was a member of the national police drug force and was reported to know Russo.

"We'll know for sure tomorrow night," said Al as he met with Rick and Charlie on the afternoon before their departure. "Remember," cautioned Al, "we need to get a good night's sleep. Our flight leaves at 7:10 a.m. tomorrow and we get to Panama City at 9:35 p.m. We'll overnight at a hotel near the airport there. Lt. Cruz will pick us up on Friday morning and we'll get the search going. Any questions about what to take?"

Truth was, Charlie and Rick had been packed for three days. They just wanted to get on their way. Al was packed, too, but he had taken care of last-minute details right up to the time he left his office to head for Charlie's.

"I'll pick you up at 4:30 a.m. tomorrow, Charlie—and, Rick, we'll get you about 4:45. That should give us the time we need to take care of the transport of our firearms. No one has any packed, right?" He got the nods he wanted, then said, "Well, I'm gonna head home for dinner with Jo Anne. I'm not going anywhere tonight, so I will get to bed early. Both of you should, too. See you in the morning."

When Al got to Charlie's the next morning, his pal was sitting on the steps down to the driveway from his lawn. He had one large duffle and two guns—rifles—stored in carrying cases. The ammunition was in a separate military traveling container.

Fifteen minutes later they were at Rick's, duplicating the loading process they'd gone through at Charlie's. Rick had only a duffle, since Al and Charlie were supplying the weapons that he would use. He was familiar with both the M&P 15-22 Sport and the Sig Sauer P226 that he would be carrying in Panama. Anything heavier was to be supplied by Panama.

Panamanian authorities were aware of why they were coming, and Al had had several conversations with Cruz—who seemed to be a nice guy, and who told him he had met Frank Russo on several occasions. "I know him well enough to call to him and try for an audience," he assured Al.

The first two legs of the flight passed uneventfully. As they waited at Hartsfield in Atlanta, Charlie was hungry. "Lots of great smells out there," he said. "We oughta go sample some food. I think I smell barbecue."

"Charlie, I'm not gonna go back outside security just to appease your appetite. If you're hungry, see what you can find on this concourse, okay?" Al was impatient but also a little out of sorts on this Thursday afternoon. His demeanor and Charlie's appetite were having a bit of a tiff. Rick, as always, stepped in to provide the voice of calm. "C'mon you guys, settle down. We've got two hours until plane time and then we'll be on our way to Panama. My guess is you'll get something on the plane, Charlie."

"Okay, okay, I got it. No one wants to eat. Fine kettle of fish this is—no one wants to experience the famous Atlanta cuisine. Oh well, I'll save up for tacos, I guess."

Two hours later, they were finding their seats on the Boeing 737-800. In deference to Charlie's large frame, Chief Brent Whigg and Sheriff Dwight Hooper had popped for business class so Charlie could be more comfortable. When they found their row, Rick gave up his aisle seat so Charlie could stretch out his legs. But until dinner was served, Charlie wasn't happy.

As he ate, his temperament improved substantially. "Ya, know, this chicken ain't half bad for airline food." And after he had polished off the grilled chicken breast and roasted new potatoes, he also enjoyed the square of coconut cake. "Tasty, tasty," he declared as he licked his fingers, then carefully folded his napkin and laid it on the tray. "Wine was good too—right, Rick?"

"If you say so," his doctor friend replied. "You know I'm a wine snob, Charlie, and while this wasn't bad, it definitely wasn't up to my standard."

"Geez, what a trip this is going to be. On one side I have cranky Al and on the other snobby Rick. Give me a break, you guys, give me a break."

Charlie was still muttering when they deplaned in Panama City, but his complaints reached epic proportions when he felt the heat and humidity which permeated the terminal in spite of the air conditioning.

Miguel Cruz was waiting for them when they reached the terminal gate. He hustled them to baggage claim and spent only a couple of minutes with the security personnel on duty to get their handguns and rifles cleared. When they walked out of the terminal, the heat and humidity hit full force, almost instantly wiping out the visitors from Wisconsin.

Aware that the climate was, at least temporarily, taking it's toll, Cruz drove them toward La Chorrera with the air conditioning in his

Land Rover cranked to maximum. But what put them most at ease was his news that he had visited with Frank Russo the day before. "He extended an invitation to meet with him at his estate tomorrow afternoon. How's that for a surprise?"

52

When the foursome of police officers arrived at the Russo villa the next afternoon they found themselves staring at a formidable stockade. A fence made of massive timbers stretched as far as the eye could see on either side. The front gate was guarded by a force of some 10 tough-looking Panamanians. As Cruz inched his Land Rover up to the guard post, the SUV was quickly surrounded by heavily armed guards. Three of them also carried long poles, to the ends of which were attached magnifying mirrors. They efficiently checked the undercarriage of the vehicle. Finding nothing, they ordered Cruz to pop the hood, after which two of them did an exhaustive check of the engine compartment. Those two searches over, the occupants were asked to leave the vehicle. They were searched efficiently, finishing with a once-over by wands used by TSA agents in the U.S. Their guns were removed from the vehicle as the result of a search. Finally, they were told to get back into the vehicle, one of the guards sat in the driver's seat and drove them along a path that was literally a tunnel in the forest.

After a short drive, they emerged into a clearing that held a large house and lawn. A swimming pool shimmered in the back yard and a small tent-like structure was set up in front of the house. The guard, speaking Spanish to Cruz, told them to wait in the tent for "el jefe," the boss.

As they sat in comfortable chairs, shaded from the sun by the tent and cooled by fans stationed around the perimeter, servants served ice-cold lemonade and wonderful pastries of a kind none of the visitors had experienced.

"This el chiefee guy does right well," assessed Charlie. "This is damn good stuff."

As Charlie licked his fingers, Rick noted, "Charlie, that's your fourth – I believe they are called torrijas. Maybe you could save some for the rest of us."

Charlie's face reddened, causing the sweat beads on his forehead to assume even more prominence. "Uh, Rick…I'm sorry." As Charlie began to put a half-eaten pastry back on the tray, Rick stopped him. "Charlie, you'd better finish that one. Just save the rest for us, okay?"

Charlie daintily placed the pastry in his mouth, then smiled and nodded at Rick. "You'll love 'em. They are superb."

As they were talking about the delicacies, a servant came up to them and in unaccented English asked about drinks.

"I'd have a beer," said Charlie. "Whatever you have."

Rick asked for a glass of red wine and Al said he'd like more lemonade, "If you have it."

The drinks were delivered a few minutes later. First sips taken, a big man in a white linen suit, walked up. "Aha, gentlemen, I hope you find the fare to your liking?" He was at least 6-foot-6, weighed well over 200 pounds and Rick, the most discerning among them, supposed the suit he wore cost more than $8,000. A white silk shirt, a blood red tie and handkerchief tucked in the chest pocket of his coat and highly polished white shoes completed the ensemble. His face was handsome, his wavy white hair crowning a proud forehead that gave way to ebony eyes and an aquiline nose. His jaw was chiseled and his mouth prominent. It was altogether a face of nobility and Frank Russo acted that way.

"You must be Al," he said, striding to the La Crosse detective and shaking his hand. "And you're Charlie. How's the beer?" When Charlie nodded, the man smiled, then moved on, extended his hand and said, "Rick, welcome." Then he turned to Miguel Cruz. "Aha, my good friend, Miguel, welcome to Fortaleza en el Oceano."

Miguel turned to the other three and translated: "Fortress on the Ocean."

The big man then said, "I am Frank Russo…welcome" and took a vacant chair, snapped his fingers and a servant appeared with a large humidor. From it Russo extracted a large cigar then waved and the servant offered cigars to the rest. Rick selected a fine Cuban cigar as did Miguel. Charlie and Al declined.

Settled back now, Russo looked at his guests, eves roving from one to the other. "I understand you are looking for Shirley Sovereign, is that right?"

"It is," said Al. "We understand that she might be living here as your wife."

"She is my wife." Russo was smiling now, although his eyes gave no hint of humor. "She has told me about her abrupt departure from her home in La Crosse. She was kidnapped, apparently, and taken to Chicago and forced into a life of prostitution, I am sorry to say. I met her when she moved to Costa Rica, we fell in love, married and now have settled here. Does that take care of this matter?"

"Mr. Russo, with all due respect, we're police officers from the U.S. And we have come here to find Ms. Sovereign, to make sure she's all right and, if she wishes, to remain here. Surely you know we must meet her to make that determination?" said Al, his words translated by Miguel.

Russo looked at Miguel, then waved him off. "I speak English," he said to the Panamanian officer. And I am afraid, detective, that Mrs. Russo is ill today and unable to join us, as I had hoped. Tomorrow, if she is better, we are scheduled to leave for vacation in Europe. So I'm afraid I must disappoint you."

Russo had suddenly turned from friendly to stiff. He rose from his chair, nodded to each of his guests, then said, "I must leave you, gentlemen. I have other obligations. Please enjoy your drinks and your cigars. When you are finished, Mateo here will show you out." Then, with a curt nod, he strode back across the lawn.

Al turned to Miguel with a mystified look on his face. Charlie and Rick look puzzled, too.

"Did we say or do something wrong?" Al was getting up from his chair as he continued to look to Miguel for guidance. Then the man known as Mateo said to him, "No, no…no trouble. Big boss he just very short…is how you say it? He get impatient easily. Must be things on his mind. I think he say you leave now, okay?"

As they nodded at Mateo, he took the lead, moving them down across the lawn to another path. As they entered the path through flowers and trees, they encountered a female servant sweeping the tiles. As they prepared to pass, she stumbled and fell headlong toward Al.

"Lo siento. No sinifico dano…lo siento," she cried as Al's steady hand helped her to her feet.

Mateo barked at her in Spanish and she cowered as the Americans and Miguel walked past.

"She only stumbled," said Al, feeling sorry for the woman.

"She is clumsy one. Always stumbling." Mateo walked on resolutely, refusing to offer any type of concern for the woman.

Soon they were outside the gates and Miguel's Land Rover was waiting for them, facing out of the plantation.

"Surly sort," said Charlie as he climbed into the front seat. Al and Rick got into the back seat. Miguel started the vehicle and they drove down the winding driveway.

"He was," agreed Al, "but that woman had something she wanted me to have." He held up his hand to reveal a carefully folded sheet of paper. "She pressed it into my hand as I helped her."

With everyone watching, he unfolded the paper. As he read the message, his face took on a frown that turned to a grimace.

"Well now, that's very interesting."

53

As they drove along the highway to the heart of La Chorrera, where they were staying, the silence was overwhelming, but both Rick and Charlie decided they would let their friend speak when he was ready. Miguel was more fidgety as he piloted the land rover.

Finally, Al looked up and broke his silence. "I know you are wondering what the note the woman gave to me says. I've just been considering the message and trying to figure out how to handle it."

"Well, how about dealing us in and letting us help you think?" suggested Charlie.

"That was my conclusion," Al replied, looking at Charlie, then turning to face Rick. "I was just trying to think about what our next move will be. Rather than read the note to you, here, Charlie, you read it first, then if Miguel would like to pull over and read it, fine, and then it should come back to Rick."

Charlie took the piece of paper, carefully unfolded it and hummed as he read it. "Very interesting," he said finally. Then he offered the note to Miguel, who slowed the car, finally pulling off at a side road and stopping to read. Taking out his glasses, he read, then handed the note back to Rick, put his glasses away and started the car, as he drove, he glanced over the seat. "A fine kettle of fish… is that how you say it?"

"I agree," Al told him as Rick continued to read.

With everyone now knowing what the note said, Al finally spoke up. "Do you think we can trust the message? Or will we be walking into a trap?"

"That is the crux of it, isn't it?" said Miguel. "My conclusion is that the handwriting is in a female hand. But is it in the hand of the female you came to get?"

"I think we have to trust the note," asserted Rick. Charlie nodded his agreement. "If she is going to break away, as the note says, we can't have her captured because we were not near to pick her up. We have to be there. At least that's my belief."

Al looked again at the sheet of paper. "She says, *'Please help me! I must escape this fortress and this man. I must hope that you will help me. Please, please, be outside the gate of the fortress nearest the ocean at 1 a.m. I plan to make my escape then. I shall need you to help me. Shirley.'* Seems pretty straight forward."

Miguel seemed deep in thought. His brow furled and he studied the road. "I agree that it seems to be a believable message, but either way – true or false – we're going to need help. I think mobilizing our SWAT group might be a good idea. At least that way we would not be on our own in that wilderness. Do you agree?"

As they reached their hotel, Miguel pulled to the curb. Al opened his door. "Miguel, could you park for a moment so we can talk about tonight and how best to handle the situation?"

A few minutes later they were seated on the outdoor of the patio. Since this was the siesta time, they were the lone occupants of the large, shady area. Palm trees bordered the cobblestones, bending to shade the entire patio. Although it was very warm, the breeze afforded a pleasant cooling affect.

When Miguel joined them, they ordered a pitcher of citrus coolers. The combination of grapefruit, pomelo, clementines and blood oranges was a favorite of the Panamanians. The Wisconsin visitors agreed that it was a great drink.

As they sipped on their cocktails, Miguel talked about the SWAT force he was recommending be enlisted to help them that night. "They're highly trained and very skillful. They know what they are doing. If we tell them stealth is a necessity, they can use their hand-to-hand combat training. In the past, there have been some worries that their ranks had been penetrated by the mob but we have never been able to prove that."

In light of Miguel's report, the group decided not to talk to the SWAT force until after 6 p.m. Miguel left to head to his office and Al, Charlie and Rick decided to stroll around the city center of La Chorrera. "Charming," said Rick. "I'll bet our wives would love it here."

"I think they would," agreed Charlie, and Al nodded in agreement. "Can't believe the prices," he said. "Hotel at $28 a night is a steal. And it's rated five stars, too."

"I hope we can see some of the countryside. What we have seen, which isn't much, has been spectacular. The area along the ocean is some of the prettiest scenery ever, don't you think?"

Both Rick and Al agreed. Al, however, broke the soft mood. "When do you think we are going to see the country, Charlie? If we rescue Shirley tonight, we should be getting out of here just as quickly as we can."

"I guess that's right," Charlie said. "Maybe someday we can come back."

"I think I might," agreed Rick. "I like it here. It's urban but laid back, too. And the scenery is supposed to be beautiful. I think it would be a great place to vacation."

A long walk behind them, the three retired to their rooms for a late siesta. They had agreed to meet Miguel for dinner at 7 at the hotel, after which they would reconnoiter with the SWAT team at police headquarters before heading for Fortaleza en el Oceano and a date with Shirley Sovereign, they hoped.

Over dinner, Miguel told them the SWAT team would be assembled when they got to police headquarters. He said he thought it best if one of the visitors briefed the team. "Some of the men only speak Spanish, but we have a member who will translate, so language will be no problem."

Although anxious to get the mission underway, they dined on a delicious dish of ropa vieja, a beef stew rich in spices. Charlie was especially taken with the dish. "Legend has it," Miguel told him that a man was once crossing Panama when he ran out of food, so he made a stew out of the clothes he wore, thus the name ropa."

"Doesn't taste like ropa to me." Charlie smacked his lips after another bite of the tender, spicy beef. "I love this. Hope I can have it again before we leave."

When they appeared before a group of 12 swat officers just before 8, they found six men and six women, all dressed in combat uniforms.

Al explained where they were going and what they were going to do. When he finished his briefing, having detailed their reason for being there and reading the note, allegedly written by Shirley Sovereign. He asked for questions.

One of the women, a strikingly beautiful female of middle-age with raven hair and dark, sparkling eyes, raised her hand. "Is this fortress the home of Frank Russo the former United States' mobster?"

"It is," Al told her. "We met with Mr. Russo there this afternoon. He was very pleasant until we asked about his wife, the woman we are seeking. Then he grew angry and made it clear that we were no longer welcome at his house. So we left. It was when we were leaving that a woman servant, tripped and fell into my arms, passing a note to be as I helped her up."

"Do you think they will be expecting us?" asked one of the seemingly younger men.

"We have no reason to believe we will be expected," Al told him, "but we should be prepared for anything we encounter."

"Señor Rouse," said another of the women, "we are highly trained in all types of situations. You can be assured we will be ready to handle anything that comes our way."

"Miguel has told us that you are Panama's elite force. We are very happy that you will be with us on this mission. It makes us feel much more at ease. We thank you for being here."

Then Al, Charlie and Rick shook hands with each of the Panama force's members, chatting briefly with those who could speak English. When Al came to the woman who had asked the first question, she put her hand on his arm, leaned forward and whispered, "Please don't worry, detective. We are the best there is in Central America.

All of you will be safe with us. Do not be worried, please." Al thanked her and moved on.

When the introductions were finished, Miguel took over and told the force they would move out at 10:30…"about an hour and 18 minutes from now," he said, checking his watch. The hour was spent checking and double-checking arms and ammunition and making plans for how the 12-member force would be deployed.

"There are three entrances to the estate. Half of you will be stationed at those three entrances. The one nearest the ocean – here," he said pointing to the location on the map, "is where the woman is to be at 1 a.m. If any alarm is raised, I expect the point of exit for any guards would be here." He pointed at the rear exit. "Do you think two of you can handle the duty there, or should we station two more there?"

The leader of the force said two would be sufficient, so Miguel moved on. "This means that eight of you will be focused on this exit." He pointed at the map. "We want two of you to protect our vehicle as we head back to Panama City. The other four will try and shut down any attempted pursuit from this exit. Everyone fine with their assignment?" All 12 SWAT members nodded.

Miguel then spent time with the Wisconsin visitors, working with them to check their handguns and rifles. "I'm hoping she can get away cleanly and without surveillance," said Miguel. "But we have to expect trouble. I am hoping we won't need these weapons, but it is good to make sure they are working properly."

Then it was time to go. The SWAT force had three vehicles, two SUVs and an armored troop carrier with a .50-caliber machine gun mounted on it. The troop carrier would be positioned in front of the gate Shirley was expected to use. It would move into position precisely at 1 a.m. to cut off any pursuit from there. The other two vehicles would do the same at the other two exits.

Miguel told them as he drove that his Land Rover would be used to pick up and carry Shirley from the plantation to the airport, where a private jet would be waiting to fly her and the Wisconsin group back to the U.S., assuming they were able to determine it was the woman they were seeking.

As they drove, Miguel noted that heavy rains were expected to move across Panama around midnight. "That may provide additional cover. But it could also interfere with your plans to leave the country, so we have to hope that is not the case."

"If we can't fly, what is the back-up plan?" Al wanted to know.

"We have a safe house three miles from the airport," Miguel told them. "We will take you there, planning to get you out as soon as it is safe for takeoff. But let's hope that doesn't happen."

The rest of the ride took place in silence. Each of the men was lost in thought. Charlie thought of Kelly and his children back in Minnesota and hoped for his safe return. Al's thoughts were much the same. Rick hoped he would not be called upon to do any shooting. Although he had tested expert each time he had accompanied Al to the police range, he had never shot at a person and he didn't want to."

Then they came to a "T." Ahead was the ocean, the waves barely visible in the inky blackness. "Okay, señors, we're two minutes away. Get your handguns ready and have the rifles where you can quickly get hold of them."

Miguel slipped out of the vehicle but was back in a flash. "Just coordinating with the group behind us. Here we go."

He started the Land Rover and moved toward the gate. As he passed just beyond it and stopped, the troop carrier pushed into the ditches on each side of the road, its front and rear fenders nearly pressed against the standards that held the gate in place.

At two minutes past one, the gate opened slightly and a tall, older woman slipped out. She was helped into and then out the other side of the troop carrier. One of the SWAT team females helped her to the Land Rover. When she was safely in the back seat with Al and Rick, Miguel turned the car and roared from the scene.

As they turned the corner onto the road back to La Chorrera, their passenger gasped, "Oh, thank you...thank you. I'm Shirley Sovereign. Are you really from La Crosse, Wisconsin?"

As Al was about to answer, the radio in the Land Rover crackled to life. "Shots fired! Shots Fired! Hold your positions," they heard the SWAT commander say. With the message, Miguel pressed down on the accelerator and the vehicle shot forward.

After about two miles, the rain started, steadily drumming on the roof of the Land Rover and punctuating the running conversation of a gun battle back at the Russo plantation.

With every transmission, Shirley scrunched herself into a smaller and smaller ball, tucked between Al and Rick. Her eyes were covered with her hands and she had not spoken again.

As they reached the outskirts of La Chorrera, Miguel steered the vehicle onto a wide boulevard nearly devoid of traffic. "Airport about two miles," he announced. But now it was if the skies emptied. The rain poured down, causing Miguel to dramatically reduce speed.

He toggled a different channel on the radio and asked if the private flight to the U.S. was going to be able to take off. "No. No. Desviar a Plan B."

"Just what I was afraid of," Miguel said. "Twenty minutes and you would have been out of here. As it is, we're going to head for the safe house back-up. I have asked that there be plenty of guards to protect you. They should be there shortly after we arrive."

Miguel drove them to, then around the airport, turning into an industrial park at the backside of the regional airstrip. As he turned a corner, they saw a huge building ahead of them and as they sped toward it a side of the building began to open. The Land Rover sped through the opening and they found themselves in a sizeable hangar. Inside was a sleek private jet, but Miguel skirted the plane and drove to the rear of the hangar, stopping before a set of stairs that led upward into blackness.

"Out and up," he commanded. "Protection should be here within minutes."

As they climbed the stairs, the door at the front of the hangar began to open and four troop carriers filled with combat troops entered. No sooner were they inside than the door closed again. The vehicles swept to the rear of the hangar, offloading troops as they stopped.

It appeared that half the force climbed the stairs. By this time Al, Shirley, Charlie and Rick had reached a landing. Miguel raced up behind them, threw open the door at the top of the stairs and ushered them into a comfortably furnished apartment.

"We're safe here," Miguel told them. "We have half the troops stationed on the landing, with the other half down in the hanger, covering all the doors.

"What is happening back at Russo's place?" asked Al.

"Nothing good," said Miguel, a taut grimace on his face. "A ferocious gun battle is continuing. Both sides have suffered casualties, although there are no reports yet on how many."

"Have they contained Russo's men?" Al asked.

"Fraid not," said Miguel. "The troop carrier held its position, but Russo's troops broke through the other two exits and are headed to La Chorrera."

As Miguel made his report, Shirley began to shake uncontrollably. "They'll come to get me," she cried, obviously terrified. "Frank is a monster when he's upset. Oh, what am I going to do? What can I do?"

54

As Shirley's rant continued, the door opened and a man walked in. Tall and thin, face covered in beard and mustache, he carried a small black bag. "This is Dr. Torres," said Miguel. "Shirley, he will give you something to calm you down, okay." She looked at them wild-eyed and was ready to scream when Miguel clapped his hand over her mouth. Dr. Torres quickly removed a hypodermic needle from his bag, filled it from a bottle of medicine and quickly prepared to inject her arm. As he was about to administer the shot, Rick Olson stepped in.

"Before I do that, can I ask what's in the shot?"

Torres stood back, face reddening. "And just who might you be?" His English was broken but understandable.

"My name is Rick Olson, Dr. Torres. I am a medical doctor along to care for the members of the Americans in the contingent."

Torres studied Olson carefully. While Al and Charlie were ready to step between the two men, Torres stepped forward, arm extended. "Dr. Olson, welcome, sir. I didn't realize there was another doctor along. I am sorry I questioned you."

"Not a problem … not a problem at all. My interruption was probably rather abrupt, but I am interested."

"It's probably not something you would have used," Torres told him. "It's actually an old Mayan remedy for people who were 'crazy.' Our scientists have adapted it."

"I appreciate your discussion," injected Miguel, "but our patient isn't getting any less agitated."

Olson looked momentarily at Torres, then said, "I have no meds along that would help this."

"What I can tell you," said Torres, "is that this would fall into the benzodiazepine family. We have used it with great results because, if it has side effects, we have not seen them."

Olson stood back as Torres stepped in and quickly administered the shot.

Almost immediately Shirley's struggling ceased and she slumped in Miguel's arms.

Dr. Olson looked at Dr. Torres and said, "I would surely like to know more about that. I have never seen an anti-anxiety drug work so quickly."

"I shall share its makeup," said Torres, "but your FDA has not approved it for use in your country. The only idea we have as to why is that your big pharma folks don't want their stranglehold on the category disrupted."

Olson and Torres talked for a time, the U.S. doctor making copious notes as they talked. Finally, Torres said. I was prepared to remain with you in case further of my services were needed. But I am quite sure, she will be calm now, although the drug I gave her will not make her unconscious. She will be able to communicate, although I hope softly. I shall take my leave now."

Having said that, he looked at Shirley, now seated on a nearby sofa with Miguel. "Ms. Sovereign?" said Dr. Torres, "How do you feel now?"

"Oh, very well, thank you." Her response was soft but clear and the look on her face had changed from fear to normal, it seemed. "Very well," he told her. "I am sure these people have questions for you. So I will leave that to them."

The doctor moved to the small kitchenette, where his bag was on the table. He returned the hypodermic tube to the bag after disposing of the needle.

"At that point Olson stepped forward and said, "Dr. Torres, again I apologize if I was rude, but I hope you will stay with us."

Miguel arose, faced his Wisconsin friends and told them, "I am hoping that we will be safe here until the rain ends. Then the plane outside in the hangar will be used to ferry you back to your country with Ms. Sovereign. So please, rest and relax here. The troops outside will remain vigilant."

Al moved to the sofa and seated himself next to Shirley. "Would it be all right to ask you a few questions?" he asked.

She nodded to him and smiled. He looked at her, thinking she had aged remarkably well. Her face was basically unlined by age

"So you are the Shirley Sovereign who has been missing from La Crosse since 1979, is that correct?"

"It is…Mr…detec…what shall I call you?"

"Al would be great."

"Okay, Al. Yes. I am the Shirley Sovereign who was kidnapped and taken from La Crosse."

"So you were kidnapped?"

"Yes, from that house where I was babysitting. It was October, I think. Or September, maybe?"

"Did you know the people who took you?"

"Yes, yes, I did. They came to where I was babysitting. I had met them a week or two before, in Hazard. I guess I was kind of a wild kid. My folks were very strict. They didn't let me do anything. Oh, once in a while, they would let me do a sleepover. But otherwise I had to be home before eight."

"Do you remember the night of your kidnapping?"

"I do." She looked at her hands, which she had clasped tightly in her lap. "I was babysitting for a friend of my dad's – another professor at the university. They had a very young baby that I was watching that night. About 8 or so, I answered the door and was surprised to find two men I had met a couple of weeks earlier. I met one in a bar at Hazard and the other drove a few of us home that night."

Al waited for a moment. Shirley seemed a bit frazzled and he wanted her to continue when she was ready. Finally, she squared her shoulders, sat up a bit straighter. "I said I was kind of a wild kid. The summer after I turned 15 was sort of a renaissance time for me, I guess. I think I was feeling the urge to break out of my shell. Some of my friends felt the same way and we sort of conspired to help each other find out what was out there."

As she paused, Al said, "What was out where, Shirley?"

"You know, just out in the world. We'd plan sleepovers at a house where the parents didn't bother to check on their kids. That way we could do what we wanted and get in when we wanted. On a night during the week before I was taken, we stayed at the house of a friend whose folks were gone. That way we had no worries about them checking on us. We were seeing some older boys – freshmen from the university. That was a bit of a problem for me, because my dad was a professor, so we used different names. They picked us up and took us to Hazard. We were at a bar there where no I.D.s were required. We all were drinking. I got pretty drunk and the college kids left three of us there. Guess they thought we were too drunk to mess with anymore.

"Anyhow, we talked two older guys – men, really – into taking us home. They parked along the way home and made out with us. It got a little out of control. They did things to us that I didn't like."

"Like what?"

"Like hands all over my body. The only thing that saved me was I had just gotten my period, so they left that part of me alone. But then, on that Saturday night, they showed up where I was babysitting and knocked at the door. That really upset me and I told them to leave, slammed and locked the door.

"About a half hour later, I was studying and I heard sounds in the basement. I was scared, but I finally decided to look. I crept down the stairs and turned on the light. One of the men was in the basement. He grabbed me and told me to keep my mouth shut or I would be hurt. He twisted my arm behind my back and walked me up the steps. He threw me on the couch and then went and opened the door, so his partner could come in. They sat on either side of me and began to touch me and make comments to me about my breasts. Then they began to touch them. If I moved one set of hands, the other would grab me. I was so scared. I was crying. And I was afraid that the baby would wake up and they would harm her."

"Are you all right? Is there something we can get you?" Al was leaning forward, ready to secure anything that Shirley asked for. He wanted her to feel comfortable enough to continue talking.

"They kept getting more and more bold, both of them touching me. And the older of the two – the man who had driven us back to La Crosse a few nights earlier – was the boldest. He kept pushing his hand up my skirt. The younger one stopped when I began to cry but not the older one. His hand kept sliding farther and farther up my skirt until he was touching my underwear."

She paused, put her hands to her face and sobbed for a few seconds before straightening up, composing herself and then continuing.

"Look at me, detective, I'm an older woman. I'm 56 years old. My body has been used in every conceivable way and yet talking about that night long ago has me acting like a school girl. I am sorry."

"Shirley there is every reason for you to be upset, no matter what you have done or experienced since then. We feel your pain … and we want to help. I must tell you, you surely don't look like a woman of 56." Al talked while Charlie, Rick, Miguel and even Dr. Torres paid rapt attention to what the woman on the sofa, head in her hands, was saying.

After again sobbing into her hands, Shirley straightened, shivered and tried hard to compose herself, continuing even though sobs wracked her body.

"Eventually, I concluded I could not fight them off, so I pretended to be docile and cooperative. They got very aggressive. The older one removed his pants and underwear. It was disgusting. I think the younger one sensed the situation and let his guard down just long enough for me to squirm away. Thinking I could protect the baby if I could get the older guy out of the house, I ran through the door into the yard, yelling for help. It was about 9 on Saturday night, kinda dark but there was no one to help. I ran for the neighbors' house and as I got to the corner of the yard the older one tackled me from behind. I hit my head on a brick from the flower bed. I stood up and that's the last thing I remember until I awoke in the backseat of the car. The younger man was driving and the older one had me nude and was trying to…to…to…"

"We have the picture," Al said. "Without trying to explain the rest of the night, could you tell us what happened then?"

"I sorta have to explain," she stammered. "He got on top me… told me he had to make sure I was a good fit for what he had in mind, otherwise, he said, he would just kill me and throw me in the river. I fought like … like a tiger, but there was no way I could get him off me and he got what he wanted. My fighting must have thrilled him, because he said, 'Bucky, this is one sweet ride. She'll bring plenty of bucks.' Eventually he rolled off me. They took me to a woman in … I think … Richland Center. She helped me. I showered, she had clothes for me and she cared for me for several days. Then three really tough guys came and got me. We went to another town and picked up another girl. Then they drove us to a little town where they got a motel room. They raped us all night long, holding guns to our head. It was … was … horrible."

Now another group of spasms swept her and she again sobbed uncontrollably. Eventually she quieted and went on.

The youngest of the three was kind of nice. He took me to his room where we were alone. Then he taught me what it was like to be made love to. In spite of the horrors of the night, he was kind. Cleaned me up, gave me something that helped with the pain. Then he spent time talking to me before he … before he … made love to me. I hate to say this, but it's the truth. He was nice, touched me to make me ready then, for the first and maybe only time, he made real love to me. I can't explain it, but after what had happened earlier, it was wonderful. I know that sounds terrible, but it's true … I can't deny it."

"Then you pretty much know the rest. I was taken to Chicago and became a prostitute for the mob. They called me 'Sweet Momma.,' I guess my age and build made me a favorite and so I lived pretty high. Most of the … you know … Johns … were pretty nice guys. I liked the guys best who wanted a loving night. Once in a while there were rough guys, but I had my own muscle…don't know how else to describe it. They took good care of me. And I always had my own big boss that I went home to. Mr. Rouse, could I have some water, please."

Miguel fetched a bottle from the refrigerator. She took several big swallows, then began to talk again.

"I was actually popular into my 50s. I kept my shape and looks pretty well and by then I had learned how to capture a man's attention, so I stayed in circulation longer than most of the women. But there's always a point when you get too old. That happened when I was about 51, I think. They sent me to Frank Russo in Costa Rica. He tried to be nice to me at first, but I never liked him. He was … was … slimy." She shivered again.

But I became Mrs. Frank Russo, although we never were married. After a time we moved to Panama. I liked it there. I had a number of good friends among the servants. They did all they could to protect me. But Russo was an evil man." She rolled up the sleeve of her dress, exposing burn scars.

"Cigarette burns?" Al was set jawed now and his eyes were glaring black holes.

"Yes, cigarette burns." She shook her head, a look of sadness on her face. "Oh, my poor folks, I hope they never find out what happened to me. They have to be dead, don't they?

Just then Miguel broke in. "We have to board the plane. They want to make a hot taxi to the runway and be off moments after leaving this facility. Let's go. Let's go."

Al took Shirley's hand, helped her to her feet and put his arm around her shoulders. Then the hurried down the stairs. Lights were now visible in the jet. They reached the steps and quickly climbed them into the luxurious cabin.

As Al entered the cabin and directed Shirley to a seat, Rick and Charlie were waiting to help her. He turned back just as the co-pilot was ready to pull up the door. He waved to Miguel. "Thank you, my good friend."

Miguel smiled and said, "But, my friend, I am going with you. I need to make sure you are safe."

Al was both surprised but happy. Quickly he focused his attention on the door, waving to the people in the hangar as the co-pilot activated the switch and the door rolled up into the cabin. The handle was snapped into place, the seal checked, after which the co-pilot returned to the cockpit.

Before the cockpit door was closed, Al saw the huge hangar doors begin to fold in and up. He hurried back and took his seat next to Shirley, then grasped her hand as if to assure her things were going to be all right.

The engines whined and the plane began to move slowly until they could see the lights of La Chorrera around them as they taxied.

As the plane turned, a sharp voice came over the speaker system. We have outlaws at the airport. Everyone hang on tight. This is going to be a harrowing takeoff."

Then the cabin lights were extinguished as the plane began to gain speed.

55

Suddenly the plane was gaining speed dramatically, its passengers pushed sharply back into their seats, then the plane tilted sharply backward as it shot into the air. As Al watched out the window, he saw darts of light streaking toward them. He realized they were being fired upon. He ducked as he sensed bullets coming very close to them, then sat back and chuckled to himself as he thought that, given where he was, bullets from the ground had little chance of hitting him. But, he realized, they had a much better chance of hitting the plane.

Shirley, who was holding Al's hand in a tight grasp, seemed to have crawled inside herself. Her eyes were closed and from time to time she shivered, although Al thought the temperature in the plane was comfortable.

As they rose through the clouds, Al was relieved there were no more streaks outside his window. Soon they were flying smoothly, the moon splashing the clouds beneath them with shimmering light that faded, then reappeared, and faded again.

The pilot came on the intercom, apologizing for the abrupt departure from La Chorrera. "As you may have seen," she told them, "we had to avoid gunfire as we left the airport. We had heard there were bandits waiting outside, which is why we decided to do a hot taxi from the hangar. We knew there were rebels stationed near the end of the runway. We also knew they had no idea where we were, or even if we were at the airport. Although they fired on us as we flew over, we're not sure that they knew who was aboard this flight. We're also not sure that it was us they were looking for. We're out of range now and we have just turned back over Central America on our way to a landing in William P. Hobby Airport in Houston, Texas. Flight time tonight should be about four and a half hours. If there's anything you need, just let us know."

With the announcement made, Charlie got up and began to inspect the cabin. "Wonder if there's anything on here to eat?"

"Geez, Charlie, is that all you think about?" asked Al.

"It's been a long time since supper … and we didn't have enough of that. What time is it, anyway?" Charlie studied his watch, then reported, "It's just after 4 a.m. Damn right I'm hungry."

Al pushed the intercom button, talked to the pilots and then told Charlie, "If you look on the credenza back there," he said, pointing, "I'm told you will find fruit and pastries, along with beverages in the fridge."

Soon Charlie hoisted a bottle of Orange juice in triumph. "Found it. Anyone else thirsty or hungry?"

Miguel and Rick joined Charlie around the credenza. Soon they were eating and chatting noisily.

"Keep it down a little, will you? Shirley's sleeping. The rest will be good for her."

Rick and Miguel grabbed bananas, pastries, and coffee and returned to their seats. Charlie remained in the back, sampling the pastries and fruit at will. The air had grown uncommonly smooth, given the turbulent takeoff, and Al began to doze, Shirley's head on his shoulder.

The two of them slept soundly for an hour when the captain again came on the intercom. "Folks, we're going to make an unscheduled stop in Cancun. We seem to be burning fuel at an alarming rate. We need to get some things checked. Fact is, at this rate of consumption, we are going to land with almost no fuel in the tanks. We're hoping the folks in Cancun can give us a quick read on the situation and get us on our way shortly after landing. We'll start our descent in about thirty minutes. We'll let you know when that commences."

At that point, most of the passengers went back to sleep, too tired to think much about what might be happening. Al was not among them. He was awake, listening to the gentle whisper of air past the fuselage as Shirley slept, her head on his shoulder, and her hand tightly holding his.

Before he knew it, the captain came on the intercom again and told them "folks we really are cutting this close. Please fasten your seat belts tightly just in case we fail to make the runway. We have the airport in sight and are on a glide path that will put us on the tarmac in two minutes and forty-five seconds."

Al prayed quietly as Shirley continued to doze. Then suddenly there was no motor sound. The plane rocked slightly as the captain said, "We have lost both engines, no doubt due to empty tanks. I am confident we are going to make the runway. We are not going to show any lights as we land … just in case there are any bad guys waiting for us. We still hope that a quick inspection and refueling will get us on our way quickly."

Several seconds later the wheels made a soft touch down, there was a slight bounce and the aircraft settled back to the runway and rolled along with only inertia to push it. It stopped soon, and the captain said, "We should have several vehicles with us shortly. There are two fire engines, a tug cart and two troop carriers full of armed combat veterans, we're told. We have asked them to approach without warnings lights. I would like to get into a hangar without any fanfare. I will keep you posted as we know more."

Watching out the window, Al saw several shadowy shapes pull up to the plane. Then they both heard and felt the tug cart being connected to the plane. Slowly they started to move and as they neared a more well lighted area of the airport, Al could see the two firetrucks following, one on either side of the plane and behind the wings. As he watched, the plane was towed into a hangar.

"We have just been towed into a hangar," the captain, Carol Van Dijk, told them. We are going to lower the stairs, and my colleague and I will take part in the inspection. You are welcome to deplane and stretch your legs, but please do not leave the hangar. Thank you."

Al and Shirley were among the first on their feet after the stairs were lowered. They followed Van Dijk and her co-pilot off the plane, then stood off to the side as the two pilots, using powerful flashlights in the dark hangar, began to examine each inch of the plane, starting with the wings.

"Got it," Van Dijk reported. "Olaf, come here, will you?"

The co-pilot joined her under the wing where she was standing. "Look here," she told him, pointing. Al inched closer to the two so he could see. He immediately saw the problem. The otherwise spotless wing now showed a hole in the wing's underside. The co-pilot called for and was brought a stairway on wheels. As he mounted the stairs, he trained his flashlight on the wing they were studying. "Yup, exited here." He was craning toward the wing in an effort to get a better view. "Must have been firing some pretty powerful ammunition."

The pilot looked at her passengers huddled in the hangar near the plane. "We're fortunate," she told them. "Bullet passed through the wing cleanly and without starting a fire. A few inches either way and we likely would have had a fire. And if it had hit the fuselage, it could have taken out the pressurization system. I think we should all say prayers of thanks. However, that's the good news. This plane is not going any further tonight. I will be working on an alternative ride. While I do that in the office, please remain near the plane, so any communications can reach you efficiently."

Then she and the co-pilot were led by one of the men in overalls to what Al presumed was the office area. Another of the men in overalls pointed out where the rest rooms and the lounge area were located.

Half an hour later, the pilots returned to the hangar. "We'll be moved to another hangar in a few minutes," Captain Van Dijk reported. "I will be with you until the transfer is made but you will have two new pilots. I managed to find one of the few private aviation operations still open because of the weather system moving through. They say the weather will clear in about thirty-five minutes. They will have the Gulfstream ready to fly when the break comes. Olaf and I will see you safely to the new operator and aboard their plane, and then we will return here to supervise the repair of our plane tomorrow. We are very sorry that we were unable to complete your flight as scheduled."

Thinking that something should be said, Al spoke up. "Captain, we appreciate all you did to get us here safely. It was an act of bravery to get us out of La Chorrera. We all are very grateful for what you did for us."

The captain seemed genuinely touched by Al's words and then assured them, "I will make sure that you are on the way home safely, so you aren't quite rid of me yet."

As they waited for instructions on what came next, Al spent time thinking about the almost unbelievable set of circumstances that had brought them to this hangar in Cancun on this rainy night in Mexico. *I can't believe the luck that surrounded this trip. How could a bullet punch its way through a wing, pass through a fuel tank, exit the top and not set things ablaze? How amazing is it that there was no fire. Angels among us? For sure … absolute and for sure.*

Al was jogged from his reverie by the stirring around him in the hangar. Almost silently the doors began to open. As the gap widened they saw another small jet taxiing up to the door. It made its way into the hangar, then stopped and the stair dropped from the fuselage. While they made their way up the steps, the engines continued to whine.

Inside, the noise was blanked out and the cheery cabin lights greeted them. The pleasant interior was arranged in a series of seating areas. Shirley kept her hand tightly on Al's arm. He led her to a sofa, where they sat. Charlie and Rick took seats next to them.

Miguel boarded the plane. He simply wished the Americans well, asked them to keep him apprised of their progress and then left the plane. Captain Van Dijk was the next to wish them well, shaking hands with her former charges before leaving the aircraft. Then the co-pilot exited the cockpit to pull up the stairway and lock it in place. Before he returned to the cockpit, he made them aware of refreshments and the location of the refrigerator. "Whatever you want, it should be there." Then he turned and walked to the front of the plane, disappearing into the cockpit, latching the door and soon the plane began to move.

They taxied swiftly to the runway and swept into the air. With joy in their hearts, they felt the plane bank into a turn that they be-lieved put them on a homeward course.

Shirley grasped Al's hand tightly. "I just feel as if something is terribly wrong, Al. Please don't leave me until we are back in the States and I am safe. Please, promise.

"I promise." His response came just as the plane encountered se-vere turbulence and began to be tossed wildly about the sky. "Tighten your seatbelt," he told her. I'm sure we will be out of this soon."

The pitching and rolling continued for another half hour. By the time they arrived at smoother air, Charlie was heaving into the bags provided, Rick looked green around the gills, and Shirley had confessed that she was too frightened to be ill.

Al, too, had had all he wanted of the rough air, and when the plane settled onto a monotonous path of smooth sky, he uttered a short prayer of thanksgiving to the gods of the heavens. Two hours later they were on final approach for HOU. When the wheels touched down, the captain came on the intercom and told them, "Shirley, we have been ordered to have you surrender to the border patrol at the terminal."

"What does that mean?" Shirley was looking at Al, her eyes large with fright.

"Whatever it means, we'll take care of it," Al assured her. As the plane came to a stop, gently rocking back and forth, Shirley tightened her grasp on Al's arm.

The co-pilot came out from the cockpit, lowered the stair, and gestured to people waiting for them. Within two minutes, two mus-cular men had boarded the plane, each holding credentials for Al to examine. The credentials identified them as Agents Matias Garcia and Stanley Westendorf of the CIA-SOG.

"What do you need?" Al had thoroughly examined the creden-tials before looking up at the two men.

"It's been reported that you have a Shirley Sovereign with you." Westendorf was the spokesman. "Is that true?"

"It is." Al now handed his shield and credentials to Westendorf. As the agent looked over the leather police pocket folder, Al said, "We have been searching for Ms. Sovereign, who was kidnapped more than forty years ago, Agent Westendorf. We are now returning her from Panama to Wisconsin."

"Is she facing charges there?" Westendorf wanted to know.

"She is not, but insofar as she's been a missing person for more than forty years, she is now in my custody. I fail to understand what the issue is involving the agency?"

Westendorf looked Al up down, finally he lounged on the arm of a seat. "We have a report from a U.S. citizen in Panama that Ms. Sovereign was taken against her will from a plantation near Panama City. Is that true?"

"Negative. But perhaps Ms. Sovereign should tell you herself."

"I think that would be a good idea." Westendorf now fixed his gaze on the very attractive figure of Shirley Soverign, who had dropped back into the seat where she had been for the flight. Westendorf addressed her in his best south Texas drawl."Well … Ms. Sovereign?"

Shirley held his gaze with her own steely regard, then spoke. "Yes, Agent Westendorf?"

"Ms. Sovereign, we have a report that you were kidnapped from your plantation near Panama City. Is that the truth?"

"It most certainly is not, Agent," Shirley asserted in a clear, no-nonsense tone, her blue eyes snapping. "In fact, I was being held at the Russo compound against my will, and under armed guard. These officers came to my rescue—which was no small thing. They freed me from a mob boss, who apparently is using every means in his power to promote a ruse that I was kidnapped. That is decidedly not the case."

Now clearly confused, Westendorf shook his head. After thinking for a minute, he decided. "I'm not sure what's going on here, but I am definitely going to find out. Matias, we are going to take Ms. Sovereign into custody. And we are going to invite her companions here—Mr. Rouse, Mr. Berzinski, and Dr. Olson—to accompany her to our offices, where we will get to the bottom of this and proceed accordingly."

Westendorf turned, nodded to Garcia and left the plane. As he disappeared down the stairs, Garcia nodded to Shirley and her party and gestured for them to deplane. "We will make sure your luggage accompanies us to our offices." He waited as they exited down the stairs, then searched the cabin, and left the plane.

Waiting for them was a large black SUV with dark tinted windows and three bench seats. Charlie and Rick clambered into the rear, Al and Shirley took the second row, and Agent Garcia rode up front with the driver.

The SUV left the airport. Al looked at his watch and realized that the time was somewhere around noon. He glanced out the window and confirmed that notion with the position of the sun, then watched as the streets of the city zoomed past. Shirley held on to his hand as they wound their way into downtown, finally stopping in front of the impressive building towers that dominate the downtown Houston landscape.

As they left the SUV, Al looked the building up and down with curiousity. "Isn't this the old Enron headquarters?"

"It is. Remarkably perceptive memory, Detective Rouse." Agent Garcia studied him with renewed interest. "I don't think many out of state visitors would have picked up on that. Where are y'all from, exactly, if you don't mind my asking?"

"La Crosse, Wisconsin," responded Al. Then, noting the blank gaze on the agent's face, he clarified, "It's about eleven hundred miles straight up the Mississippi from New Orleans."

Garcia thought about that, then brightened and said, "Nice country, I bet?"

"This time of the year, absolutely. Now, come November, I might have a different answer."

"Gets cold there, does it?"

"It does," Al agreed, "and we often get lots of snow to go with the cold. That's when we'd like to be here. But, the reasonable summers in Wisconsin are far preferable to this," Al gestured at the heat rising from the Houston sidewalk.

Garcia nodded. "Yeah, we're looking at ninety-eight degrees

humidity and 102 degrees of heat today. Hot and sticky. Just like I like it."

Al acknowledged the agent's quip with an amused half-smile, then took Shirley by the arm and lead her to the door of the building. A building guard held open the twenty-foot glass door, and they walked inside to a welcome blast of cool air.

Garcia led them to the elevator banks, "How tall is this puppy?" Charlie was looking at the numbers.

"Fifty-one floors," the agent said.

"Humph," grumbled Charlie. "Looks to me like the numbers only go to fifty."

"Fifty-one is the mystery floor," Garcia said. "That's where we take problem visitors to teach them a lesson."

Charlie looked at him in amazement. "You're kid…" he started. "You're just foolin' me."

"I am," Garcia admitted. "And with the group all assembled now, why don't we go up and see what we can do to sort out your situation?"

Garcia pushed the button for the forty-first floor, and then entered some kind of code on the panel before the door closed and began ascending.

"Direct flight," he said smiling.

After a breathtaking ascent to floor forty-one that left them all feeling slightly light-headed, they were soon seated in Westendorf's office. The agent wasted no time in providing Al and Charlie the document received from the U.S. Embassy in Panama. It alleged that "one Shirley Sovereign Russo was seized and taken from her home against her will, brainwashed, and then taken to the United States."

"You will notice that this instructs U.S. agents," said Westendorf, "to apprehend Ms. Sovreign and her kidnappers, and immediately return her to the custody of the Panama Consulate General in Houston, Texas. They are further asserting that her kidnappers must be extradited to Panama to face charges. Now, tell me how all of this came to be?"

Al began the story with Shirley Sovereign's disappearance from

La Crosse, Wisconsin, in October of 1979. For an uninterrupted hour, Al—with help from Charlie, Rick, and Shirley—laid out the facts of why and how Shirley had been rescued and reclaimed for her home country, fleeing Panama and the man she alleged had bought her to be his sex-slave, Frank Russo. Altogether, it was a compelling story, and Westendorf was open in his regard for the operation undertaken by the officers from La Crosse.

"In summary, Stan," Al leaned forward a bit, studying Westendorf across the table, "Charlie and I were following up on information we received from an informant *who had a hand in taking her from La Crosse*. Not inconsequentially, we have also coordinated parts of our investigation with the FBI, in Chicago, who I am sure will attest to the legitimacy of this mission to return Ms. Sovreign to her former life in La Crosse.

"We are not asserting at this time that she was kidnapped. We may later move to bring charges against Mr. Russo, but we have not yet even had time to debrief Ms. Sovereign. That, we feel, should come first. But I am interested in your assessment of how we should proceed." Al felt confident that he had made his case, and had claimed the high ground.

Westendorf looked at Al over his glasses from behind his large desk. The look on his face was serious but understanding. "Well, a warrant from another country to hold her for extradition to Panama isn't a trivial matter. However, in light of the involvement of Wisconsin and federal authorities, I am going to have to consult my bosses to sort this out. I'll need your agent contact at the FBI." Al started writing it down for him from a card in his wallet. "Meanwhile, will y'all be comfortable here for an hour or so while I take this upstairs?"

Al looked to Shirley for confirmation and, when she nodded, he replied, "Agent Westendorf, we haven't had much sleep, thanks to events of last night. I think an hour to an hour and a half is no problem. But if it drags beyond that point, we may appeal for a hotel so Ms. Sovereign and all of us can get some rest. We have had rather more than we bargained for with this latest snag."

"Perfectly understandable. I will do everything I can to expedite a conference with the officials involved, and get a resolution on what we are looking at here. Give me that time to do my job. In the meanwhile, y'all can make yourselves at home in my office. If you need anything, my admin, Rosalie, will get it for you.

"And I might point out, that sofa over there is quite comfortable." He nodded toward an expansive leather couch in front of the corner windows. "I can vouch for it, having spent many nights there during investigations."

When Westendorf left the office, Matias smiled at them. "Stan was uncommonly genial," he said in perfect English. "And that isn't like him at all. What it seemed like to me is that he was telling you, in his own way, that he is going to fight for you." Al nodded at that with an appreciative smile.

Al saw to it that Shirley headed toward the sofa, where she took off her shoes, swung her legs onto the cushions, and languidly stretched out. "It is amazingly comfortable. I doubt that I shall be awake too long."

Then she closed her eyes and soon was asleep. Charlie and Rick grabbed the two other easy chairs.

"Thanks, pals," quipped Al as he sat on the floor, removed a pillow from a chair and stretched out on the elegant maroon carpet. "I bet this carpet was here before you moved in. Doesn't seem likely any government agency would spring for a pile this plush."

"You're right, it was here. In fact, all the furniture was here, too. We just took it over as it was. Hard to believe some junior Enron exec had an office this cushy, isn't it?

"Sure is, Matias." Then Al rolled on his side and closed his eyes. Charlie and Rick already seemed to be asleep, so Matias closed the drapes tightly and sat down behind Westendorf's desk, took off his boots, and propped his feet up.

No one was going to lose a second of down time.

56

"Well, just look at this," Westendorf smiled and muttered under his breath, walking back into his office, where he was greeted by a chorus of snores from five people who obviously were sound asleep. He strode to his desk, gently shook Matias by the shoulder and watched as his eyes flew open.

Westendorf whispered, "Boy howdy, I leave you to watch these folks, and you wind up having a slumber party with them. What kind of surveillance is that, Matias?"

"Sorry, boss," Matias said sheepishly as he hastily got up, but his boss put his finger to his lips. Matias whispered his apology. "Everyone was sleeping and I just sort of nodded off. Didn't intend to—it just happened."

Westendorf wasn't angry, and he shook his head. He, too, would have liked a nap, but his meeting with the AIC had precluded any slack time in this day. He had been working hard on this case upstairs.

"Matias, we have a new set of orders. Let me wake Al and we'll talk about it."

He went over to where Al appeared to be out cold on the carpet, shook him gently. When Al jerked awake, Westendorf put a finger to his lips. Al sat up and quietly got to his feet. Then, with Matias, watching the other three, Al and Westendorf left the office.

Out in the hall, Stan stopped, faced Al and whispered, "The AIC and I just talked to your boss in La Crosse, Al, and he verified that your mission is 100 percent legit. And he appealed to us for help in getting you back to La Crosse. He even offered to pick up the tab for private aviation. He's concerned that you get back quickly, and I think we can help with that."

Al looked at him in amazement that the situation had been so easily resolved.

"And you ought to know that Chief Whigg provided a few more details on the case, Al. Seems that you have been far too modest in discussing the situation. I had no idea the amount of detective work that you and Charlie had done in tracking down this woman. As for Shirley, she is fortunate that you were able to extract her from what was clearly a dangerous situation. In any event, my boss is going to put a private plane at your disposal. As soon as you are ready to leave, we'll have you on your way to the airport, and then on home to Wisconsin."

Greatly relieved, and almost buoyant, Al walked back into Westendorf's capacious office and roused Charlie and Rick, who scrambled to their feet. Lastly, Al moved to the sofa, shook Shirley gently by the shoulder and held his hand out to her when she awakened. "You're going home," he said. She allowed a brilliant smile that Al imagined had inspired many hearts, took his hand, slowly sat up, then rose to her feet—seemingly with a renewed sense of well-being.

Al brought them all up to date on his talk with Westendorf. As he finished, Shirley looked at him with a steady gaze and said, "You know, I hope I'm ready for this. I'm not sure I will recognize my old home town. Not to mention that you, Al, Rick, and Charlie, are probably the only people I will know. But I'm ready for whatever comes next."

Al excused himself and went out into the hall to call Jo Anne. After catching her up on developments, he asked if she would call Kelly Berzinski and Peggy Olson and arrange to have the three of them meet the airplane. "I'll call you when I have an ETA," he told her. "And by the way, Shirley Sovereign is understandably disheartened by the prospect of landing in a city she will hardly recognize, and where she won't know anyone. I think the three of you could help, if you're willing."

Assured that she would put together a small welcoming party, Al returned to the group in Westendorf's office. With a wink at Rick and Charlie, he looked toward Westendorf. "Stan, I think we're more than ready to complete this journey. Why don't we get going?"

Westendorf led them to the back of the building, then summoned a freight elevator to carry them to the basement where a long black SUV waited for them, along with four other cars. The traveling party fit in the SUV with Westendorf occupying the front seat passenger seat. The fact that the agency's "person of interest" had been involved with the mob had induced an abundance of caution on the part of the agency.

On Westendorf's command, the caravan began to roll—three of the cars preceded theirs and one followed. When they left the building, two of the cars fell in alongside, one ahead and one behind. "This will work for the first mile or so," Stan told them. "Then the car on the left side will fall back with the car behind to help protect the rear." Westendorf was indicating to Al that they had taken the threat of danger very seriously indeed. Al was impressed—and grateful.

Ten minutes later they were at the airport. Shirley declined Al's help in managing the stairs and ascended the steps into the small jet under her own power and with elegant ease. Charlie and Rick followed, along with two other agents. Al waited behind to shake hands with Stan before boarding.

"I'm going, too," Westendorf told him.

Surprised, Al realized he was glad to have his company. "Great! After you, then," as he swept his hand indicating he could go first. Al followed him up the stairs and into the pleasant passenger area of the small business jet, a twin-engine Gulfsteam g650.

"Wow." Al entered the cabin and stopped to look around. There were three clusters of three seats, arranged around tables.

"It's a beauty, all right. It's assigned to the boss, who has made it available to you. Behind that bulkhead," he pointed at the back wall of the cabin, "is a double bed ... and, Shirley, the boss said you're to make yourself comfortable on the flight home. Agent Cortez, here, will be our attendant and will take good care of you."

A pretty and competent looking brunette stepped forward and said, "Call me Martha, and I'll be taking breakfast orders once we're airborne. I think you will like the accommodations, Shirley, and you can get some rest. As for the rest of you," she pointed toward the seat clusters, "those chairs are recliners, so you will be quite comfortable, too."

Martha then introduced Joel Jacobson, captain, and Leslie Priefert, co-pilot. Joel told them, "We'll be cruising up to Wisconsin at 47,000 feet today, a good altitude to insure a smooth ride. I estimate the flight should take about four hours—allowing for a detour around some weather over Missouri. When y'all are all set, we'll get going. We are pre-flighted out of here in ten minutes. Martha, you're in charge—just let me know when we're ready for liftoff."

Joel stepped into the cockpit while Leslie retracted the stairs and checked the seal before going forward to take the co-pilot seat. The engines whined and the jet began to taxi. Soon they were airborne and in mere minutes they were at cruising altitude.

"Nothing like a private jet for comfort," said Stan, stretching his arms. Martha stood and made her way to the kitchen in the back of the cabin. "We have omelets for breakfast," she told them. "I can make them with ham, cheese, onions, peppers, and mushrooms, or any combination." Charlie's eyes sparkled at the menu.

Soon heavenly breakfast smells filled the cabin and everyone was busy eating and talking. Conversation was light, with most of the banter centering on the merits of the Brewers versus the Astros. All agreed that the Astros were ascendant. Shirley was reserved but amused by the lively talk that was almost a foreign language to her. Finally, Martha efficiently cleared the dishes, served another round of decaf, then led Shirley to the rear of the plane. When the hostessing agent returned, she smiled. "She is going to be asleep soon, but before I closed the door, she wondered if she could have a word with you, Stan. ."

"Me? Really? Wonder what that's about. Let me go visit. I'll be back soon." He walked to the back of the plane and closed the door behind him.

Twenty minutes later he re-emerged, a grim look on his face and sat down to talk to Al.

"She's worried, Al. She definitely wants to be home, but she fears the news coverage and what that would do to alert the bad guys. Do you think we can keep this on the hush-hush?"

"Geez, Stan, not sure how we can do that. The news is going to leak, you know that. It's just bound to. Someone will say something without realizing it and then it will be all over the place."

"Do you think we could try and put a net over it until we've got a protection plan in place?"

"We can try, but we better get a plan in place in short order."

For the next half hour, the two law enforcement officers, with Charlie listening in, put together a plan. One they had the details, Stan and Al went forward to make contact with their bosses. Ten minutes later, Al returned and told Charlie, "We got to Brent right away and he's cool. He's going to go over and brief Dwight. We're going to try and keep it to the four of us locals, plus Rick and Peggy. We are going to have to impress on our wives the importance of not talking. When Stan is back, the three of us will go up, one by one, and call our wives from the cockpit and clue them in."

Stan returned fifteen minutes later and, one by one, the La Crosse contingent filed forward to talk to their wives. When Al reached Jo Anne, she told him she had organized a small greeting party.

Dismayed, Al sharply replied, "How many, Jo Anne.

"Well, I tried to call some of Shirley's former friends, but the only one I reached was Mary Nordstrom. She is home all alone, so she is happy to come."

Irritated at himself for not foreseeing the potential problem when he had talked to Jo Anne earlier, Al said, "Geez, Jo Anne, we have to keep this thing quiet. Call her right away and put a muzzle on her. Make damn sure you know who she's talked to. Have you talked to anyone else?"

Assured she had not, Al was not comforted when he concluded the phone call. He huddled with Rick and Charlie. Each assured him their wives had assured them no one had been contacted.

"Well, we better damn well hope so," replied Al sullenly, "or this is going to be another C.F."

Al then walked back to where Stan was sitting and told him about his talk with Jo Anne and also what Rick and Charlie had found out.

Stan nodded and then said, "We have to hope that the lid is on, Al. Nothing else we can do. You should know, there's another small surprise for Shirley before we land." Al's eyebrows shot up as he gave Stan a questioning look, but Agent Westendorf was suddenly a man of few words, and merely smiled as he leaned back in his lounger and closed his eyes.

The flight passed uneventfully and smoothly. Before they knew it, the pilot announced they were beginning their descent into La Crosse and should be on the ground in thirty minutes.

"We'll give you a gentle descent. Want to save everyone's ears."

True to his words, the trip down was barely noticeable. Agent Cortez, who had spent most of her time in the rear of the cabin with Shirley, returned to the main passenger area all smiles.

"I think our female passenger was delighted to find that her compartment had a shower and a completely stocked vanity area. When I left her, she was happily applying fresh makeup, and I think you will all be pleasantly surprised to see the transformation. She will be ready to meet people when we land. Will there be a large crowd?"

"Absolutely not—at least I hope there won't be. Just a few of our family members and maybe a friend of hers from high school—a small gathering." Al finished, winked at his colleagues and was about to speak again when the rear bulkhead door opened and Shirley walked into the room.

57

The woman who walked into the forward cabin was a different Shirley than any of them had seen. And she was stunningly beautiful.

She could have been in her late thirties, certainly no older. Her medium length blonde hair was swept back, her electric blue eyes were dancing, and expertly applied makeup provided a natural glow. The sleep had also helped. She looked rested and confident.

She pirouetted for them in a simple form-fitting black dress with three-quarter sleeves and a scooped neckline that was deemed elegant and yet perfect for any occasion—the quintessential "little black dress" that every woman has in her closet. She asked, "Am I presentable?"

"Wow." Al's response brought nods from the others. "Where did you find the outfit?" Charlie whistled, then said, "You look beautiful, Shirley."

"Martha went shopping!" It was clear that Shirley was thrilled with the thoughtful attention that had been provided by the agency. "*Someone* gave her a good description, too," as she shot a look at Stan, who returned an admiring look, "because she purchased this with a bit more than just a woman's intuition."

Stan was clearly pleased with the result, and smiled broadly. "I sent Martha over to the Houston Galleria, and told her to find something she liked. I don't know how much it's going to cost me, but Agent Cortez has discernment for style, it would seem." He winked at Martha.

Shirley made her way over to Al and Stan, who both immediately jumped up to offer her a seat at their small table. All eyes were on the woman who had effortlessly taken over the room. "Before we land, there are a couple of things I want to say," she said, speaking to all of them, but keeping eye contact mostly with Al and Stan. "First of all, I am, of course, very apprehensive about returning to a town I hardly know. I haven't been in La Crosse for forty years. But when I woke up, I decided that—even if the only people I will know in La Crosse are the ones right here in this cabin—I am fortunate indeed. But I also want you to know I am scared to death what might happen if Frank finds out where I am."

"Shirley, you have nothing to worry about." Al was smiling as he recovered from the shock. "I expect that our wives will all be there when we land, and they will take a liking to you, I have no doubt. We will make sure you feel welcomed home."

Shirley put her hand on Al's arm. "Al, you have been very gracious, and have gone above and beyond to provide a soft landing for me. But, my other concern—and I am sure you and Stan and Charlie will agree—is that I am not out of danger wherever I go from here. The mob has deep connections, and Russo is not a man to cross."

All three law men nodded at that as she continued. "So, for good measure, I hope you will stay close, at least until I can figure out how to manage my new life under more secure circumstances." Rick was studying the "new" Shirley with a clinical regard for any signs of shakiness in her composure. He found none. *This is a remarkable woman,* he thought.

Shirley leaned back in her seat slightly and crossed a pair of quite shapely legs. It was not hard for any of the men in the cabin to see that, when she wanted it, she had command of the so-called stronger sex with a well-practiced ease. "There's one other thing. I don't want to be a burden to any of you, so it would be preferable if you could arrange for a hotel room. Believe it or not, I have ample resources, and I've been thinking that a room at that new Radisson Hotel down by the river would be lovely. Is it open?"

The La Crosse residents laughed when Shirley asked her question. "It's been open for forty years. Must have opened just before you were … err … left," said Charlie.

Al nodded in simple agreement, pleased by Shirley's clear grasp of the precarious nature of her situation. As he looked out the window, he realized that the plane had looped around La Crosse and was landing from the north. As he watched, the wheels skimmed over the waters of Lake Onalaska, the plane's shadow a dark mark on the water. Momentarily, they crossed the shoreline, topped the chain-link fence, and gently settled onto the runway.

As the plane taxied to the private base operation on the east side of the airport, Al shook his head. "Damn, I forgot we are flying private. I bet everyone is waiting over at the main terminal."

His fears were unnecessary. As they neared their destination, he saw Jo Anne waiting with several other women—among them Kelly Berzinski and Peggy Olson. And he was pleased to see that Sheriff Hooper and Chief Whigg were on hand as well, behind the main welcome party Jo Ann had put together.

But then, just as they slowed to stop, a large bang echoed through the cabin and the plane listed to one side.

"Down! Get down!" Stan ordered, reaching for his gun in a small forward compartment, uncertain of what caused the noise but unwilling to risk harm to anyone on the plane. Charlie and Al automatically dove to shield Shirley, who had quickly ducked under the table, as Rick and Martha hit the floor under another table.

The co-pilot came out, dropped to the floor, crawled to the door, activated the release, and pushed a button to lower the steps to the ground. No further sounds were heard. The cabin was flooded with cool air.

The co-pilot—standing and indicating to Stan that he would take a look with Stan covering him—carefully exited the plane, as Stan took up a position by the door frame. Soon Leslie returned to report, shouting over the engines up at Stan, "It's okay. Looks like we somehow managed to blow a brand new tire."

The pilot had appeared behind Stan to say, "Well, if it had to happen, this was better than on landing." Then he added, "Don't worry about your luggage—we'll get that after y'all are off the plane."

Al exited first, with Charlie and Rick following him down the steps and moving onto the tarmac. As Al had moved toward the group waiting, Jo Anne rushed into his arms. "Welcome home, star," she gushed as she smothered him with affection.

"Star? What's that all about?"

"You're gonna be big news when this gets out, that's what."

Al gripped her by the shoulders, looked her in the eye and said, Jo Anne …"

"I haven't said a word. I promise. But I thought there would likely be a news release on the homecoming."

"I sure as hell hope not," he snapped. Then, as he saw the look on her face, his grimace softened., "Jo Anne, we're really worried about Shirley. We took her from some real bad guys and they are going to be looking to get her back. That's why we are so concerned. We can't say a word. Not one word!"

"I know, Al, and none of us has said a word. We got the message. But I still think you're a star."

After being lost in thought, Al came back to the present and smiled. "Jo Anne, you're a dear. I'm so glad you got Nancy here on such short notice."

"Got her on the first try. Couldn't keep her away."

Turning toward the plane, Al saw Shirley peek out the entrance as she prepared to deplane. "Look who's here," Al announced to the group, loud enough for Shirley to hear. Shirley waved, then ducked back in. Stan came out first to offer her a hand and escort her down the steps.

As Shirley reached the tarmac and walked toward the group on Agent Westendorf's arm, she gave them a homecoming queen smile. Al went forward a few steps to take Shirley's free hand, put it on his own arm, and Shirley laughed as she got a double escort to meet the welcome home delegation.

After forty-one years, Shirley Sovereign was home.

58

Al began making introductions. "Shirley, there are some people here I'd like you to meet, starting with my wife, Jo Anne." Jo Anne stepped up and hugged the woman. "Welcome home, Shirley—it's been a very long time, but we are so happy you are here." Shirley returned the hug and murmured her thanks for such a gracious welcome.

Al then introduced Kelly and Peggy, both of whom were warm with their own hugs and a kiss on the cheek.

"And I want all of you to meet the real hero today in getting us here—this is Agent Stan Westendorf of the Houston special branch." As was protocol in law enforcement circles, he maintained radio silence on what "special branch" Stan represented—the CIA-SOG. Al signaled to Sheriff Hooper and Chief Whigg, who had been standing off to the side of the welcome party, to come over and introduce themselves to Stan separately.

While these introductions were taking place, Nancy Nordstrom was hanging back. Now she walked up smiling. As Al began to speak, Shirley's face lit up—and she held up her hand. "Nancy? Nancy Hornberg ... is that really you?" Shirley squealed with delight and held out both arms to receive a hug and a laugh from her long ago friend.

Stepping back a little but still holding Shirley by her shoulders, Nancy said, "It's Nancy Nordstrom now—I married Bill right out of high school." Shirley exclaimed and laughed at the news. The two women hugged again, and looked at each other. Nancy said, "I have to say, Shirley, you are as beautiful as ever—and it's so good to have you home."

346

Shirley was beaming at her childhood friend and said, "Thank you for being here for me, Nancy. I never thought I'd see you again, let alone be able to hug you."

With misty eyes and a deep smile at her prodigal friend, Nancy quipped, "Well that sure goes double for me. And you still know how to make an entrance!" Everyone on the tarmac laughed and clapped at her quick wit that broke any remaining homecoming tension.

The welcoming activities going strong, Al talked briefly to the pilots, thanking them for the smooth trip home, and then letting them go to tend to the unfortunate flat tire before beginning their trip back to Houston. Stan remained behind for a brief word with Al before joining his flight team in the hangar.

Then Al—his message soft but firm—suggested that Shirley, Charlie, Rick, and he were all weary from their recent experiences, and that it was time to go. He thoughtfully added that they needed to get Shirley to dinner and then on to her hotel for the evening.

As Al was trying to herd them all to their cars, Shirley and Nancy expertly corralled him for a word. Shirley was the first to speak. "Al, it has been great to meet Jo Anne and the others, but having Nancy as part of the welcome home party has been a special treat. And we have so much to talk about. Do you think I could ride home with her and have dinner there?"

Something about it made Al uneasy—he wasn't comfortable with the lack of a security arrangement, but he didn't know how to turn her down, either. Nancy intervened in the brief silence and said, "Detective Rouse, we have so much to catch up on. I hope I didn't overstep my bounds here. That wasn't my intention."

"No, nothing like that, but we are worried about her safety. Will you mind having a police car parked outside your house while she's there?"

"Heavens no, that will be fine."

"Then I think it will work out."

Al conferred with Chief Whigg and Sheriff Hooper, then made certain everyone was aware of the change in plans. That handled, he escorted Shirley to Nancy's car, signaled the police car containing two detectives to follow, and watched the two-vehicle procession leave the airport.

Later, Al and Jo Anne were just finishing dinner when the phone rang. Jo Anne checked the caller I.D. "It's Nordstrom, better take it." She handed the phone to Al.

"Al Rouse."

"Hi, Detective, it's Nancy Nordstrom. We're just talking nonstop over here, and I'd like to ask a favor of you. Would it be all right if Shirley stayed here tonight? We have lots of room, my husband is gone on a fishing trip, and it would be great to just keep talking."

Al thought for a minute about the request, then smiled, thinking of the two women catching up on forty years of very different stories.

"I think that would be all right, but I have to check with the Chief and get back to you. We do have a room booked, and police stationed, to make sure she's got protection."

"You know, Detective, if it's no trouble, perhaps your officers wouldn't mind being stationed here at the house? I have given it some thought, and we only have the front and back doors. And it's well lighted out on the street." Clearly, Nancy Nordstrom was capable of marshalling a good argument for her cause.

"Let me see what I can do. I'll get back to you in a few minutes."

Al dialed the chief, who answered on the first ring. It was a short chat. Brent Whigg agreed with Al that no harm should come to Shirley if she spent the night with Nancy Nordstrom as long as there were officers in place. Whigg agreed to call the two officers assigned to guard duty and to redirect them to the Nordstrom house. Al then relayed the plan to Nancy Nordstrom, and all was settled.

That done, Al returned to the table and finished bringing Jo Anne up to date on the investigation and recovery operation at the Russo estate on the shores of the Pacific in Panama.

Jo Anne shuddered when Al came to the part about Shirley sliding out of the gate to the SUV where they waited for her, and then making the getaway. When she heard about the failure of the SWAT team to hold one of the other exits, her eyes were large with concern.

"Jo, the gunfire was nowhere near us," Al told her soothingly.

"We were already on our way back to the airport to head for the U.S. and home."

Jo Anne Rouse knew that a few details had likely been left out. "I sense, Al Rouse, like always with you, there's more to this story than you're telling me," his wife said, with her customary understanding smile. "But I'm satisfied that you're back home safe and sound. And, there's apple pie for dessert. Want some?"

59

"**S**he's gone!"

Al had just answered the phone. With the one eye he had open, he noted that the time was 5:15 a.m.—too early. "Gone? Who's gone? Who is this?"

Sputtering, as if choking back tears, the woman on the line managed to croak out, "Shirley's gone. This is Nancy."

Al was fully awake now. Upright and sitting on the bed, he was pulling off his pajamas with one hand.

"Nancy—are you sure she isn't just outside?" His voice was soothing now as he tried to calm her down. "Could she just have gone out for a walk or something? Have you talked to the guys in the car outside?"

"No, I went to wake her. We were going to take a walk. I just searched the house."

"Tell you what, you go outside and check with them. I'll be there in five minutes." He was talking softly, his voice controlled. He was hoping his tone would calm Nancy Nordstrom.

He dressed quickly, scrambled down the stairs, gunned his car out of the driveway, and headed north toward the Nordstrom residence.

As he drove, he dialed the officers in the car at the Nordstrom House. Tim Burke answered immediately. Al identified himself and asked for an update.

"Al, we've been here and awake all night. In fact, Hank spent much of the night, except for a couple cups of coffee with me, sitting in a chair watching the back of the house. Neither one of us saw a thing, but the woman is gone. I helped Mrs. Nordstrom search the house again. We went through every room, every closet, the attic and the basement plus the garage. Not a sign of her. Hank drove the neighborhood but says there is no one out yet. Sorry."

"I'm just a few blocks away. Be there in a minute." Al signed off and told his hands-free unit to dial the home of Chief Brent Whigg.

Whigg answered. "Al, here, Chief. We've got a problem. Seems that Shirley Sovereign disappeared from the Nordstrom house overnight. There's no sign of her in the neighborhood and the house has been searched several times. She's nowhere to be found."

Al was surprised how calmly his boss handled the news. "Where are you now, Al?" the Chief wanted to know.

"A block from the Nordstrom house, Chief."

"I'll be on the way in a minute. When you get there, make an assessment. By the time you have that done, I'll be there and we'll get things going."

The chief hung up abruptly and Al turned onto the street where the Nordstroms lived. He was pleased to see several police cruisers ahead, but none of them with emergency lights flashing.

After he had parked, he left the car, closed the door quietly and began looking for Tim Burke. The first officer he encountered was Bill Hanratty, who was looking through items in the Nordstrom garage.

As Al approached, Hanratty straightened up and told him, "Not one sign Al ... nothing. It's as if she evaporated."

Here we go all over again. Many thoughts were racing through his head as he processed what Hanratty had said.

"We gotta keep looking, Bill. If there is no trace here, move to the backyard and see if there is anything there. Look for anything that is out of place. A garbage can moved against the fence, for instance. Challenge everything you see out of the norm. There is something here, we just have to find it."

Hanratty, a new policeman, had a bit of a dazed look on his face as Al turned to leave. Although Hanratty might have liked more, Al didn't have the time. He headed for the house where he found Burke seated at the kitchen table with Nancy Nordstrom. As he approached,

Nancy's eyes were red-rimmed, but she looked ready to deal with the situation. Al hugged her, then greeted Burke.

"Anything new?"

"We were just talking about that," Burke told him. "No, nothing new. Nancy and I were discussing things we haven't done. We were just getting ready to take a closer look at the bedroom Shirley used. Nancy's going to take the bed apart and I'm going to search the furniture. We've been through the room but not in fine enough detail."

"That sounds like a good plan, but why don't you wait until the crime bureau people have a chance to cover the scene, okay?"

"Sure, Al. I'm afraid the scene has been badly compromised, but perhaps they can find something we missed."

"How about the two of you just continue talking. Go through everything ... think hard, both of you."

Then Al was off to wait for Chief Whigg. As he exited the front door of the house, the Chief was just pulling to the curb on the opposite side of the street.

The two greeted each other, then returned to the house to talk.

"Have the crime bureau boys been here yet?" the chief asked.

"No, and to be honest, I'm not sure what they will find. The house has been searched twice, so the scene's compromised. We have also been through the neighborhood and we found no sign of her. When it gets a little later, we are going to do it again, this time talking to people. And we are not going to mention names. I'm not sure where else to turn, Chief. Nordstrom's car is here and her husband and his car are gone. The bed had been slept in. But, apparently she made it before she left. My guess is she slipped away. Why? That's the question. And I don't know the answer."

You think returning here was just too much for her?"

"Could be, but she seemed okay yesterday. I never thought twice about asking you to allow her stay here. She and Nancy were getting along okay, and although I haven't talked to Nancy yet, my guess is she will have little to tell me."

"I guess you ought to do that ... talk to Nancy yourself. I can get some folks on all the public transportation outlets and the taxi services, too."

"Better check rental car companies, too, Chief. Not sure where she could have bought a car, but maybe take a look at the 'slippery' companies … the small used car guys anxious to make a quick buck."

"I'll do that, but my thought is we don't say anything about her being missing. Not many people knew we had found her and were bringing her back. Thank God the media didn't know we had found her."

The two lawmen stood there, thinking, each ticking off assignments in their heads. Finally, Al faced the chief. "Boss, any chance that anyone in our shop leaked the fact that we were bringing her home?"

"Who would it have been? As far as I know, we're the only two guys who knew. I know I didn't talk to anyone."

"I didn't either. Anyone in the Sheriff's shop?"

"Just Dwight and Charlie, far as I know."

"Our wives knew," mused Al, "but we called just prior to landing and they were busy getting some folks together to greet the plane. That group was restricted to Kelly, Peggy, JoAnne and Nancy. I'll ask Nancy, but I'll be surprised if she talked to anyone."

"Okay, Al, you get busy with Nancy, and I'll head downtown to organize the search effort. If we don't have any leads by late afternoon, we'll have to think about dealing in the media."

The chief turned to leave when Tim Burke and Nancy Nordstrom burst into the room. "Al, Al! We've got something!" Burke was loud as he waved a sheet of paper.

Al signaled him for quiet, then quickly walked over to him.

"We found this under the mattress of the bed that Shirley slept in," reported Burke.

Al took the paper, opened it, and, with the Chief looking over his shoulder, began to read:

Dear Nancy,

I'm sorry to leave this way but I hope you will understand. Coming home to La Crosse was much scarier than I thought it would be. There are too many memories here for me … too many ghosts. My folks are gone. I have no idea where they are buried. My sister and brother may be alive but no one knows where they are. So, while I am grateful we had our time to talk, I hope you will understand that I just cannot stay. I must move on. For one thing, my being back is bound to become a big news story. When that breaks, the people who were holding me will know. They will come after me. If they find me the torture will be unbearable. Thank you for your kindness and friendship. Nancy, you will always be my bestie. But now it's time for me to vanish again. Please do nothing that will get yourself in trouble on my behalf. That's why I am telling you nothing—because the less you know, the better. I doubt our paths will cross again, but please know, dear friend, I love you!

Your friend,

Shirley

Al finished reading, handed the note to the Chief and scratched his head. The chief shook his head, studied the ground, then said, "It would appear she slipped away on her own. It doesn't sound to me like she had help. You?"

"I agree," replied Al, nodding. "Besides, when would she have had time to enlist someone to help her?"

60

He stopped, turned to Nancy and said, "Was there a phone book in the room she used, Nancy?"

Nancy thought for a time, her hand on her chin and her head turned down. Eventually she said, "There might be." She talked slowly, seemingly still considering the question. "I think there might." She was a bit more assertive now. "I think there was. I think my daughter might have had one in there the last time she was home, a couple of months ago. But there's one in the kitchen and one in the den. Shirley could have slipped down there any time after we went to bed. I passed out almost right away, given how emotional and tiring the day had been."

Al had been thinking the same thing.

"Chief, we have a good plan. Why don't you go ahead and get things started downtown. Nancy and I will have a little chat. I've gotta call Charlie, too."

"I should also let Dwight know," the chief said as he turned to cross the street to his car. "See you about nine?"

"I imagine that's about right. Not much more to be found here."

As the chief drove away, Al ushered Nancy back to the house.

"Would you like some coffee? I really need some." Nancy's hand was on a cupboard door now, just after they entered the kitchen.

"I'd love some."

"What flavor? I've got hazelnut, breakfast blend, or DoNut Shoppe stout. For my Kuerig," she clarified.

"Hazelnut sounds great." Al pulled out a chair from under the back window. In the yard, two officers were going over the area with a fine-tooth comb.

"How about some coffeecake? It's fresh. Planned it for breakfast with Shirley, but when it was done and I knocked at her door … well, you know the rest of that."

"Sure, I'd have some. It's been an early morning."

As they ate, they talked. Al employed all his special talents and skills to try to get Nancy talking about their visit.

"Anything surprise you about your talk with Shirley?" he asked finally.

"No, nothing she said was surprising. In fact, I was more surprised by what she *didn't* talk about."

"Really? Like what?"

"Well, she asked not once about—nor did we talk about—her sister, her brother, or where her parents are buried. Doesn't that seem like something she might have wondered about?"

"Maybe she didn't think you'd know?"

"I don't think so, Al. I told her that I had stayed in touch with her sister for a few years after she disappeared. She didn't seem interested. I always thought she and her sister were pretty close."

"Perhaps the whole situation frightened her. You know, having been out of touch for almost forty years and then suddenly being introduced to your past sets up some daunting circumstances. But I just can't believe she slipped away."

Nancy paused with her piece of coffeecake halfway to her mouth. She got kind of a funny look on her face. "You know, Al, there was only one thing that sparked any interest. That was Hazard. We had gone there a couple of times as sophomores—you know, when it seemed fun to run around with older men. She asked if I had gone there after she disappeared. I told her I hadn't. She remembered every one of the men who used to come and pick us up to take us down there. She wanted to know all about them."

"Hmm, really." Al had already made a mental note to check out Hazard.

They had visited for another half hour when Al excused himself, saying he had better get back to police headquarters to see if there was anything new. He also knew he had to call Charlie.

Before he left for the office, he talked with the officers who were working in the area. "Anything new?" he asked as he approached Bill Hanratty and his partner.

"Maybe, I really don't know. Wanna take a look at this, Al?" said Bill walking to the yard's back gate.

"We found this gate like this," Bill told him. "Pretty hard to tell if it was like this, though. It surely could have been."

Al examined the gate, then walked back to the house, rang the bell and waited for Nancy. When she answered the door, he asked about the back gate being ajar.

"I doubt it," was Nancy's reply. Bill—my husband, Bill—makes sure it's fastened tightly every day he's home. The neighbors back there are very fussy. I suppose it could have been, but I doubt it. I am sure Bill would have checked it before he left, and I haven't been out there. That is surprising."

Al made note of it, thanked Nancy, and the officers and began the walk to his car. As he reached the curb, two other officers were walking down the street toward him. The oldest, Mark Hoeppner, was laughing.

Al smiled at them. "Hey, what's so funny. Care to share?"

Hoeppner stopped, shook his head, then looked up. "Well, Al, me and Jerry here have been walking a two-square-block area. Haven't heard one damn thing that's useful. I was laughin' because Jerry was tellin' me about this old woman he bumped into who told him this wild story about black SUV's, men in black, spacecraft, and aliens. It's hilarious. Tell him, Jer'."

His partner stepped forward, tipped his hat and said, "Al, I'm Jerry Berger. I don't think we've met."

"Oh, sorry, you two. I guess I just assumed you had," said Hoeppner.

"About the story?" asked Al.

"Oh, it's nothing really," said Berger. "I actually talked to quite a few more people than Mark. No one knew or saw anything ... except this one really old lady. She told me she's going to be 102 in a month. She lives along the next street over, and often is up during the night. She told me this really wild story. She said she was sitting in her living room—in the dark, mind you—at 2 a.m., when two black SUV's pulled up to the curb and six guys got out and walked off. Pretty soon, she said, three of 'em came back with another person. She said it could've been a woman. They pushed this person into the car, which took off like a shot. She said the other three didn't come back until just before four. They got in and drove off, too."

"When I asked her about the spaceship, she didn't think it was very funny. Told me to get my ass the hell off her walk—exact words— and not to come back."

"Sounds like quite a story, Jerry. Did she look the type for a big imagination?"

"Sure did. After she calmed down, she told me she thought these men were meeting a group of aliens. She said she often sees these little gray creatures roaming around between midnight and 2 a.m."

"Hope you got her address," said Al. "If we get any reports of spaceships or aliens, we may want to talk to her."

"Don't worry, Al." said Berger, "I've got names and addresses of everyone I talked to, including Maude St. Peter, the 102-year-old."

Al then said his good-byes, got into his car and began the drive to his office.

He called Charlie on the way back to tell him about Shirley's disappearance and all the details. The big guy was dumbfounded, and belligerent.

"Are you kiddin' me? She up and took off again? After all the trouble we went through to bring her home? Pisses me off. Maybe we ought to just let her go. Far as we know, any crime she committed is long ago, and all of those were misdemeanors. To hell with it. Let her go. As far as I'm concerned, we closed this cold case. That's good enough for me."

"Charlie, c'mon. It's not good enough. What if she didn't take off on her own? What if she was kidnapped again?"

"Well we have the note, don't we? Have it tested. Make sure it's her handwriting. If it is, end of subject. Enough. Finito."

"Charlie, you're being a little cynical. Don't you think we have to find her?"

"No, I don't. If she ran off on her own, she wanted it that way. I say, let 'er go. We solved the case, brought her home…and away she went. That's my position. I ain't lookin' for her. Not gonna spend one minute worryin' either."

"Geez, Charlie, that's pretty harsh. It's not like you."

"Hell, it ain't. I ran all of the Americas lookin' for her. Avoided gunshots. All to get her outta Panama. And on top of that, there was more trouble in Mexico. That's enough of my time, Al, more than enough. I'm out of it now. Thanks for lettin' me know she took off, but I don't have time to look for her."

61

Still stunned by his buddy's attitude, Al sat down in front of Chief Whigg's desk, shaking his head. Chief looked up from his work, noted the look on his chief detective's face, and his own face took on a quizzical look. "You look like JoAnne left you along with Shirley, Al. What's wrong?"

"I'll tell you what's wrong, boss. I called Charlie to let him know Shirley was gone and I got an ear full of advice—all of it bad, in my opinion." He got to his feet and began pacing the room, hands behind his back. After a few passes, he stopped. "Charlie effectively told me to take the Sovereign kidnapping case and stick it where the sun don't shine. He was downright mean about it, too."

Al shook his head, stopped pacing and sat. "I just can't figure him out. It was like he washed his hands of the whole matter. He told me he was out of it."

The Chief studied him for a few seconds, then a kindly smile spread across his handsome, craggy face. "You know, Al, that's kinda the way I feel, too. I hate to tell you that, but it's true. We spent lots of time and money chasing her down and helping her escape from that despot in Panama, and it seems that all the thanks we get is having her run away again. As far as I'm concerned, that cold case is closed. Hate to be cynical about it, but I think we should just let her go."

Al couldn't believe what he was hearing. *Really? Is that really how the Chief and Charlie feel? What's wrong with me? Why don't I see it that way?*

Al backed out of the Chief's office, bewilderment oozing from every pore in his body. *Case closed? How can it be? Seems like there is something else I should be doing. Is there?*

Back in his office, as if on autopilot, he made a cup of coffee, then sat at his desk, head in his hands and thought … thought about what he was missing, thought about why the Chief and Charlie felt as they did, thought about what he wasn't seeing in the case, and thought about why he was concerned. After half an hour, he straightened and decided to check on the plan that the Chief had put into play after getting the word that Shirley was gone.

He checked with the people working on the public transportation outlets. Joe Moore was a good cop, but he didn't have an original thought in his head. "We've been to them all, Al—cabs, limos, buses, trains, and planes. No one matching the description of your gal was remembered by any of them. They didn't have any unusual requests from people they didn't know. Cab fares were all routine, and no one bought last minute tickets on any of the rest. Sorry."

Anxious for something to do, Al thought he'd check the used car dealers himself, starting with the seediest. They were, at best, a colorful lot … long-haired, in bright bandanas, tobacco chewing, and not very talkative. He started on the south side, theorizing that might have been the way she went, especially if she expressed interest in Hazard. By noon, he had talked to eight dealers, not a one of them happy to be visiting with him, and not a one with anything of relevance to tell him. Not a one said they'd seen her or anyone remotely resembling her, and not a one professed to have sold a vehicle in the last two days. They were, to a person, dodgy personalities, even the one woman—Diane Cromley.

In fact, Cromley might have been the seediest of the lot. Somewhere in her sixties, he guessed, her dirty gray hair bound in a bun at the back of her head, she was wearing a cardigan sweater unbuttoned to her waist revealing an old sports bra so ratty and begrimed he guessed it hadn't seen a laundromat for months—probably the last time she had a bath, he thought, as he maneuvered to stay upwind. She was both chewing tobacco and smoking a corncob pipe—the stem of which levered up and down between the gaps in her teeth like a see-saw as she talked. It was both hard to watch and hard not to stare.

"How the hell many of youse is gonna come around? Had two guys in here this morning already. One gal, too. You're the fourth. I don't appreciate the bother, and it's bad for business, so you can just get your ass off my property and head on down the street." Then she stomped back into the trailer that he surmised doubled as office and home.

As he looked around before leaving, he decided the cars she was selling seemed to resemble her personality. Rundown and disagreeable.

The clock was touching two when he gratefully left Diane's Great Used Cars, got into his car, and headed west (which would have been north to most people). Nothing. Shirley Sovereign had vanished, gone like a wisp of gossamer.

Not hungry, he grabbed a cup of coffee at a southside McDonald's, then parked across from Gundersen Lutheran and thought.

Is it possible for someone without a vehicle to simply vanish? Was La Crosse that porous? Could I do it? He pondered that last thought until only the dregs were left in his cup. *Might as well get on with it. Maybe I'll get lucky.* He chuckled at what seemed to be the irony of the thought. Lucky? At what? Where?

By four-thirty, he was dog-tired. Nothing he had tried had produced a single clue—not one. He stopped at the office, returned a couple of messages, and checked with the dispatcher to see if any of the searchers had found anything useful. She messaged them and got nothing in return—all reported fruitless searches.

He headed home, anxious for a cold beer and a nap on the couch. He got the beer, not the nap. JoAnne had other ideas. She had spent her day painting an upstairs bedroom, and she wanted help taking off the masking tape and uncovering the furniture. And she wanted to go out to eat ... the last thing he wanted to do. But Jo Anne had had a hard day, too, so he changed into jeans and a tee shirt and off they went to Schmidty's. It was rib night, the place was crowded, but Schmidty himself found them a quiet table in the back corner of the barroom.

After a beer, they ordered ribs and baked potato, and visited about their days while they waited. Al confessed his frustration at turning up nothing on his new search, and on being the odd man out. JoAnne was sympathetic, but truly was dumbfounded that Shirley had vanished. "She seemed so happy to be home. Do you really think she was just too frightened to stay?"

"No, no I don't. As you say, she seemed happy. She and Nancy seemed to pick up where they left off forty-some years ago. There was nothing that I saw or heard that predicted this kind of situation. Not one thing."

As they talked aimlessly about Shirley and where she might have gone, Al quickly tired of the thread and was happy when their order arrived. They busied themselves with their food, ordered another beer as they finished up, drank it, talking little, and finally made their way home, arriving around seven-thirty. Professing tiredness, Al made his way upstairs, showered, and then propped himself up in bed at eight-thirty to catch a game. The Brewers were on TV. He listened to the game mostly for its noise value, and then began to think. By nine-thirty he was snoring.

When he arrived at work the next morning and checked the notes on his desk, nothing had changed—no word, no sightings. That's the way it went for the next two weeks—until no one cared and the search was ended.

And, that's the way it was when summer began and when it ended, when fall and its bright colors and crisp air made its appearance, then rode out on the wings of a snowstorm as winter came in.

"I think we're in for a long one, how about you?" Charlie asked the question as they enjoyed lunch at the La Crosse Club a couple of weeks before Christmas. Although nothing in the reshelved cold case had changed, everything else *had*. It was Chief of Police Al Rouse now, and Assistant Chief Charlie Berzinski.

Chief Brent Whigg was retired and living in Florida. The changing-of-the-guard in the Chief's office had occurred as Whigg turned sixty-five in early December.

The two former confederates were even closer as La Crosse police executives. And although their tenure was only three weeks old, already the word was out: if you want to do crime, better do it somewhere other than La Crosse.

Thinking about his assistant's prophecy about the weather, Al smiled over his hot beef sandwich. "Could be." He took a bite of the hot, juicy sandwich and let his mind go back to a wistful corner. "You know, Charlie, I just keep wondering what happened. Where did she go? The media has had a field day ... for once, I can't fault them ... and yet nothing has surfaced. Not one darn thing. Where do you think she went?"

"Hate to say this, Al, but, as you darn well know, I don't know and I don't really give a crap, either. We busted our asses to find her and bring her home. As far as I'm concerned, that's a cold case that can get freezer burn for all I care. I've moved on. You should do that, too."

"Oh, well, I guess you're right."

But later, as they drove back to work, Al found himself deep in thought. *What I wouldn't give for just one report ... just one clue.*

When the long winter ended, and the greenery of spring spread over the valley, a new set of case boxes were wheeled into the city hall warehouse and stacked in meticulous order by date on the shelves ... to molder in the cold layers of dust.

EPILOGUE

A bird twittered melodiously outside her window, gently stirring the nude form of Shirley Sovereign from peaceful sleep to semi-consciousness. Most days she awoke alone in her sumptuous king-plus sized bed, but tonight would be a different story. Tonight her best friend and lover Stan Westendorf would share her boudoir, warming her heart and definitely heating up her body.

It was nearly two years since she had fled La Crosse, Wisconsin, after she had returned there in a private jet arranged for by Westendorf, who had accompanied the group north from Houston, Texas.

As that flight neared an end, Westendorf, at her invitation, had visited her in the private bedroom at the rear of the plane. It was there that love had suddenly blossomed, and there that the plan had been made to use the jet to spirit her away again hours later. In the middle of the night, they had disappeared under the noses of the local police from the south side of La Crosse to Meigs Field in Chicago, and from there to the forests of Oregon, then further on to this beautiful site in California.

Her new home was a modest but comfortable Victorian outside Ferndale, a city of a thousand souls, guarded by majestic redwoods, with the Pacific Ocean at its front doorstep.

The house that Shirley lived in was on a large functioning dairy farm. More than 2,000 Holsteins were milked there on a continuous cycle each day, and the sprawling farm produced crops sufficient to provide for the sizable herd.

Shirley allegedly was the mistress of the manor, a story understood and accepted by all her neighbors that had her transplanting from the urban jungle of New York City to take over the placid but successful operation begun by her father's great-grandfather in 1856, just four years after Seth and Stephen Shaw crossed the Eel River by canoe, proceeded up the Eel's tributary, the Salt River, and through St. Francis Creek to a level piece of ground that eventually became Ferndale.

When the area was settled massive ferns up to six feet tall populated the savannahs and gave rise, ultimately to the city's name. The house that Shirley—now known as Shelby Shaw—inhabited was built by Seth Shaw, in 1856, the second dwelling that he had created. The first house, which Seth named Ferndale, became a post office as the area drew more settlers. As the city sprang up around him, Seth moved to the country and built this house, which was on the National Register of Historic Places.

But through the years, Seth had managed to ensure privacy for the dwelling by acquiring property that placed the house at the center of the farm, two miles from the nearest highway. Acquired by the federal Witness Protection Program in 1993, it might be the most idyllic site in the program's inventory of properties.

Westendorf had his eye on it from the beginning, and when Shirley had talked to him—on the flight from Houston to La Crosse—about her fear of re-capture by the mob, and had sparked his first feelings of love for her, he pulled every string necessary to place her here.

Now he visited her every third weekend as his career neared its end. He had already made the deal to acquire the property from the program for them.

As Shirley thought of the night ahead, she knew Stan would sweep in about eight. Their first stop would be in this bed, and after their passion had been satisfied—thought Shirley with a smile—she would once more ask Stan if he had let Al Rouse know there was no need to worry about her. And he would once again say, "I am working on it, Little One. Patience, please."

And then they would once more lose themselves in each other until the sun sank on Sunday and he would leave her at 8 p.m. for the 36-mile drive to Eureka-Arcata Airport on the coast. At 9 p.m., a Gulfstream would swoop out of the sky, pick him up, and deliver him back to Houston, Texas, 2,000 miles away.

ABOUT THE AUTHOR

Gary Evans has turned his passion for novel writing into a post-retirement career, with book four soon to be released, and book five already in the works. Evans spent 30 years in Midwest newsrooms as an award-winning writer, editor, and publisher. He spent 12 years as vice president at Winona State University. He ended his career as the president and CEO of Hiawatha Broadband Communication, one of the nation's first alternative entrant telecommunications firms, after 15 years. Married to Ellen, they have two grown children, Gregory and Natalie.